S0-AWD-864

LADY LIBERTY

"There is no question that Vicki Hinze has delivered a tour de force thriller that will leave readers gasping for breath. LADY LIBERTY is the ultimate thrill ride! This book would make one hell of a movie!"—*Romantic Times* Top Pick

"With its candid view of Washington, a complex plot and perceptive handling of the heroine's gradual realization that she can love again, Hinze's timely offering should attract thriller and romance readers."—*Booklist*

"Political intrigue with nonstop action. You'll read this one from the edge of your seat!"
—Christina Skye, bestselling author of *My Spy*

ALL DUE RESPECT

"Five stars. Dramatic and moving, finely crafted military fiction that weaves a touch of romance, intrigue, and danger into every page . . . the find of the year. Hinze has definitely made her mark with her latest release, earning herself the title of "Queen of Romantic Suspense."
—*New Age Bookshelf*

"A diverting romantic thriller."—*Publishers Weekly*

"A must read for lovers of suspense, military thrillers and classic romance."—*Romance Reviews Today*

ACTS OF HONOR

"Gripping and adrenaline-charged, Hinze's plot will appeal to fans who like their suspense razor sharp."
—*Publishers Weekly*

"Absolutely riveting."—*Philadelphia Inquirer*

"An excellent story of awakening love."—*Miami Herald*

"Suspense filled and very well written."—*The Jackson Journal*

"Utterly thrilling from beginning to end. So suspenseful you don't want to put it down. Hinze has proven herself a true master of military romantic suspense tales."
—*Romantic Times*

"Five stars. An entertaining thriller."—*Painted Rock*

"A nail-biting psychological military romantic mystery. This is one book that won't let you put it down!"
—*Affaire du Coeur*

DUPLICITY

"Written in the tradition of A Few Good Men, this highly suspenseful story of a solitary woman's fight against an evil military conspiracy is one readers won't want to put down."
—*Library Journal*

"Hinze's suspense-filled novel is one that will keep the reader turning pages and trying to guess the next moves in a complex and intriguing plot."—*Raleigh News and Observer*

"An exciting read. Guaranteed to keep you entertained."
—*Rocky Mountain News*

"A page-turner that fuses thriller and romance. Hinze has a knack for combining compelling, realistic characterizations with suspense and a romantic plot."—*Publishers Weekly*

"Keeps the suspense going until the last page. Hinze's books demand justice."—*The Bay Beacon*

"If you like well-plotted suspense with your romance, if you like clues and curves at a roller-coaster pace, DUPLICITY is for you. It's a page-turner, and don't skip a page."
—*The Courier Herald*

"Clear an entire shelf for this author's work, she doesn't disappoint, making her a sure candidate for the bestseller's list. Very highly recommended."—*BookBrowser*

"A blazing new star!"—*Romantic Times*

"Wow! A spellbinding book. A true page-turner. The way [Hinze] pulls into the action with the characters is so incredible. There are so many hurdles to overcome, so many emotions, feelings and situations that leave you reeling, you won't want to put it down until you see the story through the very end. Bravo!"—*Old Book Barn Gazette*

"[A] tautly crafted thriller . . . a roller-coaster ride of sizzling suspense, deadly betrayal, and courage."
—Merline Lovelace, Colonel USAF (Ret), author of *Call of Duty*

SHADES OF GRAY

"With her impressively realistic portrayal of the jeopardy faced by Special Ops members, dynamic author Vicki Hinze guarantees her readers an edge-of-their-seat thrill ride. You want intrigue, danger and romance? Ms. Hinze proves she can supply them!"—*Romantic Times*

"A winner for fans of romantic suspense."—*Affaire du Coeur*

"A roller-coaster ride of suspense and terror. Hinze may just have initiated a new genre. A page-turner from beginning to end."—*Suite 101*

"High tension, riveting action, and characters of extraordinary integrity and self-control make SHADES OF GRAY informative and entertaining."—Amazon.com

LADY JUSTICE

Vicki Hinze

BANTAM BOOKS

LADY LIBERTY
A Bantam Book / August 2004

Published by Bantam Dell
A division of Random House, Inc.
New York, New York

This is a work of fiction. Names, characters, places,
and incidents either are the product of the author's imagination
or are used fictitiously. Any resemblance to actual persons, living
or dead, events, or locales is entirely coincidental.

ISBN 0-553-58353-0

Manufactured in the United States of America
Published simultaneously in Canada

OPM   10   9   8   7   6   5   4   3   2   1

To Dr. Donald A. Urban,

Because a promise is a promise,
with a grateful and humble heart,
I offer you this book.

★   ★   ★

Acknowledgments

I must express my most sincere gratitude and appreciation to the following individuals and their staffs:

Dr. Donald A. Urban
Dr. Douglas J. Wirthlin
The University of Alabama Hospital
Dr. Mark Schroeder
Dr. Samuel Poppell
Dr. Ralph Zappada

Your willingness to share your expertise, skills, and knowledge has profoundly impacted my work and my life. Thank you.

I would be equally remiss if I neglected to thank my dear friends Lorna Tedder and Marge Smith for their support, expertise, and advice. My life is far richer because you are in it.

And my most humble gratitude to the Bantam dream team who worked on this book, including Kara Cesare, Anne Bohner, and Micahlyn Whitt.

LADY JUSTICE

Chapter One

It *couldn't* be broken.

Canceling the mission was not an option; he would have to proceed regardless, and if it had broken, he would not survive.

Panic shot through Cardel Boudreaux's chest, hollowing his stomach, and the stale air inside the sedan seemed to spike twenty degrees. He dodged the steering wheel, bent double to the floorboard, and looked closer at the glass vial he had dropped.

No spillage. No milky white serum on the floorboard. The vial seemed intact. . . .

Afraid to believe his eyes, he lifted it, pinching his forefinger and thumb, and then gently rocked the vial end to end. There was no seepage, no serum, slicking the outside of the vial.

He let the truth that he had survived a near miss settle in; lower his pulse, his heart rate. When his hand stopped shaking, he slid the vial back into its sheath, rewrapped the sheath in bubble wrap, zippered it into its gray pouch, and then returned the pouch to his backpack.

Carelessness kills, Cardel.

It did. In his profession, religiously. Leaving his damn backpack open . . . he must have been out of his mind.

He abandoned his rental car in long-term parking, where it would be a little more difficult but not impossible to locate, and eased his backpack's strap onto his shoulder. Near the main terminal, he tugged his white cap down on his forehead, so its visor shielded his eyes and the U.S. flag pin attached to it was clearly visible, and then he entered the airport.

Every second of his time had been structured specifically to maximize his odds for success, including booking his flight during the airport's heaviest departure-and-arrival traffic.

Weaving through the thick bustle of people, Cardel blocked out dins of insignificant noises and made his way straight to the concourse dedicated to international flights. Security would be tightest there, but the Consortium, who had hired his organization, had connections worldwide, and his own superiors anticipated no challenges. Yet, like any other Global Warrior worth his fee, Cardel had prepared for unanticipated events that sometimes popped up, particularly on international missions. That preparation made his fee seven figures, rather than the typical six earned by the majority, and clients always seemed eager to pay it.

For fifteen years, he had worked hard to build and maintain a sterling reputation. He left no loose ends, offered no excuses, rarely made mistakes, and had never compromised a client.

Sidestepping a mother who was half dragging, half cajoling a crying little boy, Cardel entered the restroom and took stock. Only four of the sixteen stalls were occupied.

The two open rows of urinals were all in use. Surveillance cameras bolted to the wall were positioned high overhead, focusing on the entrance and exit.

Seeing nothing that hadn't been included in his briefing, he stepped into the nearest stall, shut the door, and unzipped his backpack. Inside, he found the gray padded pouch. He pulled it out, removed a syringe and the small glass vial. His mouth went dry.

Swallowing hard, he banded his upper arm with a thin strip of rubber, filled the syringe, and then injected himself. As the milky liquid entered his vein, his fear the vial might break before he could inject himself died.

He set the vial and empty syringe on the tile floor behind the toilet, crushed them with his shoe, then mopped up the bits of glass with toilet tissue and dumped them in the toilet. Next, he saturated the stall floor with chlorine bleach. No trace of the serum could be found; the Consortium had been emphatic about that.

"Flight one twenty-seven to Miami, Florida, is now boarding."

Hearing the tinny loudspeaker announcement, Cardel glanced at his watch. He had seven minutes and twenty seconds to finish his work and get on that plane.

Moving quickly, he uncoiled a thin, clear hose, stuffed it down the waist of his slacks, further down the inseam of his right leg. The tip cleared the top of his shoe, remaining concealed by the hem of his slacks.

He pulled a quart-size canister out of his backpack, put it in a special holster crafted to carry canisters of the same size and shape, and then strapped it to his chest. A second canister remained in his backpack.

This is almost too easy.

It was. And normally that would have concerned Cardel. But this mission *should* be easy. The entire operation had been in the works for over a year. Every facet of it had been scrutinized, studied, tested, and then scrutinized again.

Calm and controlled, he connected the holstered canister to the hose, slid on a nasal oxygen mask, and then buried its unconnected hose from sight inside the holster. A quick twist and the canister's valve opened.

A clear liquid drained through the hose and puddled on the floor near his feet. Stepping into it, he coated his shoes, and then left the stall.

After walking a path before the urinals, the stall doors, and the sinks where men stood washing their hands, Cardel left the restroom, careful to keep his chin tucked to his chest so his cap would block the security camera from recording a clear picture of his face. He stepped out onto the crowded concourse and tapped a release button on the canister near his waist. A thin trail of the liquid contaminant seeped onto the floor.

Obscured by heavy foot traffic, it was not noticed.

Because these passengers were heading for destinations worldwide, they would spread the contaminant to their various flights, infect others, who would go on to infect still others, and the diffusion would be accomplished. Tracing the contaminant back to its source would be impossible. In political circles, both Paris and Miami would have plausible deniability. That was vital to Cardel's client. Why, Cardel didn't know, nor did he care.

"Attention, passengers. Flight one twenty-seven to Miami, Florida, this is your final boarding call."

Cardel stepped up to the only middle-aged male security screener on duty. Slumping beside his machine, he looked bored. Heavy, dark circles rimmed his eyes. *Definitely innocuous.* Cardel approved the mission planner's choice. "Long shift?"

"A double," the screener said, grimacing. "Cutbacks."

Offering a sympathetic nod, Cardel passed over the canisters and the oxygen certification provided by headquarters, which would get the canisters on the plane. "Rough times all over," he said, then adjusted the nasal tabs in his mask and smiled, knowing it wouldn't touch his eyes.

The screener didn't smile back. He gave the certification and the canisters a cursory glance, and then passed them back. "Better hurry." His voice sounded as flat as the loudspeaker. "They've already made the final boarding call."

"Thank you," Cardel said, and then made his way to the gate, where he produced the certification, the canisters, and his ticket for the flight attendant. It had been purchased weeks ago with a credit card that would soon disappear. These days, cash transactions and one-way tickets raised red flags with monitors. "Sorry I'm late. I got held up by Security."

"Doesn't everyone these days?" Totally forgiving, she quickly reviewed the certification and the numbers on the canisters. On verifying the match, she returned them, smiled, and then rushed him onto the plane.

In short order, the plane took off. When it leveled out at high altitude and they were gliding over the Atlantic, Cardel checked his watch. As if on cue, the seat belt sign went off. *Right on schedule.*

He left his seat and headed toward the back of the plane to the restroom. On the walk down the center aisle, he depressed the canister button and held it, silently dispensing the contaminant. Odorless and colorless, it failed to draw the flight attendants' attention, or that of the passengers seated along the aisle.

With a casual effect, he smiled at a blue-haired grandmother seated across the aisle, and then made his way to the restroom. At this moment, only a fool wouldn't be on edge. *If the canister failed to eject . . .*

Cardel entered the restroom, closed the door to secure the OCCUPIED sign, and removed the canister from its holster. Coolly, he dropped it into the toilet, flushed, and waited to see if the mission planners had properly prepared for the disposal.

The canister disappeared from sight.

A moment of pure joy lifted him. There was no broken vial, no jammed canister, and no evidence. Expelled from the plane, the canister would end up somewhere in the Atlantic, and the truth of its origins would be lost for all time.

He loosened his limbs, relaxed. His portion of the mission would be a success. He was out of danger on the flight, and nearly finished. Once the plane landed, he had only to holster and connect the second canister, and then to take a stroll through a couple of Florida orange groves.

Piece of cake.

Pleased with himself, Cardel stepped out of the rest room—and came to a dead halt.

Bright red, yellow, green, and blue plastic cubes littered the contaminated center aisle. And among them crawled a curly-haired toddler.

In a cold sweat, Cardel stared at the child. Over the years, the mission planners had been flawlessly professional, but this time—on the Global Warriors' most intensive U.S. attack ever—the planners hadn't considered that a parent might put a child on the aisle floor to play so early in the flight.

Cardel blinked hard, forced himself to look away and return to his seat. He snapped on his safety belt and then signaled the flight attendant for a drink. "Scotch and water, please."

"Yes, sir." She smiled down at the toddler.

Cardel's gaze invariably followed. If the child died before the plane landed, the mission would be a disaster. "Make it a double."

Chapter Two

Hundreds of U.S. flags flew on the docked cruise ship.

Tonight there would be a fireworks display that would set American passengers' spirits soaring, but Jaris Adahan would no longer be aboard to see it. He would, however, enjoy the irony in Americans celebrating Independence Day on the very day he made them dependent.

After checking the brim of his white baseball cap to make sure the U.S. flag pin was secure, he tugged it on and then gave himself the injection that would protect him from exposure to the contaminant. He ran a length of thin, clear hose down his sleeve, holstered the canister under his arm at his side, and mentally reviewed his checklist. He had already contaminated the ballast tanks, and the handrails and decks at the ship's exit points he would not be using to depart the ship. He had bleached his quarters, destroyed all evidence of his ever having been aboard, exchanged his passport and visa for new ones, claiming yet another false identity, and, while still at sea, he had disposed of the empty contaminant canister.

He had three more canisters: one in the holster, and two in his backpack. All were full.

After a last look to make sure he hadn't missed anything, he left his cabin and went down two floors to the largest common area on the ship. On the far side, just down from a boutique, he ducked into an obscure alcove and then soaked the soles of his shoes. He paused then for a moment and hoped Cardel Boudreaux hadn't used all of the Warriors' luck on his leg of the mission.

A woman walked by, holding the hands of her twin girls. Remorse pricked at Jaris. They weren't as young as Cardel's toddler—these girls were five, or maybe six—but they had pink ribbons in their hair and they were laughing.

Jaris liked the innocence in the sound, and resented liking it. *Don't notice*, he reminded himself. Noticing brought nightmares. Nightmares, regret. He'd learned that the hard way.

He shut out the sights and sounds and smells of all the people in the busy lobby, and then left the alcove. It was time to get off of the ship.

Dispensing a thin film of clear, odorless contaminant through the tubing in his sleeve, he saturated every handrail in his path and a tempting-looking luncheon buffet set out on deck.

No one stopped him, or slowed his progress. He walked off the ship, then the dock, and made it to the U.S. border without incident.

There, foot traffic was heavy, and people waiting to enter the country stood in long lines. The noon sun beat down on them, raising sweat and tempers. Jaris moved from line to line, scanning the customs officials' uniforms, looking for his Consortium contact. Finally, he spotted him. Middle-aged and nondescript, he was wearing a U.S. flag pin on his lapel.

Jaris stepped into the man's line, and when his turn arrived, he handed over his new passport. "Blistering sun today."

"Blistering." Recognition shone in the man's eyes. "They say tomorrow will be hotter."

Certain now he had made the appropriate contact, Jaris passed over a canister from his backpack—a canister the official had been well paid to use to contaminate an imported shipment of fruit. What kind of fruit, Jaris was not told, which meant, in the foreseeable future, he would avoid eating any.

The official waved him through, and he walked onto U.S. soil.

The canister in his holster was now empty, and he had made delivery on another. *Two down, and one to go.*

One that required only an afternoon walk through a few maize and cotton fields . . .

Chapter Three

Sebastian Cabot sat in his car at the Canadian border, too consumed by thoughts of his family and memories of his youth to spare any concern on getting caught.

The trunk of his Chevrolet Impala was filled with contraband cans of pâté. Simply put, he was smuggling. He had made no declarations to the customs official but, if what the Consortium had told him proved true, he wouldn't be challenged.

After September 11, that alone was enough to scare the hell out of John Q. Public. But because there was more, it made Sebastian sick.

He slung an arm over the steering wheel to cool the sweat from his armpit, and inched the car forward in line. Who would have thought that having a few celebratory drinks after winning the biggest case of his twenty-seven-year legal career would lead him to this? To Sebastian

Cabot, attorney extraordinaire, friend of the court and champion of underdogs, smuggling pâté?

And soon, to worse.

His stomach slid into knots under his ribs. It was a tragic end to a life lived with purpose, but he was powerless to change it. The Consortium's director and then its chairman had made that clear—and they'd hired an entire cell of Global Warriors to deliver the message proving it.

He was not safe. His wife and their three children were not safe. Even his secretary, his second cousin, Oscar, whom he hadn't seen in twenty years, and his damned dog were not safe.

And there was only one way to make any of them safe again.

"You're clear to proceed, sir." The official nodded.

"Thanks." Sebastian nodded back. The U.S. flag pin on his white golfing hat bobbed. Driving on, he headed south.

By early afternoon, he was in California's Napa Valley: the heart of wine country in the United States. He thought about pulling into a truck stop for an artery-clogging meal of the cholesterol-packed, fried foods he had avoided for the last three years under doctor's orders—today he could eat anything guilt-free—but his stomach churned, and he decided against it. The work he was about to do had his system riled up enough without throwing it a grease-fest. So he drove on, to a vineyard, and then pulled off onto the shoulder of the road.

The tires turning on the loose, dry dirt raised a little dust cloud. He waited a moment for it to settle, looked up and then down the asphalt road. Heat rippled off it in waves. The entire area seemed desolate. No people. No cars, or trucks. Nothing in sight except row upon row of lush grapevines basking in the hot, summer sun.

Sweating profusely, Sebastian gave in to his foul mood. He didn't want to be doing this. The only saving grace in this whole side trip to hell was that, after it all happened, he wouldn't see the disappointment in his family's eyes.

His whole life he'd heard the kind of warnings now playing in his head. The conscience tugs that had kept him in church on Sundays; in the band in high school, when he wanted nothing more than to quit; when he avoided drugs in college, even though everyone short of God was experimenting with them; and in law school long after he wanted to drop out.

Then, those warnings had helped keep him on the straight and narrow.

Now, nothing could help him, or save his ass.

He got out of the car and opened the trunk, and then the first can of pâté. He didn't give himself an antidote injection. There wasn't one. Not that it mattered.

Stooping low, he used his pocketknife to empty the tin onto the ground, among the grapevines. His stomach clutched. How many years of sweat and dreams—how many lives was he destroying?

Son of a bitch, he hated this. He loved his country and the people in it. But who would believe that now? He was a smuggler and a saboteur. Call a spade a spade. He was a traitor.

He blinked hard, his chin trembling. What difference did it make what anyone else thought? His wife and kids meant the most and they would hate him. Yes, this was wrong, but the bottom line hadn't changed. As much as he loved his country, he loved his family more.

His chest tight, he closed his mind, shunned the guilt, and moved on to the next vineyard. And then to the next, contaminating them one by one with the tainted pâté.

When he had emptied the last tin, he tossed it back into the trunk. It clanged against the others, bled dry and hollow. Sebastian slammed the trunk lid shut, got back into the car, and then drove north, into the Sierra Nevada Mountains.

His conscience nagged at him. Merciless. Unrelenting. Each tin contained millions of biologically engineered grape lice, which would demolish the grapevines from the roots out. By the time the poor growers realized they had a problem, they'd have lost seventy percent of their plants—and the grape lice would have spread to even more vineyards.

The California wine industry would be crippled, if not destroyed.

And European vineyard and wine stocks would soar, generating significant profits for the Consortium.

Sebastian didn't personally know any of the Consortium members, much less its chairman or director, but he hated them all. They considered themselves a profit-seeking, strategic alliance of international businessmen, but they were a self-serving group of terrorists who would manipulate anyone by any means necessary to achieve their financial goals. What they were forcing him to do proved there was no limit to the amount of damage they were willing to inflict, or to the number of lives they were willing to crush. The bastards had no consciences, no morals or ethics, and no mercy.

And most terrifying of all, they had forced him to be just like them.

Sebastian mopped at his throbbing forehead. If only he could go back . . .

Regret and resentment burned deep in his gut. He hadn't had a single drink since that night, yet his abstinence changed nothing. He had tried everything; there was no way out. The Consortium had him by the short hairs and the chairman had offered Sebastian only one option that kept his family alive. Only one. And though it went against everything he had believed in and had worked for all his life, he had taken it.

God forgive him, he had taken it.

Near Lake Tahoe, the temperature plunged. He cranked

down the air conditioner to warm up, pulled out his phone, and then dialed the number he'd been instructed to call.

"Yes?" A man with a thick European accent answered in a clipped tone.

The chairman. Clamping down on the steering wheel, Sebastian glared into the taillights of an eighteen-wheeler on the road in front of him. "It's done."

"Very well."

"My family—"

"Will be safe, Mr. Cabot. In our line of work, keeping one's word is essential. Your debt is paid—provided you stick to the terms of the agreement."

Sebastian broke into a cold sweat. "Done." He disconnected, drove on for twenty minutes, and then dialed a second number.

A Cayman woman answered in a crisp voice. "First Island Bank."

"I need to verify a deposit, please." He waited until she put him through to a second woman, and then made his request, adding the account number.

"And the account owner's name, sir?"

"G. D. Cabot." Sebastian revealed the name of his wife, Glenna, and then added the additional personal information that would be requested to prove he had authority on this account.

"Yes, Mr. Cabot," the woman said. "A five-million-dollar deposit was credited to your account today. Certified funds."

That was it, then. "Thank you." Sebastian hit the end button on the phone, considered calling his wife and kids, but then thought better of it. A call home wasn't on the list, and who knew what dangers the Consortium or their Global Warriors would attribute to an unscheduled call. They could feel Glenna or the kids were a threat.

No, as much as he craved hearing Glenna's voice, Sebastian couldn't risk it.

But he wished he could. She had the most soothing voice he had ever heard. He had married her for that voice. When nothing else could, it relaxed him.

Soft-colored memories of happy times flowed through his mind, bittersweet in the way of good things ending. They'd had a good marriage, good kids, good everything. And he'd lost it all because of one night. One night, and one too many martinis . . .

Remorse and soul-deep regret gnawed at him, warred with dark, sharp-edged resentment. Sebastian stiffened in his seat, clamped hard on the steering wheel until his fingertips turned numb, drove on down the winding roadway. Steep cliffs lined the road. Twice, so far, he had seen pretty waterfalls. The next one he saw—

Bridal Falls. Off to his right. At least a hundred-foot drop.

He pulled an image of Glenna and the kids on the sailboat last summer from his memory, holding it fast in his mind's eye. He stomped down on the accelerator. The car lurched, ripped through the guardrail. Metal crunched, glass shattered, and the car sailed out, over the gorge.

Moments stretched into lifetimes and a strange noise filled his ears. His own primal weeping.

As the Impala plunged and tumbled, crashed into tree branches and trunks and sharp rocks, it burst into flames.

The Consortium had issued an ultimatum.

Sebastian Cabot had followed his orders explicitly.

Including the order to die on impact.

Chapter Four

"You're busted, Lieutenant Gibson."

Senior Special Agent Gabrielle Kincaid stalked around the conference table, as rigid and tense as only the infuriated Queen Bitch of the highly skilled Special Detail Unit of the Secret Service could. She stopped behind him, just off his left shoulder, and then bent low and with a growling whisper put the question to him.

"How does it feel . . . to know . . . that you . . . killed seventeen civilians, three seasoned SDU operatives, and two FBI agents?"

Gibson bowed his head, looked down from the copper-lined wall in the top-secret Home Base headquarters conference room to the scarred table that had seen too many crises and even more ass-chewing debriefings. He didn't dare to answer. In his days as a security monitor at Home Base, Gibson once had seen her boil. It wasn't an experience he was eager to repeat, much less to instigate.

Mildly put, Agent Kincaid did not suffer in silence.

"You know . . . we're America's last line of defense," she said from behind him in a tone that raised the hair on his neck. "Our missions are critical to the nation's safety. They require total and complete anonymity—absolute secrecy. There aren't a hundred people in the entire country who know SDU exists, and that's essential to our effectiveness." She paused, lowered her voice a decibel, and added, "This was training, Gibson, but if you're going to survive the transition from active duty military to SDU operative, then you'd better get one thing clear . . . in your head . . . right now. SDU is a stealth operation. You never, *never*, sacrifice its secrecy. Good agents who have devoted their lives to this unit have popped cyanide or been killed by other good agents in this unit to protect it. That's a fact of life here. Burn it into your brain if you have to, but don't ever forget it again."

He risked a glance at her. "It was just a momentary lapse."

Dressed appropriately in sleek black, she tossed her sun-bronzed hair back from her face and glared at him. "Then you also know that if you had one of these momentary lapses on an actual mission, everyone in the unit—including Commander Conlee and every single operative currently on missions worldwide—would be killed. Inside of twenty-four hours, all evidence that SDU existed would be eradicated. *All* evidence, including us." Her green eyes burned nearly black with disdain and fury. "I'm not ready to die because you're sloppy or incompetent and are having momentary lapses, Gibson."

Gibson's stomach heaved and stuck somewhere in his ribs. "It won't happen again, ma'am."

"It can't happen again." She walked around the table, leaned across it, and planted her spread hands on its scarred surface. "Understand this, too. My first obligation is to the security of the United States. You screw up again and I'll kill you myself."

How could anyone so beautiful be so vicious and merciless?

Her partner, Maxwell Grayson, would say it was God's sense of compensation and balance, but Gibson considered it more likely God's twisted sense of humor, reserved to make men crazy—or His secret weapon, used to scare them spitless. Either way, Gibson believed her every word from his toenails up. It was common knowledge in the unit that if Gabby Kincaid said something, you could take it to the bank and cash it. Or, in his case, to the graveyard and bury it. "Yes, ma'am."

She folded her arms across her chest. "I'll be back in two weeks to either bust you out of SDU or to certify your final training mission. I have no mercy, Gibson. Remember that and be prepared," she warned him. "Now, get the hell out of my face."

Gibson wasted no time leaving the conference room. He felt shamed and scorched and totally pissed off at her for being unforgiving, and at himself because he had screwed up and created a need for it. He knew better.

Special Agent Maxwell Grayson stood leaning against the hallway wall. He straightened and then clasped Gibson's shoulder in an unspoken gesture of sympathy. "Rough one, huh?"

"Oh, yeah." Gibson looked back, grunted. "I've got a debrief with Commander Conlee next, and I'm not sure I've got enough ass left for him to chew."

Conlee wouldn't have to chew; Gabby had done a thorough job. But that was her job and vital to Gibson's training. "You'll probably survive it." Max nodded to lend weight to his words. "She's tough—"

"She deserves her reputation," Gibson interjected with feeling.

Max could disagree, but Gabby wouldn't appreciate it.

She'd worked hard around the unit to earn her unofficial title, "Queen Bitch," and even harder to keep it—it was essential to her high-risk performance. No one had called her that to Max's face, but Gibson had just come close. She must have really worked him over.

Rightly or wrongly, Gabby made an all-out effort to be hypercritical of other agents' job performances. In the last six years, she had alienated everyone in the unit except Commander Conlee and his second in charge, Jonathan Westford. Both relationships were atypical, and being her professional partner had told Max nothing. But being her personal friend had told him plenty that Brad Gibson and the others didn't know. "She's my partner, Brad. Show a little respect."

"Sorry." His face reddened and the pulse at his throat throbbed. "She just gave me a really hard time."

"Kiss her feet for it," Max said in all earnest.

Gibson's surprise had his jaw hanging loose. "What?"

"She's hands down the best active operative in the unit," Max told him. "What she rips you a new one for can—and probably will—save your life down the line. It has others, including mine. That's worth remembering."

"Okay, okay. You're right and I'm wrong. But, man, she's as subtle as a tank." Gibson dragged a hand through his short, spiky hair. "At this point, I'll be amazed if I get down the line without her killing me first."

"There is that." Max bit back a smile and stuffed a hand in his pocket. "Consider it an opportunity to rise to the challenge."

"I could strap my ass to a booster rocket and not rise high enough to please her." Resignation flickered over Gibson's face. "She meant exactly what she said, didn't she?"

"I've worked with her for five years, and I've never known her to make an idle statement or empty threat."

Gibson's face leaked all its color.

Ah, she'd threatened to kill him, Max deduced. Glad

her anger wasn't squared on his head, he nodded at Gibson. "Better get a move on. Commander Conlee is waiting."

"Wish me luck." Gibson rolled his shoulders, shook off some tension, and then took off down the hall.

"You got it." Not envying him the next half hour of his life, Max watched him go and then walked in the opposite direction, down the hallway, and into the conference room.

Gabby stood near the far wall, her arms folded over her chest, her eyes closed, her chin tilted to the ceiling. It was her classic pose for on-the-job meditating to harness her temper.

Max gave her a moment, then spoke up. "Still terrorizing the troops, I see."

"Only when it's necessary to keep them from killing others, Agent Grayson," she answered in a tone stiffened with mock formality. "Perhaps one day, you." She stood behind one of the hard-backed chairs. "I'd hate to lose my favorite absentee husband over a trainee with an attention deficit."

"I'm sure you would." Max nodded, letting her hear his sarcasm. Their marriage was part of their cover: a common means of keeping backup available on undercover, covert missions. "Especially considering how much you rely on your husband in your missions."

She rolled her gaze, moved to his side of the table. "You're essential to me, Max."

"As a friend, yes. But as a partner? No way."

A sigh heaved her shoulders. "Are we going to fight about this again?"

"We've fought over it for five years without resolving anything. My guess is, it'll be on the agenda for some time."

She crossed her chest with her arms and cocked her head. "You're a pain in the ass."

"Yeah." He smiled just to annoy her. "I'm nuts about you, too."

"Then show a little mercy. I'm pretty much beat." She

swiped at her chin and leaned forward against the chair. "Bitching out trainees isn't nearly as much fun as it used to be."

Max laughed hard and deep. "But, honey, you do it so well."

"Someone's got to do the dark and ugly around here." She shrugged, serious but sparkling mischief. "Can I help it if I have a talent for it?"

"I suppose not." Figuring he'd get slammed for his next comment, he crooked his arm close to his side and braced. "You do have a knack for exposing a mean underbelly."

She slid him a sultry look, stroked his tensed arm. "Baby, I have a knack for exposing a mean everything."

Heat sank into his skin from her trailing fingertip. Pretending to be unfazed by it, he rubbed a fingertip to his temple. "Actually, you're a tad short on a sweet disposition."

She feigned disdain. "You want me to breach my cover?" A smile touched her eyes. "I do try hard to honor my covers, Max."

He bit his lip to keep his expression neutral. He wasn't talking about her cover; he was talking about her life. Yet Gabby saw them as one and the same. "In that case, you're safe." Venting her temper on Gibson and bantering with Max had left her face flushed. It looked good on her. He caressed her cheek. "As Queen Bitch, you reign unchallenged."

She studied him, clearly looking for sarcasm, and found it. Laughing lightly, she gave him a hug. "That's what I adore about you, Max." Her voice muffled against his chest. "You're so appreciative of my finer qualities."

He closed his arms around her. "Isn't that a husband's duty?"

"It certainly is." She patted his back and then pulled away, still smiling up at him.

The lightness left his voice. This time she'd scared him. "You were gone too long, Gabby."

"No choice, really." She lifted her hands. "But I'm here now."

"You up for dinner?" He cocked a teasing brow that was more than half serious. "Conjugal rights?"

"Only in my dreams, darling." She sighed, checking her watch. "I'm in hustle mode."

"Now why is that always the case when it's your turn to pick up the tab?"

She hiked a cocky brow and suggested, "Great karma and a phenomenal streak of luck?"

"Unquestionably." He grunted to let her know what he really thought of that remark. "If you don't want sex or suds, then why the summons?" They'd often shared dinner and drinks, never had sex or shared more than hugs, though Max sure as hell had thought about it plenty and Gabby had made it clear she could be interested. Yet the idea of losing their easy rapport had both of them avoiding those "highly combustible" complications. They hadn't discussed it, just sort of come to an unspoken understanding of how things would be between them.

Half the time Max thought that understanding was clear, sound thinking. The other half of the time he stood in cold showers, swearing he'd lost his mind.

"Commander Conlee thought it would be a good idea to brief you on the Four Grande operation before I fly back to Florida."

Max nodded. Gabby had been undercover in Florida for the past seven months, investigating judicial corruption claims involving a suspected cell of extremely effective mercenary assassins known as Global Warriors and their connection to a local judge named Abernathy. The Four Grande operation was a secondary high-risk mission she'd taken on. Max hadn't thought much about it—simultaneous missions were common to seasoned SDU covert operatives—and Gabby habitually requested assignment to every one classified "high risk." Why, he could only speculate. But missions with ten percent survival odds stacked up against you fast. Max sat down across the table from her. Was it the rush? The woman was definitely hooked on danger. Why else would someone so vibrant and alive court death?

"Max." She sidled over, slid a hip onto the tabletop, and snapped her fingers in front of his face. "Are you listening to me?"

"Totally," he lied. "Go on."

"Succinctly put, Four Grande is in the mop-up stage. I turned it over to the FBI late yesterday. They've handled the resulting arrests."

SDU worked totally behind the scenes. Overt agencies handled the public aspects of all missions. "How many arrests were there?"

"Three." She shifted, sat on the table, and swung her dangling leg. The heel of her shoe brushed against his slacks. "All senior members of Four Grande, in the U.S. to buy arms through a phony charity they'd set up on the Web. That's been shut down and the FBI is tracking all transactions back to their points of origin. Homeland Security's all over it, so we're done."

Another success—and a hollow victory because she'd achieved it without him. "Excellent." Max admired her— not for her devotion, all SDU operatives were devoted— but because as hard as she was on everyone else, including Gibson, she was harder still on herself. Max respected that, and all of SDU respected her work. Who could argue with her stats?

Gabby shrugged, resigned that he intended to ignore her brushing his slacks, hinting for a foot rub. "I would have liked to dig down another layer in their organization to make sure we'd totally disrupted their operation, but they were within forty-eight hours of taking delivery on dirty nukes. Couldn't risk it."

"Good call, in my humble opinion." On rare occasions, she consulted with Commander Conlee or Assistant Commander Westford, but she didn't bother with anyone else, including Max.

"Thanks." She managed a nod. "So, we delivered. Close your file on Four Grande."

"*You* delivered, and *I* never opened a file on Four Grande." His jaw clamped tight and he crossed his arms over his chest. "If I had, it'd be empty."

"Max, please don't get pissy about this again." She lifted a pleading hand. "If I'd needed help I would have activated you. I swear."

"Funny, I'm hearing everything in this briefing except how you were nearly killed by one of the men arrested. You should have activated me to cover your back." He pointed a finger at her chest. "You keep shutting me out and you're going to wake up dead, woman."

"You're being melodramatic." She frowned. "Who briefed you? Gibson?"

"Gabby—"

The skin between her brows furrowed, deepening her frown. "It wasn't *that* close."

"It was *extremely* close," he countered with a level look. "You're a lousy liar."

"Actually, I'm quite an accomplished liar—being undercover more often than not does that to a woman—but it really wasn't that close. The guy was a lousy shot."

"Lousy?" Max raised his voice. "Jesus, Gabby. He missed giving you a Mohawk by three inches."

"See?" She hiked her shoulders. "Three whole inches. The man couldn't hit a barn door on a good day. My back was fine." She cranked her neck and stared at the ceiling, then turned pleading eyes on him. "Don't raise hell, Max. I know the lecture by heart, okay?"

That comment earned her a solid frown—and he held it so she wouldn't miss it. "I don't know why I waste my breath."

"Me either, but I forgive you." She pinched his cheek and again checked her watch. "Probably because you're gorgeous, and now and then you give a really good foot massage."

"And you give me gray hair and shut me out." She drove him nuts—and left him scratching his head. How the hell did she twist him up so much? Regardless, she'd won another battle in their ongoing war. "Okay, great." He consoled himself with a resigned sigh. "You lived—*this time*—and I'm glad."

"Me, too."

The wistfulness in her tone warned him something was off, and he really looked at her. Gabby was his age, thirty-five, and five-eight, though she had long legs that made her appear taller. Her blond hair hung long and loose down past her shoulders, framing her classic face. She commanded double takes, and even the most critical man couldn't consider her anything but beautiful. The whole package was striking, but it was her earthy sensuality and distinctiveness that made her compelling—qualities that helped her play a wide variety of undercover roles. She was complicated and, combined with a steely exterior—induced by either a sense of duty or a protective shield; only God knew which—very sexy. He understood exactly why men felt drawn to her and told her their secrets. At times, Max had felt compelled to spill his guts, too. The woman was also incredibly sharp and flexible and fast on her feet. And, blessing or curse, her work was her life.

Unfortunately, work was his life as well, which added a whole new dimension to the challenge of being her shutout partner. "I take it your investigation is going well down in Florida?" Max asked, relatively certain it must be since the commander hadn't told him otherwise. Though Max wouldn't bet his career she kept Conlee up to speed twenty-four, seven.

"*Our* investigation is fine," she said. "Complex. Moving at a snail's pace, but fine."

Pouncing on that deliberate *our*, Max opened his mouth to ask if he could help with anything, but she stayed him with a raised finger. "I've got it all under control. There's no need to pull you off your missions here to assist me there."

So much for *our*—and for her needing him. "You know, a guy could get a real complex partnering with you, Gabby."

"What kind of complex?" Glancing up at him, she turned serious.

"Feeling about as useful as gum stuck to the bottom of a shoe."

"That's absurd." She tossed his comment aside. "You're priceless."

"Yeah, right."

"To me, it's a fact, Max." She glanced at her watch again and frowned. "We'll have to finish this fight later. If I don't leave now, I'll miss my flight." She snagged her purse. "Unless something significant breaks, I'll catch you up on developments in two weeks, when I come back to bust Gibson. We'll have dinner and a couple drinks. Hell, I might even dance with you."

"Be still, my heart." Thumping his chest with a flat hand, he glanced toward the ceiling and slowly rolled his eyes.

"Okay, okay. Two dances, dinner, and a couple drinks. My treat. But I get a foot rub."

"What about conjugal rights?" He openly challenged her. "I'm priceless, remember?"

"Honey, they're amazing." She shot him a look that was deadpan serious. "As real and fulfilling as our marriage."

The dreamy lull in her voice held promise.

"Oh, yeah." She cast Max a wicked whisper that could

steal a man's sense. "Stretch your imagination a little, darling. We're very . . . creative."

Flooded with vivid images, he growled. "Get the hell out of here before you miss your plane and I have to feed you."

Laughing, she turned toward the door, headed back to Carnel Cove, Florida, to the Global Warrior/Judge Abernathy corruption case. Back to her primary cover assignment as a judge.

"Gabby?" Max stopped her, wondering if his assessment could be totally off the wall.

"Yeah?" She paused, looked back at him.

"Is Gibson that bad?" She'd said she'd be back to bust him.

Sparing Max a groan to signal he should know better, she slung her purse strap over her shoulder, walked back, and pecked Max on the cheek. "No, darling. He's that good."

"Of course." Max bit back a pleased-with-himself smile. He had a lot of faith in Gibson. "You wouldn't waste your time ripping a lousy trainee a new ass."

"I wouldn't?" Near the door, she slanted Max a sly glance back over her shoulder.

"No, you wouldn't." Max knew how her mind worked. "You'd just shoot him."

She didn't smile, but she did look tempted. Walking out of the conference room, her heels clicked on the ceramic tile. "Try not to get yourself killed while I'm gone. I'm in no mood to be a widow, and wearing black would be torture. It's sweltering hot in Florida in July. The humidity is murder."

"I'll do my best not to inconvenience you by dying." She looked fabulous in black—and sweltering. "Same to you."

The echo of her steps grew faint, and Max smiled. "I'll be damned."

For the first time in five years, Gabby Kincaid had expressed a professional interest in his survival. Did he dare to hope she was getting used to the idea of having a partner? Not a chance. For five years, she'd been direct about not wanting one, and when he'd had the audacity to suggest he could be helpful to her, she had flatly reminded him that she *always* worked alone.

Max rocked back on his seat. In the sheen of the copper wall, he remembered their first conversation after he'd been assigned as her partner under the absentee-husband cover, which was standard operating procedure on Special Detail Unit missions, and he'd had the temerity—some would say, bad judgment—to offer to help her.

Unless Commander Conlee orders you to put a bullet through my head, don't interfere on my missions. Any of my missions. Actually, it'll be best if you just stay out of my way. SDU missions carry high stakes and higher kill rates. If I die on one, it's going to be because I screwed up, not because some partner I don't even want got me killed. Now, let's go get a beer and you can tell me all about your love life. It's got to be fascinating—you're gorgeous.

Flabbergasted, Max had stuttered, *Excuse me?*

Gabby never missed a beat. *When you get your ass in a jam and I come rescue you, it'll be as your wife. I need to know details.*

She'd been fired up, loaded for bear, and deliberately pushed every one of his buttons.

To get around her aversion to having a partner, Max had worked at making her his friend. He'd succeeded, which was both blessing and curse—Gabby wasn't the easiest woman in the world to figure out and trying often left him dizzy. Yet she continued to refuse his professional assistance and it had taken a while for Max to shake off the feeling that by refusing his help on missions she was slamming him and his personal worth. Commander Conlee had sworn her attitude had everything to do with Gabby's view of Gabby and nothing to do with Max. When it came to SDU covert operations, Conlee had said, Gabby Kincaid was top-notch and knew it. She trusted only herself.

In time, Max had come to believe that. Professionally, she had earned his respect and, more than once, his admiration. But in SDU, working with a partner without trust was a mark for certain death. Between Max's reluctance to die and Gabby's shoe-scum professional treatment, Max had no choice but to concede that she *did* work best alone.

Even if it would eventually kill her.

Chapter Five

Carmel Cove, Florida ★ Friday, August 2

"Sources tell Fast-Track News that, while the timing of the biological contaminations of U.S. crops in Texas and Florida has sparked a wildfire of speculation and suspicion, there is no evidence these incidents were terrorist attacks. After extensive testing, authorities are confident the incidents are unconnected, natural occurrences.

"An authority, speaking on the condition of anonymity, says the Texas contamination happened as a result of two separate incidents that occurred near the same time. The first involved fruit imports that arrived from South America, tested clean, and were shipped to grocery stores before the infestation manifested. Flies likely acted as carriers and introduced the infection to the food chain. Already, flies, mosquitoes, birds, squirrels, and other wildlife are testing positive as carriers. The second incident occurred on Independence Day, when a cruise ship full of passengers returned to Texas from Mexico, where the infestation is prevalent.

"As we previously reported, the ship's medical officer said no passengers had reported feeling ill or symptomatic at departure, yet during the first forty-eight hours after the ship's return to the United States, twenty-seven passengers died. Today, over two hundred passengers and fourteen health care professionals, all of whom treated the first wave of passengers to arrive at local hospitals, remain hospitalized in serious to guarded condition."

Standing in his kitchen, Judge Andrew Abernathy stilled the knife covered with mayonnaise he had intended to spread on two slices of bread for a turkey sandwich. He held it in midair, praying his gut instincts were wrong, and listened to Jade McDonald, the pretty redheaded reporter whose image filled the TV screen.

"In Florida, orange growers report this same infestation already has claimed more than half of this year's crop. Due to the abnormally high rate of ill passengers, investigators suspect the contaminant was inadvertently introduced to Florida via an international airline flight from Paris. Florida state and Paris officials, however, deny responsibility, citing that identical cases have been confirmed simultaneously in seventeen countries.

"Currently in the U.S., forty-one are dead, including a two-year-old boy who was on the Paris flight, and an additional eighty-seven are hospitalized and remain in critical condition. Back to you, Tim."

Tim Fargate, the anchor seated at the news desk, looked skeptical. "Are authorities telling you we've seen the worst of these 'natural occurrences,' Jade?"

The wind whipped at her hair. Standing near the main entrance of Carnel Cove Memorial Hospital, she dipped her chin and responded. "On the record, no one is willing to commit. Off the record, they fear the loss of life and crops will mount significantly before the problem is arrested, Tim. Cipro, the current top antibiotic, is ineffective. Patients are just not responding."

Judge Abernathy's knees went weak. He put down the knife and then slid onto a kitchen chair, his lips thinning, his somber expression turning grim.

On the screen, so did Tim's. "Has the infection been identified? And what physical impact is it having on people?"

"Initially, doctors reported never having seen this exact infection, Tim. But in the last ten days, there's been a growing consensus in the medical community that the infection is a mutated strain of encephalitis. Patients are suffering neurological damage similar to that seen in cases of EEE—eastern equine encephalitis. That means, doctors are reporting everything from flulike symptoms with various degrees of memory loss to total shutdowns of the autonomous nervous system, and as we've reported, of course, death."

Tim retained his on-camera composure, but a muscle in his cheek ticked and his eyes looked haunted—about as haunted, Judge Abernathy supposed, as his own would look if he were brave enough to check them in a mirror, which he wasn't. Not now. And maybe not ever again.

Jade ended her report, and her image disappeared.

Tim's returned. "Today, on the West Coast, yet another biological outbreak has been labeled a natural occurrence by authorities. California wine growers reported that, in the last two weeks, a rapid-spreading grape louse infestation has claimed sixty percent of all plants in the Napa Valley. State authorities report that this louse has genetically mutated and is resistant to all known pesticides. While every possible effort is being made, inspectors and growers fear that California's wine industry and perhaps crops in other states will be destroyed.

"In other news, the weather system we've been tracking has been upgraded to Tropical Storm Darla. Darla has been churning up the northern Gulf of Mexico for nearly a week. Chief meteorologists claim conditions are favorable for further, rapid intensification. Currently, sustained winds are fifty miles per hour, and the storm is moving due north at eight. Pressure is ten fifty-seven and dropping. Warnings have been issued from Tallahassee, Florida, to Biloxi, Mississippi. Highest strike probability is between Panama City and Pensacola, Florida. From all the models, it looks as if Darla is going to be a hurricane and she's going to bear down on Carnel Cove. Local authorities have issued alerts, telling residents to take all necessary precautions immediately and warning people living in low-lying areas to be prepared for possible evacuation orders in the next few hours. Darla's development during that time will be critical . . ."

A hurricane *and* all this? The judge muted the TV's volume and then held his head in his hands, atop the table. In his mind, he heard his dead wife's voice. *You did this, Andrew. You, and your lust for revenge. Why didn't you just let it go? Why?*

Liz was right. Queasy, Andrew squeezed his eyes shut. He had wanted revenge so desperately; he had betrayed his country, the memories of his wife and son, and himself to get it. But sanity had returned, and when calm had prevailed, he had tried to turn things around. In December— within a week of Kincaid being appointed to the bench in the Cove—he had retired.

His retiring from the bench should have been enough. Yes, he had betrayed himself personally and professionally, but he had lost his family; serving as a judge was all he had left. Retiring really should have been enough.

But it hadn't been. And now . . . this.

Nothing about these biological disasters is natural, Andrew.

He looked up from the table, out through the breakfast nook window. A robin sat on a low-slung branch in the magnolia he and Liz had planted the day they had moved into this house, nearly thirty years ago. She had known his mind then, and she knew it now. *No, Liz. Nothing about them is natural.*

Natural or, he feared, unrelated. These incidents had to be parts of a coordinated attack launched for the Consortium by those bastard Global Warriors.

Guilt churned with regret and bulged inside him. As usual, Liz was right. His lust for revenge had seduced him into getting mixed up with the Consortium. Its senior manager, some mysterious man the local director referred to only as the chairman, supposedly called it a business alliance, but in truth the Consortium wasn't a hell of a lot different from the Mafia. It just ran corporations that manipulated stock, industries, and other corporations rather than illegal horse races, drugs, and gambling. Once a person was in with them, even on the periphery, he soon found out that the two were very much alike. Andrew, unfortunately, was in on the outer edge of that periphery. His only way out was death.

His eyes burned. Blinking hard, he glanced back at the TV screen, watched the names of the dead scroll by. So many innocents . . . gone.

And so many more would die.

A dark pall settled over him. His own death couldn't come soon enough. It would be a welcome relief, far easier on his conscience than living with knowing he could have done—

What, Andrew? What could you have done?

"Something. Just . . . something!" Frustrated, he lifted the knife and stabbed the turkey breast, and then swiped at the cutting board. He hit the mayonnaise jar. It fell to the tile floor and shattered.

You couldn't have stopped them alone, Andrew. But you should have at least tried. You should have gone to the FBI.

He would have been dead before he had reached the field office door. And for that same reason—he stared at the mayonnaise splatters, at the jagged shards of glass—even now, he would not do a thing.

Self-loathing washed over him. He ripped two paper towels off the roll mounted under the cabinet, and then bent to his knees on the floor to clean up the mess. In his position, he should welcome death. But he couldn't. Not really. God forgive him, Liz and Douglas, his only son, forgive him, he should welcome death, but Andrew Abernathy, retired judge and formerly a man who lived his convictions, wanted to live.

The telephone rang.

Grabbing the edge of the counter, he heaved himself up. His knees cracked, protesting, and he answered the phone. "Abernathy."

"It's me," a man said. "Did you see the report?"

The director of the Consortium. "I saw it. I suppose you've called to gloat." With the coordinated timing of the biological incidents, and having tracked them all back to Independence Day, the authorities had to strongly suspect they had been acts of terrorism. Yet they clearly had no evidence of it. If they had any at all, they never would have labeled the incidents "natural occurrences."

"Gloat? Me?" The director chuckled. "Well, maybe a little, provided they believe these are natural occurrences and they aren't just spreading misinformation under the protective umbrella of 'national security interests' to catch us off guard."

"How likely is that?"

"Considering the political repercussions of leaving civilians totally vulnerable, and us giving Paris and Florida plausible deniability of responsibility by infecting seventeen—soon to be twenty-one—countries? Slim, I would say. But either way, our interests are protected."

Andrew was disgusted. Why hadn't he expected that the director would kill indiscriminately? Why had he assumed the director had a moral conscience? That even if he did not, the chairman did? Nothing came between that man and his profits.

For someone who had spent a lifetime on the bench, judging people, Andrew had grossly underestimated the character of the director. And he had known the man nearly half his life. "Tell me there's a vaccine." The loss of crops could devastate the economy, but the loss of lives could devastate and cost far more.

"Of course, there's a vaccine. In fact, it was developed under a DOD contract for military applications, though, naturally, we've seen to it that its developmental progress has been grossly underreported."

A Department of Defense contract. This wasn't good news. The contaminants could be part of the nation's biological arsenal. "So the DOD has the vaccine, then?" Why weren't they treating the people hospitalized?

"Actually, they don't. We do."

Oh, God. "What about food supplies?" The U.S. fed most of the world. If the Consortium played too loose and free with their contaminations, the country and a large segment of the world would face famine and starvation.

"Relax, Andrew. Our storehouses are full. The supply is more than adequate, and we've got an effective pesticide."

Relax? He was holding people hostage for a life-saving vaccine and pesticide, all while sounding like a gleeful kid who had gotten his cake and now gets to eat it, too, and the director expected Andrew to relax? No one in his right mind could relax. "When are you going to release the vaccine?" Hundreds were hospitalized. Without the vaccine, they would die, and both men knew it.

"Soon enough. Bidding is still in progress."

Icy fingers tapped his spine, and Andrew cringed. "You're selling it to Americans, too?"

"Of course. We're in business to make money. Who has more to lose than the U.S.?"

Until now, nothing had been said about involving Americans. Had the Consortium solicited bids from research centers? Pharmaceutical companies? Andrew grimaced, snatched up the turkey, slung it into the trash bin under the sink, and then slammed the cabinet door. "People need that vaccine now."

"Trial studies haven't yet been done, Andrew. We need them to prove the military applications to potential buyers. The chairman assures me that once that's been accomplished, bidding will close, and the vaccine will be supplied to victims."

The son of a bitch was running trial studies on the public without their knowledge. Appalled, horrified, Andrew snagged the knife and cutting board, rinsed them off in the sink, and then dried his hands. Still feeling dirty, he washed them again. "What about the food?" Food imports were one of the few aspects of the U.S. economy that operated without a trade deficit. It was the spine of the economy. Without food, not only were people facing starvation, the U.S. economy was facing collapse.

Collapse the economy, and you collapse the government.

Andrew stiffened, his hip bone slamming against the edge of the counter. Pain shot up through his stomach, cinched his chest. During the course of history, that economy-to-government relationship had proven true. With the Consortium manipulating events, and their Global Warriors implementing them, the possibility of that strategy happening to the U.S. now seemed only too real. Was that the chairman's ultimate goal? The director swore it was strictly financial gain, but all of these attacks felt like . . . more. "I asked, what about the food?"

"I told you to sell off your agricultural stocks. You did it, didn't you?" the director asked, sidestepping a direct answer.

Andrew felt nauseous. He had followed the director's recommendation and had dumped all agricultural investments right after quarterly earnings reports had driven prices up six percent. That was just days before news of the biological incidents had first hit the wire. It would be months before U.S. authorities definitively determined the economy had been targeted and attacked—if they ever figured it out. The Consortium's Global Warriors never left loose ends. Andrew knew that for fact. He'd turned every stone and found nothing; no way out. "Yes," Andrew said, suddenly weary to the bone. "I cashed out."

"Then you're finally a rich man. I suggest you invest in Egyptian cotton," the director said. "Soon. And enjoy being at peace, Andrew."

He sipped iced tea from a chilled glass, hoping to ease the raw burn from his throat so his stomach would settle down and he wouldn't vomit. "I'll be at peace when I know for fact Gabrielle Kincaid is the judge she's supposed to be and not the Justice Department investigator I'm afraid she could be."

"What's the difference? Either way, beyond your acting as judge, she can't tie you in any way to the Warriors or their cases. How many times must I tell you that before you believe it?"

"How many times must I tell you there's something about her that isn't right?" Her image flashed through his mind. "She's too smart and pretty, and she's too skilled. In my experience, women are either mental or physical. Few excel at both. She does, and I'm telling you, she's dangerous."

"You're worrying needlessly," the director said. "No one in the Justice Department—or in the entire government, for that matter—knows the Consortium exists." His tone changed, placated. "Look, forget about her. Forget about all of this. Go up to the camp, do a little fishing, and just relax. Everything is under control."

"You're underestimating Gabby Kincaid." The robin

left the magnolia branch and flew off, beyond Andrew's line of sight.

"I'm not. Listen to me, Andrew. She's irrelevant."

"Irrelevant?" Andrew couldn't believe it. "She can bury us."

"No, she can't. That's why I called. Orders have been issued, my friend."

"What the hell are you talking about?" The orders had to be from the chairman. The director issued orders to everyone else and only took them from the chairman.

"Gabby Kincaid will be dead by dawn."

Chapter Six

Carnel Cove, Florida ★ Friday, August 2

Gabby snatched up the receiver and punched down the flashing line. "Judge Kincaid."

"Please hold for Vice President Stone," a woman said.

A few seconds later, Sybil came on the line. "Gabby?"

She removed her reading glasses and dropped them onto the desk in her chambers, eager to talk with her best friend. "Tell me this is good news. I've had a wicked day."

"I take it you're busy—it's nine P.M."

"Up to my ears," Gabby said, rolling her shoulders to work out the crackles. "An angel came out of nowhere today with a gift that's going to help me wrap up this mission. As soon as we get off the phone, I'm heading to the lab to verify a few suspicions." Soon she would know if Judge William Powell's unexpected death had been innocent, or if he had been murdered.

"I hope it pans out. You've been down there too long."

"You sound like Max." No huge surprise that the two

people closest to her would pick up on her thoughts. "I swear I've had it, Sybil. When this is over, I'm never going under deep cover again."

"Right."

"I mean it."

"You always mean it."

She did. She had meant it when she had been active duty Air Force in Special Operations, and again now as a senior covert operative in the Special Detail Unit, where she worked only high-risk Special Projects. Personally, she'd had enough. "This time is different. I'm burned out. Totally."

"Uh-huh," Sybil said, still lacking conviction. "Either way, you're still on for the first week of September, right?"

Vacation. "Absolutely. It's a ritual." They had vacationed together every year since they had been college roommates. Gabby stretched back in her chair and rubbed at her stiff neck. "Where are we going?"

"Jonathan votes for Tibet." A hint of laughter tinged her voice.

"Veto. You're the one who is engaged. I'm still single. Do you really want me to risk my soul by snagging myself a monk?" She stared down at the lamplight glinting on her desktop. Reflections of her gold gavel and crystal ball shone in the glossy wood. "How about England?"

"Honestly, Gabby. If I try to drag Jonathan through another castle, there probably won't be a wedding. Besides, I was hoping for something a little more obscure."

As only old friends can, Gabby interpreted Sybil's true meaning. She wanted to go someplace where she was less known and more apt to blend in with the masses. It wasn't a realistic thought, considering a detail of Secret Service agents guarded her every step, but Gabby understood Sybil's craving to get out of the public eye. "You could tell Jonathan I vetoed Tibet and then let him choose someplace else." Pure mischief seeped into Gabby's tone. "How about we commune with nature? The Florida swamps are obscure. Actually, they're private and impressive, I hear."

Sybil laughed, hard and full. "You're such a bitch, Gabby. Crazy, too, if you think I'm going through that again. I've had all the swamp time I can stand in one lifetime. Maybe two."

"But I'm sure it'd be far more relaxing this time. No jumping out of a plane with a bomb strapped to you to get to it—"

"Gabby." Warning edged Sybil's tone. "These are not pleasant recollections. It was hell out there."

"Hey, you survived." Movement caught her eye at the window. She looked over and watched a car creep down Main Street. Traffic on Main at this time of night was unusual enough that it piqued her curiosity. She moved to the window, but the car had disappeared onto Highway 98 and was now out of sight. "You should feel fantastic."

"You thrive on danger, not me."

"I'll take my kind of danger over yours any day. Swimming with political sharks is not my idea of a safe haven." Rocking back, Gabby propped her feet on her desk. "How about Spain?"

"Spain." She paused a moment. "Mmm, Spain could be interesting. Fascinating, actually. Sounds good. I'll tell Jonathan."

"Shouldn't we get his input before making a final decision?"

"Why?" Sybil asked in all seriousness. "If he disagreed, we would just outvote him."

"Works for me." Gabby smiled. Jonathan might get outvoted now and then, but he held his own with the two of them just fine. Sybil loved the man, and Gabby adored them both. "I'm so ready for a vacation."

"Me, too," Sybil said. "Are you going to invite Max this year?"

"I don't know." Gabby grinned. "I sent him a birthday card. He might not be speaking to me for a while."

"What did you do to him now?"

"Nothing serious, I swear. Just a little inside humor I'm not sure he'll appreciate."

"Gabby, if the man's still going to be ticked off in September, it's a good bet whatever you did is at least minorly significant."

Gabby ignored her droll tone. "I'm not telling."

"You're incorrigible."

"One of my finer traits." She rubbed at a knot in her neck. Long days and longer nights were catching up with her. "I'll tell you about it after I hear from him."

"Uh-oh. It's got to be bad if you're certain you're going to hear from him."

"Max calls at least once a week." The calls were short, flirty, touching-base calls, but she didn't mention that to Sybil.

"I don't know why you don't just stop dancing around and take the man to bed."

Gabby frowned, hoping it carried through in her voice. "It's not like that with us, Sybil."

"I know. But it could be, and don't bother telling me that isn't how you want it."

Gabby hated it when Sybil was right, which was too often. She went serious, refusing to give in to her or to her own emotions. "If I had a guarantee that sleeping with the man wouldn't screw up what we've got, yeah, I'd do it in a heartbeat. But I'm not willing to lose what we've got and it would screw things up. It always does."

"Not always."

Jonathan. He and Sybil finally had connected and their relationship was terrific. Enviable. "For you, no, not always." Gabby squelched a pang of jealousy. "But for me, it's as certain as sagging boobs in old age."

"Okay," Sybil agreed. "But he could be worth the risks,

Gabby. If taking a chance after divorcing Austin taught me nothing else, it taught me that. I don't want to imagine my life without Jonathan now. But I was afraid to take the risk, too. Look at what I would have missed."

"Max isn't Jonathan. He was in love with you for years. This is . . . different." She tried hard to keep the envy out of her voice. The envy and the wistfulness she so hated hearing.

"Not that different." Sybil sighed. "They're summoning me to the West Wing. I've got to go."

"Give President Lance my regards, and take care of you."

"I will—unless they corner me on running for president. David is pushing hard."

President Lance was a smart man. "You'd make a great president."

"Not all cultures are as open-minded as ours about women, Gabby. You've spent a lot of time in the Middle East. You know exactly what I mean. Women can't drive, can't vote; they can't get medical treatment at a hospital without a man saying it's okay. They can't go out on the street unescorted by a man."

"Well, if they're dealing with us, it's time they catch up."

"At Americans' expense?"

Gabby's mouth tightened in a frown. "We need to educate their women."

Sybil laughed because she was supposed to laugh, not because she had changed her mind. She was convinced that her candidacy would be a U.S. foreign affairs liability, and the one thing Sybil Stone, soon to be Sybil Stone-Westford, would never agree to was being a liability.

"You're wrong about this gender thing," Gabby said with passion. "Give the rest of us the opportunity and we'll follow you, Sybil. Give the world a shot at judging you as a leader and they'll follow you, too. You're giving in to bias and low expectations."

"I'll think about it." A buzz signaled, sounded through her phone; her second warning on the West Wing summons. Sybil paused and then added in a hushed, almost reverent voice, "Gabby, I've got an uneasy feeling about you. I don't like it."

"Well, thank God for that."

"Stop it. You know what I mean."

Unfortunately, she did. They often got these feelings about each other, and too often they had proven to be precursors of life-threatening danger. "Don't worry," Gabby said, knowing she was wasting her breath. "I'll be extra careful."

"Promise?" Sybil sounded vulnerable.

Gabby hated it, but she understood it. Aside from Jonathan, Gabby was the only family Sybil had, and she was extremely protective. "Hey, listen. I'm ready for a lot of things, but dying isn't one of them. I've got a future to anticipate. Spain, sangria, and gorgeous men are a scant month away."

"And if you're lucky maybe one of those gorgeous men will get your mind off Grayson?"

That was the problem with good friends. They knew too much about you. "I'd prefer that to doing or saying something stupid and Max filing sexual harassment charges against me."

"Mmm, the way you shut him out of your missions, he could be angry enough to want to do that. I'd sure be itching to get even. You have done some pretty outrageous things to him, Gabby. Like that clown stripper you had highjack him in the grocery store last year for his birthday—and what about the time you rigged his boat motor and he was stuck in the Devil's Triangle for two days?"

"He had everything he needed on board to fix that motor," Gabby said, hotly defending herself. "He wanted to be out there, so he deliberately waited to fix it."

"Right."

That *was* right. She rubbed a finger over her crystal ball. "He came back to work totally rested." And Commander Conlee hadn't so much as whispered a word about forcing Max to take a couple days' down time. "Don't worry, Sybil. I can handle him."

"Be careful, Gabby. Max isn't a 'handle me' kind of man."

"Maybe not," she said, mulling it over. "But we're doing dinner and drinks and he owes me two dances."

"Only if you're handcuffed to him so you can't leave him behind and go alone."

That stung. But because it was true, Gabby couldn't snap back with a witty remark. Instead, she took the conversation off on a tangent. "Max and handcuffs." She let out a breathy sigh. "Oh, my. I've been alone too long to have those kind of images in my head."

"Okay, okay." Sybil laughed, and the background buzzer summoned again. "Third time's a charm. Really have to run. Talk to you soon."

Gabby hung up the phone, and an immediate weight settled on her. Sybil's warning had her tense and uneasy, and she again checked the window.

Heavy black clouds churned low in the night sky, obscuring the stars and building into a whale of a thunderstorm. The tropical system NOAA had been watching, "Darla," must be strengthening. She checked her watch—nine-thirty; if she hurried, she could catch the tropical update on the radio on her way to the lab.

She snagged her purse and locked the office. The deadbolt clicked. Darn. She'd left the "gift from an angel" on her desk. Needing to put it in a safe place, she fumbled with her keys, and recalled stashing it on her last restroom break. *You're definitely burned out, Gabby. Huge.*

Chiding herself, she made her way to the elevator and took it down to the parking garage, then climbed in her red Jeep and headed for the Logan Industries lab.

Fifteen minutes later, Gabby arrived at the sleek brick facility. She drove straight through the lab's parking lot, beyond its asphalt and lights, into a small bank of trees. In the darkness and out of sight, she parked her Jeep, and then hugged the edge of the wood, working her way around the perimeter of the lot toward the private entrance.

The lot itself was empty. Pangs of sheer gratitude shuffled through her weary body. It had already been a long day. The last thing she wanted to do was to have to wait in the Jeep until everyone left the building, especially with a storm hanging heavy in the air. When she'd first arrived in Carnel Cove, Florida, she had nearly melted from the high humidity and hadn't been able to tell the difference between threatening rain and dangerous storms. Now she easily noted the differences, and unless she was mistaken, the sky was about to split wide open.

A branch cracked off to her left.

Gabby stilled, stared through the darkness toward the sound, seeking its source. Only L.I.'s—Logan Industries'—major shareholder, Candace Burke, Gabby's neighbor and friend, knew Gabby had access to the lab, and for her own safety—and Candace's—it had to remain that way. At best, exposure would be risky. At worst, it'd be lethal.

Gabby keyed the lock, punched in Candace's security code, and watched the door open. She locked it behind her, and though it was solid steel and weighed a ton, she gave it a habitual shake to make sure it was secure.

Of course, it didn't budge.

Moving through Candace's plush but rarely used office, Gabby took the hallway down to the lab, passing L.I.'s CEO and Chief Researcher Dr. Marcus Swift's plush and well-used office. Dealing with Swift had been easy—Gabby had totally avoided him—but Swift's second-in-command, Senior Researcher Dr. David Erickson, frequently interfered with Gabby's work here. The man was so devoted he rarely went home.

Dr. Erickson was responsible for a Department of Defense contract to develop a vaccine and pesticide to battle Z-4027, a vicious superbug that had unexpectedly surfaced in the U.S. last February, in New York. Homeland Security, and all Intel agencies, had been caught flat-footed by it, and President Lance had issued an executive order funding the research, seeking a solution. He'd also quietly turned over the challenge of finding out who was responsible for developing and turning the superbug loose in the U.S. over to the Special Detail Unit.

Erickson, who had years of researching EEE under his belt, had hit the ground running on the project, and he remained in high gear. Considering that Z-4027 had proven to be a genetically altered and extremely lethal derivative of EEE, the American in Gabby appreciated his going the extra mile. But in the last few weeks, since the July 4 incidents, Erickson had gone the extra mile in overdrive. The sensitivity and top-secret nature of the work required Logan Industries' full disclosure for reasons of national security—not to mention the political advantages of not disclosing to the world that a new superbug that had no cure was on the loose in the U.S.—which meant every event, note, calculation, and test on Erickson's project was observed and reviewed by Intel. That taped surveillance proved Dr. Erickson rarely left the lab. His work habits made for a lot of three A.M. visits to the lab for her, and there was no alternate facility within a reasonable distance.

Logan Industries was one of the top three cutting-edge government-contracted labs in the biological warfare defense program located away from Washington's and Nevada's arsenal storage. It had the added benefit of being the facility closest to the Centers for Disease Control in Atlanta. Six hours by car. Hours she had driven often in the past few months. But most importantly, Logan Industries was the only lab where Gabby could get full access, no questions asked. So she'd sucked it up and sustained the god-awful hours.

Ten minutes later, she stood to the left of a long row of mosquito-filled tanks at the first of four stainless steel lab tables, staring up at the white ceiling. She couldn't see the secure remote viewer, but she knew Intel had installed one there, complete with audio. When occurrences warranted, Intel passed top-secret information along to Home Base's Commander Conlee. Lagniappe for Gabby was that the viewer provided her with direct, secure communications with SDU. And secure contact between Home Base and a covert operative under deep cover was essential to staying alive.

She prepared the tissue specimen received on Judge Powell today, and immersed it in testing solution. Her nostrils burned. She sniffed and blinked hard to stop the stinging in her eyes, her nose, and waited. The specimen and fluid turned purple.

Oh, God. Oh, God, no. Her stomach pitched and rolled and she went clammy from the inside out. She tested again, and then a third time, to leave no room for error.

The results never changed.

Queasy, she pulled a mobile communicator from her purse, and inserted its earplug into her ear. It took two tries to seat it; her hand was shaking. Adjusting the lip mike, she bumped her mouth, cutting her inner lip with her teeth. "This is Lady Justice," she said, identifying herself and her security clearance to Intel by using her code name. "I need a direct feed with Dr. Richardson—stat."

Home Base's chief medical officer was one of the sharpest medical minds in the world. Gabby had often relied on his expertise, but never had needed it more than right now.

Gabby checked her watch. Two minutes ticked by. It seemed like two lifetimes. Finally, she heard a man's voice through her earpiece.

"We've established the patch, Lady Justice," the Intel officer said. "Tropical Storm Darla is charging down your throat, challenging communications. Wait twenty seconds for scramble to assure security."

Tropical Storm Darla? "It was a depression this morning."

"Yes, ma'am. And it'll be a hurricane by midnight, according to the Hurricane Hunters' ten P.M. advisory."

Oh, please. She did *not* need a hurricane complicating matters.

Dr. Richardson spoke first, his voice crisp and clear. "I'm on the line, Lady Justice. What do you need?"

"A verification request on the specimen testing, Doc." She couldn't, wouldn't, reveal the results until she confirmed.

"Striation or color?"

"Color," she said from around a lump in her throat, clearing the lab table and preparing the specimen for transport.

"How did you prepare the specimen?"

Relaying specific details on the specimen and then the procedure, she locked the specimen in place inside a foam-lined steel transport box.

"You're certain the entire specimen was totally immersed?"

"Yes, sir. I double-checked and validated."

"Then we want pink."

Pink meant the coroner had been correct. That Judge William Powell's cause of death was due to a natural genetic mutation of eastern equine encephalitis. That Gabby and Commander Conlee had been wrong, and the genetically altered superbug, Z-4027, deliberately created and black-marketed by God only knew who, had not murdered the judge.

"Lady Justice?" Dr. Richardson prodded. "What color is it?"

Gabby opened her mouth to answer him, but something moved just outside the lab door. Someone was coming. She couldn't risk a response.

Hurriedly, she shoved the transport case under the lab table and then dropped to the floor, rolled underneath it.

The door opened, and Dr. Erickson walked in.

She didn't move, didn't breathe. Whistling, he walked down the aisle on the other side of the lab table until he reached the fourth table, near the only window in the lab. She crouched, slid on her stomach, cleared the edge, and then risked a glimpse to see what he was doing.

Washing his hands at the sink. Turning his back, Erickson stretched for a towel.

Now or never, Gabby. There'll be no better time.

Adrenaline rushing through her, she grabbed the case and eased to the door. Slipping out, she scrambled down the hallway and, finally, exited the building.

Hard, cold rain pelted her head, her face, her arms, stinging her skin, drenching her clothes. Darla's feeder bands—the foremost lines of the storm—had arrived. Powerful gusts of biting winds whipped at her, tugging at her eyelids, plastering her hair back from her face, pushing her back toward the building.

Shielding her eyes, she avoided the amber-lit parking lot and headed through the trees, winding between branches that bent low, threatening to snap. The shrill wind sliced through the leaves, piercing her ears, slapping at her legs. Lightning flashed. Hellacious thunder rolled over the ground and rumbled through her, vibrating down to her bones. She stubbed her toe on an exposed tree root, muttered a curse, and kept moving through the dark thicket to her hidden Jeep.

Fighting a violent gust of wind, she forced the car door open wide enough to crawl inside.

It slammed shut behind her. The sudden silence was

deafening. Dripping wet and cold, she reached into the backseat for her judge's robe. A sharp stick. "Ouch."

Her skin crawled. She had nicked her fingertip on a knife that should have been under the seat.

An icy chill crept down her spine. She paused in removing her blouse, to focus, and recalled cutting twine from around the oak she'd picked up at the nursery and planted in the front yard. It had been larger than the ones she usually bought and planted on missions. Slinging her blouse onto the floorboard, she recalled her every move, pulled on the dry robe, and specifically remembered dropping the knife onto the seat while wrestling with the oak.

Relaxing, she fished in her purse for her keys. Her fingertips grazed the cool metal of her .38, a tube of Jive Java lipstick that was supposed to last eight hours but she managed to eat off in four, and finally hooked her key ring. She had to connect with Home Base, tell them the test results, and request someone to pick up the specimen. It was now valuable evidence that couldn't be replaced. But Dr. Erickson had been carrying a coffee thermos; clearly planning on pulling an all-nighter. Which meant she couldn't get to the remote viewer and be assured of secure communications. Until then, she had to keep the specimen someplace safe.

Her windshield wipers clacking, she drove back toward the courthouse and cranked up the volume on the radio to check the weather. But the rolling thunder and horizontal rain beating against the car drowned out the sound.

The traffic light suspended above the road on Main Street swung like a kid on a playground swing. Gabby hung a left, dipped into the empty courthouse's parking garage, and then parked in a slot next to the judges' private elevator. Shortly, she passed Judge Powell's old office, and a lump stuck in her throat. William Powell had been a good man. Stiffening, she walked on to her adjoining courtroom, bent low, and then tapped a button that opened a secret compartment under her bench. She placed the specimen into the cubby only she and the now-deceased Judge Powell knew existed, and then tucked notes of the test results inside the black leather notebook—the "gift from an angel" anonymously delivered to her office—that could prove helpful to Gabby. With luck, it would. But right now, she had no choice but to establish strict priorities, and anything ranking as "could" had to wait.

Beyond weary, she locked up and headed home. She'd grab something to eat on the way, shower and change clothes, and then return to the lab to wait out Dr. Erickson and reconnect with Home Base. She remembered Sybil's warning—another thought she couldn't shake.

She should activate Max.

Of course, she wouldn't do it. Things were heating up too fast. She stared out the windshield at the Silver Spoon Café. The parking lot was full. Sheriff Coulter's patrol car was parked next to the mayor's Caddy. Her jaw clenched and she had to make herself stop grinding her teeth. "Maxwell Grayson, you have no idea what I go through for you."

* * *

Max drained the bottle of beer and was about to signal the bartender for another when Brad Gibson circled the pool table and walked over to him, carrying a white envelope. "Agent Kincaid called and said to deliver this to you right away," he said.

"Thanks." Max nodded to the bar stool beside him. "Want a beer?"

"No, sir. I've got to get back and hit the books. One slip and she'll cut my throat."

Gabby. Gibson was talking about the SDU operative's certification exam. "Or break your balls."

"Most likely both, sir." Gibson still felt the sting of his last meeting with her. He turned and left the bar.

Max opened the envelope, pulled out a brightly colored card. Gabby had remembered his birthday. As he read the words, his heart beat faster.

To my gorgeous husband,
I hope this birthday is filled with laughter and joy
and a lot of celebrating. But not too much
celebrating or too much joy—not without me.
Laughter is okay.

At the bottom, she'd handwritten a note:

Envision me there, now, dancing with my favorite
shoe-scum and looking forward to . . . Use your
imagination, Max, and remember, we're very
creative.
                    Long, lush kisses and lots of love,
                    Gabby

Max stared at the card a long moment, willing his body to let go of the heat he was generating. He smiled to himself and tucked it into his inner jacket pocket. "Creative. Oh, yeah." On a whim, he pulled out his cell phone and dialed her number.

She answered on the second ring. "Kincaid."

His throat clutched. "I got your card."

Gabby smiled and braked for a red light on Highway 98, two blocks east of Main. "Happy birthday, darling." She glanced out the windshield to the rainy night. Thankfully, she had a little latitude, and the endearment wouldn't surprise Max. Cell phone conversations were a snap to monitor, so the cover had to be accentuated.

"Thanks. I just had a beer with you."

She smiled. "Did we dance?"

He dropped his voice, low and husky and hot. "Among other things."

She turned the corner, drove down the block. The lights were on next door, at Candace's house. "That sounds very interesting. I'd like to hear more, honey, but I'm in transit—need to stay focused on driving." Repressed laughter shimmied in her voice. "How about I call you when I get home and we engage in a little phone sex?"

He stared at his reflection in a mirror above the bar. His ears were red and he was grinning like the village idiot. "You're a walking violation to a man's discipline. Have you no shame, woman?"

"None." Three cars were parked in Candace's driveway—one, a Mercedes belonging to Elizabeth Powell, Judge William Powell's widow. "Love you."

"Of course. I'm a loveable guy," he said, then ended the call.

Grunting, Gabby stuffed the phone back into her purse. Just once, she wished he'd say he loved her, too. But he never did. Of course, he didn't love her, but that was beside the point. In their cover, he should love her to distraction.

Turning into her gravel driveway, her lights shone down the length of Elizabeth's Mercedes, and an unexpected shot of pure jealousy raced up her backbone. Elizabeth and William had been married twenty-five years. They'd had a history together that had spanned their entire lives, two great kids, and a lot of fun. They'd had home, family, marriage—a life.

Gabby had had a lot of lives, none of which had been her own, and she'd never had a relationship with Max or anyone else like Elizabeth and William's—and feared she never would. Something hardened in her chest, and she avoided looking at her own dark house, reached up to the visor, and punched the button to open the garage door.

It isn't your house, Gabby. It's your cover's house.

Either way, it was dark and empty. Her apartment in Georgetown, her cover house; it didn't matter. It never mattered. All of her houses were always dark and empty.

Hey, hey, hey. What's this? You have your work, Gabrielle Kincaid. That's the way you wanted it, remember? You have exactly what you wanted.

She did. Yet maybe she had been a little shortsighted. She had but didn't have Max. Had but didn't have an intimate relationship with any man. Had but didn't have a real life with a real family—good and bad and indifferent.

Grinding her teeth, she swept her wet hair back from her face, determined to leave this depressing pity party. "I need a vacation." She watched the garage door glide open.

Her headlights reflected off the freezer and hot water heater onto the concrete floor.

On two sets of wet footprints.

Chapter Seven

The hair on Gabby's neck stood on end. She couldn't back out of the garage and go for help; not without a lot of explanations she couldn't give.

The Special Detail Unit didn't officially exist and fewer than a hundred people—all with security clearances exceeding Top Secret—ever had heard of it. Military members assigned to SDU were formally assigned to "Personnel" along with most "Intel" and "Black World, Special Operations" folks, where their classified jobs could be easily concealed in the interests of national security, and civilians like Gabby were intentionally buried in the system's "Human Resources" maze. Good operatives *had* died to protect SDU's anonymity. But she wasn't eager to become one of them.

She tucked her Smith & Wesson into her waistband under the robe, wishing she'd kept on her wet shirt. Weapon access would have been so much easier.

One set of footprints led into the house. The other disappeared behind the water heater.

Fabulous. At first chance, the intruder by the heater would attack her from behind. She'd have to eliminate that threat without alerting the second person inside. The gun was not an option; no silencer. She needed the knife. She could just reach back for it, but it would be wiser to control the timing of the attack rather than to let the intruder choose it.

You're going to wake up dead, woman.

Max's warning replayed in her mind. She shut it out, took in three slow and steady, deep breaths. "Hold it together, Gabby. Focus. Focus. Focus . . ."

Feeling the familiar flood of calm that comes only with years of intense training and experience, she turned off the engine, got out, and then opened the back door and bent to the backseat. Her fingers closed around the knife.

A shoe squeaked on the floor behind her.

She spun around, saw his gun, and stopped. He stood too far away to disarm; she'd reacted too quickly. Her heart rate doubled. Adrenaline shot through her veins.

Dressed in black, ski mask to shoes, he motioned. "Drop whatever is in your hand."

Gabby stashed the knife through a slit in her robe, let her car keys fall to the concrete floor. The tinny clang surprised him; he startled. "Now your weapon," he said.

She forced herself to whisper brokenly, not wanting to alert the owner of that second set of prints. "I—I don't have a weapon."

He studied her for a long moment, dark eyes glaring, judging her, through two holes in the mask. She stretched her eyes wide, let her chin tremble, and hunched back against the car.

He believed her feigned fear, but not that she was weaponless. "Where's your purse?"

"In—in the front seat."

"Get it."

Perfect. Better than she dared to hope. Gabby snagged her purse, turned, and feigned a slip. When he automatically charged forward to keep her from falling, she kneed him in the groin, pulled out the knife, and stabbed the man in the chest.

Stunned, he grabbed his chest, opened his mouth to scream. She had to stop him before he alerted the second intruder. Quickly and efficiently, she slashed at his neck.

The man slumped to the floor, dead.

Gabby turned her attention to the doorway from the garage into the house. She'd never make it to the back or front door undetected. Going in through the garage was risky, but it provided the best shot for catching the second intruder. Hopefully, she wouldn't have to kill this one before she could question him.

She entered using normal tactics, gun first around the corner. No reaction from inside. Risking it, she peeked around the doorway. The light over the stove cast a sheen on the ceramic tile in the breakfast room. *Wet marks.* They led away from her, through the breakfast room, into the kitchen.

Her every sense heightened, every instinct alert, she eased inside, sliding her back against the rough, stippled wall. *Nothing.* Past the table and chairs, the hutch. *Nothing.* Off her right shoulder, the refrigerator motor clicked on and the icemaker dumped cubes into the bin. She nearly jumped out of her skin.

Focusing, she moved on, her footsteps silent. Near the corner, the sounds of rain outside grew louder. The back door must be open.

Afraid of falling for a deliberate trap, she maintained caution, checked above and below, and then made the last corner to the back door.

It stood wide open and the wet footprints continued

outside on the concrete, off the edge of the covered porch to the wet patio.

He was either gone, or he wanted her to be convinced he had gone. From the size of his footprints, this second intruder had to also be a guy—or a woman who wore about a size twelve.

Tightening her grip on the .38, Gabby went back inside and locked the deadbolt on the door. Her fingers trembled on the bolt's slide. Darkness wasn't an asset to her anymore, so she flipped on the lights, pulled a methodical, deliberate search of every inch of the house, and then the attic. When convinced she had an all clear, she breathed easier. The second man had cut and run. "So much for the benefits of having a partner."

Right now she didn't need a partner. She needed luck. A lot of luck, to figure out who the hell these men were and why they wanted to kill her.

She returned to the closed garage and then searched the dead man. In his jacket's left inside pocket, he had three sets of identification and two visas that looked totally authentic. But Gabby took a good look at his face and knew all of the identification was bogus.

The man she was looking at was Jaris Adahan, a Global Warrior on the Special Detail Unit's watch list.

And he'd come to kill her.

Tom Hanks's *"Houston, we have a problem"* ran through her mind. Boy, did she. A problem that carried ninety-percent odds of killing her.

Had the Global Warriors attempted to assassinate her because she was a judge looking into cases that might tie them to judicial corruption in Carnel Cove, Florida? Or did they want her dead because they had identified her as an SDU covert operative?

Chilling, but the truth didn't matter. Either way, she was a compromised operative. Her cover was blown and someone, either a warrior or an SDU operative, would come for her and do the killing. She had to notify Home Base.

Her stomach knotted. Resisting panic—she'd known the risks before getting into SDU and she'd elected to take them—she laid out her options. The secure phone line in the house could have been tampered with or corrupted; that left her one choice: the remote viewer. She got back into the Jeep and drove to the lab.

Dr. Erickson's silver Volvo was still parked in the lot. Neck-deep in her own problems now, she had little patience for him or his. She pulled out her cell phone and called Candace—the only one with total control of the lab.

"Hello."

"It's me," Gabby said, watching the trees bend under the forceful winds. "Listen, I have an emergency. Get Erickson out of the lab. He's parked and I need to get in there now."

"Gabby, are you okay?"

I just killed an enemy of the United States and I'm about to be rewarded for it by being killed myself. Of course, I'm okay. Why wouldn't I be okay? "I'm fine. Just get Erickson out fast, Candace."

"But he's securing the lab. Haven't you heard? Warnings are up all along the Emerald Coast. Hurricane Darla's going to hit us within twelve hours."

Another complication. Terrific. "That's in twelve hours. I need lab access now."

"I'll take care of it," Candace said, picking up on the urgency in Gabby's tone. "Do you need help? Elizabeth and I—"

"Not at the moment." Gabby hesitated, then went on. "I think Max is coming home."

"You're kidding." Candace's voice sounded deadpan flat.

Gabby clenched her teeth. She should have had him come to the Cove sooner. So his visiting wouldn't seem so strange. Honest to God, she never had intended to activate him, but now she had no choice. "I'm serious," she said, falling into his cover of helping Third World countries develop water purification systems. Currently, he was supposed to be in Africa. "He's finally at a point on the project where he can take a break."

"I'll be damned. I thought he was a figment of your imagination," Candace said. "Hey, Elizabeth. Max is coming home." A pause and then, "I swear, Gabby just told me herself."

They sounded delighted. Elated, even. But then they had no idea what his "coming home" really meant. Gabby's stomach hollowed. She gritted her teeth, disconnected, and then forced her mind to the immediate challenge and away from her personal crisis. Tapping the butt of the phone against the steering wheel, she waited for Erickson to leave the building.

Her thoughts raced and dragged her into despair. Not one scenario left her alive.

Erickson walked out of the building, ducking under a folded newspaper. The wind caught it, ripped it from his hands, and it tumbled across the parking lot. He ran for his Volvo, parked under an amber street lamp. When he cranked the engine and hit the lights, Gabby whispered, "Bless you, Candace."

Erickson finally pulled out of the lot, passed the neon Logan Industries sign, and hooked a left on to Highway 98, the main thoroughfare in Carnel Cove. His tires kicked up a spray of water; then, seconds later, his taillights disappeared from sight. Gabby waited another flash and then put on her headgear, adjusted the lip mike, and made for the lab door.

Minutes later, for the second time that night, she stood at the steel lab table staring up at the ceiling to communicate with Home Base through the remote viewer. "I need a direct feed to Commander Conlee."

"He isn't available, Lady Justice," the Intel monitor said, clearly recognizing her voice from her earlier transmission.

Isn't available? He was always available. "Is he dead?"

"No, ma'am. He's in conference with the President."

Great. Just great. "Okay, fine. I want you to record what I'm telling you and get it to Lieutenant Gibson. Tell him that I don't care how he does it, but I want this message in the commander's hands within the next ten minutes. Tell him he's got an SCO in a Code Red."

Hearing *Senior Covert Operative* and *Code Red* in a single statement conjured an immediate reaction in the man. "I'm sorry to hear that, ma'am." The timbre of his voice proved he genuinely meant it. "Are you coding the operative or the mission?"

She, not the mission, had become the high-risk liability. Though sorry, too—they were discussing her life—she refused to so much as blink. "The operative." She swiped at her forehead, unsure whether she was mopping at sweat or raindrops. "The mission remains at Level Three." Midlevel. Important, but not a situation currently threatening widespread destruction of life or assets. Those challenges were deemed Level Five missions.

The operative. They both knew what that meant. Her death was inevitable. The only question was would hostile or friendly forces kill her?

"Are you ready to record, ma'am?"

She cleared her throat, debating. If she disclosed Judge Powell's test results, she would be dead before daybreak, and she needed time to find a way to survive, if one existed. She needed help. She needed Max. She hadn't wanted him involved in any of her missions. The risks were too great. But this wasn't just about what she wanted for him anymore. Her back was against the wall and her ass was on the line.

Probably far more than just her life was on the line.

They weren't here just to kill her. They were here to kill others. Lots of others. They're Global Warriors. No one hired Global Warriors for a single hit—not even for a senior SDU operative. They would kill others unless stopped, and she couldn't stop them alone. Max was her only logical course of action. She blew out a silent breath and looked up at the remove viewer. "I'm ready whenever you are."

"Go ahead then, ma'am. We're running . . . three, two, one . . . now."

"This message is classified Eyes Only. Lady Justice to Commander Donald Conlee." She paused to give Intel time to officially abandon their ears. "Commander, it's Gabby. I'm issuing a Priority One request to activate Agent Grayson immediately." *Sorry, Max. I can't protect you anymore. I need help—even if it just means someone I respect kills me.*

He was her partner. He owed her that much.

He owes you a lot more, not that he will ever know it.

Tuning out her internal dialogue, she focused on the recording. "There is one stipulation to this request, sir." Obligated to lay out the situation in blunt terms, she swallowed hard and let the tremble in her voice reveal what she couldn't express with words even on a secure communication. Issuing your own death sentence was extremely difficult, even for an SCO. "I'm in a lousy position here, Commander." She broke into a cold sweat and dread covered her like a shroud. "Make sure Agent Grayson is up to doing whatever proves necessary. Otherwise, keep him at home and I'll handle it myself."

Are you crazy? Handle it yourself? You can't do that.

I can, and I will.

Silence, heavy and thick, hung in the air. Then the Intel monitor spoke up. "The commander will need to know the extricate-or-eliminate odds, Lady Justice—to make the best decision. Did you cover that, ma'am?"

He was right, of course. That she hadn't given it to him

automatically proved how rattled she was by all of this. "Not yet. Odds of extricating me?" With Hurricane Darla bearing down on the Cove and a Global Warrior hunting her down? Sucky. "Ten percent." And that was being optimistic.

"Elimination odds?" he asked.

Her heart thundered, knocking against her ribs. Worse. "Ninety percent."

Unfortunately, that prediction was even more optimistic.

Chapter Eight

There is no justice.

If there were any, Max would be in his apartment, kicked back in his recliner, sipping a cold beer and watching the Yankees kick ass on TV. If there were a lot of justice, Gabby would phone him back for a robust session of phone sex, which was about as likely as her activating him on a mission. He'd settle for a call within the next three days—her equivalent of "right away"—and a sassy sparring session of flirting and matching wits, which he would relish until their next sassy session, knowing it proved just how pathetic his real life had become.

That, of course, was Gabby's fault. She had breezed into his life and highjacked his senses. Her pit stops ruined him for other women and her birthday card had his imagination in overdrive. But instead of baseball or stimulating calls from Gabby, Max was responding to Commander Conlee's summons to Home Base on an SCO Code Red.

Everyone in the unit understood the likely outcome of a SCO Code Red. The scum being investigated by a Special Detail Unit operative would live, and the senior covert operative doing the investigating would die. Where was the justice in that?

Driving down the dark, dusty road to the top-secret A-267 site housing headquarters, Max swiped at his pants leg, hoping to hell he hadn't been summoned to do the killing.

A fence topped with razor wire stretched across the road, a gate and brick security shack in its center. A guard pulling duty walked out, wearing camo gear and carrying an M16. It was Fowler. Max braked, dimmed his headlights, and opened the window to flash his ID and reel off the day's security code.

Fowler waved Max through, and he drove on through A-267—a site that housed so much sensitive intelligence and technology that the entire site had to be classified—to the three drab-green hangars buried under a canopy of thick foliage that protected them from satellite view. He parked outside the far left hangar. It still housed Home Base headquarters—at least, temporarily.

A short while back, during a missile crisis, several members of the press had breached site security. SDU, of course, hadn't been compromised, but now Home Base needed new quarters to retain its anonymity. And just as soon as the commander put in a formal request to President Lance on a new location, it would have them. Odds were running four to one that Conlee already had the place chosen and a sleeper cell of operatives on site, smoothing the transition. Odds were one hundred percent that site would be in a rural community, away from Washington and any densely populated area. After the missile crisis, when D.C. and the surrounding states were in jeopardy of annihilation, adopting that policy seemed like a no-brainer to Max.

Inside the cavernous hangar, he cleared Level One security. In the hallway, his shoes squeaked on the white tile floor, grating on his raw nerves. He stopped outside the elevator that would take him down to headquarters and processed through the biometric iris, bone structure, and DNA cross-match rituals, clearing Level Two.

The elevator door opened. Max stepped inside and, moments later, he descended to the area most SDU operatives referred to as "the tomb." Home Base was buried so deep in the bowels of the earth that no missile known to man could penetrate it. That added protection wasn't essential to Home Base's mission. It was a perk the unit enjoyed due to other classified concerns at the site.

The elevator stopped and the door opened.

Just outside, Brad Gibson stood behind the sleek station desk, pulling Level Three security. Though young and brash when first assigned to Home Base a year ago, Gibson had lost a little of his attitude and a lot of his innocence. Narrowly averting a national disaster that had started on your watch could do that to a man, and that missile crisis had done it to plenty of them. Even President Lance hadn't been exempt. He'd taken Oversight, which monitored Special Detail Unit's mission activities, away from Senator Cap Marlowe and had put it directly under Vice President Sybil Stone's wing.

SDU undeniably had benefited from the change of command. The veep had made it her business to make sure the honchos knew how important it was that the nation have a strong last-line-of-defense. "Well," Max said to Gibson. "I see you're still hitting the books." He'd stated his intentions earlier in the bar. "How's the mentoring going?"

Gibson set the Regulations binder he had been studying aside and grunted. "Commander Conlee used to make me nervous. But after getting reamed by Agent Kincaid, talking to the commander's a breeze."

A new respect for Gabby that hadn't been there before

registered in Gibson's voice. Max was glad to hear it. "I'll take one of his chewings over one of hers any day," Max said, and then reeled off the day's clearance code.

Gibson double-checked it, verified, and then nodded. "You're clear to proceed, sir."

Max took the corridor to the conference room, where he would meet with Commander Conlee, who ran SDU with an iron fist and the full weight of the Presidential hammer. Seeing a Secret Service agent standing just outside the door put dread back into Max's step. The honchos had been called in, too. *Bad sign.*

Nodding, he walked past the man, and entered the conference room. For the moment, it was empty; security must have just finished its sweep. Without Gabby standing in it, the place felt different. Colder. More distant. Intense. And it looked as barren as it felt.

Lined in copper to decrease the odds of conversations being intercepted by hostile or friendly forces, the conference room held only the scarred conference table and straight-back wooden chairs—nothing to invite a man to sit or encourage him to linger. That seemed appropriate, considering anything that brought people to this table, brought them there to resolve a crisis that couldn't be resolved through ordinary means or by overt U.S. agencies.

As soon as Max took a seat, the still silence and the weight of what he feared would soon happen here bore down on him.

If there were *any* justice at all, he wouldn't be here, and he definitely wouldn't be about to receive orders no covert operative—whether assigned to the elite Special Detail Unit, or to the more typical CIA or FBI—ever wanted to receive. On his birthday, no less. He sighed. *You're batting a thousand, Max.*

"Grayson." Commander Donald Conlee strutted into the conference room with the gait of a man in his twenties, not his mid-fifties. His mouth was twisted into a sour curve, his unlit, stubby cigar clenched between his teeth. "Thanks for coming."

The light from the overhead fluorescent shone down over his short, spiked gray hair and onto a face hard-lined from too many tough decisions and too little laughter. Max respected Conlee. He was tough, but fair. Still, he was the last man Max wanted to see tonight—and judging by the grim line of Conlee's mouth, he wasn't any happier about having to see Max.

A bitter taste filled his mouth, and Max stood up. "Commander."

"I've asked Agent Westford and Vice President Stone to join us." Conlee motioned for Max to sit and took his own seat at the head of the table. "They'll be in momentarily."

Oh, man. A consensus briefing. Jonathan Westford was SDU's Assistant Commander, Conlee's right hand. He was also Vice President Sybil Stone's fiancé, and she was the head of Oversight. That they both had been asked to attend this meeting had Max's stomach doing double gainers. Conlee clearly intended to issue Max the orders he had dreaded receiving from the moment he had been summoned to headquarters.

Only one order required the veep's consensus prior to Conlee issuing it: an order to cancel an SDU covert operative. And knowing it left just one question in Max's mind.

Which operative would he be ordered to murder?

Chapter Nine

At exactly twelve minutes after midnight, Conlee launched the briefing and, gauging by their sober expressions, both Vice President Stone and Agent Westford had no illusions about why they had been summoned to Home Base's conference room. Clearly, they found the meeting as distasteful as Max.

"About a year ago," Commander Conlee said, "the director of Homeland Security asked me to review three criminal cases that Intel had red-flagged for suspected judicial corruption. All three cases had transferred from other parts of Florida to Carnel Cove for trial. Judge Andrew Abernathy heard all three cases, and in each one, he ordered a suspended sentence."

"Am I missing something, Commander?" Sybil asked. "I don't understand why this isn't being handled through the Justice Department. What makes it significant to Homeland Security, much less to us?"

"All three defendants were on the SDU watch list, ma'am." Conlee's mouth flattened to a slash. "We think they were Global Warriors."

Max leaned forward, riveted. Of all the challenging adversaries SDU faced, the Global Warriors were currently the most worrisome. The reason stemmed from demographics. The Warriors weren't loyal to any country, or motivated by any set of ideals, any religion, or any convictions. Simply put, they were an international group of hired assassins who would murder anyone for the right price. The Warriors enjoyed killing and they were good at it. That made them extremely dangerous, extremely difficult to locate, and extremely difficult to eradicate.

Conlee stuffed his cigar stub into his shirt pocket. He always carried one, but hadn't lighted up in years. "During our initial review, a fourth suspected Warriors' case was transferred from Miami to Carnel Cove. Since the opportunity presented itself and I was on the verge of ordering deeper investigation, I inserted Agent Gabrielle Kincaid in Carnel Cove as a judge."

"Gabby?" Vice President Stone stiffened. "This is about Gabby?"

Max's stomach clutched. Gabby. Not Gabby. She was his partner, but she was also the closest thing the veep had to family. They had been college roommates and best friends; like sisters.

Pity flashed through Conlee's eyes. Regret chased it. He didn't answer the veep directly, just continued his briefing. "Gabby's mission was to identify the players, investigate the circumstances, and gather sufficient evidence for the appropriate overt Homeland Security agencies to prosecute and convict Judge Abernathy—if guilty—and all Global Warriors she could directly link to the corruption, or to any other incidental crime. Frankly, we wanted whatever she could get to arrest or deport them."

"Are they still in the country?" Westford asked.

"Not legally, but who knows? Our borders are still like sieves."

Max stole a glance at the veep. Her coloring had gone from a flushed pink to pasty white. She was controlled, but this news wasn't going down easy.

"I followed typical protocol, in case Gabby required emergency backup or extraction, and assigned Agent Grayson—" Conlee nodded toward Max "—as Gabby's absentee husband. His cover is that he's a subject matter expert, a governmental consultant who primarily works in Third World countries, establishing health and safety standards."

Sybil slid Max a look heavy with accusation. "If Gabby is in trouble, then why aren't you there, helping her?"

Max had been aware of the assignment, of course, but he hadn't been told particulars. Hell, he'd only learned mission details while sitting at this table, and he hadn't been given an opportunity to review the records. The commander had followed standard operating procedure on that, too, and had sealed them. The veep knew that every case designated a "Special Project" and referred to SDU by an overt agency for disposition required the mission records being sealed. It minimized interagency leaks that could blow the case. She also knew that Conlee granted access on a "need to know" basis, and that on this mission, until now, only he and Gabby'd had a need to know. Max hadn't been activated. But while the veep knew all this and more, she wasn't immune to her emotions, and this was personal. Holding that in mind, Max softened his response. "She hasn't permitted me to or asked for my help, ma'am."

"Actually, she has." Conlee corrected Max, and then looked at the veep. "That's why we're here now, ma'am."

She nodded, and Conlee went on. "Shortly after Gabby was inserted in Carnel Cove, Judge Abernathy refused to hear the fourth case. He cited failing health and retired."

"Did he get tipped off about Gabby?"

"No evidence of that, ma'am. She thinks he just had a keen sixth sense about her."

"Or a guilty conscience."

"That's possible, ma'am," Conlee agreed. "Regardless, Abernathy retired and that left Judge William Powell in charge."

Westford spoke for the second time since entering the conference room. "What's Abernathy been up to since his retirement?"

"He spends most of his time at his fishing camp, which is on a lake about twenty miles north of Carnel Cove. His best friends, Mayor Faulkner and Carl Blake—he's a bank president and local businessman—"

"What kind of business?" Westford interrupted.

"Several," Conlee said. "Car lots, a fleet of school buses and pest-control trucks, a lot of real estate—nothing out of the ordinary." Conlee set down his coffee cup. "Anyway, Faulkner and Blake often drive up to Abernathy's camp for the weekend. Judge Powell used to go up fairly often, too."

"When did Powell stop going?" Westford asked.

"When he died." Conlee gave Westford a flat look. "As mentioned, last February, he contracted EEE, according to the coroner's report."

"Do we think it was something else?" the veep asked, picking up on the commander's strange wording.

"Within forty-eight hours, he was dead, ma'am."

Eastern equine encephalitis that ran its course from incubation to death in forty-eight hours? Max barely suppressed a curse. The usual incubation time on EEE was ten to fourteen days. Powell's version had to contain an accelerant. "EEE or Z-4027?"

"Gabby's determining that now." Conlee stabbed the

point of a pencil to the blank yellow pad on the table before him. "FBI contacted the local coroner. He swears it was EEE."

And for reasons of national security, Conlee hadn't openly challenged that diagnosis, though he clearly doubted it. Max mentally reviewed the details of the New York incident where an accelerated EEE, dubbed Z-4027, had first surfaced in the U.S. It had occurred last February, too, on a hotel elevator and had killed eight people. The accelerant hadn't been seen before, and Max hoped they weren't seeing it now. But with all the contaminations lately, only a fool would rule out that they could be. Regardless, in February Conlee had recommended counterterrorism grants and contract awards be issued immediately through the Department of Defense to study the EEE accelerant. President Lance had approved them, and the Special Project had been code-named Z-4027, though as a national security precaution, everyone referred to it as EEE.

The U.S. could hardly announce that a deadly superbug had been turned loose inside the country when it had no defense against it. Whoever had unleashed this monster would ransom it off on the black market to every terrorist group in the world with an ax to grind, and they would use it against the U.S. Work on a vaccine and a pesticide, since the superbug worked equally well at destroying vegetation, crops, wildlife, and humans, was ongoing. Max blinked hard and fast. "Judge Powell was one of the victims?"

"Maybe. But he wasn't in that New York elevator." Clearly worried, Conlee thumbed the handle on his coffee cup. "If Powell got Z-4027, he contracted it in Carnel Cove. We'll know as soon as Gabby finishes running the tests on the tissue specimens."

The Vice President frowned at the commander. "The man died in February. It's now August. Why haven't these tests already been done? Obviously, you've had these suspicions Z-4027 was involved."

"We couldn't get authorization to test the tissue, ma'am. Powell's widow, Elizabeth, refused on religious grounds to give anyone official authorization."

"But," Westford interjected, turning his gaze from Conlee to Sybil, "national security overrides religious grounds."

"Not without a public constitutional challenge."

Max looked at the veep. The operative word in that explanation was *public*. Exposure was the last thing they wanted. "So Elizabeth Powell won by default."

"And gauging by her objection, Judge Powell apparently had some suspicions of his own," Westford added.

The commander nodded. "Gabby says Powell didn't know which authorities could be trusted so he told Elizabeth to trust none of them."

Sybil touched the tip of her finger to her temple. "If she doesn't have the specimens and the overt agencies can't get authorization, then how is Gabby doing the tests?"

Conlee looked down his nose at her, his chin dipped to his chest. "Elizabeth gave the specimens to Gabby personally. We suppose, because Gabby worked for Judge Powell, but it wasn't due to blind trust. Elizabeth and a few female friends in Carnel Cove ran a respectable background check on Gabby," Conlee said, offering rare praise. "Fortunately, we were prepared with her cover. When they were finally convinced that Gabby was trustworthy, Elizabeth approached Gabby about the specimens and her suspicions. She demanded Gabby's solemn oath that she would tell Elizabeth the truth about the results and give her access to them. Gabby agreed because frankly that's the only way we could get the specimens and test them."

Max mulled that over. "Maybe these Carnel Cove women are tied to the corruption cases. They have influence with Elizabeth Powell and investigative skills. Hell, they could have hired the Global Warriors to take out Gabby."

Conlee's eyes shone, but not with suspicion; the commander was clearly amused. "We've been watching the ladies of Carnel Cove for a long time on other matters, and we've run extensive security checks. They're safe."

Surprised, Max wasn't sure what to make of that. Conlee rarely deemed anyone outside of the unit safe, and that included former Oversight chairmen.

Westford frowned. "So this superbug first appears in February, and it shows up twice. Multiple testing attacks?"

The thought alone chilled Max's blood, but it was highly possible. "The timing between the New York elevator attack and Powell's death can't be coincidental." Staggering implications. "If the February attacks were the testing phase, it's feasible that the Z-4027 has already hit the black market. That could explain the rash of Independence Day contaminations."

"Good God, I hope not," the Vice President said, swiping her hair back from her face. "Reasonable speculation but not proof, Agent Grayson." She looked back to Conlee. "We don't have proof of that, do we?"

"Not conclusive proof, ma'am. Not at this time."

"Okay, then. We go on what we've got." Sybil turned the topic back to her situation, eager to determine Gabby's status. "What about Judge Abernathy's personal contacts? Or following his money?"

Conlee answered. "He's had no interaction with known or suspected Warriors and no irregular, traceable financial transactions."

"So why are we here?" The veep's patience gave out. "What's wrong with Gabby?"

Max heard the fear in her voice, and saw Westford reach beneath the table for her hand. This was going to be bad. If what Max suspected would happen did happen, whether or not she granted her consensus, the veep would never again look at Max without hatred in her eyes.

Conlee sipped from a steaming cup of coffee at his elbow, then met her gaze head-on. "About an hour ago, Gabby contacted us through a remote viewer we installed in Logan Industries' lab in Carnel Cove, Florida."

If memory served Max, Logan Industries was a research firm currently working on a couple of Department of Defense biological contracts.

"Is she hurt?" Sybil asked in a hollow, wooden voice.

"No." Conlee shoved his coffee cup away. "But she asked me to activate Max immediately—provided he has the guts to extract or cancel her. She placed elimination odds at ninety percent, ma'am."

A sharp breath lifted Sybil's chest. She smoothed her hair back from her face and shifted on her seat, struggling to temper her reaction.

Westford glanced from Conlee to Max, then back to Conlee. They all were clear on what this activation meant. "Did she say why?"

"Her report was interrupted. I suspect she's discovered a connection between Powell's death and the other Z-4027 incident. And I further suspect she's somehow tied them both to Global Warriors. That's speculation, but she's believed it for a long time, and the Warriors have marked her as a target."

Due to the veep's personal relationship with Gabby, Conlee was tiptoeing, trying to let her digest the gravity of the situation in bits. But Max needed hard data fast. If Gabby had requested backup, she needed it yesterday. Only an act of Congress or a monumental crisis could convince her to ask for his help. "I'd like to review the tape."

"Sorry." Conlee gave Max a negative nod. "She's classified it, my eyes only."

"How can I help her if I'm not briefed?"

"You'll be told all you need to know."

Max's stomach dropped into a sour pit.

Westford scratched at his temple. "If Gabby's cover is

as a judge, how the hell did she get access to a medical research lab to get to the remote viewer?"

"Her neighbor, Candace Burke, is Logan Industries' major shareholder," Conlee said. "Strictly a figurehead. She's a financial whiz. Not into research. But she keeps an office there and she provided the access—according to Gabby—no questions asked, no explanations given."

"Candace must be friends with Elizabeth," the veep said.

Conlee nodded. "She wasn't the primary investigator in their group when they checked out Gabby—that honor went to a computer whiz who works for Candace, Miranda Coffield—but Candace was involved and, yes, they're all friends."

"That explains lab access, then," the veep said, seeming completely satisfied that the rationale was logical and sound.

Max wasn't buying it. This group of women had to know Gabby was more than a judge for Candace to give her unfettered lab access. With the bio contracts being handled there, Candace had to know the security breach carried penalties too steep for a friend to do a friend a favor. She could be looking at charges of treason and life at Leavenworth, for Christ's sake.

He looked over at the commander, whose stoic expression said he wasn't buying the unfettered, unquestioned access either, and he intended to order Max to cancel Gabby, which was indeed why the veep and Westford were here. No doubt about it, this was a consensus briefing. Professionally and personally, Conlee wanted the veep to sign off on the kill order before he ordered Max to execute it.

He leaned back in his chair, grateful that he wasn't standing in the commander's shoes. Killing Gabby was bad enough. Having to ask her surrogate sister to authorize it had to be hell.

Conlee looked straight at the veep. "You know what we have to do, ma'am."

She stiffened. "Don't be ridiculous, Commander."

"Gabby gave herself ninety percent elimination odds," Westford said. "Ninety percent."

"No!" The veep's face turned the color of paste. "For God's sake, she's one of us."

"Yes, Sybil, she is." Westford kept his voice calm, his tone firm, and looked straight into her eyes. "And she knows best. We have to trust her judgment."

"Ma'am," Conlee said softly, leaning toward her over his yellow pad on the table. "I know how difficult this is for you. I'm fond of Gabby, too. Hell, I handpicked and stole her from Air Force Special Ops." A frown creased the skin between his eyebrows. "I feel responsible for all my people, but even more so for her—because of the nature of her missions. Yet, we've got an entire nation depending on us to do what's right for it. We can't compromise—not even for Gabby. We've had several close brushes with the Warriors. Gabby is human and she will crack under torture. Everyone does. We can't risk exposure. If SDU is exposed, we lose the entire unit's capacity to act, and we put every operative we've got worldwide in mortal jeopardy."

"Killing her has to be wrong," Sybil insisted. "She's sacrificed so much to protect this country. This isn't right. It can't be right—"

"Sybil," Westford said softly. "We've had to sacrifice operatives before, and we'll have to do it again. Everyone in the unit knows the risks, including Gabby. She chose to take them because she believed what she was doing mattered more than any one individual's life. Even if that individual life she had to sacrifice was her own. She made the call. Then and now."

"Jonathan's right." Conlee pulled out his stubby cigar and mashed it between his forefinger and thumb. "If we fail to do what's right here, then we're going to do what's wrong, knowing we're probably signing death warrants on everyone in SDU and on the unit itself." Conlee lifted a hand. "Anyone disagree? Deny it?"

Max didn't and couldn't. No one could.

"It's a bitch of a call," Conlee said. "But when we get down to brass tacks, I have no choice, Sybil, and neither do you. We took oaths. So did Gabby."

"She's protecting all of us." The veep darted her gaze to Westford, her eyes too big for her face and filled with despair.

Westford didn't cringe, and somehow he held her gaze. "Yes."

Max's chest went tight. He'd never been close to anyone like the veep and Gabby were, but he'd imagined what it would be like. Evidently, he'd been pretty good at imagining because what gripped his chest right now felt an awful lot like a bullet wound. Sharp, shattering pain.

For a long moment, the veep stared down at the conference table. When she lifted her head, her face looked as set and fixed and blank as a stone statue's. Blood from her nails biting into her flesh dotted her palm. "Do it."

"Yes, ma'am." Conlee looked to Westford. "Jonathan?"

His jaw clenched to the point of cracking, Jonathan nodded.

Conlee swiveled his gaze to Max. "Agent Grayson?"

Max wouldn't make the call. He'd follow orders, but he wouldn't mark his partner and friend. He didn't have enough friends to squander the one who best understood him. Yet he couldn't refuse to follow orders. Too many others would be compromised. "I serve at the pleasure of the United States."

Something softened in Sybil's face. Close to losing her composure, she pushed her chair back from the table. "If there's nothing else, Commander?"

Recognizing the question was a formality and nothing

could keep her in the conference room another minute, Conlee shook his head. "No, ma'am. Thank you, ma'am."

Max swallowed hard. The woman had made the call. It hadn't been easy. But it was the right call for the country— and sad enough to rip the heart right out of a man's chest.

He had admired the veep for some time, but never had Max understood the personal costs of her office as well as he did at that moment. The urge to do or say something comforting that acknowledged her sacrifice rammed him hard. "Madam Vice President?"

She stopped and looked back at Max, her blue eyes huge and haunted. "Yes?"

He searched past platitudes, wanting to give her something, *anything,* of substance. She loved Gabby. He hadn't known love and doubted he ever would, but once in a while he thought about it, and he'd gotten a hint of what it'd be like with Gabby. What would he want to hear?

Finally, a worthy response came to him. "She won't suffer, ma'am."

The veep's chin trembled and she nodded. "Thank you, Agent Grayson. One day, I know I'll find the comfort you intended in those words."

But not today. Today I'm losing the only family I have. My best friend.

Feeling futile, he stuffed his hands in his pockets and avoided her eyes. "I hope so."

Westford nodded, then followed her out of the conference room.

Minutes lapsed, and neither Conlee nor Max seemed eager to fill the silence with empty words. In Max's mind, that silence was already bulging with the pain he had seen in Sybil Stone's eyes. If Gabby looked at him like that when the time came to kill her, God help him. He'd be haunted forever.

"She took it pretty well, considering," Conlee said, talking about the veep. "I wish I could say I was taking it any better." He reached for his cup, tapped its rim with his thumb, and opened up for a rare unguarded moment. "You know, Max, a commander gets stuck with a lot of duties that suck. But canceling one of his own . . . that's the worst."

"I'm sure it is, sir." It wasn't a picnic for a partner, either. Max blew out a breath he hoped would clear his lungs. His chest still felt like lead. Maybe he was better off, not loving or being loved by anyone else. "I take it that I'm activated."

Conlee sent him a level look. "Can you kill her?"

"If I have to, yes, I can." Max's stomach soured. "I took an oath, too."

"Then, yes, I'm activating you. Insert in Carnel Cove and cancel Agent Kincaid."

"There's a ten percent chance I can—"

"No, Max." Conlee held up a hand. "This is a cancellation order. No heroics, no intercession. We can't afford anything else. Even Gabby agrees."

Leave it to her to make that call. The professional in him admired her; the man who was her friend wanted to box her ears. Max nodded, wishing he were anywhere else, doing anything else. That he was anyone else. "Yes, sir."

"Fine." Conlee cleared his throat, regained his composure. "Carnel Cove sits on the Gulf of Mexico. Darla—a Class Three hurricane—is currently hitting it hard. Nothing is flying in, power is out, and the roads are impassable due to debris and fallen trees."

"How am I inserting?"

"A Special Ops helicopter is standing by to transport you as close to the site as possible. From there, it's up to you."

Max nodded, his emotions mixed. He liked Gabby. Half the time he didn't understand her, but that was a common problem between men and women. Lust probably had something to do with it. It was hard to focus on communication when you had a clouded mind. She was beautiful but arrogant, hypercritical and adept at making him feel as useful as shoe scum, but Max couldn't remember a time when he didn't respect her skills or her work, or a time when he hadn't been attracted to her and wondered what loving her and being loved by her, and making love with her, would be like.

He hated the thought of canceling any other operative, much less his partner—despite the fact that she didn't want to be his partner. But he particularly hated this order. Gabby mattered to him and it didn't take much imagination to see that any operative could be wearing her shoes.

But Gabby had had the guts to make the call.

And Max had to have the guts to answer it.

"I'm sorry as hell about this, Max," Conlee said. "You're closer to Gabby than anyone else in the unit."

With the exception of Westford, Max was. But being engaged to the veep had taken Westford out of the running on this assignment. Love pulled off miracles, but if Westford killed Gabby, it'd take more than a miracle for Sybil to ever look at him again and not see him killing her best friend. No relationship could stand that kind of strain. "Thanks, Commander."

"Transport's waiting." Conlee stood up and extended his hand.

Max gained his feet and clasped it. "Yes, sir."

Conlee tightened his grip, and dropped his voice, deep and gruff. "No pain." His eyes looked as haunted as the veep's. "She hasn't been warned that I'm activating you. I doubt you'll be able to, but if you can, blindside her."

"No pain, Commander. You have my word on it."

Conlee nodded, looking as if there were something more he wanted to say. Instead, he clenched his lips flat, drew back his hand, and then lowered his gaze to the floor. Obviously he needed a few moments alone.

Max understood, considered himself dismissed, and

headed for the transport. On the walk, he wondered. How many years would it be before he could walk back into the conference room and not think of the meeting that had just occurred? How many years would it take him to get over killing Gabby? And just how many more times in his life would he have the truth shoved in his face?

There is no justice.

*　　*　　*

Sybil sat quietly in the back of the darkened limo, her eyes filled with tears she tried hard not to shed, her heart filled with fear so strong she tasted its bitterness and fought not to throw up.

"You okay?" Jonathan asked.

She looked at him as if he'd lost his mind. "I just took the biggest leap of faith I've ever taken in my entire life, and I took it with Gabby's life. Hell, no, I'm not okay. Are you okay?"

Jonathan hadn't missed the silent communications between Sybil and Commander Conlee in the conference room, but he couldn't interpret them then and he had no idea what leap of faith she was talking about having taken now. Still, he understood the worry and grief and guilt that came with putting someone else at risk, deciding whether that person lived or died. And this person was Gabby. "No," he confessed. "I'm not okay. I'm so not okay I want to beat the hell out of something."

Blinking hard, Sybil slid closer to him on the seat, buried her head against his chest, and whispered as if speaking softly would keep the fear from growing or becoming too big for her to hold. "I'm scared, Jonathan. I'm so scared." Her chest went tight. "If Gabby dies, I'm going to have to live with killing her the rest of my life."

"Yes, you are. So am I."

He wrapped an arm around her shoulder, but didn't do

anything to shield her from the stark reality of what they'd done. That would insult her, him, and more than both of them, Gabby. She swallowed a sob.

"But we will live with it, Sybil. We'll do what we have to do because we have a greater responsibility, beyond Gabby, and she'd be the first one to remind us—"

Jonathan paused, thinking of what Sybil had just said, and then frowned at her. "What do you mean, *if* Gabby dies? You just ordered her canceled."

"Yes." Burrowing against him, Sybil stared unseeingly out the window, her voice edged with an even more anxious whisper. "Yes, I did."

Chapter Ten

"Conlee sent *you* to kill me?"

So much for blindsiding her. Hovering against the wall just outside her bedroom door, Max stifled a curse with a frown, and walked inside.

His footfalls echoed on the hardwood floor and he was still dripping water. It had taken almost twenty-four hours to get here, and thanks to Hurricane Darla, he'd spent most of that time out in the rain, fighting squalls in destruction that resembled a war zone.

Stopping just inside the door, he opened his senses to impressions. *Spartan, slick dresser tops, bare walls. Unadorned and hollow. Empty.* Everything about the room shouted to stay out and not to bother to look for clues on its owner; everything except the bed. It dared him to look away. So did the woman in it.

Gabby lay pale and nearly lost in its rumpled middle, bathed in the shimmering light from a slender candle in a copper holder on the nightstand. The bronze coverlet and a half-dozen pillows had been tossed aside, but she rested against a mountain more of them. Some were square, some round, and they were all deep jewel-toned, rich fabrics. Even the sheets were a shiny bronze silk—no Egyptian cotton for her—and she had pulled the top sheet up over her chest. Still, a scrap of ivory lace from her gown peeked out from under the sheet's scalloped edge, and seeing her, looking sultry and sexy, had him attracted tenfold.

"I asked you a question, Max. Did Conlee send you to kill me?"

Her hair was damp and the sheen of sweat glistened on her forehead, but it wasn't sleep that glazed her green eyes.

She had been waiting for him.

And not for the first time, Max hated his job and just maybe himself. But for the luck of the draw, he would be lying in her bed and she would be standing at the foot of it with a .38 tucked into her shoulder holster that held a bullet bearing his name. "Yes, Gabby. Conlee activated me and ordered me to kill you."

She blinked hard. Once. Swallowed. "Well, then. I guess that's that." Her questioning look faded.

"I'm—sorry." Lame. Totally lame.

"I know, Max." The empathy in her eyes proved she did. "I felt sure Conlee would refuse to activate you and send someone else—a non-friend, you know? But to tell you the truth, I'm glad he didn't. I would have missed this chance to say good-bye." She patted the covers smooth beside her hip. "Sit for a moment and talk with me."

Did she think he had the emotions of a stone? They were partners and friends. How could she expect him to sit down, converse with her, and then put a bullet through her skull?

Swallowing what felt like an elephant parked in his throat, he reminded himself that Gabby was the consummate professional who slid in and out of identities with the ease snakes shed skins. Canceling her was part of the job. She didn't expect Max to be made of stone. It wouldn't occur to her that he wasn't. "I don't think a chat is a good idea. Maybe you're reconciled to this, but I haven't had much time to adjust."

"Sorry." Her tone turned matter-of-fact. "Your adjustment is low priority. I'm going to be dead and, comparatively speaking, a few minutes of your time isn't asking for too much."

A cold chill sank into his bones. On the surface, her calm and courage seemed unnatural—and it would have been for other women. But Gabby was nothing like other women. He checked his watch for emotional distance. The numerals looked an eerie green. Eleven P.M.

Gabby picked up on the obvious stall. "If you're going to be a smart-ass about this, I could pull rank on you, or remind you that you wanted me to activate you. I could even play on your emotions by reminding you that we're friends." She shut an open book beside her, and set it on the nightstand next to her gun.

Wuthering Heights and a .38 Smith & Wesson. Uniquely Gabby. Her comments had the intended impact. Killing her would haunt him either way, and she was making the ultimate sacrifice. He should try to make it easier for her. She would appreciate the effort and maybe later he'd find some solace in it. "Underhanded tactics aren't your style."

"No one knows my style, Max. Not even you." She looked up. "Maybe not even me."

Max knew more about her than most. From her dossier, he knew Conlee had recruited her six years ago from Air Force Special Operations, where she had already earned a chest full of medals for distinguished service and an impressive array of covert ops successes. No one doubted she had guts and grit; Gabby was focused, deliberately distant, and determined to succeed on all fronts, at all times, and at any costs. She could convincingly be anyone she chose to be—a doctor, a mercenary, and now, a judge—which was vital in covert operations. From five years' first-hand experience, Max knew that she was independent, sharp-tongued, abrupt, critical, less than diplomatic within the unit, and that she conducted even the never-discussed, dark-underbelly parts of her job without qualm.

Because on occasions like this one Max did have qualms, he hated and admired her for that. Nerves of steel rated as an asset only when they didn't get you killed. So what was this "chat with me" business about? "What are you doing, Gabby?"

"Thinking about my life." She blinked slowly, held his gaze. "Do you think I don't know what they say about me in the unit, Max? I've always known. Half of them think I suffer from multiple-personality disorder. What else could explain how easily I juggle identities and diverse roles? And because I'm disciplined, the other half is convinced I'm some kind of freaky secret weapon—the result of some advanced robotics experiment, and not human at all." She let out a self-depreciating grunt. "I'm dying alone, misunderstood, and it pisses me off."

That confession tugged at his heart. "Well, to be honest, honey, you've never exactly tried to disabuse anyone of those ideas." He congratulated himself for that bit of diplomacy. At every opportunity, Gabby had deliberately fed the rumors.

"I couldn't. Not and do my job." She rolled her gaze toward the ceiling. "I'm getting maudlin. It's disgusting." She grabbed a long-neck bottle of beer from the bedside, kicked back a long draw, and shed her resentment. "Come on. Sit," she said, reclaiming a flicker of sass. "I know you're soaking wet and you don't want to, but I'm the one who'll die tonight." She scooted over on the bed to make room. "Indulge me."

How could he refuse? Resigned, Max sat down on the edge of the bed, hitched his slacks on his thighs, and then braced the flats of his arms on his knees. "What do you want?"

"Oh, baby. What a loaded question." She sighed, slumped back against the pillows and headboard, and closed her eyes. "What I want has been the million-dollar question all my life."

Regret had stolen into her voice. He pretended not to notice, stared at the candle's flame, and wished Hurricane Darla hadn't knocked out the power. Gabby's windows were all closed—no doubt to prevent anyone from sneaking in on her—and it was hotter than hell in her house.

But more than the steamy heat, she troubled him. This woman wasn't acting like Gabby. In the soft candlelight, she didn't look like Gabby, either. She had Gabby's exquisite looks, her deep and sultry voice, but where was her arrogance, her razor-sharp tongue? She was always at her bitchiest under pressure—bitchy and flirtatious. But both were absent now, and while he wouldn't venture so far as to say this woman looked vulnerable, she looked . . . soft.

Even at her most relaxed Gabby had never looked soft. It fascinated him.

"When push comes to shove—and I'd say we're there, Max—what I want doesn't matter anymore." She swept at her damp hair. It sprang right back down onto her forehead. "So, it's on to business. There are a few things I didn't report."

An understatement if ever he'd heard one. "Things like the dead man in your garage?"

"That would be one of them, yes," she said. "I couldn't get him out because of the hurricane, but I left the body where you couldn't possibly miss it." She shrugged. "There was no sense in Housekeeping making two trips. One for him and one for me."

"Is he why you activated me?"

"He could be," she admitted, clearly uncertain. "His three passports and two visas are all valid but issued under bogus names."

"Who is he?" Identifying him in the dark had been impossible, and Max hadn't dared to use a flashlight while operating under Commander Conlee's "blindside her" order.

"Jaris Adahan."

A Global Warrior on the SDU watch list. Oh, this was definitely not good.

"The problem is . . ." Gabby reclaimed his attention. "I'm not sure if he came after me because I'm SDU or because I'm a judge here investigating the judicial corruption cases."

That complicated the issue. "So your cover might or might not be compromised."

"Exactly." She smiled. "And that's why I activated you, Max."

And why she had insisted he be able to extricate or eliminate her. He walked to the foot of the bed. "Do you have a reasonable explanation for Candace Burke giving you lab access?"

"As a matter of fact, I do."

He stuffed a hand into his slacks pocket. "Would you care to share it?"

"It's complex," she warned him, the candlelight flickering in her eyes. "Didn't Commander Conlee tell you about the ladies of Carnel Cove?"

"Only that they were safe."

She digested that with a slow nod. "Then let's leave it there."

"Let's not." Droplets of water dripped from his hair down his face.

"Like I said, Max. It's complicated."

He pointed toward the adjoining bath. "Mind if I grab a towel? I'm more than a little wet. Doing a number on your sheets." He was soaked to the skin and had been most of the twenty-four hours it had taken him to get here.

"Just be sure to take it with you when you leave. Evidence, you know?"

"I know." She was insulting his competence. He knew his job. "Go ahead with your complicated explanation. I'll do my best to keep up."

If she caught his sarcasm, she ignored it. "Mayor Faulkner has a zero-tolerance policy against crime that no one questions, including Sheriff Jackson Coulter. Most Carnel Covers moved here to get away from crime. In practical terms, that's significant. You can't report suspicions of criminal activity to any local authority without everyone in the Cove knowing it—including, unfortunately, those who might be involved in the criminal activity."

"Candace suspects some of the local authorities are involved in criminal activity." Max rubbed the water out of his hair.

"Yes. And she's confided them to me."

Max slung the towel around his neck. "Because you're an outsider."

"Because Judge Powell vouched for me. Candace's best friend is Elizabeth Powell."

Judge Powell's widow. "Did EEE really kill him within forty-eight hours?"

"He died within forty-eight hours, but that's not the most interesting fact in the incident." Gabby sat up, cross-legged. "According to Candace, William was in New York in February. He was at the Grand Hotel when the elevator incident happened."

Max suddenly stopped mopping at his face with the towel. "Conlee doesn't know this?"

"There's no evidence Powell was infected there," Gabby said. "But Elizabeth told Candace that if William hadn't forgotten his wallet and gone back to his room to get it, he would have been on that elevator. He was sure the incident had been a terrorist attack, so he bugged out and returned to the Cove. Then he went up to Judge Abernathy's fishing camp."

"The same judge you're investigating for Global Warrior corruption?"

"*We're* investigating, Max," she corrected him. "And, yes, he's the same man. Twenty-four hours after this visit to the fishing camp with Abernathy, Judge Powell died."

Something tingled low in Max's gut. "You think the eight people on the elevator were collateral damage. That Powell was the target."

Again she nodded. "He went up there for a meeting, but even Elizabeth doesn't know with whom or for what purpose."

"So Judge Powell didn't contract EEE in Carnel Cove."

"Apparently, he did," Gabby disputed him. "Candace photographed three mosquito bites on the back of his neck. She pulled blood, hair, and skin scrapings on him, too."

"Without him knowing it?"

"He told her to do it, and to bring them all to me. That's why Candace gave me access to the lab. To run preliminary tests on the samples."

So Judge Powell had been Gabby's in-house contact on the corruption investigation. He knew she had been planted to investigate, though Max felt sure Powell had thought she worked for the Justice Department and not SDU. "I assume you've done that."

"Some of them. I only recently got the samples."

"Conlee told me. Candace and Elizabeth wanted to be sure they could trust you."

"They're not paranoid. Caution is a necessary evil here." Gabby stiffened and forced herself to look at Max. "William Powell did die from EEE, Max." Worry flooded her eyes. "But it was EEE laced with the same accelerant we found in the New York elevator cases."

Max's blood ran cold. "You're positive it's Z-4027?"

She nodded. "I checked twice."

A pit dropped open in Max's stomach. The superbug was definitely on the loose in the U.S. "Son of a bitch."

"Yeah."

Max tossed the towel toward the bath. "So Powell was murdered." A secondary thought hit hard. "And whoever killed him knew you were running lab tests to prove it. That's why the Warriors targeted you."

"Maybe, maybe not. But I have no choice except to make that assumption."

"So SDU and your judge cover could be intact."

"Too high-risk to consider that probable—especially with a dead Warrior in my garage."

Commander Conlee would agree, which left Max with no choice but to cancel her. Her resigned expression proved she'd drawn the same conclusion. "Anything else unreported?"

"My evidence brings the Global Warriors center stage, Max. They've murdered before, and they're about to do it again. This time, on a larger scale."

"Who hired them?"

"That's another million-dollar question."

She didn't know. Bad news all around. He turned to her. "You're sure about this?"

"I'm not sure about the nature of the attack, but I know there's going to be one."

"Have you identified specific Warriors?"

"Only the one on the garage floor. But there were two here. I suspect the next attack will be in Carnel Cove or they wouldn't have been here."

Not two Warriors to hit one judge, or one SDU operative. "Here, where?" Carnel Cove wasn't exactly a metropolitan area. It was a small tourist town. If not for Logan Industries and a couple of nearby military bases, it would be totally dependent on tourists.

"I don't have a specific target, but I have a window for

when." She passed him a slip of paper, licked at her lips, and motioned for a glass of water. "According to Jaris Adahan, you've got five days, Max."

The paper was an airline ticket from Atlanta to London for next Friday. The attack would be before his departure. Max had five days to fill in the blanks. Not much time to discover, much less to protect and prevent an attack. He filled the glass on the nightstand, and then passed the water to her. "Individuals or mass?" he asked, seeking her best guess on the number of intended victims. Gabby's best guess often had proven more accurate than Intel's, even with all their high-tech gear and inside sources.

"According to my anonymous tipster, mass." Pity filled her eyes. "Hundreds. Maybe more." She tugged at the strap of her gown. "I can't peg the nature of the attack. I'm sorry. I tried. They've used Z-4027 in New York and on Powell. I can't imagine why they'd need to use it again here."

"New York, Powell, and only God knows on how many were misdiagnosed as EEE."

A frown creased the skin between her brows. "They've most likely black marketed it already, Max. You do realize that."

"Yeah. The worst of it, aside from what they're going to do next, is that—"

"Makes tracking the evidence on the Independence Day attacks next to impossible."

"Anyone could have bought the bug and used it by now. Maybe even multiple parties."

She agreed. "Dr. Richardson still hasn't determined definitively that those were attacks and not natural occurrences."

That remark was a test. Max knew it, and responded to it. "They were attacks, Gabby. Proving it is one thing, but we know it."

"Yes, we do." She looked relieved that he hadn't disappointed her.

"So do you think they're testing something else now, or broadening sales of Z-4027?"

"I have no idea," she said. "It could be either—especially considering the nature of the Independence Day attacks. They did as much crop destruction as harm to human beings."

She had no idea, and he'd be left to try to untangle this mess without her insights and stop an attack scheduled for sometime during the next five days.

The news kept getting worse and worse. The country was still struggling to heal from the World Trade Center and Pentagon attacks. For that reason, SDU overt affiliates hadn't disclosed the dozens of subsequent attempted attacks it had thwarted. Another attack now, even on a smaller scale, was the last thing Americans needed. "Where's the evidence?"

"Tucked away." She drank thirstily, then handed the glass back to him.

So she had succumbed, conceding her personal superiority and joining the rest of the mere mortal operatives. The legendary Gabby Kincaid would bargain the evidence for her life.

"You can stop looking so worried, Max. You won't have to torture me to get it." An almost amused lilt lifted her voice. "God, you look guilty. You thought I wanted to cut a deal."

Because he had, he felt guilty, and he gave her a solid frown. "I would have helped you, Gabby. On any or all of the missions. All you had to do was call."

Her thigh brushing against his hip, she pressed a gentle hand to his face and shared a tender smile. "I know."

"Then why didn't you?"

"It doesn't matter now, Max." She dropped her hand, scooted over to put distance between them.

"It matters to me."

She pivoted her gaze from the far wall to him. "I

thought I was doing the right thing. That's all you're going to get." Her focus drifted to the sculptured ceiling. Worry knit her brows and filled her voice. "Sybil is going to have such a hard time with this."

She already was. The sadness in her eyes at the consensus briefing could have drawn tears from a rock. "Westford will help her."

"Yes, he will." Gabby smiled because she had played a part in getting them together. "If Sybil asked, Jonathan would harness the universe for her."

"He'd try." Max shifted, looked at her hard. Tousled, Gabby was even prettier than usual. Classic bones, promising emerald eyes that held more secrets than they told, and generous lips that made men forget their lies and bare their souls. Had any man ever tried to harness the universe for her?

No one significant had been mentioned in her profile. Only parents she rarely saw, an older brother who had been in and out of addiction treatment centers for years, and a younger sister who was self-absorbed and clueless about anything that didn't directly affect her. Gabby didn't seem to fit in that family. Had she ever been close to any of them?

It was hard to imagine, but maybe Max'd had the easier life. Six foster homes, an unknown dad, and a crack mom who forgot he existed for days at a stretch might have been easier to handle than a family that wasn't really a family. He had known what to expect. Gabby had been stuck her whole life, hanging on to the hope things would get better.

But she did have friends who would miss her, and at least one of them would hate the man who had taken her from them: Vice President Stone. Westford, too, was fond of Gabby, muttering that she was a royal pain in the ass. From him, that was high praise. Aside from Max, were there other friends who would mourn her?

He doubted it. Most operatives avoided close relation-ships. Life as a loner, though it was hell on holidays and special occasions, was easier. It required fewer vague an-swers to unwelcome questions, fewer evasive explanations and outright lies. Special Detail Unit operatives simply had too many secrets to keep.

How had Gabby handled the loner challenge? It sud-denly seemed important to know.

He knew better than to get mired down in a cancella-tion—especially when the target was a friend. A rookie knew better than to let his thoughts venture beyond the mission requirements. Problem was he had been involved with Gabby from a distance for a long time. But the job took precedence over everything else. She was a cracker-jack senior operative; there was far more at stake here than a slip of a woman and her life—and a man who wanted ab-solution and peace for his own conscience for taking it. The Global Warriors were about to attack. Lives were at stake.

Gabby's own warning replayed in his mind. *You've got five days, Max.*

By daybreak, he'd care. But right now, standing in Gabby's bedroom under orders to kill her, he didn't give a damn about any of them. He gave a damn about Gabby. About *her* life.

She shoved aside what he thought had been a pillow clutched to her chest. "What's in the box?" he asked.

She let out a sharp little laugh that held no humor. "Very little."

Even now, getting information out of her was like pulling nails. "Gabby?"

"My life." She shoved it toward him. "Have a look." It rolled across the bed halted near her hip. "You won't be im-pressed."

Max reached over her, lifted the box, and then took off its padded lid and set it aside. It was nearly empty. Just a fistful of photos of fledgling oak trees, a yellowed piece of notebook paper, and a silver pair of wings rested on its bottom. "Your first pilot's wings?"

She nodded.

"Why are these significant?" He held up some of the photos.

"My indulgence."

He didn't get it. "What indulgence?"

Her lips flat-lined, clearly expressing her resentment of the question. "My only indulgence in remembering who I really am while I'm inserted under cover. I plant oaks, okay?"

That he understood. It was easy to get so deep into the cover that you actually forgot it was a cover. It became your life. You needed something physical to remind you who you really were. "I use a coin. A liberty silver dollar."

"Really?" That revelation pleased her; her lips softened. "I didn't know that."

No one knew that. "Now you do, and I know you plant oaks. Sad commentary for a man married to a woman five times, don't you think? To know so little about his wife?"

"It was necessary."

Necessary. Doing the right thing. What was it with all these bases for her shutting him out? "Why?"

She jutted her jaw. "Because I considered it best."

Best. Another basis to add to her list. "For whom?"

"Both of us."

"I see," he said, not seeing at all but knowing she was done explaining. He returned the photos to the box and lifted the folded paper. Age yellowed it; made it fragile. "May I?"

"Why not?" She glared right into his eyes. "You're my only husband."

Interesting remark. Telling, too. Really being married to her wouldn't be any more a walk in the park than being her partner or friend. But he had the feeling that it would always be fascinating. He unfolded the page, wishing he could fully decipher the look in her eyes. It was cold, but somehow vulnerable. Or maybe, wounded. Very un-Gabby. He read the note, scribbled in a child's hand:

I don't like you, Gabby. I like Shelly.
She's special. You're not.
Harlan T. Crumsfield

Surprise rippled through Max. People kept mementos of good things and happy times. This wasn't either. Who would want to remember this?

"We were in fifth grade," she said. "My first broken heart." A sad smile twisted her lips. "Later, the boys became men, but no matter how intense, the relationships were short-term and the reason for bailing was always the same. Other women were special." She blew out a breath and glared up at Max. "When women are strong standing alone, and are with you because they want to be, not because they need to be, you bastards are heartless. Do you know that?"

"So I've heard." Max refolded the note, put it back in the box, and put the lid in place, knowing he had been privileged to see a rare glimpse of the real woman: the Gabby who had placed second to other women with the important men in her life. The box snapped closed, sealing her life inside. His emotions a tangled jumble he couldn't begin to decipher, Max cleared his throat. "Gabby?"

She draped an arm over her forehead and her eyes drifted closed. Thick clumps of her lashes rested against her pale cheeks. "Yeah?"

His chest went heavy then tight, and warnings flashed through his mind not to ask, but he had to anyway. "Are you going to die with regrets?"

"Aren't we all?" Her tone dripped sarcasm.

Was it ingrained from habit, or a defense? He

shouldn't care, but he did, and he was going to remember this night, remember the sight of her in this bed, remember killing her for the rest of his life. When those irreversible memories haunted him—they always haunted him—he would need insights only she could give him. "I need to know, Gabby."

She opened her eyes, searched his, and understanding dawned. She clasped his hand and gently squeezed. "You have nothing to feel guilty about. You're just following orders."

Could any man come up with a reasonable response to that? He was going to kill her, and instead of bargaining for her life, she's giving him absolution. "I don't understand you."

She let out a humorless laugh. "Hell, Max. I don't understand me. Why should you?"

"Because I'm going to be the one doing the killing." And the living with it. He'd definitely be doing the living with it.

"Poor, Max." She caressed his face. "It's a bitch of a job, isn't it?"

"At times, yes, it is." Especially when her touch was tender and her voice didn't even hint at sass or sarcasm. She understood his inner struggle. Had she ever been in this position?

"Just keep your eye on the big picture," she suggested. "What you do, you do for the greater good. Remembering that helps."

She had been in his shoes. "Is that what you're doing? Focusing on the big picture?"

"You don't need to analyze me, Max. You've read my profile." As her husband on five cases, he had read it often. "You know all that matters."

"I know nothing that matters," he disagreed. The woman he had known and the woman she was tonight stood worlds apart. This woman intrigued him. She seemed real and in-

vested in others. She had vulnerabilities and wounds and acknowledged them. The Gabby he had known professionally—and as a friend—was none of these things. "Does
anyone really know you?"

She thought a moment and then, as if the answer troubled her, abandoned it. "Probably not. But at this juncture
in my life it's irrelevant. If I were Commander Conlee, I'd
order this hit. That's what's relevant." She took in a shud-
dering breath and pulled her hand back from Max's face.
"I'm ready now."

That comment startled him. He met her gaze, expecting to see fear. Instead, he saw acceptance. It unnerved
him. "All right, Gabby." Swallowing hard, he leaned forward to stand.

★   ★   ★

The twelfth potential buyer moved down the aisle of the
darkened screening room on the arm of a tuxedoed escort.

Like the others, this one was blindfolded and led to a
seat portioned off from the rest of those seated in the room
by red velvet drapes that hung suspended from the twenty-
foot ceiling. The drapes concealed and blocked the view of
each man on three sides, leaving him only a frontal view of
the screen.

Privacy from each other was essential. Guaranteed.
And smart business, considering any breach would result
in death.

The director had taken precautions to assure privacy
for his own benefit as well as for theirs. The Consortium
was a complex network with specific rules; no member
could be certain if the most minute breach marked them
for retention in the Consortium or for elimination from it.
One thing, and only one thing, made the risks of being a
member worth taking: the financial gains were astronomical.

So amazingly astronomical that the director, who had grown up penniless on dusty backwoods roads in Alabama, had recently purchased his own little island and a voluptuous twenty-five-year-old redhead to keep him company whenever he was on it. His proper and respected wife of thirty years, of course, knew nothing about either. Or about how filthy rich they had become in his five-year association with the Consortium.

The thirteenth potential buyer took his seat.

Moving into place at the back of the room, the director stepped into a mirrored cubicle, closed the door behind him, and then activated the security locks. No one could see inside. He could look out and see everything happening in the procession. A bank of monitors to his left gave him a bird's-eye view of each of the men. He wouldn't miss a single reaction.

The fourteenth and final man sat down, and his escort gave the director the nod. Everyone was in place, facing the wide screen that stretched across the front of the room, waiting for the demonstration to begin.

On the surface, it seemed odd that there were no women in the group—typically there were—but these buyers, being from their corner of the world, considered women of little value, and they were the ideal clients for the two products being offered for sale.

A red phone rested on the ledged desk in front of him. The director lifted the receiver. "We're ready to go, sir."

"Excellent." The chairman's voice lifted. "Let the games begin."

Chapter Eleven

"Max, wait." Gabby clasped his arm, her fingers digging into his flesh. She opened her mouth, hesitated, and then closed it without making a sound. "Never mind."

"Never mind? Gabby, you don't have the option of telling me later. There won't be a later." He wanted to shake her until she raged and ordered him not to kill her. Instead, he waited, having no idea what to expect from this intriguing woman he had been friends with and married to on paper five times and didn't know at all. "What is it?"

Silence and the sweet scent of the burning candle fell between them. The clock beside her bed ticked off seconds that became minutes, but something innately warned him she wasn't stalling to delay her death, she was working through a weighty challenge. In her own time and in her own way, Gabby had to make peace with herself. Max couldn't begrudge a woman about to die the chance to make peace with herself.

Finally, she looked up at him, fear lighting her eyes. He hated it. "What is it, Gabby?"

"You asked me if I had any regrets." He nodded, and she went on. "I do, Max." Her chin trembled. "I lost my brother to drugs, I never found my sister, and my parents never found me. I'm about to die and I've lived my entire life invisible to all."

Gabby invisible? He could dispute her, but she wouldn't believe him. "Is that why you left active duty in the Air Force and came to SDU?"

She cocked her head. "Commander Conlee needed me."

Harlan's note, the important men in her life resenting her strength. "But now the job isn't enough?" That Max understood. He'd had no one to rely on his entire life. He'd always been invisible to all and disconnected. So he'd found a job where being disconnected connected him and what he did mattered. That meant *he* mattered. Finally, working in SDU, he mattered.

"Hell of a time to realize it, isn't it?" She frowned. "But 'She worked hard' is a sorry epitaph. All my life, I believed in something greater and more worthy than me. But now . . . I want to know I did something significant that only I could have done. I have no one, Max. Not one person knows what I've done or why, and when I'm dead, no one will even notice I'm gone." She swallowed hard, as if her words tasted bitter. "I'm lying here, and I'm mad as hell because it's hit me that I want *someone* to notice. The job isn't enough." She let out a little laugh that held only loss and anger at the irony of this. "My job isn't enough, I'm invisible, my memory box is empty, and the man closest to me is one I've been married to five times on paper who doesn't know I plant trees."

"I know you plant trees," he said softly. "I even know they're oaks."

"Only because I just told you." She shook. "Look, I'm

serious here. I'm going to die alone, Max, and I have no proof that I lived well or with purpose. I thought I was happy. Well, mostly happy. But now all I feel is empty. Just . . . empty."

It would happen to Max, too. Gutted and hollow, he admitted he didn't want regrets. And he damn sure didn't want to have to remember hers.

She went on, thankfully too deep in her own dynamics to notice his. "I've never committed myself to a relationship or been head over heels in love, and I never will. Worse, I'm not leaving anything behind anyone will cherish. No one will even think fond thoughts. Call me weak. Say I'm just feeling sorry for myself, but I'm going to die, Max. It matters."

Their gazes locked, and there was no hiding from the truth or from understanding. It shone there, raw and brazen, bold and undeniable. And it urged Max to give her something good and real to hold on to for strength. He *wanted* to give to her. "You've saved thousands of lives, Gabby," he said softly. "Every mission you've performed saved lives. That's a hell of a legacy."

"For other people. But not for me." She squeezed her eyes shut, then reopened them. "I've been undercover so long I don't have a life anymore. Being someone else has become my life." Resignation slid over her face. "No one is going to remember me as special."

Something hard in his chest went soft. He let his fingertips slide down her jaw and cupped her chin. "Gabby, this is the life you chose. We all did—for the greater good of a nation." Throwing her philosophy back at her should have made him feel lousy, but tonight he would take any help he could get.

"But I thought I'd have something left over for me, and I haven't, Max." A warning tinged her tone. "Don't make the same mistake. It matters . . . now."

He had heard enough deathbed confessions to pass as

a priest, but this from Gabby? She was trying to protect him. Did she do that often? He thought about it and soon was convinced that the reason she had worked alone wasn't that she was an arrogant snob; she had refused to activate Max or to call him for emergency backup assistance to protect him. He was supposed to be her friend. Why hadn't he seen that before now?

Shameful, but he'd never looked. He had judged her by what everyone else thought about her: that she believed she was so good she didn't need help. And he was scared of her; of what she made him feel. Some friend.

Guilt started a war between his head and heart that had him swearing he should have never allowed himself to feel the slightest attraction to her. But he wasn't kidding anyone. He had tried to squelch it, and nothing worked. The woman got to him then, and she got to him now.

"You're a kind man, Max," she said. "A good friend and my favorite husband."

She had meant for him to smile, so he did. But inside, a small ache expanded and spread through the guilt. "You've been my favorite wife, too." Seeing opportunity, he seized it. "A wife who doesn't nag, doesn't interrupt a man during ball games, doesn't snitch all the covers, or send him out for ice cream at two in the morning—hell, Gabby. You're every man's dream of the perfect wife."

She laughed out loud. "You forgot my greatest asset."

"What's that?" he asked, finding himself smiling.

"My excellent taste in men."

Pure sass. But he could hardly dispute her since he was her favorite. "Excellent taste."

Her eyes held onto her laughter a moment longer than her generous mouth, but then sadness seeped in. "Max, you'd better do it now." She clasped his hands. "I'm trying not to be a coward, but my brave front is slipping."

It was all an act. Another Gabby performance. A knot lodged in his throat. He gave her hand a gentle squeeze, then stood up. Inside, he was a rat's nest of nerves and conflicting emotions. But he had to do this. He had his orders.

"Could I impose on you for one more thing?"

Anything. Anything at all. He nodded.

"It's going to sound crazy but, well, I want it for me." She gave herself a little shake and then looked at him, her eyes calm and clear and intent. "Would you please kiss me, Max?"

Too stunned to hide his surprise, he frowned. "What?"

"Will you kiss me—please?" she repeated, and then shrugged. "For five years, I've wanted to know what kissing you would be like. I'd like to find out before . . . well, before . . . you know."

He couldn't believe it. She had to be razzing him, sidetracking him to break down the emotional intensity that had blown up between them. "Are you serious?"

"Would I joke now?"

Her earnest expression said she wouldn't. Ordinarily, he would gladly oblige her. She wasn't the only one who had wondered what it would be like. But under the circumstances, he wasn't crazy about the idea. Who would be now?

Kiss her, kill her. The two just didn't mesh on the actions-of-a-rational-man front. Especially when that rational man recognized that, in the last half hour, the woman had come closer to arousing every sense in his body and emotion in his soul than any other woman had come in thirty-five years.

"I'm not asking you for the rest of your life, Max. Just for a kiss."

"Knock it off, Gabby." He swiped a hand through his hair and paced beside her bed, then paced again. Stopping near her, he let out a burst of breath. "You took me off guard, okay?"

"Well, when you can get back on guard, will you answer me?"

Amused. Her eyes were actually twinkling in the candlelight. Damn it all, she knew she'd knock him off center, asking that. "I'm on guard. Believe it or not, I don't stay on my ass when I get surprised. I'm good at my job, too."

"But this isn't about your job," she said softly. "It's about you. And I have a feeling you're about as good at being you as I am at being me."

Torture couldn't get him to admit she was right. But one look, and she knew.

She tilted her head back on the pillows, looked up at him. "Well? Will you kiss me?"

Absolutely right he would. He wasn't giving into temper, or proving anything to her, though. Flat out, he was insane. That was the only logical explanation for it. Bending deep, he pecked a kiss on her lips. "There. Okay. You got your kiss," he said, oddly breathless. "It's done."

"That's not a kiss, Max. It's an insult to my imagination. Five years of thinking about this, and that's the best you believe I can come up with?" Frowning, she lifted her arms and looped them around his neck. "Believe me," she whispered against his chin. "My imagination is far more fertile." Steering his mouth back to hers, she kissed him deeply, lavishly, with an unexpected mix of tenderness and heat.

Finally, she separated their mouths and looked up into his eyes. "Do you agree?"

"Oh, yeah." He finally found his voice. "I agree." Her imagination was dangerously fertile, and her kiss wasn't friend to friend but woman to man. Now, he'd have to live with knowing that, too.

The twinkling light left her eyes and they grew serious. Sad and serious and pleading. "Max, I want something else from you."

He tilted his chin into her hand on his jaw. "What?"

"No guilt. Promise me."

He couldn't do it. He couldn't deliberately make a

promise he knew he didn't stand a chance in hell of keeping. But this wasn't about him. It was about Gabby. She'd be doing the dying, and she wanted to do it with her mind at ease. "I promise," he said.

"Thanks, Max." She let out a satisfied sigh and then released him. "Hurry now."

More rattled than he'd ever been in his life, he moved away from the bed and pulled out his gun. "Close your eyes."

She dutifully lowered her lids. "You're a good kisser. I wish I had known that sooner."

"I wish you had, too." He checked the chamber, though he knew the gun was ready to fire. It was always ready to fire.

"So?" She opened one eye a slit and peeked at him. "Was I a good kisser, too?"

"Oh, yeah." His knees were still knocking. He aimed the gun, saw that the shaking extended to his hands, and remembered her memory box. "I'll never forget it."

That pleased her into smiling. "Wait. I have to ask." She opened both eyes, saw he hadn't dropped his aim, and winced. "Are you as good at making love as you are at kissing?"

He eyed her sharply. She wasn't stalling, just bluntly asking. And though he saw where this was heading and he was tempted, he knew he'd already have nightmares about this for six months. No way was he intentionally going to extend that to a lifetime. "I'm not going to make love to you, Gabby."

"All right." She sighed, again closed her eyes. "I guess I'll die with a regret, after all."

Max had to work at it not to groan. He would carry around a bucketful of her regret and his guilt forever. Yet his logic sucked. He would still be here. *Without* her. He shook off his misgivings and took aim. Right in the center of her forehead . . .

★   ★   ★

The director clipped the microphone to his suit jacket's lapel. Broadcasting his message into the screening room, he greeted the potential buyers, and then began his briefing. "As you know, the Consortium successfully introduced West Nile virus to the United States in 1999. As of today, it has spread to thirty-two states. Although this proliferation has been far too rapid to be considered possible by normal means, thanks to our efforts, the scientific community broadly considers it a 'natural occurrence.'

"While the research grants and residual financial gains have been beneficial to all participants in this venture, the Consortium has been disappointed with the biological results of the infection itself. Roughly one in two hundred people infected get seriously ill, and only twenty percent even experience mild flulike symptoms that require medical treatment. This less-than-stellar performance is, of course, an insufficient return on Consortium members' investments. Therefore, we have taken concrete steps to maximize profit potential through the development of a more powerful flavivirus—a superbug, if you will, referred to as Z-4027. Naturally, we have also developed a pesticide to counterbalance its effects so that we retain full control of its impact.

"At this time, only the Consortium offers Z-4027, the vaccine to inoculate people against it, and the only pesticide developed to kill its carriers. While mosquitoes were initially used to carry Z-4027, it has been successfully transmitted to birds, horses, dogs, cats, and other wildlife indigenous to specific geographical areas. It has also successfully contaminated blood transfusions undetected. Soon, we expect to know if the infection can be effectively transmitted through a new mother's breast milk."

The image on the screen flashed, and a new one replaced it. One of a busy airport. "If you will, note the man on the left of the screen, wearing a cap with a U.S. flag pin." The man was Cardel Boudreaux; though with his chin dipped to his chest, his face wasn't visible on the screen to the buyers. "The date was July fourth. This man was performing a trial study of Z-4027. I'm happy to report the biological results exceeded our expectations. While this trial study was limited in scope, it proved that Z-4027 is five hundred times more lethal than West Nile. From this one study, the virus has already spread to seventeen countries. As I'm sure you know from media coverage, the scientific community has also dubbed this outbreak a 'natural occurrence.'"

The director paused to check the monitors. The buyers' gazes were riveted to the screen.

Smiling to himself, he pushed a button on a handheld remote. The image on the screen flashed again, and two new images appeared, side by side: On the left, a cruise ship, and on the right, a cotton field. In both, Jaris Adahan appeared, wearing a U.S. flag pin on the brim of his hat. "The date again is July fourth. I doubt I need to delve into a deeper explanation. The medical conditions of the ship's passengers and the medical staff who initially treated them have been well documented in the media. What is worthy of mention is that on this same day, at this same port, a shipment of fruit was also contaminated. With minimal effort and expense, both contaminations went undetected, and again, while limited in scope, Z-4027 exceeded our expectations by three hundred percent."

He pushed the button again. This time, images of two fields of cotton separated by only a dirt road appeared on the screen. The left field was brown. Nothing in it lived. The field on the right side of the road was lush and green with mature cotton plants nearly ready to be harvested. "Both of these fields were contaminated with Z-4027 on July fourth. The one on the left was not treated with the pesticide being offered to you today. The one on the right was treated. As you can see, the treatment was highly successful." He allowed himself a little laugh. "This study is also why we advised all of our associates to replace their existing interests in this market with ones in Egyptian cotton. Unless treated with our pesticide, the damage to crops will continue to spread through the region. In five years, the state of Texas could look like a desert, gentlemen—if we will it."

Again, he glimpsed the monitors. The men were sitting on the edges of their seats, transfixed by what they were seeing on the screen.

He flipped to the last slide. Sebastian Cabot's photo appeared. The director felt a pang of pity that quickly faded. Cabot had been a good man who had made one mistake in his life. If he hadn't been such an altruistic idiot, he'd still be alive. In the slide, Cabot was squatting in a vineyard, scraping the contents of a tin of pâté onto the ground.

"This study," the director said, "was also conducted on July fourth as a gift to potential buyers of our products. In it, the Consortium introduced a genetically altered grape louse to vineyards in California's Napa Valley. As you're surely aware, seventy-five percent of those vineyards have suffered a total loss.

"The properties will eventually be purchased by Consortium members for pennies on the dollar. Market values have already suffered a swift decline that will spiral down substantially further. Then, Consortium associates will purchase those vineyards. While the land appears to be untreatable at this time, we have the means to reverse this challenge and will do so once all of our objectives are met. In three years, California will have the best wine crop in its history.

"All of this is evidence that once again the Consortium's methods and means are effective. Our profit ratio is now satisfactory."

Setting aside the remote, the director hardened his voice. "Until now, all of the trial studies have been extremely limited in scope. But broader studies are currently under way in Carnel Cove, Florida. You'll be apprised of the results in due time."

Now came the real test. The director took in a deep breath, expelled it slowly, and then went on. "Gentlemen, we have proven that anyone who wishes to can successfully launch an economic war against the United States of America. Manipulating its economy, thus its government, and the world market is our goal. This is an opt-in proposition. Your initial investment is one hundred million U.S. dollars. We anticipate a fifty percent return within one year and a three-hundred percent return within three years, when the vaccine becomes available to the public. One question is on the table tonight. In the Consortium's economic war, will you be its ally, or its enemy?"

He paused to let the weight and implications of that choice set in, and then delivered his final message. "You have seventy-two hours to decide."

One by one, the escorts led the buyers out of the building and into their waiting limousines. When the screening room stood empty, the director lifted the receiver on the red phone. "The briefing has concluded."

"Excellent job." The chairman's voice sounded ragged, like gravel over a grate. "You have three minutes to exit the building before it explodes."

Fear slammed through the director's chest. "What?"

"Three minutes." He laughed. "I wouldn't waste them chatting with me."

The director dropped the receiver on the desktop and frantically gathered his notes and slides, taking no chances on what would and would not survive the explosion.

When he disarmed the security system and crossed the threshold of the door, the vicious sounds of that evil voice still rang in his ears, infuriating him.

Eliminating any trace of evidence, any ability of an infiltrator identifying the building or following a trail from it to a Consortium member; the director should have expected this. He'd known the chairman was cautious—hell, he'd be dead if he weren't cautious—but who could have predicted he would blow up the entire building? Much less, in three minutes?

The buyers would still be within spitting distance. They would see the flames, hear the sirens, and smell the smoke. And the chairman knew it.

The bastard was shrewd.

And twisted.

Chapter Twelve

Max lowered his aim from Gabby's face to her heart.

That would be better. Quick and clean. No suffering. And her face would be intact for her funeral. Her mother would appreciate that.

Gabby's breasts rose and fell furiously. Soft. Lush. He swallowed hard, blew out a sigh ripe with frustration. Why had he had to notice?

"Did you change your mind and decide to make love with me?"

"No." Now her voice was trembling. She was scared. He couldn't shoot her when she was scared. Her eyes looked even more haunted than the veep's.

He wouldn't forget it. Not ever. He'd endure nightmares. Cold sweats. Guilt. Pacing the floor in the middle of the night, seeing that look in her eyes, tasting her kiss; things like that made forever a long, long time . . .

"Oh."

She uttered one word on a little sigh, and yet it somehow held a world of disappointment. So was it him she wanted? Or just anyone? He couldn't believe he was even asking. Had to be anyone. She'd had no life of her own. She just wanted someone to remember her.

But she had wondered about *his* kiss for five years.

And he would remember it *and* her for the rest of his life.

His common sense slid into a nosedive with his resolve. If she wanted to make love once more, then why not? They were friends, they had been attracted to each other for five years, and they wouldn't have another chance. So what if a good man would refuse her? According to his nagging conscience, he hadn't been a good man in a lot of years. "Why do you want this?"

Gabby hesitated so long he thought she'd decided not to answer. But then she pursed her lips and made herself look into his eyes. "I don't want it. I need it. Just once, I need to feel special to one man. Not loved, or anything. Just special."

She was about to die and she'd never felt special. Neither had Max. His heart ached a little for both of them. "You have been special. In significant ways, to a lot of people—"

"But never to one man. There's a difference, Max, and you know it."

When she laid down her armor, she really laid it down. As hard as it was to look at those deepest secrets, he could see himself in her exact situation, feeling all the things she was feeling. Grieving. Mourning. Resenting. "That's the way it is for most of us, honey. You know that." Very few SDU agents married, and of those who did, very few stayed married. The risks of death were high and ever present. Operatives were frequently absent from home, often for months at a time, and always without explanation. And when they were home, they had trouble shifting away from the high-wire tension that came with the job. Love, marriage, and covert operations—especially covert ops in SDU—just didn't mix.

"In my head, I know it. But not in my heart." She hugged an emerald silk pillow to her chest. "Why do you think I kept the wings, Max?"

"Because they were your first pair, after you became a pilot."

She shook her head and sent him a telling look. "I kept them because with wings I could fly."

Finally, she'd be special. "And you did."

"But there are a lot of pilots," she countered. "My wings weren't any different than anyone else's."

To her, she'd been just run of the mill and more of the same. Frustration and empathy warred inside him and empathy won. "I hear what you're telling me, Gabby. I just don't know what I can say that will change anything."

She tossed the pillow aside. "Haven't you ever wished that just once you could be really special to someone? That a woman would look at you, and you'd know she believed her world was a remarkable place just because you were in it? That the mere sound of your voice, or the most fleeting sight of you, or one touch of your hand made her feel really lucky to be alive? Haven't you ever wished for that, Max? Even once?"

"Every day of my life," he answered honestly. The words had rolled off his tongue as if he had said them often when, in truth, he'd never before dared to utter them aloud. He'd barely permitted himself to think them.

"Really?"

No sense in denying it. "Unfortunately."

She sat up. The covers spilled down to her waist, exposing the frothy lace and the swell of her breasts. "Did Commander Conlee give you a timetable?"

"Not exactly." Conlee's *"no pain"* hardly qualified.

"So you don't have to kill me and get right back to

Home Base?" she asked, referring to SDU headquarters in Washington, D.C.

Max lowered the gun, almost afraid to ask. "What are you thinking?"

"I'm thinking I want to feel special and so do you," she said. "And I'm thinking that if our kiss is a decent gauge, we can both have our wish."

"Gabby, this is a lousy idea." It was even if it felt like a great one. "We're not talking about a couple dances and dinner and drinks. Or having an affair and keeping it quiet in the unit so we aren't banned as partners. I have to kill you."

"I know. You have your orders and you have to carry them out. I would myself." She tossed back the sheet, then crawled out of bed. Her lace gown unfolded and, as she walked over to him, it swished around her ankles. Stopping in front of him, she lifted her hands to his chest. "But tonight, or in the morning—what's the difference? Dead is dead, Max, and I can't die without knowing if you're as special as your kiss promised."

"Yes, you can." He raised the gun, disputing her.

"Okay, I can." She eased the barrel aside, pointing it toward the window, and then stepped closer; so close their chests brushed and her subtle scent filled him. "But I'd rather not." She circled his neck with her arms. "And I'd sincerely rather you not." Pressuring with her fingertips, she tilted his head and sought his mouth. Her warm breath fanned over his face. "If only for one night, I want you to feel special, Max. I want you to know where you belong."

She'd found his Achilles' heel and stomped it hard. Gabby was doing for him what no other human being, not even his parents, had ever done: taking him in, claiming him . . . protecting him. She was determined to spare him from regret. And if there was even an outside chance that either of them could experience what they'd needed their whole lives, even for one second, he wanted—no, *needed*—to take that chance.

"Max, please."

He shouldn't do it. It'd be worse to do it than regret not doing it. Good God, if he got that second, he'd never be content without it. Gabby wouldn't be there. Not ever again.

Logical. Reasonable. Rational. He should refuse. He really should refuse, but . . . He dropped the gun on the pale green carpet. "To hell with it." He closed his arms around Gabby.

"By sunrise," she promised between kisses, "you'll be glad you didn't just shoot me."

By sunrise he would have more to regret—and the stuff of his nightmares would have an entire arsenal of new fodder for tormenting him. He tugged at her lower lip with his teeth. "Spoken like a confident woman."

"Confidence has nothing to do with it." She rubbed circles on his sides, just below his ribs, and inhaled the scent of his skin at the crook of his neck.

Something in her tone had him rearing back and lifting his eyebrows in question.

She forked her fingers through his hair, lightly raked the skin at his nape with her nails. "We got sidetracked and I forgot to tell you where I hid the evidence."

Shock rolled over him in waves.

Gabby erupted in laughter. Though he didn't like being the object of it, he did like the sound of it. Gentle, but robust. Honest. In their profession, honest emotional reactions of any kind were a rare treat. "Tell me where it is now."

"After," she promised, and then tempted him with a searing kiss.

"After." He scooped her into his arms, not at all sure he would get through this kiss-then-kill scenario, or why getting through it had become so important to him. But it had.

It mattered to Gabby. And somewhere between entering her room and holding her in his arms, what mattered to Gabby had come to matter most to him. Yet there was only one way this could end, and Gabby's "big picture" and "for the greater good" comments proved she knew it.

Orders had been issued at the highest level.

There would be no reprieve, no order to rescind, and no escape.

It was his duty as a reliable, dedicated operative to execute those orders, and he would execute them. He would kill her.

Later.

The phone rang.

Gabby protested the interruption with a heartfelt groan, but he put her down, and she stepped away to answer it. Tapping a button on the phone, she engaged the speaker. "Hello."

"Gabby, it's Candace," a woman said. She sounded breathless. "I need help."

Gabby frowned, hiked a shoulder at Max. "What's wrong?"

"I'm at the lab. There's been an accident with the tanks. It's serious."

"Five minutes," Gabby said, already tearing off her gown and pulling on a pair of jeans. "Max made it home."

"In the middle of a hurricane?"

"He knows I'm freaky around storms, so he risked it." She shoved an arm into a blue T-shirt, then yanked it down over her head. "He'll come, too."

"For God's sake, hurry."

Tugging on her sneakers, she promised. "We're on our way."

When she tapped the toggle to disconnect the call,

Max sent her a look meant to melt steel. "Why did you tell her I was here? Gabby, you're complicating—"

"Stop bitching." Gabby cut him off, snagged her purse from a hook inside the closet. "You can kill me later." Grabbing him by the arm, she headed for the back door. "Right now, I need your help. We've got to try to prevent a biological disaster."

Max followed, closing the door behind him. Ignoring Jaris Adahan's body on the garage floor, he slid into the passenger seat of Gabby's red Jeep and snagged his safety belt. "What kind of biological disaster?"

"Candace's lab is filled with mosquito tanks." Gabby opened the garage door, cranked the engine, slammed the gearshift into reverse, and then stomped the gas. Outside on the driveway, she slammed on the brakes, knocked the gearshift into drive, then punched down on the gas pedal. The tires spun and spit gravel.

The fear on her face worried him more than the Jeep fishtailing down the horseshoe driveway to the street. He'd never seen her express fear so openly. "It's just mosquitoes, not sarin, Gabby," he said, referring to a deadly chemical nerve agent. "Take it easy."

"Take it easy? Did Conlee tell you nothing?" She let out a huff of pure exasperation, cracked the heel of her hand against the steering wheel. "Logan Industries doesn't have ordinary mosquitoes, Max. It's a research firm, remember? They're infected with Z-4027."

Logan Industries was one of the research firms developing a vaccine and pesticide to combat Z-4027. The truth smacked him in the face. "You know for fact that the crop infestations aren't natural occurrences?"

"I strongly suspect it, but I can't prove it. Not yet." She nodded. "I'm convinced someone was testing the waters with the New York incident and Judge Powell. Z-4027 has to be on the black market by now, and I'm scared to death someone has turned it loose on our crops."

Max didn't have five days. He didn't have five minutes. He looked at Gabby. The fear he felt, stark and solid, bitter and tinged with terror, shone back at him from the depths of her eyes and proved his worst nightmare had come true.

The attack had already begun.

Chapter Thirteen

The lab was a wreck. A quarter inch of water soaked the floor, mosquitoes swarmed everywhere, and the stench of pesticide seemed to have sucked out every atom of oxygen.

His eyes tearing and nose burning, Max blinked hard to clear his vision. A tall blonde he presumed was Candace stood bare to the waist and spread-eagle with her back to him and Gabby, stretching her blouse over the only window in the lab. Judging by the broken glass at her feet, she was trying to block the opening—and not totally succeeding.

"Gabby?" Candace called out, clearly panicked. "Help me over here."

Gabby ran to her, began batting at the mosquitoes biting Candace. "Oh, Jesus." She nodded toward the broken window. "Do something about that."

Max grabbed a stapler off a desk. "Where's some tape?"

"Third drawer on the left in Erickson's desk," Candace said from between gritted teeth.

Spotting Erickson's nameplate, Max jerked open the desk drawer, snagged a roll of masking tape, and then rushed back to the window. He stapled Candace's blouse in place and then sealed the edges with masking tape.

"Jesus, there's a million of them." Gabby kept slapping at the mosquitoes covering Candace's back. "What the hell happened? Where's Erickson?"

"Too many trees and electrical wires are down from the storm." Candace coughed hard, choking on the pesticide. "He couldn't get here. Neither could Marcus."

Gabby spared Max a glance. "Erickson heads the Z-4027 project. Marcus Swift runs Logan Industries."

Candace frantically swatted at her arms, her thighs. "Some of the mosquitoes got out. I tried—I really tried, but I couldn't keep them all inside."

Tears streamed down her face. Whether she was crying or the chemicals stinging his eyes had hers watering, he couldn't tell. But her voice sounded steady.

She swiped at her cheeks with the back of her hand. "The window was broken and all the tanks were smashed and they were swarming everywhere and I couldn't find anything to block the broken glass, so I used my shirt and—" her voice broke "—I'm not sure how many got out, Gabby. But some did." Fresh tears spilled down her face. "I know some did. We've got to warn Sheriff Coulter."

Candace was nearly at the breaking point and she was already swelling, particularly on her face, chest, and neck. Max did a quick scan. At forty bites, he stopped counting. Gauging, she had maybe twice that many. He glanced over, saw a target, and smacked Gabby's upper arm.

She glared at him. "What?"

"You were being bitten."

Gabby still stared at him.

"What?" Either she thought he had been ogling Candace, or she was still smarting from him swatting at the bugs biting her. "You want me to just watch you get bitten?"

Gabby held her glare. "Seal the lab, Max." Then what he had said sank in; it stiffened her expression. "Bitten? Oh, no." She glanced at her arms—seven bites—then at Candace, who was covered. "Oh, God." The stench of fear fell between them. "How long do we have?"

Candace swallowed hard. "Not long. Respiratory problems manifest within minutes and steadily worsen. We've got maybe twelve hours before we're in respiratory failure and coma. From what William told Elizabeth, he lived about twenty-one hours after three bites." Candace surveyed her red-whelped chest and arms. "I'd say my time is going to be shorter."

Gabby darted a frantic gaze at Max. "Are you bitten, too?"

Dressed in all black covert gear with only his face exposed, he was well protected. "No, I'm pretty well covered, and I may smell bitter. They're avoiding me."

"Thank God." Gabby turned back to Candace. "We've got to get them contained."

While they captured or killed the mosquitoes to stop the immediate dissemination challenge, Max sealed the lab and then searched for clothing for Candace.

In the supply room, a variety of cans lined the wall. He walked around, into an alcove, and then opened a cabinet. Lab coats were stacked next to masks, boxes of gloves, and other nonregulated supplies. Grabbing two coats—Gabby's arms were bare—and masks, he left the supply room and returned to the main lab.

"Put these on." He passed the items. "Masks, too." The pungent odor of pesticide still hung heavy in the air. Near the window, three cans of insect repellent had been tossed to the floor. Two were dented.

Candace buttoned up the coat. "I did that—sprayed

the insecticide. It didn't work at all. It just seemed to piss them off."

Max swiveled his gaze to Gabby. No insecticide or pesticide in existence would kill Z-4027-infected mosquitoes. "I'm sure it did."

Gabby shrugged into the sleeves of her coat. "We'll gather up the strays. You report and see what we're supposed to do now. Use the viewer. Candace knows it's here."

Surprised, Max nodded and pulled out a headset, then moved to the lab table Gabby indicated. He looked up into the remote viewer, and realized if Candace knew about it, then Gabby's cover *had* been compromised, though not by Global Warriors. By Candace—unless the commander had authorized disclosure to Candace. He well might have. Logan Industries worked on highly classified Z-4027 contracts with the Department of Defense. They'd be subject to a full review, which meant Candace would have to respond to any inquiries.

Did that mean Elizabeth knew about Gabby, too? More than likely, she did. She was Powell's widow, and Candace wouldn't have given Gabby his tissue samples without Elizabeth's agreement. They were friends, right? Of course, she knew. Though they could both think Gabby had been inserted undercover for the Justice Department.

However, none of those things would explain to Candace how Max knew about the remote viewer or why he was reporting to Conlee. How had—or would—Gabby explain? "Gabby?" When she looked over at him, he sent her a pointed, questioning look, insisting she think through her reporting suggestion.

The mask covering her mouth and nose, she nodded. "Do it, Max. It's okay."

How could it be okay? "Are you sure?"

"Positive."

"All right." This mission just kept getting more and more twisted.

Feeling futile because he wasn't fully informed or certain that he ever would be, Max cursed again, and then spoke into the lip mike. "Commander?"

"I'm here," Conlee said. "We've been monitoring. I've already contacted Burke Pharmaceutical. They're working a mirror contract for us on this. Dr. Keith Burke is on his way to Carnel Cove with a vaccine injection."

"So there is a vaccine available?" Hope filled Max. A vaccine would save Candace's and Gabby's lives. Erickson hadn't yet developed one, though according to Gabby, he was making significant progress.

"It's strictly experimental," Conlee said. "Burke hasn't yet done trial studies, so if Candace is willing, she'll be the first to test it."

Max glanced back at the women. They were still killing mosquitoes, but getting things under control. "What's the alternative?"

Conlee didn't miss a beat. "Certain death."

"I guess she'll agree, then." How could she refuse? "What about Gabby?"

The commander hesitated and silence crackled through the headpiece. Finally, he answered, his voice steely with resolve. "You have your orders."

Frowning, Max walked away from the viewer, though he could still pick up audio, and examined the mosquito tanks, the fall pattern of the broken glass on the lab floor, the rows of chemical canisters labeled with yellow bands, and one canister banded in black. He doubled back to Dr. David Erickson's desk. Next to his nameplate rested a photo of a boy about nine. Its silver frame glinted in the overhead emergency light. Was that Erickson's son? A rock had skid across the desktop, scuffing it, and lay next to the frame. What was going on with these rocks?

Fist-size rocks lay all over the lab . . . including near or inside every broken mosquito tank. Max checked more thoroughly and then spoke into the lip mike. "Commander, it looks as if someone hurled in a rock from outside to break the window." The lab had only one window. "There are rocks all over the place. Actually, most of them are stones. Polished, not natural. The kind you buy in stores." He double-checked the trajectories, window to damage points. The damage definitely had been done from outside the lab. "This isn't a result of hurricane damage, sir. And it wasn't an accident."

"Stand by. I'm having Intel run the tapes. Maybe we'll get lucky."

Max checked on Gabby and Candace, soaping their bites at the sink. Gabby had to know that wouldn't help, not with Z-4027-infected mosquitoes. So why was she doing it? "Gabby?"

She looked up, her eyes calm and intent. She knew what she was doing. "Yes, Max?"

Gabby was just comforting Candace. Helping her to feel in control and not like a helpless victim. "Never mind."

Sweat sheened on her skin. She swiped her hair back from her face. Candace was already pouring sweat and breathing heavily, though that could be a reaction to the pesticide or anxiety about what lay ahead rather than symptoms induced by Z-4027.

"Grayson?"

Max turned his attention back to Conlee. "Yes, Commander?"

"The thrower never entered the lab. The window was broken first with rocks, and then the stones were hurled at the tanks from outside. Unfortunately, that's also beyond our viewer's field of vision. Supposition is based on the trajectory of the rocks and stones."

Two good-size rocks were on the floor below the window and stones were in or near every tank. "Looks that way from here, too, sir. Nothing indicates otherwise." Why was there a window in the lab? Max had never seen a window in a lab that worked classified projects.

"Then we can't ID the thrower. Can Candace?"

"No, sir." Max had overheard her telling Gabby. "When she entered, the lab was empty and the damage had already been done."

"How long was containment violated?"

"No clear estimate on this end." Max's stomach furled. "Best bet is to clock the time of the damage on the tape and go from there."

"Is the lab sealed now?"

"Yes, sir." Max wandered back to the lab table below the viewer. "Should we notify Sheriff Coulter or the mayor?" Gabby had mentioned his name, but at the moment Max couldn't recall—wait. Faulkner. That was it. Mayor Faulkner.

"No. Not yet," Conlee said, sounding worried and agitated. "Frankly, there isn't a thing they can do about this that they aren't already doing."

"Sir?" Max didn't understand.

"Hurricane Darla has power out and mosquitoes breeding like there's no tomorrow. There's a post-storm warning to take preventative measures and a dusk-to-dawn curfew." Dread etched his tone. "Dusk is feeding time."

Max's skin crawled. "I see."

"I'll get back to you with further orders. What I want to know now is why you haven't carried out your initial orders."

Why isn't Gabby dead? Max gave in to a sigh. "It took a twenty-four-hour hike to get here and a lot is going on that hasn't yet been reported in detail, Commander. She's been gathering evidence. When this lab incident occurred, she was still briefing me." He probably should stop there, but of course, he wouldn't. "It's possible neither SDU nor her cover has been breached by those we feared." Max saw no need to mention Candace. Conlee had deemed her safe and he'd heard and seen everything that had happened in the lab—or he would as soon as he did a full review of the tapes. "I'm following Vice President Stone's orders, too, sir, making sure this is absolutely necessary and there's no other way." It couldn't hurt to remind Conlee of her orders. "I'm sure you agree that's essential."

"I don't agree or disagree. I issue orders and you follow them," Conlee said sharply. "Kincaid's cover is breached or this lab incident wouldn't have happened. It has to be related to her investigations. Do your job, Grayson."

"But, sir—"

"As soon as possible," Conlee snapped, clearly out of patience. "The risks of being wrong are exorbitant."

That was the bottom line. It was always the bottom line. An overwhelming urge surged through Max to knock the person who had devised risk assessment on his ass. "Yes, sir," he said, swallowing his bitterness. "As soon as possible." Which would be after Gabby had finished her briefing.

That could take a while. When he looked the veep in the face, he wanted to be able to meet her eyes with no hesitation or reservation. Until he could, Gabby was going to stay alive.

"Take Candace home," Conlee said. "Dr. Burke will meet you there. And get someone to brick up that window."

"Yes, sir." Max shouldn't ask, but . . . "Why was there a window, sir?"

"Erickson has a medical condition. He needs sunlight." Conlee sighed. "Secure labs can't have windows *unless* they're authorized under a disability request. Those are discretionary and I granted one. My responsibility. Totally."

Max winced. Conlee was going to suffer on this one. Fatalities were inevitable.

"Don't drag your heels executing my orders or I'll bust you out of SDU."

Was the old man reading his mind, or what? Max stiffened. He was either psychic or figuring out what he would do if he were in Max's position. Regardless, his warning was well intentioned and clear. Once an SDU operative went active in the unit, there was only one way to bust him out.

If Max delayed canceling Gabby, then he would be canceled, too.

Chapter Fourteen

Carnel Cove, Florida ★ Monday, August 5

Candace Burke's home was a contemporary minipalace on a three-acre lot that backed up to the cove for which Carnel Cove had been named. Power was out for miles, but thanks to an elaborate backup generator system, she had lights and air-conditioning to battle the sultry, humid heat.

Gabby adjusted the thermostat on the hallway wall, knocking the temperature down a couple degrees, and then walked back into the living room, where Max was pacing between the bar and the sleek sofa nearest the fireplace. It was one-thirty in the morning and he hadn't racked out in a bed in two days. He was running on sheer adrenaline and it showed in the tense set of his shoulders and the strain lining his face. Yet even now, and even under these circumstances, he still had that magical something that made Gabby notice everything about him, and made everything about him vitally important to her.

He paused and looked over at her. "How is she?"

"Not good." Gabby walked to the bar, poured herself a finger of bourbon, and knocked it back. "She's spiked a fever, Max. It's a hundred and one, and climbing. She's already suffering muscle pain, and a mild headache. Soon it'll be a wall-banger."

"But it's only been two hours."

"She's got over a hundred bites. That's a lot of Z-4027 in her system."

"We should get her to the hospital."

Coma, brain inflammation, her breathing shutting down, and organ failure—all that could and would happen sooner rather than later. "She needs medical attention but no, no hospital." Gabby thumbed the rim of her glass. "I brought it up, but Candace repeatedly refused and continuously murmured one name: Keith."

"Burke Pharmaceutical's Keith?" Max asked. Conlee had told him about Keith Burke.

Gabby nodded. "She has complete faith only he can save her. My instincts are warning me she's right. So we wait here for Dr. Burke."

"She's not exactly in great shape to be making decisions, Gabby. Is that what's best for her?" Max asked. "Look, I know you're losing more than a contact, you're losing a friend." He softened his voice. "But you have to think of what's best for Candace. The hospital has the means to make her more comfortable."

Gabby smacked her glass down on the bar and turned on him. "That's exactly what I'm doing." She rolled her gaze heavenward, seeking divine intervention to keep from choking him. "Think, Max. Powell was murdered, remember?"

Max wasn't tracking. "At the hospital?"

"Candace says, yes."

"There's a 'but' in that remark." He laid a level look on her that demanded a straight answer. "What is it?"

Gabby wasn't in the mood for explanations, but she couldn't very well ask Max to operate blind. He had delayed killing her, and if for no other reason, she owed him for that. "But Elizabeth swears he was bitten while he and Mayor Faulkner were at Judge Abernathy's fishing camp."

"This is the first I've heard of Faulkner being up there with Powell." Max walked to the bar, poured himself a club soda. "Is that verified?"

Gabby nodded, and then checked the window, anxiously waiting for Dr. Keith Burke's arrival. God, she wished he'd get the lead out. He was Candace's only shot at surviving. Gabby wasn't feeling great either, but whether it was from the virus or from Max, she was going to die, so it didn't matter. Candace, however, had a life. Purpose. She needed to live. "Faulkner mentors most of the Cove judges and businessmen. The ones with influence anyway. Some like it—Judge Abernathy and Carl Blake, the bank president, come to mind." She fingered the silky drapes. "Some hate but tolerate it, like Judge Powell. Elizabeth says he wanted to keep an eye on them, to see what they were up to. Apparently, William went to high school with Faulkner and Sheriff Coulter, and they both know what Faulkner is really like."

"What is he really like?"

Solid question. She looked over at Max. "First to take credit, last to accept blame."

"Your typical politician—Sybil and a rare few others excepted, of course."

"Not exactly," Gabby said. "Elizabeth says Faulkner is unsavory and he has no character. That's a little worse than the average politician." Gabby cocked her head and stretched her neck muscles. "But take that assessment with a grain of salt. Elizabeth's fabulous, but her ethics are up there with Jesus and Sybil's. Few can measure up, if you know what I mean—me included."

"The veep does have a worldwide sterling reputation."

"Yeah, and I'm a bitch but no ethics slouch." Gabby poured and then took a healthy swig from her glass. It burned going down her throat.

"The bitch business is your own fault. People only know what you let them know." Stopping beside a white curved sofa that looked comfortable but too perfect to sit on, Max stuffed his hands in his pockets. "So these fishing trips are when Faulkner does his mentoring. They're actually strategy sessions?"

Gabby nodded, plopped down on the sofa and tucked her feet up under her.

Max went ahead and sat down beside her. "It seems obvious that when Powell returned from New York and went with Faulkner up to Abernathy's camp, he wasn't planning to fish. But how could a strategy session between locals tie to the New York elevator attack? Did they hire the Global Warriors to hit you? What do these Covers know about Z-4027?"

"There you go again with more of those million-dollar questions, Max." She reached over, patted his thigh. "They aren't supposed to know anything—and I can't prove they that they do—but I suspect they know plenty."

"Well, are you going to share your suspicions?" He covered her hand with his and gentled his voice. "You're looking peaked. Feeling bad?"

"I'm all right." She said the words hoping they would make it so. She was feeling bad. Not anywhere near as raunchy as Candace, but bad. "I'm going to share everything I know with you." She pulled back her hand and hauled herself to her feet. It took more effort than she cared to admit, even to herself. "But first, I'm going to answer the door."

"The door?" Max looked from her to it.

She was halfway to it when the doorbell rang.

Dr. Keith Burke finally had arrived.

★   ★   ★

They weren't strangers.

Gabby looked at Keith on his knees beside Candace's bed, stroking her face. He was a large man, nearly as tall as Max at six foot one, but the likenesses stopped there. Keith was blond; Max's hair was as black as mined coal. Where Keith had that wiry, athletic build, Max was broad and solid. Both men were attractive, but Keith paled standing next to Max. At least, in Gabby's opinion.

Near the door to Candace's bedroom, Max stepped closer to Gabby and whispered, "These people are not just business acquaintances."

"Apparently not." Gabby watched Dr. Burke talk with Candace, getting what he needed both from her and in examining her to assess her condition. "Even before she spiked a fever, she kept calling for him. I guess she knows he's the only one who can possibly save her life."

"Maybe." Max watched, processed the tenderness and familiarity passing between them. "But it seems like more. They're intimate, Gabby. Connected."

"Yeah, they are. We'll talk to him after he does what he can for her." Gabby looked over at Max, a glint of surprise lighting her eyes.

Max lifted a questioning eyebrow. "What?"

"I was just thinking. It's kind of nice to have someone to talk with at times like this."

"Partners don't just try to get you killed," he whispered from behind his hand. "For a smart woman, it's taking you a long time to figure that out."

"Habit." She shut down her emotions and slid her professional mask back into place.

"I'll be right here," Burke said. "Just let me talk with Gabby and Max a second, okay?"

"Don't leave me."

"I won't, darling." Burke walked away from the bed, to the door where they stood.

Gabby didn't bother to hide her curiosity. "You two obviously know each other well."

"We were once married, Gabby. I'm surprised Candace hasn't told you."

Gabby frowned. "You're divorced *and* professional competitors on Department of Defense contracts?"

She was getting hostile. Max put a restraining arm on hers. "Honey, let him talk to us." He hoped the endearment would remind her she was undercover as a wife and judge and not a ticked-off SDU operative fearing the best interests of the United States government had been violated.

"Of course, sugar." She looped their arms and sent him a smile forged of pure steel so he felt more than heard her sarcasm. "So talk, Dr. Burke."

"Keith," he said, then turned the topic back to the matter at hand. "Candace has no interest in medical research. Logan Industries was vulnerable to takeover and an excellent investment she wanted to buy, provided I didn't object—and I didn't—so she bought it. I gave her my blessing and invested heavily in LI stock. When it comes to investments, Candace is charmed. The short version is we decided to be loving friends instead of married enemies. It's that simple. Or it was." He blinked hard three times. "Now it's not. Now, she's dying." His voice went thick. "And I don't know if what I've got will save her or kill her."

"The vaccine?" Max focused. The weight of Gabby's arm on his wasn't sexual or sensual. She was leaning on him. And sweating. And her eyes were glossy and overly bright.

The infection was taking hold in her, too.

"Yeah, the vaccine." Keith nodded. "I want her permission. I have to know she understands the risks."

Because if things went badly, her not knowing them would haunt Keith Burke the rest of his life. Max nodded, puzzled by their relationship. They obviously loved each other. So why had they divorced?

"Of course, you do." Gabby nodded back toward Candace. "Go talk to her, Keith. She took over a hundred bites. There's no time to lose."

"Over a hundred?" His eyes widened and he sucked in a little gasp.

The horror in his reaction robbed Gabby of her voice. She settled for a nod.

Keith just stared at her for a long, unblinking moment, then he squeezed his eyes shut. "Dear God." He looked down at the creamy carpet, and then turned away and returned to Candace's bedside. "I've got a vaccine for this infection, darling, but it's new." He fluffed her pillow and then dabbed at her brow with a cool, wet cloth. "I don't know if it'll work."

"Experimental?" Her voice sounded breathy, faint and tinny.

"Yes." He clasped her hand in his. "It could not work at all, Candace."

She leveled her calm blue eyes on him. "Or it could kill me, right?"

"Yes." He cleared his throat. "If it works, we'll see significant evidence of it within an hour. If it fails, it could have no effect at all." He paused and looked from her eyes to the wall and then back again. "Or it could cause immediate death." Doubt riddled his face, his voice. "I just don't know, darling. I wish to God I did, but I just don't know."

"Shh, it's okay. I know what I need to know." She pulled their clasped hands to her face, kissed his knuckles. "Without it, I'm definitely going to die. With it, I have hope." She stroked his cheek. "I'll take my chances with your vaccine."

"I wish—" Words failed him and he dropped his chin to his chest.

"No." She searched his face, her heart in her eyes.

"Married or not, I've always loved you, Keith. Death won't change that. Nothing can change that."

"For me, either."

"Just don't leave me until it's done, okay? Either way."

"I won't," he solemnly swore. "I'll be right here with you for as long as you need me."

She summoned a weak smile and motioned to his bag beside her bed. "Do it, then."

Keith moved to prepare the injection, and Candace called out, "Gabby?"

"I'm right here." She stepped forward, feeling fragile at witnessing their exchange.

"You'd better call Marcus and Dr. Erickson and tell them to lock down the lab. And get word to Mayor Faulkner and Sheriff Coulter. I have enough sins on my soul without adding innocent lives to them due to negligence."

"I'll handle it. Don't worry," Gabby said. She was shaking, scared down to the marrow of her bones of losing a friend. While she hadn't been totally honest with Candace, or any of the rest of the women in Carnel Cove, Gabby had acted like a true friend and they had trusted her. True friends were a precious thing in her life, and so scarce. "Just focus on getting well."

Keith stepped away to fill the syringe, and Candace whispered to Gabby, "If this goes badly, don't let him wallow in guilt."

Seeing that this was Candace's greatest fear, Gabby nodded. "I won't."

"Are you ready, sweetheart?" Keith stepped back to the bedside.

She nodded and smiled up at him. "I love you, Keith."

A tear rolled down his face. "I love you, too." He injected Candace, and then set the syringe aside.

"What now?" Candace asked, her long hair tumbling across her pillow in damp locks.

"We wait." Keith sat on the edge of the bed, took her hands in his, and whispered something only the two of them could hear.

Gabby sagged against Max, as if she were having trouble holding herself upright. She was sweating now, flushed, and her eyes had that fevered look. Tears leaked out and ran down her cheeks, rattling Max. Gabby never relinquished control. "Gabby?"

She looked at him, her torment unrelenting. "She's my friend. I want her to live, Max."

If Gabby could will it, it would be done. "I know." He closed an arm around her shoulder and squeezed her to him. "Let's wait in the living room. Give them some time alone."

She sniffed, nodded.

Near the door, Max paused. "Keith, if you need us, we'll be right outside."

Keith glanced back at Max, and then at Gabby. Recognition that Gabby was exhibiting symptoms too had worry flooding his eyes. He and Max shared an understanding look. Keith nodded, silently assuring he would see to Gabby as soon as he knew the impact of his vaccine.

As soon as he knew if Candace would live or die.

Chapter Fifteen

Max sat beside Gabby on Candace's sofa. Her lab coat pocket snagged his shirt button. He worked it loose. "You okay?"

She drew back her lips in a tight smile that was really more a snarl splitting her lips. "She's a good friend and she's dying. I'm freaking fabulous."

Hurting and lashing out. What did she want him to say? "I'm sorry."

She flipped up a hand. "Everyone's always sorry, but it doesn't change anything." She flopped back. "Why do we bother, Max? I mean, no matter how hard we try or how much we give up to fight them, the bad guys just keep on coming. Their names and faces change, but they never stop coming."

"We get some of them," he reminded her. "We save some of them."

"Come on, Max. Get real. We don't even know for sure

what is going on here. How are we supposed to save anyone else? I'm a dead woman walking. I can't even save myself."

He dragged a frustrated hand across his jaw. The stubble ruffled under his fingertips. "All I know is the fight is worth fighting, so I fight it. That's all I know, Gabby. It's worth fighting, and that's enough."

"Don't you dare be logical," she snarled. "I'm pissed to the gills. I don't want logic."

He finger-brushed her hair off her face. "Then what you do want?"

"A little righteous indignation. A little outrage that we're the good guys and we're getting our asses kicked—again. I want you to fight back, Max, so I can unload."

"Thanks, but I'll pass. Yelling at you won't help. We're stuck with reacting to others' actions when they get out of line. That's the way it is. Want anything else?"

She laid a frown on him that would scare Gibson out of his skin. "I don't like you when you won't fight with me. It ticks me off."

"Honey, that's when you like me best."

She jutted out her jaw but didn't deny it. The anger drained from her eyes and despair replaced it. "I—I think I want to be held. I want you to just be there beside me and hold me, Max." Her voice thinned to a faint whisper, sounding more vulnerable than he would have believed possible. "Candace has been good to me. I don't want her to die. I don't want Keith to go through the hell of failing to save her. I—I don't want to lose anymore, Max." Pain riddled her eyes. "I'm already losing everything—Sybil, you, Westford, my life. I should have some kind of immunity from anything else bad happening that hurts me."

A thump in his chest felt like a hammer swing. He circled her slender shoulder and pulled her close. "It doesn't work that way, honey." He kissed her crown. "If I could force it to, I would." Was that like harnessing the universe for her? Probably not. But it was the truth.

"Thank you, Max." She wrapped her arms around his neck, leaned into the hug. "I'm tired. So tired and frustrated, and I hurt from the bone out. Candace trusted me, and I failed to protect her. My best wasn't good enough. When it most mattered, I failed. It's almost a blessing that I won't have to live long knowing that."

She actually believed that tripe. Angry, he pulled back, stared down into Gabby's upturned face. "Oh, so you threw the rocks that broke the tanks and set the mosquitoes loose?"

"Don't be ridiculous."

"Well, that's the only way you could be responsible for what's happened."

"You know what I mean, Max." Gabby lifted a hand. "Candace called me for help and I didn't protect her. Now, she's almost certainly going to die."

He did know what she meant, and he admired her sense of duty and responsibility. But this was too far over the line. He curled her neck, pulled her head back against his chest. "You can't protect the entire world, honey. I know now how hard you try, but that's beyond the stomping grounds of mere mortals."

"I'm a mere mortal. Got it." She swung an arm across his stomach, let it fall limp, her hand on his ribs. "I'll try to remember."

He sighed, lifting her with him. "You could stop trying to pick a fight and lay off the sarcasm. That would suit me just fine. We've got enough to deal with without your attitude."

That had her pausing. "Okay." She snuggled closer to him, parked her head on his chest, over his heart. "I guess we do."

Keith walked out of the bedroom. Gabby caught a sharp breath, pulled away and straightened. "Is she—?"

"She's alive," he said quickly. "It's been thirty minutes. If she were going to die from the injection, it would have happened by now."

"Does that mean it works?" Max asked, worried for Candace and Gabby.

"No, it just means it didn't kill her."

That revelation clearly took a load off Keith's shoulders, though strain and worry still shone on his face.

"Did you mean what you said in there?" Gabby asked Keith. "That you'd be here with her until she didn't need you anymore?"

"Yes, of course." He stepped closer, leaned a hip against the bar. "I've called for some medical equipment I might need. She doesn't want to go to the hospital."

"Either way?"

"Either way, Gabby. If it can be done for her, I'll do it here."

He had just enough resolve in his eyes to prove he'd harness the universe for her, just like Westford would for Sybil. Max wondered what that kind of love would be like. He stole a sideward glance at Gabby. From the hunger in her expression, she wondered, too.

Keith moved to Gabby, and dread filled his eyes. "You're infected, too." When she said she was fine, he shifted to Max. "What about you?"

"I had protection." He nodded toward the gear he had worn during his trek to Carnel Cove that now sat in a folded stack on the opposite sofa.

Working with the Department of Defense, Keith obviously recognized the gear for what it was, but he also knew enough not to ask questions. "Good."

Relieved, Max intervened. "Would you take a look at Gabby anyway, Doc?" Max ignored her killer glare.

"I said I'm fine," she insisted. "And I'm quite capable of talking for myself."

"Yes, dear." Max gave her an indulgent look, and then turned a you-know-women look on Keith.

He smiled at Gabby. "Since I'm here, would it be okay? In the interest of science," he added. "The trial studies on the vaccine haven't been done on humans."

Her nose out of joint, she shrugged. "All right. In the interest of science."

He examined her, and his expression grew dark, then darker. Finally, he draped the stethoscope around the back of his neck. "Your respiration is off."

"I've got all the symptoms." She lifted her chin. "You don't have to soft-pedal it, Keith. I know I've got the Z-4027 infection."

"But your condition isn't as critical as Candace's. I'm not seeing the usual fatal warnings." He checked her respiration rate again. "Were you bitten a long time after she was?"

"Minutes at most." Gabby shrugged. "But I don't have anywhere near as many bites."

"I don't want to give you the injection unless we have no choice," he said. "It's too risky. I do want you to go home and rest. Drink lots of fluids and watch your temperature. If you see a sudden spike, or your head starts aching— Max, you come get me."

"You'll be here with Candace the whole time?" Gabby asked again.

She'd just asked him that. Perplexed, Max looked at her. By her expression, Gabby honestly didn't realize she was repeating herself.

Keith, however, did. He shot Max a warning, then pivoted his gaze to Gabby. "I'm not leaving her." Nodding toward the bedroom, he offered Gabby a hand to get up. "Why don't you go tell Candace good night and then get some rest? With luck, this infection won't knock you to your knees. It doesn't everyone."

"It has a seventy-eight percent mortality rate and in

multiple doses, a hundred percent. I told you not to soft-pedal to me."

He frowned. "How do you know about this?"

"Does it really matter? Soon, I'll be dead."

Torn between letting it go and pushing, he glanced at the stack of Max's gear, and understanding dawned in his eyes. Max and Gabby were a team.

Without another word, Gabby went into the bedroom. When Max could no longer see her, he claimed Keith's attention. "Don't ask anything. Nothing."

Keith grasped Max's message. Ask, and you admit knowledge. Admit knowledge and you're a threat to national security. And threats to national security must be dispensed. He didn't respond or even nod.

Satisfied, Max returned to Gabby's health. "She repeated herself. Did you notice?"

This time, Keith did nod. "Memory lapses are consistent with the symptoms of infection, Max." He let Max see his empathy. "She's right about her odds. You need to prepare yourself."

"Can't you give her the vaccine before she gets worse?"

"Not without risking killing her. I don't want that on my head, do you?"

Max didn't. He pushed past his personal reaction to his professional one. He needed her memories—her briefing—before he could do what he had been ordered to do. Otherwise, he would be fighting an undeclared war in Carnel Cove without her knowledge and insights, or her evidence. He couldn't win that war, and a lot of innocent people would die. "No, I don't. But her memory is vital."

"Her life is more vital."

To Max, yes. But he seriously doubted Commander Conlee would agree.

*   *   *

Gabby's home was nothing like the woman she had shown him. It had been decorated by a pro, but seemed sparse, clean-lined, and totally at odds with the warmth of her bedroom. The living room lacked any personal touches other than a gold gavel that was clearly a prop for her cover. No magazines littered the table. The library, adjoining the living room, was stacked to the rafters with law books. All looked well used, and that too, Max knew, was a prop. Just as his clothes in the bedroom closet had been placed there with no expectation of ever being worn. They at least had proven useful. Gabby had been here for seven months, but there were no insights to the woman in the whole house. Nothing personal, nothing uniquely Gabby—except a photo of the two of them. A wedding photo.

They hadn't been together when it had been made. The photographer had inserted them on a computer program of another couple. Sad testimony that it was, it was as real as Max got to having a family.

Gabby lay stretched out on the sofa, her knees curled to her chest. "Max?"

"Yeah." He sat a glass of lukewarm juice on the coffee table beside her. The power was still out, and she'd lit candles on the fireplace's mantel and on the sofa tables. Though the room had pockets of warm glows, it also had long deep shadows that made him want to prowl and keep watch. She seemed to have forgotten the dead Global Warrior in her garage, but Max hadn't. At this point, however, that was just another item on his worry list.

"I think the commander has wigged out on us." She punched a throw pillow tucked under her head. "We know some of the infected mosquitoes got out of the lab. We can't deliberately expose all of Carnel Cove to Z-4027. We've got to warn somebody."

"Conlee knows."

"But he's not *doing* anything." She stiffened her neck, cranked back her head. "Call him, Max. Tell him that he can't just bury this and not tell the locals. Use guilt, threats, whatever, but get him to warn them."

"Is the phone secure?"

"It was. With the Warriors here, I don't know. I didn't risk it and there hasn't been time to run a check on it."

"I'll do it, and then call Conlee." Max went outside to the box where the line came into the house, ran the check, and then checked all the phones inside. The Warriors hadn't touched the line. That was both bad and good news. It meant they hadn't been interested in taps. They'd only been interested in murder.

It also meant that it was possible Gabby had been marked merely as a judge sticking her nose into cases that they wanted left alone and they knew nothing more about her than that.

The house was stifling hot. But with that second Warrior on the loose, Max didn't dare to open a window. He returned to Gabby. She half-sat with her knees curled up, sipping at her juice. "All clear."

"Make the call, then." She set her glass back down on the table. Sweltering, it left a water ring that splashed.

Max picked up the phone and dialed. When the commander came on the line, Max point-blank asked: "The lab wasn't contained. We have no idea how many infected mosquitoes escaped into the populace. How do you want us to go about notifying the locals?"

"I don't."

"Commander, we can't—"

"I have no choice, Max." Frustration starched his voice. "If we notify Mayor Faulkner, he's obligated to contact the CDC. The media will get involved, for Christ's sake."

How the Centers for Disease Control translated to media contact, Max wasn't sure, but Conlee was convinced it was a direct line. "The word needs to get out or people here are going to start dying, Commander."

"Word gets out and we've got serious problems with the discovery process. Even more people will die. Many more people will die."

That would drive the Warriors underground, making it even more difficult, if not impossible, to discover why they were here, why they had attacked the lab, if in fact they had attacked the lab, and why they wanted to kill Gabby. "Then what do we do? Are you saying we sacrifice the lives of local civilians without lifting a finger to help them?"

"I'm saying mosquitoes don't travel far. They'll be contained in the immediate vicinity of the lab. If we can keep that area clear, we'll be okay."

"With all due respect, you're wrong, sir," Max said, feeling his temper heat. "There's just been a hurricane here. Everything is a mess, and the wildlife is stirred up. The mosquitoes will feed off birds in the immediate area, but the birds won't necessarily stay there. They'll be infected and they will definitely infect other species. Isolation will not work."

"That's not what I'm hearing from Dr. Richardson."

"He's wrong. This is a Z-4027 infection. It's hot and it's loose. Think EEE, only a hundredfold worse. That's what you're looking at, Commander. It'll wipe out Carnel Cove and start spreading outward from there, taking out everyone crossing its path. If you doubt it, I suggest you read Dr. Erickson's notes thoroughly." Conlee had hired Erickson because he was an expert on EEE, light years ahead of anyone else in his research. "I read his overviews on the ride down here. He doesn't mince words. Isolation will not work. You do nothing, and within weeks, Carnel Cove will be wiped out. Within months—"

"Okay. You've made your case." Conlee paused, then continued. "Notify no one just yet. I need a little time to reconsider strategy. You're certain dissemination from the lab has been halted, right?"

"Yes, sir."

"Okay. Follow your initial orders and check back with me in two hours."

Max checked his watch. Two hours. Four-thirty A.M. "As soon as we complete the debrief, sir." Conlee was ordering Max to move ahead on canceling Gabby. Max had to make it clear that the debrief information was vital enough to warrant waiting.

"Fine. But do it at the lab," Conlee said. The phone line crackled and hissed, a familiar sound when the security scrambler cycled. "Hurricane damage is slowing us down on getting to the scene with backup. Whoever caused the first attack could launch another. If they do, I want you in that lab, ready for them."

"Yes, sir." Max put the receiver down.

Gabby grunted from the sofa, obviously hauling herself upright. "I take it I have a short stay of execution."

"A short one." He swung around to look at her. The candlelight flames shone in her eyes. "Are you in pain?"

"Compared to the wall, it's nothing."

"The wall?"

"Two missions ago, remember? When that jerk, Ambrose, had his goons mortar me in behind that concrete wall and I had to bust my way out."

Max remembered. She'd been missing for three days. The veep and Conlee were nuts. He had been more afraid than ever before in his life. Afraid and desolate.

"That was sore. This is . . . annoying." She swung her legs over the edge of the leather, shoved with her arms, and stood up. "So what do we do?"

"Go to the lab, prevent any second attack, and wait."

"Wait?" Sliding into her shoes, she raised her voice a pitch. "For how long?"

Max felt that same futile feeling. "Two hours."

"Two hours." Gabby's head was swimming. Not aching, but not right, either. Gauzy. Misty. Definitely not clear. But nothing that seemed life-threatening. Just . . . strange. Should she mention it to Max?

No, he'd overreact and get Keith. The vaccine hadn't killed Candace, but that didn't mean it wouldn't kill Gabby. Conlee was right about notification driving the Warriors underground. A nuisance, but a good call, and she had too much to figure out before she died.

Before she died.

Gabby's throat went thick. She didn't want to die. She didn't have much of a life, but it was hers and she wanted to live it. She wanted to prevent the Warriors' attack on Carnel Cove. To stop the Z-4027 infestation before others died, to kill the bastard who had caused it. She wanted to go to Spain with Sybil and Westford in September and to make love to Max long before then—maybe during and after then, too. But to live to do any of that, she had to find out why Jaris Adahan had tried to kill her.

Who had hired the dead Warrior? The one who had escaped? And, most important to her bleak future, why?

Chapter Sixteen

By three A.M., defensive measures against a second lab attack had been taken. The Z-4027-infected mosquitoes had been relocated in spare tanks Max had pulled from the supply room; Candace's blouse had been bagged and replaced at the window with a piece of plywood Max had found down on Sublevel 2 in Maintenance, where a lot of construction seemed to be going on, and all surfaces in the lab except for the floor had been sterilized. Gabby was still working on that, sweeping the glass shards down the row of tanks into a pile on the floor near the supply room door. While she was finishing up, Max took a few more photographs of the lab from various angles and more close-up shots of the broken tanks and the placement of the rocks that had broken them.

An alarm sounded, sharp and shrill.

Max looked up at the wall-mounted security monitor.

Dr. Erickson had just entered the building through the outside door. Now, he was in the hallway, approaching the lab.

"I'll handle him, Max. No problem." Seemingly unruffled, Gabby returned to her sweeping.

Dr. Erickson entered the lab, flustered, his wind-tossed hair spiked and his face furrowed. Startled, he stopped, stared gape-jawed at them. "Judge Kincaid?" He looked at the broom as if it were a foreign object and then cast a cautious glance at Max. "What are you doing here?"

"Hello, Dr. Erickson." She stopped sweeping, swept her forehead with her hand. "This is my husband, Max."

Max extended a hand. "Pleasure to meet you, Doctor."

The doctor shook it. "David," he said, clearly expecting more of an explanation.

Gabby gave him one. "Candace is down with a headache. She said you and Dr. Swift couldn't get here because of downed trees and power lines blocking the roads, so she asked us to make sure the lab was okay. I'm afraid you had a little damage. Nothing serious, though."

Erickson glanced around and his expression went dark, then horror flooded his eyes. "Oh, my God. What happened to the tanks?"

"Hurricane damage," Max said. "We found some spares in the supply room and contained all we could. Candace said that was important."

"Oh, yeah." Erickson prowled the lab, and spotted the plywood over the window. "Did any mosquitoes get out of the lab?"

Gabby dropped the broom. It clanged on the tile floor. "Sorry." She smiled, bent to snag the broom handle. Her muscles ached, threatening to lock down. Swallowing back a groan Max wouldn't have heard if he hadn't been watching for it, she straightened upright. "I don't think so."

Erickson dragged a hand through his sandy hair, knocking down some of the spikes. "If we're not sure, we'd better follow procedure."

"Which is?" Max asked.

"Notifications have to be made to authorities." Dread filling his voice, Erickson slid his gaze to his desk, to a photograph of his son. "These are test subjects, Max, not normal mosquitoes."

Max leaned a hip against the steel lab table. "Which means?"

Erickson hesitated, moved to the row of canisters and immediately checked the black-banded one to make sure it was undamaged. "I'm sorry. I'm not at liberty to discuss it."

"I see." Max let Erickson know he understood completely.

Erickson picked up on it. "If there's any risk, we've got to call the authorities."

"There isn't." Max held Erickson's gaze, but not without costs. He personally didn't agree with Conlee's orders on this, but he had learned long ago to trust the commander's decisions. With information being disseminated on a need-to-know basis in the unit, trust was the only way to operate. He hoped to hell this wasn't the one time Conlee's judgment proved to be on hiatus. "Candace asked us to review the security tapes to make sure everything stayed inside the lab. We did. Everything's fine."

Erickson hiked a brow. "You're sure?"

"We're positive," Gabby said, not at all certain Max was up to lying again. How could Erickson look at Max's face and not know the truth? It was as clear to Gabby as the shattered glass on the floor.

Though, considering she'd been married to the man for seven years, she had insights strangers wouldn't have. God, but it was hot in here. Where was the thermostat? She found it on the wall near the door, and knocked it down ten degrees.

Married to the man for seven years?

Stunned, she leaned back against the rough wall, her knees weak. She squeezed her eyes shut, tried and failed to meditate her way to calm, then settled for something just shy of panic. What in heaven was she doing? *Married to Max?* She was *thinking* as if she were really married to Max?

This was wrong. Very wrong. What was happening to her mind? She sent Max a worried look that he missed, having his back to her while talking with Erickson. She needed more information on the effects of Z-4027. She couldn't be losing it already. She had too much to do to lose it already. But something was jumbling her real memories with the ones manufactured in her covers. It had to be the Z-4027.

Gabby tensed. Cold fingers of fear clenched her stomach and her chest, and sweat popped from her temples. Thin trickles of it flowed down between her breasts and soaked her bra. Her heart thudded, banging against her ribs. She was going to die and didn't want to; that was one thing. Becoming mentally diminished before she could debrief Max and do what she had to do was another.

Erickson would know the answers to her questions about Z-4027. But she didn't dare to ask him.

The mist thickened in her mind, and the gauze compacted, grew more dense, becoming a veil she had to claw and punch through to think straight.

She slumped onto a stool, propped her head in her hands, her elbows on the lab table. She did not need this. *Not now.*

Keith. She could ask Keith. He was working the mirror contract.

That thought stopped her dead in her mental tracks. Why was it okay for Keith Burke to know she and Max were associated with Conlee but it wasn't okay for David Erickson to know it?

Commander Conlee never did anything without a specific reason. She slid off the stool, walked over to Max, then looped her arm in his for balance. "Max?"

"Yeah, honey?" He turned his attention from Erickson to her, saw the look in her eyes, and responded to it at once. "Are you ill?"

"Headache," she said.

"You've been bitten." Erickson looked down at her forearm. Several swollen bites dotted it. "Did that happen here?"

"No," she lied. "Before I came here."

"Are you sure?" Erickson's brow furrowed and real fear sparked in his eyes.

"Oh, yes. I'm sure. Don't worry, Dr. Erickson. It's just the humidity. I don't deal with it very well." She forced a smile. The lab's pungent hospital smell had her nauseous. "A couple Tylenol and a few hours' rest, and I'll be fine."

Max hooked an arm around her waist, looked at Erickson. "You'll be in the lab?"

"Until the repairs are complete and it can be locked down, yes."

Max hedged on stating the obvious, but made his point clearly. "It wouldn't be a good idea to leave the lab until it can be sealed under full power, Dr. Erickson." Conlee would be monitoring every move. If he objected, he'd let Max know before he and Gabby could leave the building. With Erickson there, Gabby couldn't debrief. Conlee had to know that, too, and from the looks of her she needed to get that done soon. The Z-4027 symptoms were manifesting in spades.

"Full-power lockdown only." Erickson nodded, lending weight to his words. "I'll be here."

Max gauged the man and he passed. "I'll take my wife home, then." He led Gabby to the door, and then out of the lab.

She waited until they were in the parking lot to say anything. "We've got a new complication."

Max helped her get into the Jeep. She tried to snap the safety belt, but for some reason she was all thumbs. Leaning into the Jeep from the door, he reached over and snapped it for her. "What kind of new complication?"

His face was close to hers. So close she could see the pores in his skin, the little crinkles from too much squinting at the corners of his eyes, and the deep gray flecks in his irises. Something in the region of her heart softened. *Marrying him was the smartest thing you've ever done . . .*

"What new complication, Gabby?" he repeated.

Married him?

Mission covers, she reminded herself. Not marriages. Mission covers.

Her heart knocked around on her ribs. She mentally shook herself, forced herself to focus, to think straight. Okay. Okay. She had it together now. She was okay now. *Complication. Tell Max the complication.* "Conlee," she said. "He's holding out on us."

"I'm sure he has his reasons."

So Max had thought so, too. She really was okay now, in her mind. The gauzy veil parted and her thoughts seemed clear. "I want to know what they are—his reasons, I mean." Her panic subsided to a reasonable worry. "He's got something significant in mind, Max. Experience with him is warning me of it."

"You think he'll send another team down here?"

Max didn't have to say, "to cancel us." They both knew that's what he meant. "I'd be shocked if he hasn't already. But he'll pad the reason in something else to justify it."

Max stared off through the window, obviously exploring potential pads Conlee might use. "Headquarters has to move out of D.C. If he were considering moving Home Base to Carnel Cove and Oversight asked questions, he could justify the agents' deployments without raising red flags on expenses or assigning them secondary missions of canceling us. There is major construction going on down on the sublevel floors at Logan Industries—mainly one and two—that's where I appropriated the plywood for the lab window."

Gabby followed his thoughts. "That would also explain Candace, Erickson, and even Keith's reactions to us. Candace would know about the move, of course, and probably about us, but she wouldn't be any freer to discuss it than we're free to discuss our missions." Gabby stared at Max. "Conlee would do this. He'd see it as a win/win situation. You know that bottom line, we're—"

"Expendable."

"Yes." She lifted her chin. "He'd hate it, but he'd do it. He'd send a second team after us. He might even tell us they're coming as backup for us. He knows no other SDU agent, aside from Westford, stands a chance of blindsiding one of us, much less both of us."

"He already has—sent backup." Max grimaced. Conlee had levied cancellation orders on Gabby and he wouldn't think twice about issuing them on Max. Max wasn't the pseudo-sister of the Vice President of the United States and head of Oversight. "So what do we do? Just wait for them to show up and kill us?"

Gabby shrugged and sent him a sidelong look. "What else can we do?"

She said the words he expected to hear, but they didn't ring true. Gabby was planning . . . something. Having no idea what it was, Max frowned and backed away from the Jeep. On the driver's side, he got in and then cranked the engine.

It roared to life. "What's on your mind?"

"I don't want you to wake up dead because he played his cards too close to his chest."

"Me?" Max's hand stilled on the gearshift. "What about you?"

It was hard, but she didn't look away. She met his head-on gaze and held it, though her tone thinned and echoed hollow. "I'm dead anyway."

Because she was, that comment irritated Max from the toenails up. He slapped the gearshift into drive and left the parking lot. Swinging around an uprooted oak just pissed him off further. It reminded him of the photos of the oaks in Gabby's memory box. The memories she had planted lay uprooted, too, stretched across the concrete and gravel, limp and beaten by the storm.

They had been her anchors. The one thing in her life that remained real and reminded her of who she really was. And now they were dead and gone.

No wonder she felt as if her life had been wasted.

Hell, maybe his own had been, too.

Chapter Seventeen

A ringing phone in the dead of night signals one thing: Someone you love is critically ill or dead.

At least that was the case in most homes in Carnel Cove, and throughout America. But Darlene Coulter's home was different.

For the first three years she had been married to Sheriff Jackson Coulter, the frequent midnight calls always had caught her off guard. She'd get that rush of stark terror that clutches your throat closed. But Darlene had finally made peace with the midnight calls. Now, the only time she got the terror rush was if one came in and Jackson wasn't at home in bed beside her. Tonight, thankfully, she had to roll over him to grab the receiver. A bleary-eyed glance at the clock advised it was just after three A.M., but because of the hurricane crisis, he had been home for only about thirty minutes. "Coulters'."

"Darlene?"

"Elizabeth?"

With effort warranting a grunt, Jackson cranked open an eye. "What's wrong?"

"Tell Jackson it's nothing. Go to the kitchen and call me back." The dial tone buzzed.

"Is she okay?" Unable to hold his eye open, Jackson muttered into his pillow.

Poor guy hadn't slept more than a couple of hours in three days. Darlene gave him a pat on the hip. "She's fine, honey. Go back to sleep."

By the time the words were out of her mouth, he was snoring.

She slid into her slippers, shrugged on her robe, and headed for the kitchen, then dialed Elizabeth. When she answered, Darlene didn't mince words. "Is Candace dead?"

"No. Keith says she's stable for now."

Darlene knew at that moment. Elizabeth was making the sign of the cross for Candace. It was as natural to the woman as breathing, and had been all her life. If Darlene weren't a penny-stretcher, she'd bet a nickel Elizabeth had her rosary in her hand while doing it, too.

"You need to get over to my house right away."

Darlene didn't ask why. She knew that tone, and what it meant. Someone was in crisis. "Did you call Paige first?" Darlene lived further away—the rest of the ladies were clustered in the ritzy area on the cove—but Paige had a hell of a time dragging herself out of sleep. By the end of the day, she was so emotionally wrung out from the constant bombardment of her senses that she couldn't shut down. She didn't go to sleep; she fell into it. And falling in was a whole lot easier than falling out.

"I did. I told her to be conscious when she got here, too. I'll call Miranda next."

Miranda, aka "the informer," was never unconscious— or uninformed. "Ten minutes," Darlene said. It'd take her every bit of fifteen, but she'd still beat Paige by five.

When Darlene walked into Elizabeth's mansion on the cove and passed through the grand entrance, she saw a photo of the four ladies that had been taken at a fund-raiser to buy Jackson a new patrol car. She'd known it was going to be a beautiful picture and plastered all over society pages from Mobile to Miami, and it had been. Safe bet, on Darlene's part. Anytime the four stunners stood together, their group photo appeared everywhere.

Rich women had a look about them, and women who weren't so rich, like Darlene, loved looking at them, and many spent a lion's share of their discretionary income trying to achieve that look—or so said the advertising gurus. But Darlene knew "rich" was more than a look. It was an attitude. A confidence. And the other ladies had it.

Some Covers thought the ladies were all fluff and no substance, fancy former trophy wives or widows, who flitted away their days at country club luncheons, garden parties, golf clubs, tennis courts, and as token members on the boards of various charities. The ladies did do those things. But they did far more. Darlene had looked deeper, beyond the obvious, and she'd been impressed with what she'd seen.

She looked down at the photo, where the four of them stood side by side. They were stunning. All tall and lean and well honed, pampered in the way those who can afford to care for themselves. Candace Burke, bless her heart and get her well, was the most beautiful of them all, dressed in bold red that clung to every curve and fairly shouted "bombshell." Twenty-nine, blue eyes, long wheat-blond hair that tumbled in soft curls and framed a face fit for the cover of *Vogue* that had graced the cover of *People* and *Fortune* magazines. Unfortunately, "bombshell" and that she had formerly been Keith Burke's second wife, was most all Covers remembered about her.

Why he and Candace had divorced was a mystery Darlene hadn't solved. They still made public appearances together and were clearly still in love. Miranda would know—she knew everything—but Darlene wouldn't ask; she respected Candace's privacy. No other Cover would ask, either. Candace was a force to be reckoned with, owning Logan Industries and employing hundreds of locals. She was a fair, reasonable woman, if a risk taker. Why mess with her over something that was none of anyone's business anyway?

Elizabeth stood next to Candace, wearing a black crepe Dior. She was oldest at forty-four, but looked thirty with her tawny hair swept back from her face, accentuating her high cheekbones and exotic eyes. There was nothing token about her membership on any of the seven local charity boards on which she served. Elizabeth was organized and she always had a plan. If she couldn't get what you needed, it couldn't be gotten. Some of the light had died in her eyes when her beloved William had died back in February. But everyone in the Cove made it their business to give back some of the support Elizabeth had given to so many over the years.

Darlene looked on to the third woman, Miranda Coffield. As intense and quiet as Candace was bold and Elizabeth was organized, Miranda had been married to a shrink, Samuel, but had divorced him because he'd given psychiatric counseling to a pedophile and refused to give counseling to the victim's family because he said it was a conflict of interest. For Miranda, this was an unforgivable choice. He'd always taken the easy way out, the path of least resistance. That had annoyed and embarrassed her for years. Miranda felt a good man would have had the character to make the offer on his own, because it was the right thing to do. Sam hadn't, and she refused to share her life or her bed with a man who lacked character.

Dripping in enough diamonds to make Lloyd's of London break into a cold sweat, she'd taken Sam to the proverbial cleaners, used the money to build a youth center in the victim's memory, and paid for the family's grief counseling with another psychiatrist—and the Covers had loved Miranda for it. Sam had been invited to move his practice to another town. Since he'd left, anyone with a moral dilemma or a domestic "challenge" ("problems" were for those too uncivilized to seek solutions, according to Miranda) turned to her for counseling. After all, she'd been more mentally healthy than her husband, the shrink, so she was certainly qualified to offer advice, and she did, which is why she was informed about everything and everyone in the Cove.

Paige Simpson inherited a fortune from her daddy, a prestigious lawyer, and opened a dozen New Age stores across the country. Standing on the far right in the photo, she wore no jewelry and seldom did since she didn't need any adornments. Dressed in a soft gold lamé that made her flawless skin look like perfection itself—a challenge more easily met by someone barely thirty than by a woman cruising through her forties, like Darlene—Paige looked as sleek and sophisticated as the other women. Few would guess that under her polished exterior, she was an extremely creative woman with an unrelenting conscience, and an empath who felt too much and suffered mightily for it. None of them were perfect, including Paige. She talked about auras and karma too much for Elizabeth's liking, but Darlene thought the differences in spirituality were about as significant as wearing different dresses. Like clothes, spirituality has to fit. So Paige's New Age talk didn't bother Darlene a bit.

"Oh, I'm glad you're here." Elizabeth appeared at the corner from the kitchen. "I didn't hear you come in."

"You need to keep the door locked, Elizabeth." Darlene brushed by her. "Jackson would have a fit. You know hurricanes bring out scalpers and looters."

Elizabeth followed her into the kitchen. "I had it

locked. I just opened it because I knew you guys would be coming in."

"Candace really is all right, isn't she?" Darlene had to ask. Candace had always been her favorite for some reason.

"She's holding on. That's all I know." Elizabeth dropped her gaze to Darlene's feet. "I see you rushed to get here."

Darlene looked down. She was wearing one black shoe and one fluffy pink slipper. "It's a fashion statement."

"Right." The doorbell rang. Elizabeth went to answer it.

Five minutes later, Elizabeth seated the ladies at her kitchen table—including Paige. That she wasn't late reinforced their fears about this summons.

Darlene loved Elizabeth's kitchen. With its bay windows, lemon yellow and white decor, and blend of tiny florals and geometrics that should be at odds but weren't, it was modern, clean-lined, expansive, and bright. Tonight, Darlene figured, they could all use bright.

Seeing their worried looks and unasked questions, Elizabeth reassured them, "Candace is in wait-and-see mode. Keith is with her. He'll call with any news."

"His majesty had better." Miranda dropped her purse to the floor beside her chair. Keith and Candace had mutually decided to divorce, but Miranda still blamed him. "Want me to get the forks?"

"He won't leave her," Paige said with the authority only an empath can have.

Glancing back over her shoulder, Elizabeth sighed. "I think you'd better get Paige coffee first. If she slumps any further in her chair, she'll bruise her nose on the tabletop."

"Shut up, Elizabeth," Paige grumbled. "You said get over here and I'm here . . . mostly."

Elizabeth couldn't resist. "Conscious, too, I see."

Miranda put a cup and saucer down on the glass table before Paige. "Sorry, darling, we're fresh out of IVs. You'll have to ingest your caffeine the old-fashioned way."

"Some doctor's wife you are. No wonder Sam divorced you." Paige needled her, knowing full well Miranda had divorced him. She took a swallow of the steaming brew, and then another. "Sorry. That was low." She waved a hand. "Just give me a few minutes before you expect me to act civil or sound coherent."

"Of course," Elizabeth said, retrieving a pineapple upside-down cake.

Darlene picked up the knife, sliced, and passed the plates.

"You keep it up with these desserts, Elizabeth," Paige took a bite, "and I'm going to have to spend an extra week at the fat farm this September."

"Give her a bigger slice, Darlene." Miranda's mischievous streak surfaced with a vengeance. "The idea of Paige sweating her skinny backside off makes me feel terrific."

Paige glared at her. "Bitch."

Miranda grinned. "Jealous?"

"You bet." Paige stumbled to the coffeepot and refilled her cup; started to put the pot down, shrugged, and brought it back to the table with her. When she sat down, Elizabeth daintily wiped at her mouth. "Are you conscious yet, Paige?"

"Conscious." She swiped her hair back from her face, looking beautiful for a barefaced woman, if droopy-eyed. She motioned to Miranda, who had opened a burgundy eel-skin portfolio and was cranking the barrel of her gold pen, preparing to take notes. "Write for me, too," Paige said. "I need another half hour to see lines."

"Okay," Miranda said. "We've been patient, Elizabeth. Is this meeting about Candace, or Gabby and Max, or all of them?"

"Candace isn't going to die," Paige said into her cup.

"She's extremely critical," Miranda insisted. "The vaccine is experimental."

"The vaccine isn't going to save her," Paige confessed. "But she isn't going to die."

Elizabeth reached across the table, covered Paige's hand. "Keith's vaccine is all there is, dear. If it fails . . . there is nothing else."

"Whatever. I know because I know." Paige hiked a shoulder at Elizabeth. "And I know she isn't going to die—not now, anyway."

Miranda was the skeptic in the bunch, but Darlene had a feeling Paige was right. She sensed these things. "Then this is about Gabby," Darlene pulled them back on topic.

"Gabby and Max." Worry filled Elizabeth's eyes.

The droop left Paige's eyes and she sat up on full alert. "What's this with Max?"

"He's home."

Miranda groaned, and slid Elizabeth an apologetic look. "Sorry, Elizabeth. But we all know that means he's here to kill her."

"Worse," Paige said. "It's worse, isn't it, Elizabeth?"

She squeezed her little rosary bag. "I'm afraid Paige is right. I got a call from Washington. Max was ordered to cancel Gabby. He hasn't, and so—"

Darlene finished her sentence. "They want Max dead, too. They're sending another team down to kill them both?"

Elizabeth nodded. "Three operatives. They'll arrive in the Cove tomorrow night. We're supposed to aid and assist with their ingress and egress."

"I'll be damned," Darlene said.

Miranda agreed. "Not bloody likely. Gabby's put her ass on the line for us time and again, trying to figure out what's going on here. I say we tell Gabby."

"We can't," Paige reminded her. "Technically, we don't *know* about her or Max, remember? They don't *know* about us, either. We'd be signing their death warrants and our own."

"I'm not helping anyone kill her." Elizabeth spoke softly, but her mind was made up and that was clear. "She's giving me the truth about William at great risk to herself. She's my friend, and I'm not killing her."

"If we refuse, we're talking treason," Darlene reminded them.

All of the women stared at her. She didn't flinch. "I'm just making sure everyone knows what we're doing in refusing. Commander Conlee isn't going to be pleased with his new on-site unit, and he's going to be less pleased with his sleeper operatives. If we don't follow his orders, he will bust us out of SDU, and that means nasty things happen to us all. So long as you all know the facts and you accept them, fine."

"I'm not killing her," Elizabeth repeated.

"Well, that's settled, then." Darlene didn't miss mutinous expressions all around the table. "So we need a plan. I assume, Elizabeth, you've got one."

"I do." She nodded. "And if we don't screw up, it's one that will leave all of us alive."

"We're not killing the new team either, Elizabeth."

"I know, Miranda." Elizabeth sighed. "We're going to get them arrested and out of our reach, so to speak, so we *can't* help them."

"Oh, spit." Darlene propped her arm on the table, rested her head in her hand, and shot Elizabeth a glare. "Am I going to have to commit another felony?"

"I'm afraid so, dear."

She was the natural selection, of course, because Jackson wouldn't jail his wife and throw away the key. He loved two things in life: good food and great sex. Together, they had both. There were perks to spoiling your husband, getting good at what mattered most to him. Anything short of a capital crime and Jackson would move heaven and earth to keep her sentence down to a year. A year or less and prisoners didn't go to the state penitentiary, they stayed in the local jail. If he could keep her in his jail, he could take her home to cook and have conjugal rights. To save Gabby's life, Darlene could live with that.

"The new team is coming in by boat," Elizabeth said. "Three operatives. No covert gear. We're to provide them with weapons and whatever else they need to fulfill the mission."

"Right." Miranda grunted. "As if I'd give them the gun to shoot Gabby or Max."

"There'll be four of them, Elizabeth," Paige corrected her, the look in her eyes dead level. "One for each of us. To make sure we stay in line."

"Conlee doesn't trust us," Elizabeth said.

"Conlee doesn't trust anyone." Miranda tapped the point of her pen on the blank yellow page. "So what exactly is the plan?"

"We're going to get them arrested for robbing the ATM at Carl's bank."

"You're *not* bringing Sissy Blake in on this," Miranda said. She couldn't stand Carl's wife, and made no bones about it.

"Of course not." Elizabeth rolled her gaze. "We'll set Bobby up to catch them."

Darlene grimaced. Jackson's deputy wasn't the brightest bulb on the block, but he was a nice guy. She didn't want him killed over this. "Four to one are heavy odds, even for Bobby."

"We're going to minimize those odds substantially before Bobby arrives." Elizabeth frowned. "I wouldn't let Bobby get hurt, Darlene. He's fresh out of the academy. I went to his christening, for goodness' sake."

"Of course, you wouldn't." She'd been at Bobby's graduation from the academy, too. They'd sat together. "So the operatives go to jail, where Jackson holds them until— when?"

"Until Gabby and Max know they're here. Then they can decide what to do about it."

"Plant some jewelry on them, too," Miranda said. "Jackson hates looters. He'll hold them until power's restored in every house on the Cove."

"Excellent idea." Elizabeth eased her grip on the rosary. "More cake, Paige?"

"Just a little piece." She glared at Miranda. "Shut up."

"I didn't say a word."

"You didn't have to." She took her plate from Elizabeth. "Maybe I'll drag you to the farm with me."

"Not a chance, darling. My fat and I have declared détente."

"More likely mutually assured destruction."

"Whatever. I don't mess with it, and it doesn't play games with my head."

Darlene helped herself to a second slice of cake. "Aren't you going to tell us the truth about this, Elizabeth?"

She stilled her fork midair. Paige and Miranda paused to stare at her.

"Obviously Commander Conlee didn't call you and tell you to intercept the second team. So who did?"

"Why would you think anyone did, Darlene?" Elizabeth fidgeted on her chair. "You, of all people, know how fond I am of Gabby. She's been very good to me and to William."

"Because I know you," Darlene said. "And anytime you're squeezing your rosary bag so tight it leaves marks on your palms, nothing is as simple as it seems. I figure Conlee issued us the orders to assist, but someone else issued us orders to intercept these guys. Otherwise you wouldn't be torn between doing the right thing and the moral thing. So who made the second call, ordering us to intercept?"

"I can't say."

"Sybil Stone," Miranda interjected. "It's obvious. She's Gabby's best friend and Gabby loves Max. She's also

Conlee's boss, so that would negate any conflict over her orders."

Elizabeth looked down at the table.

"It wasn't Sybil," Paige said softly.

"Do you know who it was?" Darlene asked her.

Paige gave Darlene a negative shake. "But I know who it wasn't, and it wasn't Sybil."

"I can't say, and I won't," Elizabeth insisted. "I gave my word."

"Can this person keep us all out of prison?" Miranda cut to the chase.

"Yes."

"Wrong question, Miranda," Paige said. "You should have asked: *Will* this person keep us out of prison?"

Miranda looked from Paige to Elizabeth. "Well?"

"I don't know."

"What's the difference?" Paige said. "We have to do what we have to do. It's destiny."

Darlene agreed. "I wish destiny would let us just talk straight with Gabby and Max. This whole thing would be a lot easier."

"Impossible. We'd have half of Washington coming down on us," Miranda predicted.

"Destiny is as destiny is, Darlene." Paige sighed. "It's not supposed to be easy."

"Well, it's on target then." Darlene took a quick sip of coffee. "I just hope it doesn't land us ten to twenty in a maximum-security prison." She kind of liked cooking and conjugal rights, too. "What about Max? Do we have any assurance that he won't kill Gabby?"

"He hasn't," Elizabeth said. "And Conlee has enough doubt to send down another team to cancel them both."

"Means nothing," Miranda said. "Could be he just hasn't gotten to it yet."

"She loves him," Paige said. "That should count for something."

"It doesn't. Not in these situations, and we all know it," Miranda said.

"So what about Max?" Darlene asked. "What do we do? Get him arrested, too?"

"We can't." Paige stared off, across the table and out the bay window.

"Why not?" Darlene asked.

"Because Gabby needs him."

"Paige?" Elizabeth got that worried tone in her voice. "What do you mean?"

She blinked hard. "Gabby was bitten in the lab, too. She's got the infection."

Darlene's eyes stung. Candace *and* Gabby. "What about Max? Him, too?"

"No," Paige said. "He wasn't bitten."

"Why not?"

"He had on more protective clothing," Miranda said. "That's what Dr. Erickson said, anyway." Miranda had the inside track on news there, working at Logan Industries as a consultant and monitor assuring compliance with contract terms.

"So what do we do about Max?" Darlene asked again.

"Nothing," Elizabeth answered. "Gabby needs him. And unless the person issuing our orders is dead wrong, Max needs Gabby."

"Hopefully, too much to kill her."

"Hopefully, Miranda." Darlene said it, and willed it to be true. If Max killed Gabby under their noses, none of the ladies would ever again be able to meet their eyes in the mirror. And that would be just.

Chapter Eighteen

"Max, I think I'm in trouble."

It was just after five A.M. They'd returned to Gabby's from the lab. Still without power and starved, they shared a can of tuna and bottles of purified water at the kitchen table by candlelight. Max swallowed, not liking the uneasiness in her voice. "What do you mean?"

She folded a long leg under her and shifted on her seat. "The symptoms are getting worse." Clearly uncomfortable, she dotted at her mouth with the edge of a paper napkin. "It's my mind. Things are getting confused."

This was not good news. She had delayed debriefing him deliberately. He understood why she didn't want to die. Unfortunately, he also understood why he didn't want to kill her. He wanted her to live. "Confused how? What things?"

She sipped water from the bottle and set it down on the table. "I'm having a hard time keeping it all straight—

what's real, and what's not." She reached for a cracker, snapped off a corner of it. "It started at the lab. Now, it's getting worse. And I think I've got a fever."

She seemed vulnerable. So much so, he wasn't convinced he was actually talking to Gabby anymore. One thing Gabby Kincaid was not was vulnerable. He reached across the table, pressed a hand to her forehead, then to her jaw. Heat radiated from her skin, and her eyes burned overly bright. "Where's the thermometer?"

"Bedroom bath medicine cabinet. First shelf on the left."

Max slid his chair away from the table. "Be right back."

Moments later, he stood beside her chair, marking off time until he'd get an accurate reading. "That'll do it." He pulled the thermometer from her mouth and read it. "A hundred one." Tugging at the back of her chair, he scooped a hand under her elbow. "Come on, lady. You need to be in bed."

She stood up, looked up into his eyes. Serious. Calm. Too calm. "It's the infection, Max. My mind is going and it's going to kill me just like it's killing Candace."

Max wished he could deny it. But the symptoms were real and present and that she had them was clearer with each passing moment. "Let's get you to bed." He started urging her toward the bedroom.

"I can't go to bed." Even as she protested, she followed. "I have to debrief you so you can shoot me."

He swung an arm around her waist to lead her. "I'll shoot you later."

She plopped down on the side of the bed. "I'm so tired, honey. Lisa was out of the office today and it seemed as if every lawyer on every case on my docket had some motion that had to be considered right away. It was wicked." She toed off her shoes, tugged off her clothes, and naked, stretched to turn off a lamp that wasn't lighted. "I think I might sleep for a week."

Stunned, Max stared at her, curled on her side with the covers pulled up to her neck. She'd warned him the infection was confusing her. But this was more than confusion. With a sick feeling clutching at his stomach, he called Candace's number.

Keith answered the phone. Despite the time, he didn't sound roused from sleep; he sounded ticked. "This better be good."

"Sorry, I know it's early." For some, including himself, it was very late. "Gabby has spiked a fever and she's talking crazy."

"Mild confusion?"

"More." Max's throat went dry. He licked at the inside of his lips to keep them from sticking to his teeth. "She's having trouble separating truth from fiction."

"Elizabeth is here. She'll keep an eye on Candace. I'll be right over."

"Thanks." Max hung up the phone, wondering how Conlee was going to react to this development, and sure he already knew.

Gabby had too much top-secret information running around in her head to ignore her talking crazy. Mentally diminished, she could jeopardize national security, disclose top-secret information, and compromise missions or endanger operatives. She could get innocent people killed. With or without the briefing, Conlee would insist his orders be executed immediately.

Unless Max could find a way to avoid telling him . . .

★   ★   ★

Keith stepped back from Gabby's bed, where she lay in a deep sleep, and motioned Max into the hall.

From his somber expression, Max wasn't going to like hearing what the doc had to say.

"She has the infection, Max," Keith said. "I'll run the labs, but I'm sure of it."

Max felt the weight of the world bear down on his shoulders. Another complication, and one he definitely didn't need. Worse, one Gabby didn't deserve. "You'll give her the vaccine?"

"I'd rather not." Keith's expression went from serious to grim. "Candace isn't responding to it as definitively as I had hoped. She's lapsing in and out of consciousness." His worry put a tremble in his voice. "Gabby is stable for now. No respiratory distress or excessively high fever. There's no immediate reason to intervene with an extreme measure. The vaccine could kill her."

If he only knew how much extreme measures were warranted. "Keith," Max said softly. "She's all I've got. I can't lose her—"

"I know, buddy. I'm rowing the same boat next door." He clasped Max's shoulder and gave it a friendly slap. "We'll do the best we can do and that's all we can do."

"Right." Max swallowed hard. Even voicing his feelings about her under cover felt strange and alien. "So what exactly can I do?"

"Push fluids, rest. The usual things you do for flu." Keith rubbed at his neck, obviously having had a long night, too. "You mentioned some mental confusion."

Max nodded.

"Then we really do want to avoid giving her the vaccine if at all possible."

"Why?"

"Conlee told me I could speak freely with you about the contract. Don't make me sorry I did, Max."

"I won't. I'd appreciate the same courtesy." No reporting Gabby's situation to Conlee.

Keith summed Max up. "That's reasonable." Apparently comfortable with their agreement, he went on. "During the vaccine's development, my researchers have come to expect long-term memory challenges. Some mild, most significant. I've talked with David Erickson on this, and he's run into the same problem. Unfortunately, even after comparing notes, we haven't resolved it, and no one else we could approach has the necessary security clearances. We're hoping after trial studies are done, we'll have a better grip on it, though only God knows what other side effects will manifest." He turned down the hall, headed for the door. "I need to get back to Candace. If Gabby's condition worsens, call and I'll reevaluate."

"Thanks."

Max shut the door behind Keith, locked it, and then ran a perimeter security check, mindful of that second Global Warrior running loose in Carnel Cove. Confident everything was okay, he returned to check on Gabby.

The phone rang. He grabbed the closest remote from the table beside her bed. "Hello."

"Good call," Commander Conlee said. "Leaving Erickson at the lab."

"I thought if he was corrupt, he would tip his hand. Intel would pick it up. But I don't think he is, which leaves the lab protected." Erickson had homed in on that black-banded canister. Intel would be doing live monitors for the duration of the assignment on that canister. Whatever was in it had to be important; they needed to know any movement of it in real time.

"He's not corrupt, but he is motivated to succeed on this project, Max," Conlee said. "His son died of EEE a few years ago. Erickson has been hell-bent on finding a cure ever since."

Which was why Conlee and Dr. Marcus Swift, chief researcher at Logan Industries, had tagged Erickson to develop the Z-4027 vaccine.

"What's wrong with Gabby?"

Decision time. Did Max protect her, or himself? There was no way to protect them both. "She got a couple bites at

the lab. Dr. Burke checked her out. She's doing okay."
When lying, it was best to stick as close to the truth as possible. So he had. With the lie, however, came the commitment. He was in up to his neck now. He and Gabby lived or died together.

"Did he give her the vaccine?"

"No, he didn't think it was necessary."

"Good. That's good," Conlee said. "New orders for you. I've inserted you as a public health and safety subject matter expert on the FEMA team. They're inbound to Carnel Cove to provide disaster relief from Hurricane Darla."

"Okay."

"At nine A.M., you need to go to Mayor Faulkner's office to meet with him and Stan Mullin, the FEMA director. Don't leave that meeting until they agree to spray Carnel Cove for increased mosquito activity."

Max stared at a brass finial above the window at the tip of its drapery rod. Spraying would cover the potential migratory area from the lab incident, but it wouldn't kill the Z-4027-infected mosquitoes. Typical pesticides, as Candace had aptly put it, just pissed them off.

"Carl Blake," Conlee said, speaking of the banker he'd briefed Max on before coming to the Cove, "owns a small fleet of pesticide-spraying trucks. He has a contract with Carnel Cove for regular spraying. FEMA is subcontracting him to handle the additional spraying."

All well and good as far as it went, but that wasn't far enough. "What are they going to spray?" There was no known pesticide for Z-4027 superbugs.

"Logan Industries will provide the chemicals. Dr. Swift's been working on the pesticide contract for the Defense Department. It's ready for trial studies."

In other words, there was no hard data that it worked or that listed its potential side effects on the humans indirectly affected by the spray. Max stared up at the ceiling and then down at Gabby, dozing lightly in her bed, her hair tumbling across a pillow she had wadded up under her head. "Is Swift giving odds?"

"No. But it's the most effective countermeasure we've got."

"I take it all these assets are being arranged quietly."

"Provided Faulkner agrees to the spraying without disclosing the Z-4027 lab incident."

They were going to play it so this whole incident and any deaths it caused were tagged as natural occurrences. Increased mosquito activity due to Hurricane Darla. "Is this our wisest course of action, sir?"

"Would I order it if it weren't?"

"No, sir." Max didn't hesitate. "Not deliberately."

"It breaks down simply, Grayson. If the lab incident remains secret, then the Warriors won't go underground. To save lives, we've got to get to the bottom of why they're there and after Gabby. No one hires Warriors to hit one operative, even if she's senior grade in SDU."

Max should have informed the commander of the dead Warrior in Gabby's garage. But he didn't. He looked at her sprawling, her arm now slung above her head. Shoes reversed, she would do the same for him. She would try to save his life, especially not knowing if his cover had actually been breached. "What about Dr. Erickson? What assures his silence?"

"Knowing he'll be killed if he violates it."

That was a pretty potent motivation. Gabby sighed, claiming Max's attention. She turned toward him, opened an eye. Seeing Max standing, staring at her, she smiled and puckered her lips, sending him a silent kiss.

His reaction came swift and hard. Hot. And he couldn't deny the truth. He wasn't covering for Gabby because she was his partner. He was covering for her because she was going to die with regrets. And because just looking at her made him look at himself differently. He didn't want to waste his life. He didn't want a headstone that said, "He worked hard." He wanted a life. And he thought he might just want that life with her.

A woman he was obligated by oath to kill.

"Grab a couple hours sleep, Grayson," Conlee said. "Then meet Mullin at nine."

"Yes, sir." Max cradled the phone. Conlee hadn't mentioned his initial orders. He had issued "new" ones. It was stretching reason, and no doubt Conlee's patience, but for now Max could consider his initial orders canceled. Surely if Conlee had intended them to stay in force, he would have *amended* his existing orders and not issued *new* orders.

It was a ridiculously fine line, and Conlee would hit the roof, but to keep Gabby alive Max would walk it.

"Honey?"

Surprised by the endearment, he looked over at Gabby just to make sure she really was talking to him. "Yes?"

"Aren't you coming to bed?"

More crazy talk. "I'll bunk down on the sofa."

"Whatever for?" She looked perplexed and maybe a little hurt.

"You have a fever."

"In sickness and in health," she reminded him of a wedding vow. "I'm sick and I want you beside me." She threw back the covers, exposing her naked skin. "Come to bed, Max."

She wanted to feel special. Max stripped off his shoes and shirt and emptied his pockets on the nightstand. He set the .38 on the table edge, then lay down beside her.

Gabby scooted close, snuggled to his side, and resting her head on his chest, she let out a contented sigh.

Max stared at the ceiling and prayed for mercy. She was sick and not right in the head.

"Honey?"

God help him, she felt good, smelled good. "Mmm?"

"Why do you have a gun beside the bed?"

She was definitely not right. The woman had one herself on her side of the bed. "The lights are still out. You know hurricanes bring out looters."

"Right." She draped a leg across his, splayed her fingers on his chest. "I forgot."

Boy, did he need to get out of that bed. He started to rise, jostling Gabby.

"Where are you going now?"

"I forgot to set the alarm."

"It's set," she said, shoving him back down against the mattress. When he settled back, she settled in. "Night."

Not sure what else to do, Max curled an arm around her and closed his eyes, certain sleep would never come. "Night."

★   ★   ★

It was a good dream.

Andrew and Liz were standing before the assembly. He, with his right hand on the Bible, swearing the oath and becoming a judge. Liz, smiling adoringly up at him, fairly bursting with pride. She had always had a way of looking at him that made him want to live up to the admiration he saw in her eyes. And Douglas, their pride and joy and only son, who was all of seven, already thoughtful and diplomatic and sharing his father's love of the law, stood with them dressed in a navy suit with a bright tie covered with red and blue balloons. How proud they'd been of Andrew that day.

How proud Andrew had been of them every day.

Again in his dreams, Andrew relived that last breakfast with them. Their final moments together before they had died.

"I have to practice for the debate after school in the auditorium, Mom."

At the stove, Liz had flipped a skillet full of pancakes.

The smell of sizzling bacon had hung in the air, making Andrew's stomach growl in anticipation. "That's Monday," she said. "Today, Dad works, but we're going fishing in Destin."

"Charter boat! Yeah!" Licking syrup from his fingers, he saw he'd caught Andrew's eye and quickly reached for his napkin. "Sorry, Dad," Douglas said with that wry grin that had always prevented Andrew from issuing stern discipline.

"As well you should be," he said.

If only he had known those would be his last words to his son. Forever branded in his mind and heart. No "I love you." No "I'm proud of you." No "Your compassion and insights awe me." All Andrew had to soothe his broken heart and shattered soul was, "As well you should be."

He awakened to find his face and pillow wet, his mood as dark as his bedroom. He glanced over to the bedside clock. Nearly five A.M. At least, thank God, it would soon be light. He hated the dark these days. Hated the emptiness stretching and yawning endlessly before him. Hated the isolation and being damned with himself for company. Himself, and his guilt.

He stared blankly out the window until the sun came up. Just as he'd decided to haul himself out of bed for the day, the phone rang.

Tossing back the covers, he swung his legs over the side and jammed his feet into his worn slippers. "What?" he said into the phone.

"Good morning, Andrew. Have a rough night?"

The director. How Andrew had come to hate his voice. He frowned out the window, dead certain it was going to be a rotten day. "No more so than usual."

"I just received a report I thought would interest you."

A hitch lifted Andrew's thin chest. *Gabby.* "She's dead?"

"No," the director said, sounding decidedly less than happy about that. "One Warrior is dead, I'm told. The re-

maining one on that leg of the mission was unable to retrieve the body."

"Where is it?"

"I wasn't told. Better to not know that to have to lie.
But my guess is, at or near Gabby's house. Though that is
speculation."

Gabby had killed a Warrior? A trained assassin? "Well,
I hope you're wrong." The possibility alone was enough to
scare the Apostles right out of their sandals. Andrew
grabbed his skull, pressed hard with his bony fingertips.
"Has she called Sheriff Coulter?"

"No, not yet."

That was the worst news of all. "She's going to bury us.
I've said it before, and I'll say it again," Andrew said. News
of the Warrior's murder was probably all over the Cove by
now. If Jackson Coulter caught wind of it at the Silver
Spoon before hearing it through official channels, he'd be
livid.

Coulter being livid was a very dangerous thing.

"The murder hasn't been reported."

"Then how do you know it happened?"

"How do you think? The surviving Warrior told me,"
the director grumbled. "You need to calm down and get a
grip, Andrew. You're worthless, maybe even a liability now."

Icy fingers squeezed his heart. He knew exactly what
that meant. Straighten up and fly right or you'll be elimi-
nated. "I'm calm."

"No one has called the sheriff. He would have reported it to the mayor immediately. He hasn't. You would
have thought of that yourself if you weren't scared shitless
of this woman."

"But if she killed him and she didn't report it—"

"I didn't say she killed him," the director countered.
"The surviving Warrior never saw her. He thinks someone
intercepted his partner before she got there. Makes sense.

If the body were in her house, she would have reported it. She can't know the Warriors are after her."

Andrew didn't believe it. Not for a second. "Maybe she did kill him and she doesn't want you to know that she knows about the Warriors. Have you considered that? Maybe her not calling Coulter proves she's undercover on the Warrior cases, and playing us all for fools."

"Why are you obsessed with fearing this woman?"

"I have a bad feeling about her and I just can't shake it." Sounded lame, but it was the truth. "This is a mistake."

"It's no mistake."

It was, and as if to prove it, a cold chill rippled up Andrew's spine. He started sweating bullets. She was going to bury them and he was going to spend the rest of his life in jail.

He couldn't go to jail. No matter what, he couldn't do it. He knew what the inmates did to judges in jail—and so did the director. Andrew didn't have a freaking island to escape to like the director did. He'd be stuck facing the music, even if that music was the funeral march.

"Stop overreacting, Andrew. She doesn't know anything. Even if she were under cover, she'd have to report the murder to maintain the cover. Besides, her husband has come home."

"She really has a husband?"

"Apparently, she does. He risked life and limb to get to her during the hurricane."

A husband, too. This was not a welcome development. Andrew chugged water straight from his bedside carafe. "What happens now? Do the Warriors go after her or both of them?"

"For the moment, neither of them."

Had he lost his mind? "But—"

"No buts. At the moment, we have limited resources on site, and I need them in other areas. Besides, there's no reason to believe she's an immediate threat. And if she were, after the failed attempt, she'd be ready for us."

"You're making a mistake."

"Maybe," he said, taking on a haughty tone. "But as long as I'm the director, the mistakes are mine to make."

The harsh reprimand made his position clear. He was tired of the dire warnings about Gabby Kincaid. Andrew knew it, and yet the sense that she was the most dangerous of all threats to the Consortium had left a bitter iron taste in his mouth and a warning gurgling in his throat that threatened to choke him.

"Right now, Gabby Kincaid is too busy in bed with her old man to be worrying about much of anything else. By the time they're reacquainted, everything will be ready to go."

"Ready to go?" Andrew asked. What did he mean by that?

"Don't ask, and don't worry. I've got a plan."

A plan. He'd had a plan before, too, and that one had failed. It had cost Andrew his seat on the bench and, he suspected, William Powell his life. "What kind of plan?" Andrew plucked at a loose button on his pajama top and pushed anyway.

"A legal one." The director answered, surprising Andrew. "The groundwork is already in place. A meeting at nine A.M. will seal it up." He let out a relaxed sigh. "We're fine, Andrew. I'm sure of it, and I've gotten us this far, haven't I?"

"Yes, indeed you have," Andrew admitted, though he couldn't even pretend to feel good about that. He didn't, and he wouldn't lie to himself anymore.

"I hope you invested in the Egyptian cotton. I got the word about an hour ago they're going to have a total crop failure in Texas this year. As soon as the market rings the opening bell, cotton prices are going to soar."

Money. Andrew stood up and reached for his glasses.

That's all it had ever been about for the director and all it ever would be about.

Maybe if Andrew had married money and felt he hadn't measured up, he would feel the same way. But he hadn't and he didn't, and considering some of the horrors that were being committed to amass wealth, he was grateful for that.

Grateful, yes. But not stupid or courageous enough to report it.

Chapter Nineteen

"Max?" Gabby stared at the ceiling she couldn't see. The bedroom was still dark. "I'm sure there's a perfectly logical explanation why you're sleeping with me and your hand is on my breast. Would you care to share it?"

Startled from a light doze, he jerked back his hand.

Their legs were twined, and just to annoy him, she clenched her muscles to keep him in place. "Well?"

"You told me to come to bed." He shook his head, clearing it. "So I did."

"Uh-huh." She considered letting him roll away, but decided against it. She'd never seen Max off balance. It was kind of cute. She swiped at her damp hair, refusing to even try to remember whether or not she actually had issued the invitation. She was happy she wasn't dead. And if she'd had to sleep with him to be alive, so be it. But if she had slept with him, after having thought about sleeping with him for five years, she wished she could at least remember it.

Max sank deep into his pillow, clearly not ready to wake up, but he was alert. As alert as she was, and she knew it. SDU operatives often worked for days without sleep and functioned on ten-minute naps caught here or there; it was part of the training and common on the job. Operatives were generally inserted into ongoing missions under rotten conditions and with lousy survival odds. They learned quickly to think straight even when exhausted, or they ended up dead.

So say she had issued him the invitation. He was in bed with her, so he clearly had accepted it. Knowing that brought her a certain satisfaction. It wasn't as good as feeling special or knowing what he'd actually been like in bed, but considering the circumstances, it would do.

God, your mind has gone to mush.

Hearing Sybil's voice inside her head, Gabby smothered a groan against her pillow. Sybil would be rolling on the floor, laughing, swearing Gabby had become neurotic, and Gabby would be cursing a streak because Sybil was usually right.

She rubbed her nose against the bronze silk pillowslip. Its soft scent didn't dull the edge or help a bit. Maybe she had become neurotic.

And wouldn't that be a blessing . . . when your choices were neuroses or the Z-4027 infection? Maybe it was. She'd choose neurotic anytime.

She slung an arm up over her head. There was a dull ache throbbing at the base of her skull. Her thoughts still weren't exactly clear, and she felt clammy, feverish.

The superbug had taken hold in her system. Squeezing her eyes shut, she mulled over her options. It didn't take long; there weren't many. Max had to be told the truth.

Fear knotted in her stomach and she tried not to cringe. Instead, she rested a hand on his shoulder, letting the warmth of his skin seep into her. Inside, she was as cold as ice. As soon as she told him, of course, he would kill her. There was nothing to be done about that really. But maybe that would be easier on her than letting the infection run its course. Z-4027 didn't offer a merciful death. She'd watched Judge Powell die and, man, had he suffered.

"You're shaking, Gabby." Max rubbed small circles on her back. "You okay?"

"Mmm," she mumbled to avoid lying to him outright. In her career, she had seen awful things. Chemical burns, biological poisoning, the aftermath of various weapon-system detonations, including dozens of types of bombs. But those deaths had been swift. More often than not, the people had died not knowing what had hit them. With Z-4027, Powell had known. He hadn't lived long, but his pain had been unrelenting—so severe and intense that morphine hadn't touched it. When a person hurt like that, a minute could seem lifetimes long. "I'm okay."

He tried to free up his legs, but she refused to let him. "Are you planning on holding me prisoner here for a while?" he asked.

"Just a little longer," she whispered, recalling being with Elizabeth at the hospital, standing at William Powell's bedside. Gabby had been a maniac inside. Even though she had nearly seen it all, she hadn't been immune. Watching him suffer had shredded her emotions. That was the first time in her life she had seriously considered mercy killing. It had scared the hell out of her—to see that side of herself. It still did, because she knew it lurked inside her.

Cold shivers crawled up her back, and the hair on her neck stood on edge. She couldn't go through that kind of death. She just wouldn't do it. She turned onto her side. "Max?"

"Mmm?"

Her throat went thick. Facing him, she scrunched her pillow and stared at the crown of his head. "I'm dying."

He opened his eyes, met and held her gaze, and waited.

Gabby waited too, until it occurred to her that he would wait forever to say anything at all. Considering he'd slept with her and probably—maybe—had sex with her, he could at least say *something*. But, no, not Max. He would just lie there with his head propped on his hand, elbow bent, watching her. The way things were moving along, if she didn't say something, she'd be in hell three days before he uttered a word.

She wet her lips with her tongue and put it bluntly. "Death by cancellation or Z-4027, it doesn't much matter. Dead is dead. But I expect you to spare me from suffering and use a bullet, Max." She paused, terrified he would refuse, even more terrified that he wouldn't, and that he would hate her for asking this of him. "I would do it for you."

He blinked twice, swallowed hard. Understanding flashed across his face. "I won't let you suffer, Gabby." He cupped her face in his hand, stroked the line of her jaw with his thumb. "I swear it."

For the first time in her life with a man, she felt *and* believed to the marrow of her bones she was special. Max had orders to kill her. But killing her had nothing to do with them. He would honor her wishes. Act with loving compassion to shelter her. He would protect her.

Gratitude welled inside her, and her heart felt too big for her chest. Her throat went tight; she couldn't find her voice. "Thank you," she mouthed the words and managed a ghost of a smile. The urge to really open up to him hit her hard. But sharing would add to Max's guilt.

"What?" Probing, he searched her eyes. "Something's on your mind. I can see it."

Oh, the temptation was strong. But she had to fight it. This wasn't the time to grow weak-spirited or to lose her resolve. "It's nothing."

"Even now you're shutting me out. Don't do it." He let his warm hand drift down her neck to her shoulder and gently squeezed. "Tell me, Gabby."

"I—I can't." She lowered her lids, blocking the sight of him. This wasn't just a matter of her being strong. It was a matter of her wanting to just let go of all the things she had never said and had never shared with anyone. To toss aside all the years of handling whatever crisis came her way alone, on her own.

"Look at me, Gabby." Max held her face in his hands, spoke softly, encouraging not insisting, tempting her even more.

She did, and saw his tenderness and concern. Genuine. Sincere. And she saw his fear of being refused.

"Tell me," he whispered again.

Lifting her hand, she covered his on her face, lowered it and clasped his fingers. "I don't want to make you feel guilty for killing me, Max."

"You won't," he promised. "Just talk to me."

Believing him, she rolled over onto her back. She could talk to him, but she couldn't look at him while doing it. Not once in her life had she bared her soul to any man. Not once. And she'd shared her private thoughts and deepest secrets with only one woman: Sybil. Gabby wasn't even sure she knew how to share things this intimate and private. Not after so many years of burying herself under her covers and refusing to expose even hints of her real self for fear they would be used against her. Planting the oaks. That had been it. Her only concession to even remembering her real self. She'd do it. But she needed to know one thing first. "Have we slept together?"

"Slept together? Yes. Had sex? No. You're ill, Gabby," he said. "I don't take advantage of any woman, much less an ill one. Or any partner, for that matter." He turned and propped against the headboard. "Does whatever is on your mind have to do with regret?"

His homing in on her internal debate didn't surprise her. Give a man insight and you've given him ammo he wouldn't hesitate to use against you. "Yes," she admitted. "I'm in a jam, and I hate standing on shaky ground."

"What kind of shaky ground?"

She closed her mind to the warnings that he'd turn on her, and opened her heart. "I'm wishing I'd lived my life differently."

"Differently, how?" He tugged the covers up half over his chest, looking about as threatening as a teddy bear.

It was the right approach. Her defenses against him were melting. Before she decided whether or not she wanted them to totally drain away, she was answering him. "I should have left SDU years ago and married a nice guy with a dull nine-to-five job." She turned back onto her side, moved closer to Max, and rested her head on his chest. "We could have had a couple kids. I could have joined the PTA."

Max laughed out loud.

Gabby lifted her head and glared at him. "I'm bearing my soul on my deathbed, you son of a bitch. I trusted you to take me seriously. The least you could do is to fake it."

"Whatever for?" He drew her back to him, wrapped an arm around her, and pulled her closer. "Gabby, you would have died of boredom in that life. It's just not you."

"It could have been," she said, shocked at her own reaction. She sounded petulant. Good grief, she *was* neurotic! "I would have missed the edge, I admit it. But dying in that life would have had to be better than this." Because that was true, her eyes blurred with tears yet she refused to cry. She bit her lips to divert the pain. If she cried, he'd lose all respect for her. He'd know she was a fraud. And he'd know she was terrified. "No one will even notice I'm gone, Max."

"Sybil will notice," he countered, his voice gentle. "And Westford."

"I mean no one man, you moron." She let out an exasperated huff. "Could you at least try to get a grip on this? I'm human. I want a man, a family, who will miss me. Is that so hard for you to imagine?"

Max stilled, confused more than he cared to admit. Gabby. Married—with kids—and living a typical suburban life?

He tried, but he *couldn't* imagine it; it was just too alien. Yet he understood her point and what she was feeling. Strangely, he had a prickle in his gut warning him he'd feel the same way, and because he did, he couldn't insult her with platitudes. About the best he could do was to offer a truth that might or might not give her a small measure of comfort. "I'll notice, Gabby."

She looked up at him, her eyes wide and huge in her face. "Will you?"

He nodded. "I'm not much of a husband, but I am one you've got, and I will notice."

A tear slid down her face to her chin. A moment passed, and then she said, "I misjudged you, Max. You might just be worth dying for, after all." She leaned forward and kissed him.

Certain she was worth dying for, Max kissed her back.

★   ★   ★

Gabby held back, keeping the kiss tender and gentle—an unthreatening exploration intended to coax and reassure. But a telling groan signaling a need as strong as her own rumbled deep in Max's throat. It unleashed a rush of feminine prowess and a sensory assault that had her nerves sizzling and her rioting emotions imploding. She let go, melting into pure heat, with eager hands and gasped breaths, she revealed all, her naked skin seeking naked skin. They joined on mutual sighs, moving together in harmony, stretching, seeking, until finally their union expanded beyond the limitations of their bodies. Flushed and damp and breathless, they shuddered in climax, and for the first time during sex, Gabby felt connected to a man in body, mind, and spirit.

Gratified and horrified by that, she accepted it as an undeniable truth, and closed her eyes. And then, they slept. This time, wound in each other's arms without pretense or apology, aware that they were holding each other because that was exactly what they wanted to do.

For Gabby, it was her first restful sleep in recent memory. Max was here. He would be alert to any intrusion attempt by that second Warrior, and Gabby could let down her guard and just sleep. Maybe having a partner wasn't so bad . . .

*   *   *

The director reviewed the listing of buyers who had already opted in on the Z-4027 vaccine and pesticide offering from the Consortium and then phoned the chairman and gave him the details.

"What about the others?" The chairman sounded more bored than pleased or displeased, though only a fool would believe that true.

"No formal responses yet, sir, but two have significantly shifted funds. It's likely they're preparing to come on board." The director tipped up the cell phone, freeing his mouth, sipped at a coffee cup, then stared out through his tinted windshield at the front windows of the Silver Spoon Café. The parking lot was jammed; the café had been a central gathering point for Covers since Hurricane Darla had destroyed Carnel Cove's communications systems, short of satellite service. Little had been restored. "As for the others, it's early yet."

"Keep your nose clean. We have it on good authority

that that bastard Conlee is sending down a team of opera-tives to do some reconnaissance."

He had to work to keep his voice steady. Andrew's warnings about Gabby Kincaid replayed through his mind and this news made them a little harder to shove off. "Sorry to hear that." The last thing the director needed was more complications. Andrew would crack; no doubt about it. He was going to have to do something about that.

"It's manageable. Stay above suspicion, avoid risks, and don't jeopardize our position."

"Yes, sir." Terrific. For now, his hands were tied on Andrew. He'd have to make sure he didn't so much as sneeze wrong, and that the man stayed in line.

The chairman had made the director a very wealthy man. But his first loyalty was to money and his second was to the Consortium. If the director ceased being an asset to either, the chairman would have him killed. About that, the director had no illusions. And he was far from ready to die.

Chapter Twenty

Max had awakened and was in the shower. Gabby heard him stirring in the bath, but trapped in that mystical place between being asleep and awake, she couldn't seem to push herself to fully move toward either. The veil was back. Her mind felt foggy, full of sludge and confusion, her temperature was up again, and she would swear under oath that a Mack truck sat parked on her chest. Her breathing rattled. Not horribly labored yet, but noticeably different.

Max walked out of the bath and back into the bedroom fully dressed in gray slacks and a pale blue golf shirt. He looked at her and frowned. "You're worse."

Making love with him had been wonderful, better than her dreams, but in a way she regretted it, too. Max had become attuned to her and she to him in ways she didn't understand, and she wasn't sure she liked anyone else having the fast track to her innermost feelings and thoughts. "Yes,

I'm worse." Definitely no more stall time. "I need to tell you a few things."

He sat down on the bed beside her and dumped two aspirin into his palm. He passed them to her with a glass of water. "Take these, then I'll fix you something to eat."

"I can't eat, Max." Just the thought had her stomach in full revolt. She rubbed her abdomen lightly to calm it down. "I don't think the Warriors are finished attacking. I think they have something significantly more destructive planned."

"Are you sure?"

She swallowed the pills and then nodded. "No. But my source predicted hundreds, maybe thousands, would die. Even if all the mosquitoes in the lab had escaped, I can't see them killing that many people right away. Maybe over time, but the warning didn't feel like that. A devastating catastrophe is expected, Max. A single-blow attack."

"Your source?"

"Yes." Gabby couldn't make herself reveal the name. In her entire career, she had never revealed a source's name to anyone. Not even to Conlee.

Max noticed and was only slightly irritated by her withholding. He had to work at it, but kept his expression masked. Irritation or direct confrontation with Gabby had never produced positive results. "Where did you put your evidence?"

"Don't worry, darling," she said, sounding only a little caustic. "You'll get it when the time is right. Even if I'm dead."

What did Max make of that? Or even think about it? Despite her denials, he had thought for a time she had been bargaining the evidence for her life. But now she tells him that if she dies, he still gets the evidence? That didn't make sense. "Why not just give it to me?"

"I have my reasons, Max. Trust me."

Trust her? His partner, who never trusted anyone but

herself? Yet Gabby always had had her reasons, and sooner or later he had figured them out—usually later, which totally ticked him off. But being clueless and up against the wall on time now annoyed him and put him at a distinct, possibly deadly, disadvantage. He needed information and insight to make wise choices. To stop the attack she swore was coming. Only now he knew one important thing he hadn't known before coming to Carnel Cove. "Don't protect me, Gabby."

"Protect you?" She rolled her gaze. "Oh, please."

"Knock it off." All sense of subtlety faded from his tone. He would have preferred to avoid conflict—he was mellow from having great sex with a woman he had wanted for years, and she was still in his arms, and he liked having her there, regardless of orders or circumstances—but she wasn't giving him much choice, and he was just tired enough and scared enough to say to hell with it and hit her head-on. "I've been thinking about us and you, and I know now you've been protecting me. You've been protecting all the operatives. That's why you take on the highest risk missions alone. It's why you refuse to have a partner working with you, even when common sense tells everyone, including you, that you need an active partner to cover your back. It's why you're hypercritical of everyone in the unit. You're not out to destroy anyone's esteem or ego; you're hell-bent on protecting them all. You're always protecting us all." He paused, softened his voice, but kept the steel in his gaze. "I admire you for it, Gabby, but I don't want or need it. Don't protect me. Just let me do my job."

"Don't protect you?" She managed a crackle of a laugh, and artfully dodged the rest. "I'm still breathing, Agent Grayson. Doesn't that prove you're protecting me?"

She was baiting him. He'd gotten too close and she was running scared. Unfortunately, she was also right. "I need the evidence."

"And I told you you'd get it whether I'm dead or alive."

Gabby sat up, cut her eyes to look at him. "Did you lie to Conlee?"

"No." Max chewed at his inner lip, propped a hand on his hip.

She didn't believe him for a second. Not a second. He had lied, all right, and if he trusted her, he would admit it. "No?"

His jaw clamped tight and he folded his arms over his chest. "No."

"I see." No trust. Well, hell. That was fine with her, though it did hurt. She had protected him for five years, keeping him out of danger. Of course, she'd feel twinges of betrayal. But having kept him out of things had given her an advantage. Max wasn't lying to her, and she knew it. But he wasn't offering the truth, either. Bent on pinning back his ears for that, she gentled her voice. "Well, then, Max, tell me, darling. Did you allow Commander Conlee to continue believing something he assumed but you knew to be untrue?"

The lines along the sides of Max's mouth tightened, sobering his expression. Caught between the rock and the hard place, he rolled to his feet and paced a short path beside the bed, mumbling something nasty, she felt sure, under his breath.

The memory of him naked distracted her significantly. "Excuse me?"

He glared at her. "I said, more or less."

Aha. Maybe there was hope here for trust after all. "Well, which is it? More, or less?"

"More." He stopped near her feet and glowered at her. "It was more."

Ah, progress. She braced her back against the pillows. "Why did you do it?"

If looks could kill, she wouldn't have to wait for the infection or a bullet. "We're partners, Gabby. What the hell did you expect me to do? Sacrifice you without even a fight?"

"That's true, but it's not *the* truth. You're evading me again." Gabby studied him a long moment. "You do know that it's the worst kind of sin to lie to a dying woman, right?"

"Do you get some kind of perverse thrill out of pushing me, woman?"

"It's the only way I can get you to give me a straight answer. In case you haven't noticed, darling, you protect me, too."

Max blew out a breath that hiked his shoulders, clearly wishing that at this moment he could be anywhere but in her bedroom stuck in this situation. "I did it because I know how you feel," he said, his voice gruff, his tone sharp. "And I don't want you to die with regrets."

Promising. Very promising. Her heart rate quickened. "And?"

His glower faded to a distant, removed look that spoke volumes of uncertainty that his saying anything more was wise. Just when she thought he had decided to ignore her, he went on. "And because I care about you. I have for a long time."

"We've been friends a long time."

He met her gaze. "I don't sleep with friends."

A bubble of warm joy burst and spread through her chest. She smiled and held out her arms to him. "Thank you, Max."

He stepped into them, held her, and she wished that holding him didn't feel so good. He cared. And she cared about him. Yet telling him that now would be the worst kind of cruelty.

Like her, he had been alone all his life with no one to depend on for anything. With no one special person caring about him. From all she'd gathered, he hadn't even had a best friend like Sybil to lean on now and then. For Gabby to tell him she cared, and then die ... No. No, she couldn't. Finally having that intimate connection with someone and then losing it would be far worse, far harder on him, than never having known it at all.

Max waited for her to say something, anything about caring for him, but she didn't. Disappointed and a little annoyed because he'd put himself on the line telling her how he felt and now he was standing on the line alone, he went into the kitchen, found a camping stove and coffeepot, and headed for the patio.

Half an hour later, he returned to the bedroom with a tray. Gabby lay on her side, her eyes closed. Was she sleeping, or just relaxing? Considering their circumstances, either would be nothing short of a miracle. "Gabby, breakfast."

She grumbled. Moaned. Asleep and slow to awaken— amazingly slow for a seasoned operative—she muttered something about her docket being full and missing work today. "Call Lisa, baby. Tell her I'm too sick."

He set the tray down. Watched and listened. She rambled on and on about "the office," her current cases. Clearly delirious. "Gabby?"

"What, Max?"

"Are you all right?"

"I'm fine," she said automatically. "Actually, I'm not. I'm miserable. There's an orchestra of drummers beating different rhythms against my skull. My head is spinning and full of cobwebs, and my stomach is upset. It's the flu. The really raunchy kind ... unless—" She sucked in a sharp breath and her eyes stretched open. "Max, do you think I could finally be pregnant? We've tried for such a long time, I know, but maybe—do you think?"

Pregnant? Jesus, she was totally out of it. "I don't know. Maybe," he said, humoring her and reaching for the phone. This was serious *and* strange. Erickson's notes hadn't said anything about these kinds of effects, but Keith had said new effects were bound to surface with the vaccine. Was it a stretch to assume they could surface in the infection itself?

She turned on her side and curled her knees to her chest. "Are you calling Lisa, honey?"

Her assistant, Lisa Martin. "I'll call her in just a second." He dialed Candace's number. "I want Dr. Burke to come take a look at you."

"Dr. Burke?" Gabby cast him a totally blank look that sent shivers racing through his back and made his skin crawl.

"Your GYN," he lied without so much as a blink. The infection was affecting her memory. That had to be what was going on.

She looked puzzled, but nodded. "Oh. Okay."

Max stepped out into the hallway, the ringing phone pressed to his ear.

Finally, Keith answered at Candace's house. "Hey," Max said. "You'd better get over here. I have a real problem on my hands."

"What is it?" Keith asked.

How did Max answer that? He couldn't say that Gabby thought they were married. Burke thought they were married, too. He couldn't say she thought she might be pregnant. Burke wouldn't find that odd at all. What could he say? "She's having really weird delusions."

Keith muttered a curse. "Candace is stable. I had hoped Gabby wouldn't—never mind. I'm on my way."

Hearing the dial tone, Max walked back into the bedroom and dropped the receiver on the bedside table near Gabby's water glass.

"I think a girl would be nice," she said, looking up at him from her pillow. "I know you've always wanted a boy, but don't you think a girl would be nice?"

This turn of events was worse than bad, and he had to act now. "Gabby, you've got to focus, honey, and think hard.

You've got the infection; I'm sure of it. I need to know where you put the evidence."

"Evidence?" She blinked hard. "Max, you know I never discuss my cases. It's a direct violation of ethics."

"This is different, honey." He clasped her hands in his. "I'm talking about the SDU evidence, not evidence on one of your judicial cases."

She looked at him with zero recognition. "SDU?"

Oh, God. The bottom fell out of Max's stomach. She wasn't faking it. She really didn't know what he was talking about.

"Max, I asked you a question, darling. What is SDU?"

"Nothing." It would pass. As soon as Keith stepped in and treated her, she'd get her thoughts together and re-member then. Max swiped at his brow with a hand that shook.

This was Z-4027. She would get worse, not better. What if she never remembered?

That possibility was all too real, but he couldn't afford to believe it. She had to remember everything. But how? The infection would have her comatose. She would die comatose. How—when—could she remember or tell him if she did?

He had blown it. Knowing better, he had gotten in-volved beyond friendship, slept with her, and now she mat-tered. Now, he was screwed. She was going to die and there wasn't a thing he could do about it.

While he wouldn't go so far as to say he loved her, he was in serious lust and very connected to her. She pulled at him inside. Deep, in some untouched place he couldn't point to but understood was there. And though he was crazy as hell for it, he liked the feeling.

She touched him, mind, body, and soul.

And he was going to kill her.

Max stared down at her for a long moment, repulsed, his insides ripping to shreds. Guilt sank down to the marrow of his bones and he pressed a quick kiss to her forehead. *Oh, Jesus. How am I going to get either of us out of this alive?*

★   ★   ★

Sybil couldn't stand the wait any longer. She called Commander Conlee at headquarters, and barely gave him time to say hello before she hurled her question at him. "Is Gabby still alive?"

"So far."

"Commander, you'd better be right about Grayson. If not, you're going to have a cold winter commanding the weather station in the Arctic."

"I'm right about Grayson," he said, ignoring her threat.

"Care to elaborate?" Gabby hadn't exactly been kind to Max.

"Not at the present time, ma'am. Soon."

Sybil frowned. "The sooner the better." Out of patience, she clenched the receiver until her hand hurt. She was Vice President of the only superpower left in the world. Head of Oversight, which reviewed and made final call decisions on every SDU mission worldwide. And yet she lacked the power to put the fear of God into Commander Donald Conlee.

Ordinarily, and many times in the past, she had admired that about him. But this was about Gabby. And right now, Sybil Stone didn't feel admiration. She felt terror.

"I'm sending a second team. It arrives tonight."

Stark and bleak, paralyzing terror. "Why?"

"Because Grayson and Gabby expect one."

"Have you ordered them to stand down?"

"No, ma'am. Their orders are to cancel Agents Kincaid and Grayson—just as they must be." His sigh sent static through the line. "We really don't have a choice on this, ma'am."

They didn't. And Sybil hated Conlee for that. She stood up in her home office and paced the room before her desk. Usually, she enjoyed the subtle scent of peach potpourri. Today, it smelled sickly sweet. Now, Gabby and Max would be dying. Would his being with her comfort or devastate Gabby?

Sybil turned, headed back in the other direction, swiped her hair back from her face. Gabby would be devastated. Of course, she would. Just because she didn't want to recognize the signs of love didn't mean love wasn't there. To lose a loved one *and* fail to protect the nation *and* die was more than even she could take and go to her grave with any sliver of peace.

And that her best friend would suffer all of this and probably more had tears flowing down the Vice President's grieving face.

Chapter Twenty-one

Just after seven A.M., Keith finished examining Gabby and motioned Max into the hallway outside her bedroom door. He whispered, "Her condition has really deteriorated, Max."

"I know." Her lack of memory terrified him. It also created major obstacles and dilemmas for them both. "Has the vaccine done anything to help Candace?"

Keith nodded that it had. "She's still critical but she's stable and, frankly, her respiration is better than Gabby's." Worn and weary, he pinched the bridge of his nose with his fingertips. "Dr. Erickson is watching over her now."

"Do you trust him with her?"

"David lost a son to EEE," Keith said, knowing in his eyes. "He's obsessed with finding a cure, and he has more experience researching it and Z-4027 than anyone else alive."

"Are you going to give the vaccine to Gabby?"

"I can." Keith blew out a heavy sigh that rounded his cheeks, clearly wishing the decision were someone else's to make. "But there's no way to predict her reaction, Max. You've got to understand that."

"Trial studies haven't yet been done. I'm aware."

That Keith didn't ask how Max had become aware proved he already knew the answer. "Only on Candace." Leaning a shoulder against the wall, he sent Max a warning look. "The injection could kill Gabby."

"Or it could save her life," he countered.

"Her body could also reject it."

Max thought a second. "What about conventional treatments?"

"There aren't any that can compete with the accelerated actions of Z-4027. By the time anything we've got could possibly work, the patient is already dead."

Keith had avoided Gabby's name but that didn't make his words any easier to stomach.

"It's going to have to be your call," Keith said, somber and empathetic, knowing what having to make this call cost. "She's your wife."

His wife. Max stilled, stared up at the popcorn ceiling, and did his best not to outwardly react. He wasn't her husband, he was the partner she had never trusted or wanted. The man she'd slept with only because she was lonely and about to die and wanted to feel special. The man who had slept with her because he wanted her to die feeling special to assuage his guilt for killing her and to lighten the load on his conscience because he felt a lot more than he had bargained for feeling. Now he had to make a decision that could determine what little was left of her life? A woman he genuinely cared about—whether or not he wanted to— who tolerated him only because she was facing death?

As hellish as this decision was to make under any circumstances, it'd have to be easier if she were his real wife.

Then, he would at least know she trusted him to act in her best interests.

"Max?" Keith asked. "What do you want to do?"

Max stalled, unable to force himself to answer. With the vaccine, Gabby could die. Without it, she would die. When he got to that bottom line, what choice did he really have?

Still, Gabby had made him belong, and deep down she had to feel special to him, too. He'd been embarrassingly honest about that. Making love with her, sleeping with her sprawling on him, hearing her restful breathing, smelling her skin, her hair, sensing her body weight on the bed beside him—he'd liked all of it. None of it was wise or logical, but it felt right and good. He didn't want to lose her.

Oh, man, he was in deep trouble. Had he really believed that he could remain neutral? He'd never been neutral about her, and he couldn't even remember a time when he hadn't wanted her.

"Max?" Keith asked again. "What do you want me to do?"

Max shut out his selfish motives and asked himself one question: In this situation, what would Gabby do?

The answer came swift, hard, and certain. He stared straight into Burke's eyes and didn't hesitate. "Give her the vaccine."

Nodding, Keith walked back into the bedroom to prepare the injection.

Max leaned his forehead against the hallway wall, feeling its rough nubs scrape against his forehead. Not once had he asked anyone for anything. Now, he prayed.

When he walked back into the bedroom, Keith was at Gabby's bedside, giving her the injection. As he pushed the vaccine into her body, Max dared to ask God to spare Gabby's mind and her life. He had no idea if he would be heard or laughed at or answered—he'd never prayed before—but millions had, and it had comforted them through generations of recorded history, so it had to be worth a shot. Still, not knowing for sure, Max felt no comfort. And he resented that most of all.

"That's it." Keith disposed of the needle in a sharps box and dropped it into his black bag, resting on the edge of the bed. "For now, that's all we can do."

Gabby appeared to be sleeping. Max watched the rise and fall of her chest. So far, there seemed to be no disruption in her breathing. "How long before we know anything?"

"Could be a minute or less," he said, his mouth grim. "The longer it takes, the better."

It didn't kill her immediately. Minutes passed, but the tension didn't ease. It hovered around her like a canopy, and kept his chest in a vise. Every instinctive warning an operative could get warned Max to back off, gain some perspective and objectivity, but he couldn't seem to look away from her.

"I could use some caffeine. Be right back." Keith left the room.

Max sat down on the edge of the bed beside Gabby, clasped her hand in both of his. "Don't leave me, Gabby. Not yet."

His throat went thick and his eyes burned. He willed her to live, silently cursed his fear that she wouldn't, and prayed again—just in case God was real and was paying attention.

Minutes later, Keith came back with a cup of coffee and held a cell phone out to Max. "It's Elizabeth Powell," he said. "She wants to speak with you."

Max put the cell phone to his ear. "Hello."

"I'll be over in a bit."

"Excuse me?" Elizabeth Powell? Judge Powell's wife. Candace's and Gabby's friend.

"You've got a meeting at nine o'clock, remember?"

He stared at Gabby's face, still and unmasked. She'd

never looked so vulnerable before. Or so soft. That vise in his chest hitched a notch, squeezed tighter. "How did you know I had a meeting?" he asked Elizabeth.

"Mayor Faulkner mentioned it at the Silver Spoon Café this morning. Everyone's converging there to see who needs what. Hurricane Darla apparently tore down half of Carnel Cove and most of the county."

"So you're coming to stay with Gabby while I'm gone?" Could he do that? Leave her here with Elizabeth? What if Gabby started mumbling, talking out of her head again? Conlee would have Max's ass for the security clearance violation. She couldn't get anything other than an aspirin without getting clearance and having an Intel agent present to make sure she didn't breach national security or violate the integrity of any classified material while being treated.

Why are you worried? When she was delirious, she stayed in her cover. She didn't recall SDU or Conlee or anything other than her cover.

"Someone has to be with her, and obviously it can't be you or Candace. I'm electing me," Elizabeth said. "I'll be there in an hour. That'll give you plenty of time to get to the mayor's office by nine."

Before he could decide whether to protest or be relieved, the phone went dead. He passed it back to Dr. Burke, who cast him a sympathetic look.

"Getting a taste of the way the ladies of Carnel Cove operate, I see."

Max grunted. "Are they all like that?"

"The ones in her circle are." He nodded toward Gabby. "A piece of advice from a man who's been there. Don't fight them. When they close ranks, just stay out of their way. If you have trouble remembering what will get your ass in a jam or keep it out of one, just get 'Yes, dear' etched into your glasses to remind you what to do. It'll make your life a lot easier."

"Sounds pretty one-sided."

"Yeah, it does. It's hell on the ego, to tell you the truth. At least, it is at first. Then you realize there isn't one woman among them who isn't worth it." Keith pulled his stethoscope out of the black bag. "The thing is, you can fight one of them and win a few. But when they close ranks, no man stands a chance."

He checked Gabby's blood pressure, pulse, heart rate, and respiration, and then backed away from the bed. "So far so good." He looked up at Max. "She's survived the injection. Now we just have to see whether or not the vaccine is going to do her any good."

"Is she stable enough to leave her with Elizabeth? I have a meeting—with FEMA."

"No promises on what's coming, but for now, yes." Keith smiled to relieve some of Max's worry. "Gabby's the only newcomer. The rest of the ladies of Carnel Cove have been close friends for years. You can trust any of them. But Elizabeth in particular."

"Why?"

"She mothers everyone she meets, whether they want it or not. Even me, which is amazing because of the divorce."

"I'd think that would have all of them shutting you out." Didn't it usually?

"It would, but Candace and I are still close. That keeps me in Elizabeth's good graces."

"Thanks for the tips." There was an extra message buried there, and Max picked up on it but didn't go into it with Keith. "Will Gabby get her memory back?"

"I don't know," Keith admitted. "Right now, she's stable. What the next five minutes or hours will bring is a mystery to us both. This is the best I can do for you, buddy."

"I'll take it." She was alive.

Keith grabbed his bag and then walked toward the

door. "I have to get back to Candace. If she wakes up and I'm not there—"

"She'll be afraid," Max finished for him.

"Actually, I was going to say, she'll bitch me out. But you're right. She'll bitch because she's afraid." He shrugged. "Though, of course, the tortures of hell couldn't get her to admit it."

Max nodded, connecting with Keith Burke, man to man. "Strong women are that way."

"Yeah, they are." He grabbed the doorknob. "If you need me, call."

"Thanks." Max shut the door behind Keith. As the lock slipped into place, a thought struck him that nearly bent him double. Elizabeth was coming over!

The dead Global Warrior in the garage.

Racing to the garage, he grabbed a shovel, and then rushed to the wooded area on the far east of the cove, near the point that was a public park.

Downed trees and scattered debris littered the area and objects floated in the water, some clinging to the white sandy shore. An ice chest. A life jacket. A six-pack of Miller beer. A refrigerator. Someone's photo album. An oar.

Judging by the variety of the debris, Hurricane Darla had done serious storm damage. He found a muddy spot of rain-soaked ground among a clump of ancient oaks. The tree limbs were still draped with moss, though the high winds had stripped the leaves from the twisted wisteria vines choking their trunks. Storm damage could be bizarre. The tornadoes spawned in the feeder bands of the hurricane saw to that. He checked the perimeter, assuring himself he was alone, and then dug a shallow grave. In minutes, the high humidity and sweltering heat had him in a decent sweat and swearing that August in Carnel Cove should be declared unfit for humans.

When the grave was ready, he left the shovel seated in

the wet dirt, rushed back to the house, and then slung Jaris Adahan's body over his shoulder.

The dead weight stayed put like a sack of rocks.

Keeping out a sharp eye, Max saw no one on the way back to the grave. He buried Adahan, marked the grave with a shiny penny so Housekeeping could find it easily, and then returned to the house. He then checked on Gabby.

She was turned away from him, but sleeping. He watched her shoulder rise and fall with each breath. Sure that she was stable, he felt it was okay to leave her, though he'd prefer to stay by her side. Elizabeth would be here any second and he had to get to the mayor's office.

Showered, shaved, and changed into green Dockers and a tan shirt, he again found himself standing beside Gabby's bed, looking down on her. She lay sleeping peacefully, her hair tumbling half over her face and onto her pillow. Soft and vulnerable and strong and . . . and . . . he willed it away, but it wouldn't go.

This feeling was new to him. One minute he was fine. The next minute she'd invaded his thoughts. How had she done that?

He had cared about her long before coming to Carnel Cove to kill her. Still, this was different. It went beyond caring. This was love.

Man, did his timing suck. Who else would fall in love with a woman he had been ordered to kill? God help him, he was a covert operative for the most dangerous, most secret and elite antiterrorist unit in the entire United States of America, and he was also the worst idiot and biggest fool ever born.

Maxwell Grayson, who had always depended only on himself, who believed in nothing and no one other than himself, who had never connected to anyone and liked his life that way, had fallen in love.

With a woman marked for certain death.

As if he needed that reminder. He dragged a hand through his hair, felt the tension building between his shoulders. Maybe he should just shoot himself and end his misery.

The doorbell rang.

Shuffling, he went to answer it. A pretty woman about forty-five years old stood outside the entry on the landing, dressed in blue slacks and a sleeveless silk top. Her hair was gold and hung down to her shoulders, her eyes huge, and she had a gentle look about her that put a man at ease. "Morning."

"Hello, Max. I'm Elizabeth Powell." She smiled and extended her hand. When Max shook it, she added, "I'm so glad you're real, after all, and not a figment of Gabby's imagination. It's about time you came home."

Max didn't know what to say to that or what to make of her or her reprimand, and he supposed it showed. The woman laughed at him. "Relax." She walked in, dumped her purse on a chair in the entryway, and then walked toward Gabby's room, talking to him back over her shoulder. "The ladies of Carnel Cove have few secrets from each other and millions from the rest of the world. I know all about you. You're safe."

Max's stomach was flopping like a beached fish. What the hell did she mean, she knew all about him? Had Gabby broken her cover and confided the truth to these women? She couldn't have—wouldn't have. She knew the costs, and she wasn't some mistake-prone rookie. Gabby was a seasoned covert operative with a history in Special Operations; she had more cover than real life. No way would she have told them. "Who are the ladies?"

Elizabeth paused, turned back to look at him, and smiled. "I'm sorry, Max. When I checked on Candace, David Erickson told me Keith was here. I assumed he had warned you about us." The light above her head, showered down on her skin, and the glint in her eye said she knew that's exactly what Keith Burke had done. "The ladies are Gabby, Candace, Miranda, Paige, and me, of course. You'll meet them soon enough." Elizabeth wrinkled her nose. "Sissy Blake—you'll meet her husband, Carl, this morning—would like to be one of us, but that's not going to happen."

He couldn't resist. "Why not?"

"Character. Simply put, she's materialistic. All show and no substance." She wrinkled her nose. "The ladies of Carnel Cove do substance."

"Ah." Surprising. They were all wealthy women, and Candace supposedly had been some kind of trophy wife for Keith, though he sure as hell didn't react to her as if she were a trophy. They might be divorced, but he was still crazy about her and totally devoted to her.

"Oh, I forgot Darlene Coulter," Elizabeth said on second thought.

Coulter was a familiar name to Max. "Sheriff Coulter's wife?"

Elizabeth nodded. "Have you met Jackson already?"

"I will this morning at the meeting with Carl Blake and the mayor."

"You'll like him," she predicted. "Jackson is a decent man."

Were Blake and the mayor decent, too? Max waited, but she didn't elaborate. "You're sure you'll be all right with her?" He checked his watch and nodded toward Gabby's door.

"Of course. Keith's filled me in."

Now why didn't that surprise Max? Hell, everyone in the Cove would know everything he did before dusk. He'd forgotten about the fishbowl atmosphere of small towns.

"Don't you really want to know if Gabby will be all right with me?"

Shrewd and beautiful and yet still gentle. "Yes, actually, I do," he admitted.

That earned him another smile. "She will."

He believed her. "I'll get going, then."

Elizabeth hiked a sharp brow. "Without kissing your wife good-bye?" She folded her arms over her chest. "For goodness' sake, Max, I realize you've been gone a long time and you're out of practice at being a husband, but remember that women need these little things. William Powell and I were married twenty-five years and he never, not once, left home without kissing me good-bye."

"Sorry." Max apologized before asking himself why. He felt as if he'd been tested and judged and he'd landed somewhere on the list between spider and snake.

"Go on, then. I'll wait here." She tapped her crossed arms the way he'd seen a lot of mothers do—his own excepted, of course.

He went into the bedroom and placed a chaste kiss to Gabby's cool forehead. Her temperature was down. That had to be good enough, didn't it? He needed her and her memories—now! This husband business wasn't as easy as it looked from the outside. And he had a sinking feeling these Carnel Cove ladies had a thousand of those little rules. They'd see straight through him in no time.

Elizabeth walked with him to the door. "Before you go, I need to say something to you."

"What?" On edge, he paused near a six-foot potted palm.

"I know what happened at the lab. Candace called me first. I told her to call Gabby." She lowered her gaze to the floor, paused, then forced herself to look back into his eyes. "I also know Candace and Gabby are trying to prove William was murdered."

Definitely classified. He couldn't respond.

"It's okay," she said. "You don't have to say anything. I understand. I just want you to know that you have nothing to fear from me. When Gabby needs my help, she's going to get it. It's that simple."

"No questions asked?" He put it to the test. Conlee had said that Candace had let Gabby have access to the lab, no questions asked. Was it a policy among the ladies?

"She'll tell us what she wants us to know," Elizabeth said without hesitating.

Gabby very well could have told Conlee the truth, not that Max could dare to count on it.

"Elizabeth? Is that you?"

Gabby. They both looked toward the hallway to her bedroom, and Max let Elizabeth get there first. He hovered near the door, wanting to see them interact. See if Gabby felt safe.

"Thank God," Gabby said. "Grab me a gown out of the third dresser drawer, will you?"

"Naked, Gabby?" Elizabeth walked over to the dresser, slid out the drawer, and held up two possibles. "If it's because you're sick, fine. If you're naked because you've been up making love all night, I don't want to hear it."

"So abstinence doesn't agree with you?"

"Sex without William doesn't agree with me." She lifted the two gowns. "Left or right?"

"Left." Gabby chose the crisp white cotton one. "It looks cooler."

Elizabeth walked over to the bed. "I take it your answer is great sex."

Gabby stretched up her arms to slip them through the holes Elizabeth held open for her. When her head cleared the fabric, she gave Elizabeth a wicked grin. "Fabulous, to-die-for sex."

"You're shameless." Elizabeth tugged down the gown, then snagged a brush off the vanity. "You know, I really hate that about you. Even gloating you're gorgeous."

"Hey, I've done my time with abstinence, too."

Elizabeth harrumphed, and began brushing Gabby's hair. "Yes, too much. Make him stay closer to home, Gabby.

You never know when the last time you see him is going to be the last time you see him."

Gabby grabbed Elizabeth's hand, stilled it, and looked up at her. "Am I going to die?"

"I don't know." Elizabeth frowned. "Keith's doing all he can do. You're doing a lot better than Candace. That's all I know right now."

"Is she. . . ?"

"If she dies, she'll have to take Keith with her. He's not giving her up otherwise."

Gabby seemed oddly comforted by that.

Max ducked his head into the room. "Elizabeth, can I bother you a second?"

"Sure." She walked out into the hallway. "What?"

How did he explain without revealing too much? "There were some looters here yesterday. I'm not convinced they won't be back."

"Don't worry, Max. I'll protect Gabby."

Why didn't that make him feel better? He knew she would try, but she was a slender, small woman. A wife and mother and—

"I'm more capable than I look. William taught me to shoot to protect the children—judges are often threatened. I'm quite good at it. No one will hurt Gabby."

Elizabeth was a devoted mother; the exact opposite of the kind he'd had. "Thank you."

She forced herself to give him a smile. It was soft and gentle and bittersweet. "If you don't leave now, you're going to be late. Ronald—Mayor Faulkner—is a real stickler about being tardy. His mother was the principal at the high school."

Max turned toward the door, wondering exactly what secrets Gabby had shared with the ladies. It would be hard to imagine, but it was possible she had run into a situation where she'd either had to get their help or be canceled. She could have told them about everything short of SDU, though until coming to Carnel Cove and meeting Elizabeth himself, he would have denied that as a possibility.

His mind raced, playing out scenarios, and new worries piled onto the old. If Gabby had told the ladies anything classified or even hinted at SDU, Commander Conlee would have no choice but to cancel all of them, too.

And there was no way in hell Max could carry out those orders.

Mulling on the matter, he drove Gabby's Jeep down to Main Street and pulled in at City Hall. Nine o'clock straight up. Mayor Faulkner and FEMA's Stan Mullin would be waiting.

The parking lot was like an obstacle course. Trash and junk lay strewn by the storm. Huge old oaks and magnolias lay on the ground, their roots exposed to the sun. Opposite the far side of the parking lot, half in the street and half on the sandy beach, a forty-foot charter fishing boat, with the name *Daddy's Toy* painted in purple on its hull, sat leaning on its side.

Pulling into an open slot, Max turned off the ignition. Something constructive had to come out of this meeting. Luck or a miracle, he'd take what he could get. He had a lot of vital questions, too few critical answers, and not much time.

Chapter Twenty-two

Max sat at the conference table inside the mayor's office at City Hall and watched FEMA's Stan Mullin and Mayor Faulkner jockey for position in a dialogue on spraying to control Hurricane Darla's mosquito population. One thing was clear to Max—and obviously to Sheriff Coulter, gauging by his expression: The discussion would be about as productive as tits on a bull.

Just shy of seven feet tall and breezing through his fifties, Stan was clearly a basketball man back in his day, and he was still lanky and quick. Ronald Faulkner was younger, about thirty. The same age as Jackson Coulter, who sat on Max's left—and at one time, judging by the trophies on his office wall, Faulkner had been an all-star football player. Now, his "fit" had gone to "flab"—too many political fund-raising dinners could do that to a man. Before the meeting, after learning Max was Gabby's husband, Jackson had warned Max about Faulkner. "When you deal with him, cover your assets. He's slick and crafty. First and foremost, he's the mayor, and he's always running for re-election. He *never* takes responsibility for anything that goes wrong."

And he always took credit for anything that went right. Max knew the type and, during the meeting, he didn't see anything that contradicted the sheriff's opinion. Max glanced over at Jackson. He sat with an elbow propped on the table, his jaw cupped in his hand. His eyes were glazed over, proving he had no hope for anything constructive happening between Stan and Faulkner. Stan still came across as patient, but he had wearied of Faulkner's narrative, too. He'd checked his watch three times in the last sixty seconds. That move alone had Max giving Stan the upper hand on winning the debate.

When Faulkner began reiterating for the third time, Max ended the debate. "Look," he interrupted, "we've got to spray. It's inconvenient because of storm damage, but the slow cleanup is also why spraying is essential. We don't need an outbreak of West Nile here like they had in New Orleans. And if there is one, I'm sure Mayor Faulkner doesn't want to have to explain to his constituents that the reason why is he refused to spray."

Faulkner frowned. "I haven't refused to spray."

"Okay, then. You agree," Max said.

"Actually, I haven't agreed, either."

"Fine." Max folded his hands on the tabletop. "Well, then, let's call the question. Otherwise, the worst that could happen will happen, and we'll still be sitting here debating. Do we spray? Yes, or no?"

Faulkner's mud-brown eyes stretched wide and his high forehead wrinkled. "Spraying all of Carnel Cove requires a little more consideration, Max. Maybe this is routine for you federal guys, but for us it's a major decision. The expense—"

"There is no expense." Max leaned forward on his seat.

"Not to Carnel Cove." He shifted his gaze to Stan Mullin. "Is FEMA prepared to take responsibility for working with the CDC and to assume all costs?"

The Centers for Disease Control in Atlanta would have to be notified. Of course, the reports would be routed to Home Base for editing. "I could stipulate to that," Stan said, nodding.

He had orders to provide Max with whatever he needed. At least Conlee had released that much information to Stan. "Great," Max said. "That's settled, then." He stood and walked over to look at a map of Carnel Cove on the far wall of Faulkner's office. "Mayor, how do you want the Cove split up? We'll need quadrants. Where do you want the lines drawn?"

Still looking baffled at how quickly this had been settled after wrangling over a response for the past hour, Faulkner walked to the map and drew four quadrants with his fingertips. "Does that look reasonable?" He reached for a marker.

Max grabbed it first. "Perfect." The quadrant containing Logan Industries' lab needed to be sprayed first to minimize damage to Covers from the lab incident. "One." He marked the map, and then went on to mark the other three areas.

Sipping at a steaming cup of coffee, Stan joined them at the map and addressed the mayor. "Who handles the regular spraying here?"

"Carl Blake. Well, not personally," Faulkner amended. "But one of his companies."

"Were his trucks damaged in the storm?" Stan asked.

"I don't think so." Faulkner shrugged. "There was no word of his trucks taking a hit at the Silver Spoon this morning. But you can ask him yourself. He'll be here any moment."

Great. Max frowned. The mayor counted on café gossip for accurate information.

"He's not going to make it here, Mayor. He's meeting with his insurance adjuster."

"So his trucks are damaged?" Faulkner asked.

"No, sir," Sheriff Coulter said. "His home. A long-needle pine crashed through the roof in his son's bedroom. Would've killed the boy if he'd been in it and not away at college."

Faulkner slipped his hands in his pockets and slumped forward. "Is that right?"

Coulter nodded, bored and edgy and ready to get out of the conference room. "I need to get back to the office. If you don't need—"

"Naw, go ahead, Jackson." Faulkner waved a dismissive hand.

Faulkner was and had been pushing the "good old boy" routine pretty hard. And Max wondered why. It wasn't genuine or even second nature to the man; that was evident. He couldn't sustain the role without sliding out of it. Not that he had made big gaffes; he hadn't. But he had made a number of little mistakes that were glaringly apparent to a trained operative watching for them.

"Stan." Max looked over. "You'll work with the mayor and Carl Blake to get the trucks set up, right? We need to start pesticide applications today. If we wait, the CDC could declare Carnel Cove a health hazard—due to the storm-induced mosquito infestation. They could issue a mandatory quarantine of the town." That should halt any mayoral objections.

"No problem," Stan said. "Providing the trucks can get down the roads."

Faulkner chimed in. "Carl can support the city's efforts on clearing them. He has heavy-equipment rentals that can supplement the power and gas companies' trucks and our own emergency services—if FEMA's willing to pay."

"It is." Stan looked from the mayor to Max. "What about the pesticide?"

Max shot him a warning glare. Hadn't the man been briefed? Or had he failed to recall that Faulkner hadn't yet been cleared as a possible suspect for the lab incident?

Probably the former. Conlee wouldn't consider Stan had a "need to know" about the lab incident suspects any more than he would "need to know" Faulkner was a suspect in the Global Warrior judicial-corruption cases heard by Judge Abernathy. Everyone in town, including Sheriff Coulter, swore no one spit on the street without Faulkner's stamp of approval. Faulkner knew more than he was telling them about both, which so far, was nothing. Or at least, Gabby had relayed nothing. Faulkner could have told her who had killed JFK and Max wouldn't know it. Right now, Gabby wouldn't know it. And if Keith Burke's vaccine didn't arrest the Z-4027 infection, she probably never would.

If it gets bad, I expect you to do the right thing. I would do it for you.

Gabby's promise. Remembering it put a lump in Max's throat. Man, he hoped it didn't come down to that, to his killing her to end her suffering.

Worrying about that, about her, put tension in his tone. "I'll handle obtaining the pesticide," Max told Stan. "And I'll get back to you with instructions."

"No problem."

Faulkner's keen eyes missed nothing. "I thought you were the head of FEMA, Stan. Why are you taking instructions from a consultant?"

Sober, Stan grunted. "Because he's a subject matter expert and I pay him a fortune to know more than I do about health and safety. He does, and I'm smart enough to listen to him."

Stan Mullin was all right, after all. Max swallowed a chuckle under his breath. "I'll check with Logan Industries and see if they can help us."

"Oh?" Faulkner's interest level perked up.

That reaction bothered Max. The man wasn't surprised, just eager for information, and so far as Max could determine there was no reason he needed it. Wary, he looked straight at Faulkner, and said nothing.

Faulkner hesitated, but apparently he hadn't learned the power of silence as a negotiation tool. "Speaking of L.I. I ran into Dr. Erickson at the Silver Spoon this morning. He tells me Candace and Gabby are under the weather?"

"Gabby's fine," Max said, avoiding mentioning Candace. "Storms rattle her. That's all."

"I see," Faulkner said, wrapping his lips around a well-worn pipe stem.

"I'll get going on those public service warnings." Stan beat Max to the door. "We do want to mention there's a danger of EEE, right?"

"Yes," Max said, without hesitating. "A case was reported within spitting distance—Mobile—so the risks are elevated here, particularly with all the standing water due to the storm."

"Breeding ground." Stan nodded and walked out the door, swiftly closing it behind him.

"I'd better get moving, too." Max headed out, glad the objective of getting Faulkner to agree to the spraying had been met. That might buy him a little time with Commander Conlee and keep him off Max's back.

"Max?" Faulkner called out, leaning a hip on the corner of his desk, folding his arms across his chest. "Tell me something."

Max looked back at him over his shoulder. "What?"

"Tell me why the director of FEMA is taking orders from you. No offense intended, but you're just a consultant."

"Stan just answered that. I'm a subject matter expert. This is what I do."

"His explanation was lacking, and yours isn't much better."

Faulkner wanted more but he wasn't going to get it. Max glared at him, and said nothing.

"Fine," he finally said. "Then tell me, as his expert, when are you going to admit that there was an incident at Logan Industries' lab that puts the people of Carnel Cove in jeopardy?"

Max looked him straight in the eye. "What lab incident?"

"Well, that's pretty clear." Faulkner chewed at his inner lip. "One more question."

Max waited and masked his expression. Faulkner wasn't as affable as he pretended to be, but he wasn't as sly as he thought he was, either. Fine by Max. He'd often dealt with Faulkners.

"Why haven't you and Gabby divorced?"

That question Max hadn't expected. "Excuse me?"

"She's been here nearly a year, and you're just now making an appearance? Now, strangely enough, when your expertise is suddenly needed by the federal government?" Faulkner stretched out his legs in front of him, crossing them at the ankles. "Come on, Max. I'm not stupid. She's not your wife and you're not here by mistake. What the hell is going on in my town?"

Max didn't have to pretend to be offended, he felt indignant down to the tips of his toes. "With all due respect, my marriage and my wife are none of your business. You're out of line, and I recommend you don't step over it again." Max paused, doorknob in hand. "As you say, it's your town. I'm here and able to help. You want it, fine. You don't, that's fine, too."

"It's just odd. Gabby talked of you, of course. But here, all of a sudden, you show up." He tugged at the lobe of his ear. "I can't help wondering, why now? There has to be a reason."

"Wonder all you want, but keep your nose out of my private life. You mess with my wife, you mess with me."

Max looked down into Faulkner's dull, mud-brown eyes. "Frankly, you're not up to it."

"Hey, I'm sorry." The mayor slid Max a caustic smile. "I didn't mean any harm. I was just curious. No offense, eh?"

"None taken." Max smiled back as politely as if they'd been discussing the weather, and then left the office.

Max slid into Gabby's Jeep and started the ignition. He didn't like Faulkner and he didn't like the feeling of this whole situation. Not any of it. Faulkner knew exactly what had happened at the lab; his body language and eyes gave him away. He wasn't guessing there'd been damage; he knew it, and he shouldn't. The project was classified above Top Secret. That meant someone who had security clearance and knew about the incident had breached it and told him. But who with the appropriate security clearance would be that stupid?

Stan didn't know it. Faulkner had mentioned talking with Dr. Erickson at the Silver Spoon Café. Erickson had been caring for Candace while Keith had been checking on Gabby. Erickson could have told Faulkner about the project and the release of the Z-4027 mosquitoes. Seemed logical. Easy.

And that's what was wrong with it. It was *too* logical and *too* easy. Faulkner had set Erickson up. In subterfuge, only idiots drew linear lines. Faulkner was an ass, but he was not an idiot. So whom had he been protecting?

Only two other people at Logan Industries knew what the Z-4027 project entailed: Erickson's boss, Dr. Marcus Swift, and Candace Burke.

The image of Candace with her arms stretched, trying to seal the lab window with her blouse to keep the infected mosquitoes confined to the lab, replayed in Max's mind. She was a patriot, willingly sacrificing her life to save others. That narrowed Faulkner's protection list to one. Dr. Marcus Swift.

And Max wondered. If Gabby could recall all she knew, would she agree?

★   ★   ★

Gabby was hot. Why couldn't she lift her arms to wipe her forehead? They seemed to weigh a ton. Her lips were dry; she needed water, and opened her mouth to let out some of the heat.

Someone pushed a straw between her lips. It startled her. Then she remembered Max was here. Thank God, Max was here. She sipped, letting the cool water swish inside her mouth, loosen the dry flesh from her teeth, and then swallowed, feeling the blessedly cool liquid slide down her throat.

"Drink a little more, Gabby. Your fever is really up."

It wasn't Max. It was a woman's voice. Gabby tried to pry open her eyelids, but they too felt as if they had been leaded down with weights. Who was she?

Max *was* here. She knew Max was here, and shouted for him. "Max."

Why had her voice sounded like a crackled whisper? What had—oh, dear God, the mosquitoes. Z-4027. She was infected and dying. "Max," she tried again.

"It's me, Elizabeth. Max had to go to the mayor's meeting. You're sick, remember?"

It took valiant effort, but she opened one eye to a slit and saw Elizabeth bending over her bedside, glass with straw in hand. Her perfume smelled sweet, and she looked so worried. *Gabby had to be dying.* She managed to nod.

"I think I'd better call Max or Keith. I'm not happy with your temperature, Gabby."

What was Max doing with the mayor? He was supposed to be in Africa. No. No, he'd come home. The storm. He knew how much she hated storms. Ah, being a good husband.

Shh, don't tell, Gabby. Don't tell.

Something strong and important niggled at her memory, but all that held firm was that she was married to Max. "Don't tell." She croaked out and sank deeper into her pillow, exhausted from the effort.

"You don't want me to call Max or Keith?" Elizabeth said and then frowned, clearly disagreeing. "Oh, Gabby. I think we should call them both right away. You don't realize—"

"Shh." Gabby strained to keep an eye open to a slit and stared up into Elizabeth's face, her resolve evident in her sharp tone. "Don't tell."

Chapter Twenty-three

Max pulled into the Logan Industries parking lot, and then dialed Gabby's. When Elizabeth answered, he said, "It's me, Max. How is Gabby?"

"She's had a little water. Her temperature is up again. It's acting like a yo-yo."

"May I speak with her, please?"

Elizabeth hesitated. "She's not really up to talking right now."

"Do you need to call Keith?"

"Mmm, maybe later."

Her hesitancy bothered him. He didn't want to run through a liaison, but it seemed he had no choice. "Ask her what she can tell me about Dr. Marcus Swift."

"Whatever for?"

"It has to do with the lab incident," he said impatiently, though he thought she'd asked before even thinking about what she was doing. Still, Commander Conlee said the ladies could be trusted, so asking her was safe. "I need to know what kind of man he is."

"Hang on a second. I'll ask Gabby."

The phone muffled, as if she'd cupped her hand over the mouthpiece on the receiver. Then, Elizabeth came back on the line. "She doesn't know much about him, she says. But I do, if you're interested."

He needed pertinent project intelligence, but with Gabby unavailable, he'd take what he could get. "Absolutely."

"Okay." Elizabeth dragged in a breath. "He's CEO of Logan Industries, and has been since right after Candace bought controlling interest and hired him. She didn't want to assume day-to-day management, so she needed someone with impeccable qualifications. Out of all the applicants, Marcus Swift was the only one who made the cut. No one else even came close. He brought Dr. Erickson on board. Marcus makes all the decisions, but Candace has Miranda oversee everything. She has legal and specialized accountants pull a full audit every three months."

"Full audits, every three months?" Max asked, surprised at the frequency. Most corporations considered annual audits sufficient.

"That's right, quarterly. Swift hates it, but he can't dissuade Miranda and Candace backs up Miranda. When Candace Burke makes up her mind, no one short of God can change it."

"So Swift isn't happy at Logan Industries and his position is strictly administrative."

"Oh, no. He's happy. He'd just be happier if he owned it—or if he owned Candace—but don't mention that to Keith. Marcus isn't just an administrator either. He's also the head of all research and development. Candace is a financial whiz, but she's not into medical research. For her, Logan Industries was just a good investment."

The row of canisters in the lab, the one with the black

band replayed in Max's mind. "Swift is active in the lab, then?"

"Very," Elizabeth said. "Just a second. Gabby's snatching at the phone."

Gabby came on the line. "Max, how long will it be before you get home?"

"Soon. I'm at the lab now. I need to do a little legwork." He watched Erickson park his Volvo in the lot, clear security, and then walk into the building. "You okay?"

"I'm fine. My assistant said she was clearing my calendar for today, and Elizabeth is mothering me to death. I'm just going to stay in bed and rest. I love you, sugar."

He started to repeat it back to her by rote, and then remembered Gabby had said that for Elizabeth, not for him. He was surprised by how natural it had sounded to him, and by how normal his own response had seemed—as if he'd spoken those words to her many times, when in fact he had never once uttered them to any woman, in or out of bed. Stunned, he couldn't find his voice to say anything at all.

Elizabeth returned to the phone. "Max." Her voice sounded considerably lower than it had been. "Gabby's assistant hasn't called."

His stomach sank. "Keith said to expect that. It still scares the hell out of me."

"I know," she whispered. "William did it, too."

They shared a quiet moment of understanding, then Max said, "I did call her office earlier to let them know Gabby was ill. I, um, said it was the flu." His throat clenched.

"Miranda told me." Empathy and tacit agreement were in her voice. "It's for the best."

Max sure hoped so. Conlee had deemed the ladies safe, and for the moment, Max had no reason to feel any differently. Actually, Elizabeth's shared understanding seemed like a gift. "I have one more stop to make after the lab, if that's not a problem."

Gabby said something in the background, drowning out Elizabeth's voice. "Elizabeth? What did she say?"

"Don't tell," Elizabeth repeated. "I have no idea who she's talking to, Max. She's said it fifty times, but her temperature is really unstable, and right now it's way up. She's a little loopy. I saw this with William, too. We're okay, for now. Just do what you need to do."

"I'll hurry." Max slid the phone into its belt clip, then walked into Logan Industries.

At the main entrance, a woman about twenty-eight with amber hair and brown eyes met him. "Max Grayson?" When he nodded, she extended her hand. "Miranda Coffield."

He shook it. She was nearly as beautiful as Gabby, but what came to mind wasn't her beauty, it was her intensity. Experience warned him she'd be a woman who missed nothing and remembered everything: a fantastic ally and the worst kind of enemy.

"Elizabeth Powell called and told me you were on the way in. You'll need this." She passed him a security badge and motioned for him to clip it to his shirt collar. "It's for full access. You can go into any area of the facility, including the lab."

He reminded himself that Conlee had deemed the ladies safe and he shouldn't ask why she was providing unfettered access. Yet he'd never encountered this level of cooperation and he didn't quite trust it. "You agreed to this on the basis of a phone call from Elizabeth?"

"I agreed to this based on a phone call from Elizabeth *and* because you're married to Gabby, who has extremely high standards, impeccable ethics, and great taste."

It was time to probe the extent of Conlee's *safe*. "You're one of the *ladies of Carnel Cove* Elizabeth told me about."

Miranda had definitely been on the list. But would she admit it?

"Yes, but keep that quiet, will you?" She grinned.

He nodded. "Scout's honor."

She stopped at a break in the hallway. "If you need anything, I'm at extension three-one-four."

"Thank you, Miranda," he said, and then made his way down to the lab.

Maybe it was instinct, or the hint of elevated voices inside that had Max pausing at the heavy metal door in the hallway outside the lab. Even he wasn't sure. But what became blatantly evident was that Dr. Erickson and another man inside the lab had locked horns in a verbal battle. Seconds later, it erupted into a full-fledged war.

"It's okay," a woman said. "They frequently disagree."

Max turned to look behind him.

A young woman wearing a green lab coat smiled. "So far, they haven't killed each other, but there's a betting pool in Accounting if you'd like to join in."

Max stared at the curly-haired woman. "Who's the second party?"

"Ah, that would be Dr. Marcus Swift, the esteemed head honcho of Logan Industries. Brilliant but not very pleasant, as you no doubt have now deduced."

"Mmm." Max wasn't sure about Swift or Erickson, regardless of Keith Burke's insistence that Erickson was a good man.

The door opened and Swift glared at Max. "What?"

"Dr. Swift." The woman beside him intervened. "Miranda wants to see you in her office—now. Something to do with an overseas contract that doesn't look quite right to her."

"Fine, Ms. Simpson." Swift threw one more visual bullet at Erickson then left the lab.

A cold shiver raced along the back of Max's neck. "Did

Miranda really want to see Dr. Swift?" he asked Ms. Simpson.

She gave him a negative shake.

"You know Elizabeth, too."

"Of course. I'm Paige Simpson." A little laugh sounded in her throat. "You'll never find out anything with Swift around. Miranda increases your odds to seventy-three percent for deeper disclosure with just Erickson. She's *never* wrong on numbers."

Another lady of Carnel Cove. Each of them seemed to have some special gift that they brought to the group: Candace, the patriot risk taker; Elizabeth, the nurturing organizer; Miranda, the intense informer. "And what are you never wrong on, Paige?"

"Motives." She shrugged. "I'm an empath."

An empath. Great. Not a good person to be near when you kept secrets. "So Elizabeth called Miranda, who then called you to come and check out my motives for coming to the lab?" He didn't know whether to be offended or impressed. They had quite a network going here.

"Not exactly. You're married to Gabby. That grants you an enormous amount of leeway with us. But we had to be sure your motives for coming to Carnel Cove and to the lab were pure. The work done at L.I. and by Gabby isn't the kind where you take on unnecessary risks."

She was right, of course. But did she know it because she sensed it empathetically, or because Gabby had told her about her work and the work at Logan Industries? One thing was patently clear. Either the circle of people deemed "need to know" on this mission was larger than Conlee had briefed, or Gabby had taken the ladies of Carnel Cove into her confidence.

"Safe" didn't warrant full disclosure. But Gabby breaching security protocol? Hell, she didn't even trust her partner with facts, much less anyone else. That left Conlee. And the question of how much the ladies actually knew.

"You have nothing to fear from us, Max," Paige said. "When you automatically know things, it's amazing how little you must actually be told."

Did that mean Commander Conlee had confided in them, or that Paige knew the truth because she was an empath and she'd told the others?

"I know you have little reason to trust women. I'm sorry about your mother—such a horrible experience. Drugs ruin so many lives." She paused to give him a minute to absorb what she was revealing. "You could have been beaten by it, Max, but you endured and rose above the trials. Becoming the man you are wasn't the easiest choice you could have made. It took courage to develop your own code of ethics without the guidance of loving parents. You became a good man in spite of them, Max. Gabby loves that about you." She let him see the truth in her eyes. "You have nothing to fear from us." Paige walked on down the corridor.

Uneasy, feeling vulnerable in an unfamiliar and unwelcome way, Max stared at her back until she turned the corner and disappeared from sight. He had cold chills from all she'd known; things he'd never discussed with himself, much less anyone else. He felt as if he'd stood before her naked and she'd looked into his soul and deemed him worthy. Gabby had deemed him worthy—a good man—without the gifts of an empath. She'd decided on faith. No one had done that for him before. Not ever. He'd never needed anyone's approval, which had been good because he'd never had it, but knowing now he did have it—from Gabby and the ladies—well, it felt strange. An avalanche of tender, unfamiliar emotions washed through him and Max had no idea what to do with them.

Erickson peered out the lab door. "You looking for me, or just parked in my hall?"

Homing in his focus, he looked at Erickson. "I wanted to talk to you."

"Why not?" Erickson opened the door and stepped aside.

Max walked in, felt the swish of the door closing behind him. The lock clicked into place. Erickson's face still looked sunburned; he hadn't yet reined in his temper. He returned to his pacing along the row of canisters, proving it. Giving him a minute, Max glanced over at the canisters. They all had yellow bands. A hard knot formed in his throat. "What happened to it?"

"To what?" Erickson pretended not to understand, but his guilty expression proved he knew exactly what Max meant.

"When I was helping Gabby lock down the lab, there was a black-banded canister right there." He pointed to its former place in the row. "It's gone, and no work is going on here today. What happened to it?"

Erickson's expression crumbled and worry burned in his eyes. "I don't know."

"I take it Dr. Swift didn't, either."

Erickson hiked his brows but kept his mouth shut.

That was what he and Swift had been arguing about, Max surmised. Intel could give him more specific feedback on the argument itself, so Max didn't push. "What was in it?"

"I'm sorry, I'm not at liberty to say."

Which told Max all he needed to know. Z-4027. Infection experimentation. "I'm working with FEMA. We're going to spray—"

"I know." Erickson lifted a hand. "You need chemicals." He stopped suddenly. "That presents a problem, Max. Nothing currently approved will work. Malathion was showing some positive results, but it failed," Erickson said bluntly. "Everything failed."

Using the unapproved pesticide had been the basis of the argument between him and Swift. "There has to be something we can at least try."

"There is." Erickson didn't look happy about it. "We've been working on a pesticide that theoretically should work. It's supposed to kill the mosquitoes before they're old enough to bite, but we can't claim it will work with any certainty. Lab success has been positive, but who know what will happen in the field? As you well know, the two can be radically different."

"What are you thinking about in terms of side effects?"

"The standard, typical risks to humans. There's no sure thing, of course, but we're encouraged by what we've seen that we'll have few surprises."

Considering trial studies hadn't yet been done, Erickson's expectations struck Max as more rosy than realistic. "Well, we don't have a lot of choice."

"I know. But we could exacerbate the problem."

"It's my understanding that if we do nothing, we're screwed. If we try this experimental pesticide, we have a shot. Do you agree or disagree with that assessment?"

"I agree." Erickson stuffed a hand in his lab coat pocket, totally frustrated.

"That's it, then." Max shrugged. "If you need stats on the chemical quantities, check with Stan Mullin. He's coordinating and can tell you what he'll need. He's arranging delivery with Carl Blake to get his trucks gassed up and ready to go."

Erickson nodded. "We're on it."

Max turned to leave the lab. "Dr. Erickson, what would the contents of that one canister do out there?" Max nodded toward the boarded-up window to the outside.

"Within forty-eight hours, it'd wipe out the entire population of Carnel Cove. Within two weeks, the state of Florida." He looked weary and worn. "In two months, the better part of the south. An early, hard winter would be our luckiest break. Otherwise . . ."

That "otherwise" came across all too clear, and explicitly graphic. "I understand." Unfettered, with time, the contents of that one canister assisted by nature could wipe out the population of the United States.

And a Global Warrior is on the loose here, obviously attempting to unleash it.

Max picked up his pace, hurried back to the Jeep. To stop this assault, he needed information in the worst way. He needed Gabby.

Her memory.

And her evidence.

*   *   *

"Phone call." The director eased out of the booth at the Silver Spoon Café, clapped Andrew on the shoulder, silently apologizing for leaving him alone with Sissy Blake and Darlene Coulter, who were angling for a new roof for the church. "I'll be right back."

He stepped outside into the parking lot to answer his cell phone. "Hello." To his right was a water truck. People stood in line, filling jugs with clean water. The health department hadn't given the thumbs-up to use city water again yet. Hurricanes were such a pain in the ass.

"Are we ready for the spraying?"

The chairman. "Yes, sir," the director said. "We'll be starting within the hour."

"And our man?"

"Prepositioned and ready to go, sir." It gave the director enormous pleasure to report that. Once again, he was proving his value to the Consortium. He alone had manipulated events to gain the needed trial studies on the Z-4027 pesticide. That he had done so at no cost to the Consortium had the director nearly giddy.

He waved to Paige Simpson and smiled. Solemn, she waved back. He didn't believe in her empath bull, but she had snowed nearly everyone else in the Cove on it. Creepy woman.

"Film it," the chairman said. "The more graphic, the better."

"Already arranged, sir." The director rocked back on his heels.

"You've become a valuable asset."

"Thank you, sir." Smiling broadly, the director beamed, convinced he'd get a permanent position on the Consortium board for this. Not to mention an incredibly healthy bonus.

He put the phone back in his pocket. Hell, maybe he'd buy himself another island.

Heat rushed to his loins. Or another redhead.

Chapter Twenty-four

By mid-afternoon, Max had dropped in at home to check on Gabby and retrieve her courthouse keys, and phoned home twice. Each time, Elizabeth assured him that Gabby was "as expected," and she was doing all that could be done, freeing Max to do what he needed to do.

He had continued his search for intelligence and insight, searched her judge's chambers and courtroom for her evidence, and had found nothing, but he had gotten a significantly better grip on who was who in Carnel Cove.

Paige Simpson and Darlene Coulter had nabbed him at the Silver Spoon Café and fed him so much information on various Covers he'd had trouble slotting it all. They hadn't explained why they were briefing him, and he hadn't asked. Some things were better, not to mention safer, left unsaid.

The sun was sinking low as Max turned the corner and made his way down the debris-littered street to Gabby's driveway. Gabby's evidence wasn't at the house or in her chambers or in her courtroom. As he had been leaving the lab, Miranda had breezed by and mentioned in passing that Gabby didn't have a box at the bank or a post office box, and since he hadn't solicited that information, he had supposed she'd been sparing him from chasing rainbows. Again, he didn't ask how she had known he needed that information or why she was giving it to him, nor did she tell him.

He saw a little guy about eight dragging a limb as big as he was to the street-side pile where it could be picked up by the debris removal trucks that were all over town. Max felt a lot like the kid must: struggling to keep hold of the limb without getting knocked off his feet by one of its many branches.

Gabby had assured Max he would get the evidence even if she died. So where was it? Would she ever be able to tell him? He sure as hell hoped so because he didn't have a clue where else to look.

There *was* nowhere else to look.

At the head of the driveway, he braked to a stop, and then cut the engine. Before he could get out and make it up the walkway, Elizabeth rushed out the front door and met him on the porch. Her hair was tousled and her face pasty white. Worried didn't begin to cover how upset she looked. "What's wrong?"

"Max, I'm so glad you're home. Gabby wouldn't let me tell you." Elizabeth wrung her hands. "Her fever has spiked to a hundred three, and she's been asking for you nonstop. She's not in her right mind, Max." Elizabeth blinked hard. "I couldn't stand it. I *couldn't* call you, so I called Keith. He's on his way now."

Max ran past Elizabeth and into the house, straight to Gabby's bedroom. Beside her bed, he bent down to look at her. Flushed with fever, she lay on her side, knees curled to her chest, eyes closed. He stroked her hair back from her face. His hand was shaking. "Gabby?"

She looked up at him. "Max."

How could one word express such pure relief? He felt it down to the soles of his feet. Amazing considering their situation. "I'm here, honey. You okay?"

"Not really. I feel raunchy." She wrinkled her nose. "Is my work calendar clear for today? I think I might need another day or two to shake this off."

Another day or two? The bottom dropped out of his stomach. Had she forgotten what was wrong with her, or was she performing for Elizabeth? "I'll call in," he said. Gabby looked too sick to be performing, but with Gabby, who could be sure?

"I was telling Elizabeth about our honeymoon," she said. "Paris was fabulous, wasn't it? I really love Paris. We should go back there for our anniversary, Max."

She wasn't breaching her cover. Cold shivers ran up and down his back and neck, and a sick feeling stirred in the pit of his stomach. Keith had warned him about memory losses. But this wasn't exactly a memory loss. Gabby remembered her cover, her generated memories. She just didn't seem to remember her real ones. What did that make this?

They talked for a few more minutes. The air inside the bedroom was stifling hot. Elizabeth cracked open the window to let in a breeze, but the August heat made it hotter still. And muggy. Max felt as if he were trying to breathe through a wet towel. It had to be even worse for Gabby, he thought, sitting down on a chair near the window, listening while Gabby related story after story to Elizabeth about her and Max dating, what they had done on their honeymoon, the trouble they'd had adjusting to the long absences during their marriage, but how it and they endured because they loved each other unconditionally.

In less than twenty minutes, Gabby convinced Max their marriage was real.

Get a grip, Max. This is a show for Elizabeth, fool.

That reminder blindsided him. Something good and warm went hard and cold in his chest and then died. She didn't love him, with or without conditions, and he couldn't afford to forget that again.

Having distanced himself emotionally, he watched Gabby. What he saw worried him even more. Something worse, even more mysterious than memory loss, was going on with her. Something even more baffling. She seemed to have selective recall. But how could that be?

He continued to watch her intently, monitoring nebulous signs, minute details. In forty minutes, she never—not once—breached her cover. When Elizabeth went to the kitchen, Max moved over onto the bed beside Gabby and gently quizzed her. "Your recall of the specifics on Paris is amazing."

She grunted. "Every woman remembers falling in love, her wedding, and her honeymoon."

"But the details about Paris . . ."

Her blank look turned curious. "What about them?"

Don't panic. Push. Force her to remember the truth. "They never happened."

She looked at him as if he'd lost his mind. "What?"

"They never happened." He spoke softly in case Elizabeth returned unexpectedly.

"Of course, they happened. Is the heat getting to you? Maybe Keith should look—"

"The heat is fine. I'm fine," he insisted. "Gabby, we didn't go to Paris."

She ignored him, tapped a fingertip to her chin. "I'll bet it's the flu. It can confuse you, Max. Elizabeth says it's the fever. She knows about these things."

"Gabby, honey, listen to me," he insisted. "Paris never happened."

"What the hell is wrong with you? Of course, Paris happened. Look, I'm sick enough without you deliberately trying to make me worse, Max. I don't know why you've forgotten our honeymoon, but I haven't, so stop trying to tell me I have."

That set Max back on his heels, and he stilled. Gabby clearly recalled nothing of her life as a senior covert operative, her association with SDU, or even Commander Conlee. She sincerely believed her marriage to Max was real. That she was a judge in Carnel Cove, and he was a health and safety expert, working primarily in Third World countries. As strange as it sounded, Gabby had forgotten the truth.

Which meant, aside from Max's personal concerns about her, he had no idea how to stop the Warriors' attack because he had no idea what Gabby knew. Worse, Gabby had no idea what Gabby knew.

Or where she'd put the evidence.

★   ★   ★

"Wait out in the hall, Max," Keith said. "Give me a few minutes to try to get her calmed down. What did you do to her?"

"Hell, I don't know." Max was totally confused. "One minute, she was talking about when we got married, and then she said something about our honeymoon I didn't remember, and then next thing I knew she was crying her heart out and cursing a blue streak."

Keith frowned, hiked up a hand. "How long have you two been married?"

"Why?"

"Because there are certain things a man just doesn't do in a marriage if he wants any peace in his life, and one of them is to admit forgetting anything about your wedding, honeymoon, the day you met—the first of anything—or anything else remotely significant to women. Usually a man figures that out in the first year or so."

Max shrugged. "I've been out of the country a lot."

"Yeah, I'd say." Keith clapped Max on the shoulder. "A wise word from the trenches, my friend. When in doubt, keep your mouth shut. Nod and smile a lot. That's pretty safe."

"Right." Max cast a worried glance into the bedroom at Gabby. She looked waxy and pale against her bronze sheets, but at least she wasn't sobbing anymore. That was good. He didn't want to leave her—shouldn't leave her—but it had nothing to do with protecting her security clearance, though that was his responsibility. How could he have predicted she'd be so devastated by the truth? So adamant that he was wrong about it? So hurt?

He couldn't leave Gabby's side when she was hurt. Turning his gaze, he focused on Keith. "I'll be staying."

"All right." Keith gave him a man-to-man look of understanding.

Max stood against the wall next to the window. A stream of four men carried in a small power supply and medical equipment, and then disappeared the way they'd come. Keith bent over the bed, hooking Gabby up to all of it. Heart monitor, oxygen monitor, blood pressure, and pulse rate monitors. He started an IV drip and prepared an injection.

When he reached for the plastic tubing to insert it into Gabby's veins, Max interceded. How could he be sure none of the men had been Warriors wanting her dead? "What is that you're giving her, Keith?"

"Antibiotics," he said. "A lot of them."

He sounded more confident than he had about the odds of the vaccine injection working earlier, so Max kept quiet and waited, hoping when he got a chance to talk privately with Keith, he would learn Candace's condition had improved.

A good while later, Keith finally stood up straight.

Gabby had stopped crying and cursing, but she was still out of it, totally oblivious to anything going on in the room. The tense set of Elizabeth's shoulders, the worry etched in her face, expressed every nuance of Max's fear.

Pressing a hand to his lower back to work out a kink from being bent over so long, Keith stretched, turned to Max, and nodded toward the hallway.

Max followed him out and pulled the door closed behind him. "Is she going to make it?"

"Right now it doesn't look good, but Candace looked a hell of a lot worse, Max, and she's totally turned around. I wish I could say the vaccine made the difference, but the truth is I don't know what happened. One minute, Candace needed the respirator to get enough oxygen in her system to sustain life. Then next minute, she was breathing fine on her own and coming around. Maybe the vaccine kicked in and it put the antibiotics on a fast track at getting through her system, but I would have bet against it."

"Nothing that happened in the lab could substantiate it?"

"No." Keith worried at his lip. "The lab results were consistent. The vaccine's effect was either immediate death or significant improvement within an hour. After that, we saw no effect. We didn't see that in any of Candace's reactions, Max." He shook his head, still trying to figure out what had happened. "I gave Gabby the same treatment. Maybe it'll work for her, too."

"You don't think your treatment turned Candace around," Max said.

"It'd be great for my stock if I did." Keith sighed. "But, no, I don't. All I know to be true is that Candace was going down fast. I left her with Erickson to come check Gabby, and when I returned, Candace was coming back."

Dr. Erickson—who had been arguing with Dr. Swift about the missing black-banded canister in the lab. What if that black-banded canister hadn't held Z-4027? What if it was supposed to have had a yellow band, signifying it was a trial vaccine and not the Z-4027? What if someone had switched the bands? Max looked at Keith. "What if Erickson was responsible for Candace's recovery?"

"It's possible, and I'd be lying if I didn't admit I've wondered if he did something to treat her in my absence. He says no. But—"

"But you think he did."

"I honestly don't know, Max. But *something* happened. L.I. is working a mirror contract on a vaccine, and Erickson does know more than any other living human being about EEE. They're very similar—Z-4027 and EEE. I would have hired Erickson to run *my* program at Burke Pharmaceuticals if Marcus Swift hadn't beaten me to him."

That had the hair on Max's neck standing on edge. So say the bands were switched on the canister. For optimum control over the chemicals, that made the most sense. Who would have switched them? Swift seemed an obvious choice, and maybe he was. Or maybe he was a decoy set up to detract attention from the real guilty party. Could be either way. Or neither way.

Unfortunately, the bigger questions didn't come with a built-in suspect, and they were by far the most deadly.

Where was the missing canister of Z-4027? Who had it? And what did they intend to do with it?

Chapter Twenty-five

Elizabeth's hand felt clammy against the phone. She leaned back against Gabby's kitchen cabinet, and willed herself to calm down. "You're going to have to pick up that package, Miranda." Conlee's second team was due to arrive any minute. Elizabeth had been ordered to intercept and assist them, but she couldn't leave now.

"What am I supposed to do with them?"

"Follow the plan. Just fill in for me. Meet their boat at my dock. Use the rental car, not yours. Darlene has it rigged. They'll be lights out within three minutes. Then you drive over to Faulkner's house and park at the curb. It's that simple. Paige will take it from there. Just make sure you're seen outside Faulkner's house in that rental."

"What if no one is outside?"

"Honk the damn horn." Elizabeth looked heavenward, whispered a silent apology. That she'd cursed warned Miranda how frayed her nerves were at the moment. "The only other thing you have to do is drive the rental to the bank. Paige and Darlene will do the rest."

"I'll handle it." Miranda assumed control. "Darlene's ready. She has to act between eight fifteen and eight forty-five or Jackson's going to be out of his office and she'll be cutting her escape too close."

Praying Gabby still had those communications scramblers on her phone Miranda had sworn were there and they didn't all wind up in Leavenworth because of this call, Elizabeth turned toward the door to the family room. "Be careful with the oxygen, Miranda. No one smokes in the car or we'll be scraping all of you off the street."

"I know, Elizabeth. Stop worrying. We'll handle it. We can do this."

"Of course, you can." Elizabeth bit her lip and walked into the family room. Keith rounded the corner, leaving the hallway and headed toward the kitchen. Elizabeth stiffened. "Call me later." She paused by the sofa table, next to a vase of spiky twigs and magnolias. "Is Gabby okay?" she asked Keith.

It took effort, but he met her eyes. "No, not really."

"Well, where are you going, then?"

"I need more antibiotics." He motioned through the kitchen, obviously intending to cut through the garage to save a few steps. "They're at Candace's."

"No, use the front door. I mopped the kitchen floor and it's still wet."

Elizabeth's voice carried into Gabby's bedroom, and what she was doing hit Max right between the eyes. She was keeping Keith out of the garage, away from Jaris Adahan's bloodstains on the concrete floor. "Oh, God," Max muttered. Elizabeth had seen the blood. What did he do about it now?

All of Gabby's friends—Candace, Elizabeth, Miranda, and Paige—had in some way helped or protected him. He couldn't kill them.

Max walked into the living room. The news was on and a woman was giving a report outside Carnel Cove Memorial Hospital.

Elizabeth muted the sound. "It's okay. Keith's gone." Her eyes turned solemn; her expression, cautiously serious. "No one has been in the garage."

Having no idea how to respond without raising questions he didn't want to answer, Max said nothing. He couldn't lie to her. Elizabeth obviously knew far too much, and insulting her intelligence wouldn't endear him to her. Right now he was totally dependent on her goodwill, and unless he and Keith Burke were wrong about the way the women in their circle operated, that meant all the ladies' goodwill.

"Gabby is getting worse." Elizabeth drank from a sweating glass of pale tea, and then set it down on a coaster. "If we don't do something drastic, she's going to die—just like William."

Losing her husband had been hard on her. It showed in every move she made, her every glance, and every word. "We're trying everything we've got."

"I know." She rocked her head back against the sofa cushions. "But this time, it's got to be enough." She cut her gaze from the ceiling to Max. Her eyes shone overly bright, and she blinked hard. "I've buried enough people I've loved, Max. I don't want to bury any more."

"Me, either," he said. This time, he couldn't convince himself his reasons were solely, or even mostly, professional. They were personal. Simple and complex and very personal.

Elizabeth studied him, her gaze filled with skepticism. "I believe you mean that."

"I do."

"I'm glad to hear it." She stood up and grabbed her purse. "I need a shower and to check on Candace. I'll be back afterward so you can take care of whatever business you need to do."

Oh, yeah. She knew a lot more than he had thought. So much so Commander Conlee would consider her a national security threat. Hell, with their network, all the ladies probably knew too much, but Max wasn't going to report it. Conlee would only send in a tactical strike force rather than just a second team to cancel them all, him and Gabby included.

Couldn't he catch even one break on this mission?

"Don't look so worried, Max. Your secrets are safe with us," Elizabeth said.

Had he spoken aloud? "What secrets?"

She cocked her head, sending her long hair swinging forward, over her shoulder. "I cleaned up the blood on the garage floor and drowned the area in bleach."

Surprised, Max swallowed hard and kept his mouth shut.

"I'm assuming you got rid of the body and that, if you didn't commit the murder, Gabby did." She hiked her purse strap up on her shoulder, and the cross she wore on a gold chain around her neck glinted. "If Gabby killed the man, then he needed killing. I can't claim to know the same for you, but if you're married to Gabby, then I'm willing to risk that the same holds true. She isn't a woman to suffer fools, so it stands to reason she wouldn't marry one."

Stunned, Max opened his mouth, having no idea what would come out.

Elizabeth stopped him with a lifted hand. "No more needs to be said on the matter. I'll trust Gabby's judgment. In the past, it's proven sound."

He managed to nod.

"I'll be back in a few hours," she said, and then walked out the front door.

Stunned, Max stood in the living room, letting what had just happened sink in. And then something hit him that had him breaking into a cold sweat and his blood curdling.

If Gabby killed the man, then he needed killing . . .

How had Elizabeth known that there had been a dead body, and that it had been a man's?

★   ★   ★

The director locked himself in his office and used the secure phone restricted for use in his dealings with the Consortium. He dialed and waited for the scrambler to kick in; then, finally, the chairman answered.

"Yes?"

How this information would be received, the director had no idea. The chairman made a habit of not reacting as expected, and unfortunately, there was no way to know in advance when that would be. He held his cards close, which is probably why he stayed alive. "Cardel just reported in." The Warrior had been highly agitated. "Gabby Kincaid isn't dead, but she is out of the picture."

"I believe you'd better explain that."

The director looked out his window onto Main Street. A patrol car sat parked at the curb. "There was an incident at the lab. Gabby was bitten by mosquitoes infected with Z-4027."

"So she's dying." He sighed. "Vice President Stone will be in mourning."

"Cardel says she's critical. Her and Candace Burke."

"I'm aware of what's going on with Candace Burke."

How could he be aware? Who could have told—of course. Logan Industries. "Cardel is looking into Jaris Adahan's death."

"We know he's dead. What is the challenge?"

"It still hasn't been reported to the authorities."

"Where the hell is the body?"

"That's just it. It's disappeared."

"Tell Cardel Boudreaux he has twenty-four hours to find it. I want that murder reported and I want Kincaid's husband on ice. He caused problems at the meeting this morning, and I don't want him interfering anymore."

"Should Cardel see to that?"

"No, damn it," the chairman shouted. "Stacking up bodies isn't compatible with our mission. I want bodies, yes. But only those associated with the trial studies. Not ones that will have the hounds from hell coming down here, getting in our way."

"Yes, sir." The director walked to the window, looked down to the street, and saw Miranda Coffield talking with Sissy Blake. Miranda never engaged in idle chat, and she made him nervous. She saw too much and she never took anything at face value. Every time she looked at him, he had the feeling she saw straight through him. Naturally, he avoided Miranda. She was too smart and connected. Faulkner's wife and Sissy were respected, but neither was smart. So what did Miranda want with them?

"Keep me posted. And find that body."

The phone went dead, and the finality of the warning in that order rattled the director. Find that body. Right.

*   *   *

Miranda stood waiting on Elizabeth's dock. A boat's running lights drew closer and closer, then homed in on the dock. Her heart beat hard and fast. Elizabeth was better at this. Miranda was good with hard data, facts, and figures. But she found gauging people difficult and, frankly, after she'd taken the biggest leap of faith in her life and married Sam and then he'd proven he had no character and she'd divorced him, she had little patience with subterfuge. Amazing, considering her line of work, but true.

The engine's whine dropped to an idle and the boat eased into the slip. Its wake had water lapping at the pilings under the dock. Four grim-faced men dressed in street clothes stood on deck: Commander Conlee's team. "Gentlemen," Miranda said. "Any trouble finding us?"

"None." They followed her to the car, clearly not expecting introductions.

That, Miranda considered wise and possibly helpful. They piled into the burgundy rental and Miranda passed each of them a Smith & Wesson .38. Then she cranked the engine and pulled away from the dock.

Under the cover of darkness, she inserted the nasal tip of the clear tubing that ran through her sleeve into her nostrils, opened the valve to feed herself oxygen, and then turned on the air conditioner. "It'll cool down quickly. The humidity here is hell."

None of the men responded.

Obviously they wanted to do nothing to draw her notice or imprint in her memory. But she had taken a hard look at each of them, and gotten the one closest to Paige's size to sit in the left rear seat, which would make Paige's job easier.

She checked the backseat in the rearview. Her palms were slick with sweat on the steering wheel. Three of the men were already out cold. Glancing over at the passenger seat, she saw the fourth's head bob. Seconds later, it bobbed again. The third time, his chin stayed pressed to his chest. She took a two-block detour and then doubled back just to make sure they were all really out.

Satisfied that they were, she exhaled a swooshed breath, picked up her cell phone, and called Paige. "We're ready."

"Come on, then."

Miranda flipped closed her phone, turned off Highway 98, and continued onto Seashore Drive. Faulkner's house was less than a minute away.

The large Colonial was one door down from a street-light—just far enough away to cast concealing shadows.

Two neighbors with their leashed dogs, probably out for their last walk of the night, stood at the edge of the driveway across the street and three doors down—definitely within sighting distance—chatting and pretending not to notice the car. Miranda braked and pulled to the curb, directly in front of Faulkner's house.

The dogs started barking. Miranda's heart raced. Candace would love the risks in this. Miranda hated them. She reached into the backseat and shoved two men into a forward crunch, including the man closest to Paige's size, so they couldn't be seen by the neighbors, who *had* to be able to report seeing three people in the car and a fourth one getting in at Faulkner's. Then she turned away from the neighbors and opened the back door.

The light came on. Paige picked up the signal and appeared from around the side of Faulkner's house. Dressed in all black with a stocking hat, she got into the backseat and slammed the door. "Go, go!"

Miranda hit the gas. The tires screeched, the neighbors cursed, fists raised, and she took the corner and sped away.

Paige dumped Faulkner's family jewels on the backseat. "Which one is me?"

"The guy on the left." Miranda turned back onto 98, headed for the bank. "Did you open the valve on your oxygen?"

"Yeah." Paige sniffed to double-check, as she stuffed a diamond choker into the man's right slacks pocket and an aquamarine the size of a baby's fist into his shirt pocket. "It's eight forty. Haul ass or Darlene's out of time." She began stripping down to her underwear and putting her clothes on her "double."

"Did you switch the blanks to bullets in their guns?" Elizabeth had been ordered to provide them weapons in case they were intercepted en route, but no one wanted this team armed until absolutely necessary. And absolutely necessary translated to when Jackson found them.

"Working on it." Paige buttoned the last button on his shirt, changed out the bullets in one gun, shoved it into the waistband of one of the guys' slacks, and moved on to the next gun. "What about the boat?"

"Elizabeth's taking care of it." Miranda clicked on her turn signal and waited for the traffic light to turn green. At least there wasn't a car in the lane beside them. Hurricane Darla had pretty much wiped out the lane closest to the gulf. What asphalt hadn't been torn up was still covered with sand.

The light changed.

She made the turn, whipped into the bank's parking lot, and stopped next to a Mercedes, praying Darlene was right. Carl Blake had told Jackson the bank's security system was operating on reduced power, which meant only the surveillance cameras were working until full power to the bank was restored. According to Miranda's research, the car was parked out of the security camera's field of vision and Darlene had hidden Jackson's truck behind a cluster of palms, obscuring it from the street. Miranda switched cars and cranked the Mercedes' engine.

Paige sat one of the men in back upright, so he'd be captured on film at the appointed time, then crawled into the front seat. She pulled the mask in the stocking cap down over her face, pulled the car up to the front of the building, and parked directly in front of the ATM—in full camera view. Grabbing a ball bat from the floorboard, she got out of the car and walked up to the ATM machine, then sidestepped the camera's view, praying Miranda's research on what was and wasn't in view proved accurate.

Darlene replaced her, slamming the bat against the ATM machine and emptying it of cash, which she handed to Paige.

Paige took it, ran back to the rental car, got in, and

sped away—out of camera range to the other side of the parking lot, where Miranda sat waiting in the Mercedes.

Darlene took off in Jackson's truck. Paige jumped in Elizabeth's Mercedes, and checked her watch. "Elizabeth has to be back at Candace's by now. Darlene's going to the police station. I don't know, Miranda. The timing is just too close."

"Don't panic, Paige. I've taken care of it."

"Of what?" Paige looked at her as if she'd lost her mind. "You're good, okay? But you can't control time."

"No, I can't," Miranda admitted, pulling out to the street and smoothly into traffic. "But I can control when the bank alarm is triggered. And that won't be for another ten minutes."

"How the hell did you do that?"

"I have a knack with computers, darling. Remember?" Miranda shifted topics. "Elizabeth is in position at Candace's. She sank the boat. A shame, it had great twin Yamahas and the youth center needs a new motor for its ski boat."

"Good God, Miranda. You'd be crazy to do that. Think serial numbers. Think Leavenworth."

"Point taken." Miranda shivered and passed her cell phone to Paige. "Call Darlene."

A minute later, Paige smiled. "She's there."

"Good. We've got to meet Sissy Blake at the Silver Spoon."

"Tonight? What for?" Paige gritted her teeth. "Miranda, you know I have no patience with that woman."

"She's our alibi. Can you think of a better one?"

"Not really."

"Okay, then. She's the head of the altar committee and we're going to help her get restocked for communion, because that's what she happens to be doing."

"And just how do I explain this? I'm not even Catholic."

"You're filling in for Gabby." Miranda gave Paige a wicked grin. "Don't worry. She's not Catholic either."

*   *   *

Gabby lay motionless.

Max sat in a chair beside her bed, watching her breathe in the soft lamplight to reassure himself she was all right. A crew from Mississippi Power had finally restored electricity just after dark. The air conditioner had been working overtime for the last three hours, dragging the humidity out of the house and cooling it down.

Grateful for that, he tapped the remote and turned the TV on to the local news. A redheaded reporter stood in the bus yard, holding a microphone in Mayor Faulkner's face. "That's right," he said. "We divided Carnel Cove into four quadrants for spraying. FEMA's overseeing it personally and they're working on Area One now."

"Why is FEMA handling it, Mayor?" she asked. "City employees are starting up pretty late tonight. Is there something unusual about this spraying?"

"Nothing at all," he quickly assured her. "Mosquito activity is always worse right after a storm. All the standing water, you know. It's hot, and since so many Covers are still without power, they can't keep their houses closed up, so we have to make a special effort to get the mosquito population down fast. FEMA has the resources and has generously agreed to help."

Gabby groaned. Her eyelids fluttered open, and she lifted a hand.

Max automatically reached for it, to keep her from pulling the IV tubing out of her arm. "It's okay, Gabby. I'm right here."

"Watching me sleep, Max?" She clasped his hand and looked at him strangely.

So strangely at first he couldn't tag what he saw in her

eyes. Then he did, and half wished he hadn't recognized it. Gabby was looking at him with love and trust, and seeing it made him feel like a lowlife slug. And he didn't like it one bit.

She closed her fingers around his. "I'm glad you're home. I've missed you."

A sick feeling pitted his stomach. "Gabby, where did you put the evidence?"

"What evidence?"

"The evidence you said I'd get whether or not you were alive."

"What are you talking about, Max?"

She really had no idea. What should he do? Was it safe to push her? Would it cause more challenges? Gabby never had responded well to being pushed. "Look, bad stuff is cracking around here and I need help, not games. So if you're—"

"Games?" Anger flickered through her eyes. "I'm on my deathbed, you son of a bitch. You may not be happy to be home, but I am glad you're here." She hiked her chin. "At least I have been. Don't make me regret it."

She sounded sincere and looked it, too, as if she were torn between being angry and hurt. Not much liking being the cause of either, he remembered Keith Burke's advice, and backpedaled. "I'm sorry, honey. Listen, this is important, so I have no choice but to be frank."

"I think that would be wise. I deserve better than I've gotten. I am your wife, Max."

His wife. God, help him. He leaned forward in his chair. "Gabby, look. We need to talk. I wish this could wait until you're feeling better, but—"

"I'm not going to get better," she interrupted him. "This isn't just the flu. It doesn't feel like the flu. It feels . . . stronger. So say what you have to say." She stretched her neck, rotated it to work out a kink. "Except that you want a divorce. Feeling as rotten as I do, I will *not* be told that. Not now. So if that's it, hold your peace, or you'll wish you had."

"No, I don't want a divorce," he said, humoring her. What he wanted was for her to remember he didn't need one because they weren't married. He cupped her hand in both of his. "Gabby, I—I—um, we're not—" He couldn't say this. She was calmer when he was with her—Elizabeth had said so—and Gabby looked at him with love in her eyes. He'd seen lust in women many times, but love . . . it was different.

"Are you sure you don't want a divorce?" Gabby asked, unaware of his internal war. She stared at him, her eyes guarded, her emotional shields firmly in place.

"I'm sure." He pressed a kiss to her knuckles. "Absolutely not."

"Well, what is it then?"

"I have to tell you something. It's going to sound strange, but it is the truth, and it's critically important."

"You're making me nervous." She gave him a half-hearted smile.

He was nervous. "Do you remember Commander Conlee?"

She gave him a negative shake.

"SDU?"

"SDU?" she repeated, genuinely baffled and uneasy.

He grabbed her memory box and pulled out her wings. Holding them up, the lamplight caught them and set the shiny metal to glimmering. "Do you remember these?"

"Your wings?" She smiled. "Well, of course, Max. From your days in the military."

His wings. Not hers. "Gabby, tell me what you did before you sat on the bench."

She repeated her background cover verbatim. Not so much as one slip.

"And what about college?" He dropped the wings back into her memory box, put it back in the closet on the shelf, and then returned to her bedside. "Did you have a room-mate?"

"Of course, darling. Sybil. You know that." Sounding a little impatient, she prodded, "Why are you asking me these silly questions, Max?"

He heard Elizabeth call out from the living room, "I'm back."

"Keith said to ask them," Max lied, and then kissed her fingertips again. "Nothing to worry about. You're fine."

Gabby closed her eyes. Her lashes tickled her cheeks. She was *not* fine—and knew it down to the marrow of her bones—but she was confused and very sick. If she lay really still and quiet maybe Max and Elizabeth would think she had fallen asleep again and they would talk about what was wrong with her. Maybe then she could make some sense of what had gotten into Max. Who was this com-mander he had spoken of, and what did SDU mean?

If she was fine, then why had he quizzed her as if she weren't in her right mind? Keith had said to do it. But why? And for that matter, who was Keith?

Did it matter? She was dying; she felt her body shut-ting down. It was too late to change.

Shhh, don't tell.

Chapter Twenty-six

Darlene walked into the sheriff's office and let the glass door swing closed behind her, confident that Jackson's truck was in plain sight.

"Hey, Mrs. Coulter," Christie, the night receptionist, said from behind her desk. Her eyes were nearly swollen shut.

"Are you sick or just worn out like everyone else?"

"Allergies," Christie said. "Everything is so stirred up my meds aren't even touching them, much less working." She pulled a pink tissue from a box on her desk and blew her nose.

"Go home." Darlene rounded the desk, seizing the opportunity. She hated it that Christie was sick, but this worked out as well as if Elizabeth had planned it.

"I can't. There's no one to fill in." She punctuated that pitiful statement with a sniff.

"I'll fill in." Darlene hooked a thumb through the glass

wall toward Jackson's office, where he sat talking on the phone. "It's the only way I'll see my husband for the next few days."

Hope lighted Christie's eyes. "I do feel raunchy, but are you sure, Mrs. Coulter?"

"Positive."

"Oh, you're a guardian angel." Christie looked over her shoulder at Jackson, who had come up behind Darlene. "Is it okay, Sheriff?"

Jackson nodded. "Go on."

Christie left the building on winged feet, and Jackson hugged Darlene, kissed her on the forehead. "You are a guardian angel."

Darlene smiled up at him and claimed a kiss. "I love you, too."

The phone buzzed. Line one flashed. Darlene stretched and answered it. "Sheriff's office."

"Someone's stolen my jewels!" a woman screeched, positively hysterical.

Darlene cringed and passed the phone to Jackson. "You'd better take this one. It's Mrs. Mayor. She says some-one's stolen her jewelry—again."

Darlene couldn't resist the dig. Every time Mrs. Mayor got ticked off at Mr. Mayor, she "lost" a bauble and went bat-shit. He'd buy her a new one and within a few days, the old one would miraculously appear. Sooner or later, you'd think the man would catch on.

"What did he do to her this time?" Jackson asked Dar-lene.

She shrugged. "Could be looters, honey."

"Yeah, right. Out of everyone in town, some jewel thief just happens to hit the mayor's house. Not bloody likely." He took the phone. "Coulter."

Darlene shot him a sympathetic look and took her seat at Christie's desk, then patiently waited for the bank alarm to trigger.

★   ★   ★

It took every ounce of energy Gabby could muster to open her eyes. She was hot. Raging fever. Camel dry. Max sat beside her bed, sleeping, his head crooked at an odd angle. She reached over and touched his knee. "Max."

Startled awake, he jumped. "What?"

"Max, I'm dying. I can feel it."

Wide awake now, Max stiffened, his heart knocking against his ribs. "Gabby, no." Pain flashed through his chest, settled in like a ten-ton weight. Considering her memory, he was a bastard for telling her this, but he felt it, and if she was really dying, he might never again have the chance to tell her. Worse, she'd die never knowing. "I don't want to lose you. I feel like I've just found you." And he had. Lord, but he had. "I love the way you look at me and the way you make me feel. I love what I see in your eyes when I look at you. You're special, Gabby. To me, you're special." He swallowed a hard knot from his throat. His voice cracked. "Don't give up, honey. Please, just don't give up."

"I don't want to." A tear rolled down her cheek.

"Don't. You choose, Gabby. Remember? You choose." Smelling her fear and his own, he brushed a kiss to her forehead, and then called Elizabeth.

Minutes later she arrived, dressed in her fluffy pink robe and slippers, and joined Max at Gabby's bedside. "I've got to get Erickson," Max said.

"Erickson?" She asked, a frown creasing the skin between her eyebrows.

Only he could help her. "I'll explain later." Stabbing a finger in Gabby's direction, he issued an order. "Don't you die on me, Gabby Kincaid. I mean it." Then he rushed out of the house to the Jeep. Seconds later, it was spewing rock down the driveway.

★   ★   ★

At midnight, Max stomped the gas and drove around a row of seven long-bed trucks. They were working around the clock, hauling off debris. He cut a sharp left and swung around a hedgerow of cut-up limbs and tree trunks stacked alongside the road, waiting for pickup, and then hooked a hard right past the beached *Daddy's Toy* into L.I.'s parking lot.

Minutes later, he found Erickson in the lab, washing his hands at the sink.

"Gabby's dying," he said without preamble.

Erickson stiffened, paused, then continued to wash his hands. "I'm sorry, Max." He turned to face him. "I lost my wife to cancer and my son to EEE. I know what it's like."

"I don't want your sympathy." Max swallowed hard, deliberately leashed his temper and lowered his voice. "I want your help."

"If I could give it to you, I would." Erickson looked him right in the eye.

"Candace is better. It isn't from Keith's vaccine." Max knew he was risking the bank, talking openly here. Intel heard every word, which meant Commander Conlee would know everything within minutes. But Max had no choice. Not if he wanted Gabby to live, and he wanted her to live more than he feared dying.

"What's your point, Max?" Erickson rinsed his hands, cranked the water faucet off, and jerked a paper towel from the wall dispenser.

"When Keith came to check on Gabby, you stayed with Candace. Right after you left, she started improving. Keith's vaccine would have worked before then. Her improvement had to be a direct result of something you did."

"I didn't do anything." Erickson tossed the paper towel into the trash bin, setting its stainless top to swinging and casting streaks of light across the lab. "Don't you think if I could save either of them I would? Jesus, God, Max. I'm not here because Swift offered me the most money or best stock options and 401(k). Frankly, Keith Burke offered more. But here, I had the opportunity to test in ways I couldn't there. That mattered most to me."

Max needed more facts. Something had turned Candace around and whatever it was, Max needed it for Gabby. "Why did that matter most?"

"Because I failed." Erickson blinked hard, and his shoulders slumped. His burden was heavy. "When my wife was dying, she asked one thing of me. Just one thing. That I take care of our son. That's all she asked, Max." Erickson paused, swallowed hard, and his expression crumbled. "Jeremy was all I had left of her, and I let him get EEE and die. I didn't protect him."

Guilt was a bitch. Earned or not, it clung like a parasite anywhere it found a welcome sign. "You hoped the Z-4027 project would yield a cure for EEE."

Erickson nodded, his Adam's apple bobbing in his throat. "Believe me, if I could cure Gabby, I would. But I can't, Max. I . . . can't."

Erickson was telling the truth. Max's hope crushed and died. "What about the missing canister? The one with the black band?"

"It was nothing." Erickson shrugged. "Dr. Swift found it shortly after you left the lab."

"Did you verify its contents?"

"Of course." The idea of not checking them came across clearly as alien. "Everything was in order. One of Dr. Swift's team members was prepping for some in-house trial studies on the pesticide contract and had forgotten to sign the canister out. He's been reprimanded." Erickson grunted. "I don't like the idea of being forced to use this pesticide before the tests are done—neither did Dr. Swift—but considering the incident," he lifted a hand toward the plywood-covered window, "we don't have a lot of choice."

Still focusing on Gabby, Max turned Erickson's attention. "Did anyone else come to see Candace while you were there?"

"Paige and Miranda were in and out." He rubbed at his temple and thought back. "Mayor Faulkner and Dr. Swift dropped by on their way to the bus yard—oh, and Sissy came in for a moment on her way to Mass."

"Sissy?" Max had heard her mentioned, but couldn't recall by whom.

"Sissy Blake," Erickson said. "Carl's wife."

Right. The banker who owned the fleet of spraying trucks, half the real estate in town, who had missed the meeting at the mayor's because a tree had crashed through his son's bedroom roof and he'd had to meet the insurance adjuster. Max dug deeper, and recalled Elizabeth's mention of Sissy. Show and no substance. She wasn't one of the ladies. So why had she come by Candace's house?

The red phone rang on Erickson's desk. As he lifted the receiver, he told Max, "You'll have to excuse me. Classified call."

Max nodded and turned toward the lab door.

"Wait a second." Erickson sounded baffled. "It's for you, Max."

It had to be Commander Conlee. Intel sure hadn't wasted any time reporting what they'd picked up on the remote viewer.

Erickson passed the receiver, his curious look demanding an answer. "I'm a subject matter expert assigned to FEMA for Hurricane Darla," he explained, surprised Faulkner hadn't spread the news through town already. They'd been through this at the meeting. "Health risks."

"Ah." Erickson nodded and then stepped outside the lab door, into the corridor. When the heavy door closed behind him, Max lifted the receiver to his ear. "Yes, sir."

"I'm not even going to ask what the hell is going on there, but I'd better have a full report by daybreak. Withhold nothing, Grayson, or so help me, I'll send in a tactical team and shut this son of a bitch down so fast you'll get diver's bends."

Daybreak. Between now and then, Max needed a pocketful of miracles. "Yes, sir."

"Intel has tapped into Merlin. The news isn't good."

Merlin. The public health system linking Florida's public health departments to doctors and hospitals to warn officials of trends, outbreaks, or potential epidemics. Why should it be good news? He hadn't caught a break on this entire mission.

"Carnel Cove Memorial Hospital has reported seventeen cases of EEE to the CDC. At their recommendation, Mayor Faulkner is putting Carnel Cove under quarantine."

Terrific. The Centers for Disease Control levies a quarantine and no outside help can get into Carnel Cove, and the Warrior running loose in the Cove can't get out. *Batting a thousand.* "Have we intercepted the samples going to the CDC?"

"Yes." Conlee let out a pregnant sigh. "Rapid symptom manifestation in all seventeen cases suggests Z-4027 contamination."

"Damn it." Max bounced the heel of his fist against Erickson's desktop.

"There is some good news."

"I could use a little," Max admitted.

"The state epidemiologist feels all seventeen patients were infected before we began spraying in Area One."

So much for that good news. "We can't make that assumption, sir."

"Why not?"

"Logan Industries is providing the pesticide chemicals for spraying. Dr. Erickson lied about Dr. Swift finding the missing black-banded canister. I presume you're familiar with it?"

"Hell, yes." His voice muddied, as if he were chomping down on his stubby cigar. "Did Erickson confess to you?"

"No, sir. But I'm convinced the black-banded canister is still missing—gut instinct. You're aware of Candace Burke's condition, correct?"

"Keith's been keeping me posted."

"Well, she's making a miraculous recovery. The change occurred during Erickson's watch over her. The mayor and Swift stopped by there, but I'm near certain they didn't do anything to bring about her recovery. Not without Erickson knowing it."

"You think Erickson gave her a prototype vaccine he's developed?"

"That is my guess, yes." Remembering the pain in Erickson at failing his wife, uncertainty attacked Max. If not a prototype injection, then what had he done to bring about her recovery? And if the missing black-banded canister didn't contain a prototype vaccine, what was in it? He was almost afraid to add to his speculation because Conlee wanted answers, not more questions, and yet Max had to consult him on this. "Commander, ask Dr. Richardson to review the seventeen cases."

"He already has."

"Yes, sir. But ask him to do it again. Erickson and Swift were arguing over the canister being missing. If Erickson had a prototype in it that could cure, he wouldn't have been scared, and he was terrified."

"Where are you going with this, Max?"

"I'm not sure just yet. Something's nagging at me. What if that missing canister was of Z-4027, and not a vaccine or a pesticide prototype?"

"Wouldn't Erickson know that?"

"Not if someone else switched the bands on the canisters. All the others are yellow. Only that one was black."

"Carl Blake's trucks sprayed Area One, and it is closest to the lab, Max, where we'd expect to see the most dense population of the infected mosquitoes. We're under the hammer, and this could be a wild-goose chase. Considering proximity, it's highly likely the mosquitoes from the lab infected these people."

"Yes, sir. I agree this could be nothing. The number of infections reported isn't inflated beyond normal expectations. But Candace *is* better and Erickson *is* the reason. I can't prove it, sir, but I know it."

"Okay." Conlee had to be skeptical, but he trusted Max's instincts enough to agree to the request. "I'll have Richardson take a look. In the meantime, could you please focus on finding some concrete connections so we can get a grip on exactly what the hell is going on there?"

"I'm trying, sir."

"I know. But about an hour ago, SDU was called in on the other two infestations."

"Texas and California?" Max recalled the cotton crop and vineyard infections.

"Yeah." Irritation filled Conlee's voice. "So far, there's no hard evidence of a common thread. I don't have to tell you what that means."

The Global Warriors had unleashed an economic war on the U.S. And apparently, they had unleashed it all across the country.

That news was worse than it sounded because historically the Global Warriors never acted for themselves. Their goal was money, and nothing but money. Someone had hired them and paid them well to launch this attack. And as of this moment, the U.S. had no idea who.

The commander launched into a detailed briefing that lasted thirty-seven minutes: a record for the normally succinct Commander Conlee. They were just finishing up when Max's cell phone rang.

He ended the call with Conlee and then answered the cell. "Grayson."

"Max, it's Elizabeth. Gabby is really going down fast. Dr. Erickson is here. If you want to see her again . . ." Her voice cracked on a sob. "Oh, Max. You'd better get home."

Erickson was there? He'd left the lab when Max had taken the commander's call, but why had he gone to Gabby's? He'd said he couldn't help her. But not being able to help her didn't preclude him from inflicting harm. A sick feeling hollowed Max's stomach, and he headed for the door.

Swift seemed like the logical choice for corruption inside Logan Industries. He had hired Erickson; he remained in control of both Z-4027 projects—the vaccine and the pesticide; he had a thing for Candace; and he and Faulkner had been with her during Keith's absence. Swift had had access to Candace. With Faulkner diverting Erickson, Swift could have done whatever had been done to stimulate her recovery.

But what if Swift wasn't the corrupt contact at Logan Industries? What if Erickson was?

Erickson, who was now there with unfettered access to a helpless Gabby? Gabby, who if her memory was intact, could know Erickson was the guilty party.

That makes her a high risk in his book, Max. He'll eliminate the threat.

Max broke into a full run. "Elizabeth, watch Erickson. Do *not* leave him alone with Gabby. It's important," Max said in a rush, jerking open the Jeep's door and then sliding inside. The engine roared to life, and he gunned it. "I'm on my way."

Chapter Twenty-seven

Max rushed into Gabby's bedroom.

She lay sleeping, and Elizabeth stood beside her bed, holding a Smith & Wesson .38 aimed at the bedroom door. "Whoa! Put that down, okay?"

"Sorry." Elizabeth pointed the barrel down, toward the floor.

Had she shot Erickson? "Where is he?"

"He left." Elizabeth slid the gun into her slacks pocket, adjusted the covers up over Gabby's shoulders, and then turned to Max. "I don't know what happened with her. One minute, she was in serious trouble. Then the next, she was pulling out of it. I came back into the room as soon as you told me not to leave him alone with her."

"Armed? Did you feel threatened by him?"

"No, I was already armed." She glanced toward the window. "Since right after you left, I've had that 'watched' feeling that makes your skin crawl. I checked everything—

even outside. Didn't see anyone." She looked frustrated by that. "But I know someone was lurking, watching us, Max. You get a sense of those things, you know?"

He did. The hair on your neck stands straight up, a warning shoots up your back, the roof of your mouth tingles, and a little voice inside screams that there's danger. He'd had that same feeling several times here, but he, too, had failed to catch anyone spying on them. Still, he knew the man was there, and that little voice warned him he was the second Global Warrior who had tried to attack Gabby. "So Erickson didn't give you any trouble?"

"None at all." Elizabeth shrugged. "He acted normal. Finished the exam and then left."

"Did he do anything to her?"

"Not that I saw." Again, Elizabeth glanced out the window, watched intently for a moment, and then turned to look back at Max. "But I called you from the living room, so I can't be sure what he did while I was out there. His hands were empty coming in and going out of here, though." She motioned to an array of equipment littering the top of Gabby's dresser. "He used Keith's gear."

Max stepped up to the bed, looked down on Gabby. She looked comfortable, as if she were just napping, and she didn't seem as far away, though he couldn't say why or even explain how he sensed it. It was just a feeling.

"Her breathing is a lot better," Elizabeth said, sounding a little more at ease. "She drank a couple sips of water. Erickson said Keith would be over just as soon as Miranda could get there. Paige is worthless on these things."

She was a strong empath. Situations such as this would be sheer hell for her. Max glanced over. "Did Keith say how Candace was doing?"

"Better." Relief flooded Elizabeth's face. "Her fever broke, Max."

She didn't understand that any better than he did, though he strongly suspected Erickson or Swift had facilitated it. "That's good news." It was for Candace but not for Gabby. Envy swam through Max, and guilt.

She didn't stir. Max sat down on the foot of her bed. Elizabeth walked from the window to the chair beside it and then sat down.

Automatically, Max clasped Gabby's hand, held it in both of his. He probably should let this wait, but he couldn't hold off on everything. Not if he wanted to find out about this attack and get the situation here controlled. "Elizabeth," he said, deciding to tackle the matter now. "Earlier you said there had been a man's body in the garage."

She crossed her legs at her ankles and swiped her hair back from her shoulder. "Yes."

The woman had no intention of giving an inch. He'd have to be blunt and ask her directly. "How did you know that?"

She dipped her chin, looked at Gabby, and then back at him. "William and I were married twenty-five years, Max. We kept no secrets."

Okay. He supposed that was pretty normal for some married couples. But what did that have to do with this situation?

Elizabeth went on. "During his days on the bench, William often reviewed evidence, including blood splatters. I was a sounding board for him. I listened, and I learned." She leaned forward, laced her hands atop her knees, and looked Max in the eye. "I've listened to Gabby talk about you for the last year, too." She softened her voice. "And while I know she loves you, I also know she isn't married to you."

Max should deny it. If he had any sense at all, he would deny it and not break his cover. Yet something warned him against it. Elizabeth wasn't the kind of woman who would be placated with lies. *Substance, not show.* The last thing he needed to do was jeopardize being in the ladies' good graces. He couldn't lie, so instead he held his silence.

She softly smiled. "Have you swept the house for listening devices?"

He nodded, relieved his decision had been a smart move.

"Months before William told me, I concluded that Gabby was an SDU covert operative."

Shocked, Max nearly fell off the bed.

Elizabeth didn't skip a beat. "I'm assuming you're also SDU since you're Gabby's absentee husband." She stared pointedly at their clasped hands.

Max finally found his voice. "Do you know what SDU is?"

Elizabeth nodded.

"How?" Conlee would have had her killed. It wasn't possible.

"William was a legal adviser for SDU before we moved to Carnel Cove."

"He told you?" Max couldn't believe it. Why in the name of God would William Powell put her in that kind of jeopardy? But it did explain Powell's picking up on Judge Abernathy's judicial corruption here. He was trained to pick up the threads and see the signs.

"Of course he didn't tell me. That wouldn't be ethical. William was always ethical, Max. That aside, he would never willingly put me in danger." She smiled to take the bite out of her sharp tone. "I've always known it, but I wasn't aware that William knew I was aware of it until just before he died."

"He realized you knew?"

She nodded. "I'm not sure for how long." Leaning back, she propped an elbow on the arm of her chair. "When he was dying, he told me and Candace to go to Gabby with anything we found, and to get her to run some lab tests on his tissue samples. He said we could trust her—only her."

"But he didn't mention SDU."

"Not specifically. William wouldn't. But I knew, and he knew I knew." She paused a second, as if giving her emotions a moment to settle down. "Commander Conlee is not a stranger to me, Max—to any of the ladies, actually. He wanted William's blood and tissue samples, if you'll recall, and Home Base is having to move to a less densely populated location."

She paused as if weighing what next to reveal. "Conlee investigated us, but we also investigated him. Miranda is a whiz with computers, and you'd be positively awed at Candace's capabilities. After Paige came with me to meet him, she filled in the blanks for us. Candace and Miranda had already met him, of course, through their defense contracts at Logan Industries."

Conlee knew what they had learned and he hadn't canceled them. How had he avoided it? Did it have something to do with Home Base's move? Carnel Cove would be an ideal location. SDU had a built-in cover with L.I. already working defense contracts. There was also that construction going on downstairs on Sublevels 1 and 2, where he'd snagged the plywood to cover the broken lab window. The move would have protected Candace and Miranda, but not Elizabeth and Paige. Perplexed, he continued to think this possibility through, but Elizabeth reclaimed his attention.

Her voice softened. "William asked us—the ladies, as he and Keith call us—to protect Gabby. Because of the judicial corruption. That's when we brought her into our circle."

Max couldn't believe it. He just couldn't believe it. So all the ladies knew. Good God, Oversight was going to blow a gasket. "Did Gabby tell you—?"

"Gracious no, Max." Elizabeth guffawed. "Gabby doesn't know we know about her. Of course we all have known for months, but we can't tell her. It would put her between a rock and a hard place. She'd have to turn us in or be eaten alive with guilt for not turning us in. We'd never put her in that position."

"So why have you put me in it?"

"Because Gabby loves you, and we think your motives are pure. You don't believe her feelings go beyond friendship, but her best friend says Gabby's loved you for five years."

Sybil? Stunned, he had to search for his voice. "I don't believe it."

"Believe or not as you choose, Max." Elizabeth reached for a cup of tea he suspected had long since gone cold. "But know we have protected and will continue to protect her." She looked him straight in the eye. "Which is why, if you're here to cancel Gabby, you need to insist Commander Conlee revise his orders."

It was a moot point. Even Conlee knew by now Max had no intentions of executing those orders. "Elizabeth, I haven't admitted that there is an SDU or a commander, or a Conlee. I haven't admitted anything."

"Are you denying it?"

If he did, she'd probably shoot him. "I'm saying everything you've said is conjecture."

"Do you know underestimation is the number-one cause of death of SDU operatives?"

The training manual quoted verbatim. Miranda had snagged the operatives training manual? She was good. Pushing, he said, "You have no proof."

"I don't need any. I'm not preparing a case for a court of law."

"What are you doing—other than conjecturing yourself into a corner with no escape?"

"This conjecture is fact, Maxwell Grayson, and don't waste your breath or insult my intelligence by trying to intimidate me. I fear no one short of God. William's gone.

I've walked through grief's hell and survived it. What could possibly hurt me that much again?"

Elizabeth didn't bother waiting for him to answer. "My point is that we gave William our word to protect Gabby. I had hoped that wouldn't include protecting her from you, too, but if it does, then so be it. None of us is going to stand by and watch you murder her in the name of national security." Elizabeth lowered her gaze to his hands, still holding Gabby's. "Not that I'm sure you could kill her. But just in case you think you can, you had better talk to Conlee. If one hair on her head is touched intentionally, we'll stir up such a ruckus you'll all pray for death to escape. That's a promise, not a threat," she warned him. "The ladies of Carnel Cove might be a small group, but we both know small groups can be very effective, don't we, Max?"

SDU certainly had been. Because he couldn't answer, he just stared at her.

"Among us, we have a lot of powerful friends—on both sides of the law, and in influential positions."

Dangerously stubborn, but he had to admire her passion. She made no bones about protecting Gabby, regardless of what it took. He respected her conviction, a lot. "Does Gabby know that you're aware?"

"I told you, we'd never tell her."

"But does she know it?" he insisted. "The way you knew with William?"

Elizabeth hiked her chin and refused to answer. "I think I could use another cup of tea." She picked up her cup and saucer and left for the kitchen.

Watching her go, he frowned at her back. She obviously wasn't worried that he would report the ladies to Commander Conlee. Max scratched his head. Exactly why was that?

★   ★   ★

What in the world were they talking about? Gabby wondered. *So cryptic and mysterious.* They had clearly been talking about her, and yet nothing they said made the least bit of sense. They might as well have been speaking Greek.

Gabby opened her eyes. She looked at their joined hands resting on Max's knee, and groaned in earnest.

"Are you okay?" Worry lighted his eyes.

"My head feels like a road crew has been taking turns at it with a jackhammer." Her stomach was full of knots, too. Some of them because she felt like hell, but some stemmed from not understanding what was going on. What was this SDU thing Max and Elizabeth had been discussing? It sounded so ominous. If Gabby should know about it, why couldn't she remember it? She remembered them. And why hadn't Max straightened Elizabeth out on the matter of their marriage? Of course, they were married. So why hadn't he disputed her? These things just didn't make sense. None of them made sense.

Some people hallucinate with this infection, Gabby. If it happens, don't be frightened.

Erickson had told her that. Obviously, he had been right. Everything except Max seemed alien to her. He felt familiar and right on every level: from his looks to the feel of his hand holding hers to the scent of his skin.

Max blew out a breath that could only be interpreted as intense frustration. "You've worried me." He gave her hand a squeeze. "Are you okay?"

Why would he worry if they weren't married? He wouldn't. She remembered their wedding . . . more or less. She remembered her wedding gown. The seed pearls and lace and long train, and Max in a warm gray tux, looking like the hero of every Cinderella's dreams. She definitely remembered posing for that photograph. A little of her tension melted. "Much better."

She didn't remember the ceremony, the church or flowers, or making vows to Max. But she was a sick woman;

everything in her mind was jumbled right now. She rubbed the sheet between her forefinger and thumb. The rough grating felt good. She just needed to relax to remember. She certainly shouldn't lie here and give herself garbage for memory problems—especially not after the torture she'd put herself through on finally taking the plunge.

She *had* taken the plunge! Sybil had teased her mercilessly about getting married. She'd mailed Gabby a noose, shackles, and a ball and chain. Candace had seen the stuff and freaked, certain Gabby was being stalked by a crazy person.

That she remembered in humiliating detail, but not her wedding.

Max checked her temperature. "Fever's down substantially. When Dr. Erickson was here, did he give you something?"

"I don't remember." She swiped at her hair, tangled and loose, sweeping it away from her face. "My mind's been playing tricks on me, but—I just don't know."

"Gabby was dying," Elizabeth said. "She couldn't string three words together and she wasn't lucid. Not even remotely lucid. She's turned the corner on the infection. Erickson had to have done something to her. There's no other explanation."

"Was anyone else here?"

"No." Elizabeth frowned. "No one."

What a quagmire of a mission. Regardless of what Max did now, he had loose ends and a bigger maze. And still no evidence.

He'd searched and re-searched every possible place, found nothing, and there just wasn't anywhere else to look.

"There's a plate of food in the fridge for you. Pot roast and new potatoes." Elizabeth walked over and clasped his shoulder. "It's really late and I know you haven't eaten all day. I'll keep watch over her."

He glanced out the window wondering what to do.

Everything he learned revealed something that appeared important but unconnected. Yet, the connections had to be there. He just had to find them. He could further interrogate Elizabeth, but shouldn't. She offered aid without it, and what she didn't reveal on her own, all of SDU was safer with him not knowing.

"Go on and eat." Elizabeth urged him with a tug at his shoulder. "I imagine the mayor is going to want another meeting soon, especially since Carl Blake missed the first one. I just heard on Fast-Track News that they've started spraying Area Two."

Max didn't know how to react to that news. Commander Conlee had Dr. Richardson looking at the Carnel Cove victims' records, and Stan Mullin from FEMA was checking the contents of the pesticide spray, but so far, there was no word on whether the spray was preventing deaths in Carnel Cove or facilitating the infection's spread and causing them.

At the moment, Max wouldn't bet a nickel either way.

Chapter Twenty-eight

Darlene tapped her fingers on Christie's desk, staring at the bank alarm signal, willing it to go off. Miranda's ten minutes had long since come and gone.

"I'm going to take Mrs. Mayor's report." Jackson tugged on his cap. "Radio Bobby to check in with the waste trucks as time permits. Make sure they report seeing anything suspicious. We want to keep down the looting."

"Why don't I just radio the trucks?"

"Storm damage, babe. There isn't a truck in the county with radio power right now. They went hi-tech. Not equipped with CBs anymore."

Darlene's stomach plummeted. Would the bank alarm still work? Miranda had said it would, but had she known this? And so much time had passed.

Jackson left and Darlene resisted the urge to call Miranda by the skin of her teeth. Instead, she put on a fresh pot of coffee. She'd give it another two minutes. If nothing had come in by then, she'd have to act. Jackson could pass the bank and not notice the rental. The men could be waking up or even be long gone.

The alarm signaled exactly one hour late.

"Thank you, God!" Darlene grabbed the radio headset and paged Jackson, relayed notice, then listened to him confirm and radio Bobby to meet him at the bank. Daylight Savings Time. Carl hadn't altered the alarm's clock.

The knots in her stomach that should loosen up tightened. She dialed Miranda's, let the phone ring twice, and then hung up.

Miranda would pass the word that the alarm had sounded. She sipped at her coffee, answered two calls about people breaking curfew, dispatched Bobby to cover them, then waited.

Finally, Jackson radioed. "Bobby, get to the bank, pronto."

"Yes, sir, Sheriff. Minor delay. A tourist got tanked up and needed calming down."

"You take him to jail?"

"Naw, Sheriff. He got bad news today, so I just helped him get to sleep."

"Are there going to be bruises?"

"Only the ones his wife swears he got falling off the roof."

"Darlene?"

She nearly tipped her chair in an effort to reach the radio. "Go ahead, Jackson."

"Make sure all four cells are ready to receive prisoners."

"All of them?" She let out a held breath. He had the team in custody! "Did you bust up another hurricane party?"

"No drunks, tonight. It looks like a bank robbery. Get Carl Blake and have him run the ATM security tape over to the office."

"Right away, Jackson."

"And, you're not going to believe this."

"What's that?" She released the button to transmit, anticipation building in her stomach.

"Faulkner just pulled me over. Looks like Mrs. Mayor really was robbed this time."

"Seriously?" *Yes, yes, yes!* Darlene bounced on her chair. "Well, I'll be."

"Seems these bank robbers have had a busy night."

The ladies had done it! Darlene bit her lips to hide her excitement from her voice. She'd been married to Jackson too long for him to miss it. "They robbed the bank *and* the mayor?"

"Sure looks that way. The aquamarine she reported stolen last winter showed up in a shirt pocket during patdown."

Remembering who those men were, the training they had, and their abilities, worried her. "You be careful, Jackson."

"Always," he said. "Get busy on those cells."

Darlene phoned Carl Blake and then Elizabeth, keeping one ear on the radio.

"Hello," Elizabeth said softly, sounding half-asleep, though Darlene knew all the ladies were wide awake, awaiting word.

"It's Darlene Coulter, Elizabeth," she said, mindful of the recordings. "Sorry to phone so late, but I'm in a jam."

"No problem, dear," Elizabeth said. "Can I help?"

"I'm hoping you can. I was supposed to take care of Candace in the morning, but Christie is suffering something awful from her allergies so I sent her home. I'm filling in for her at the station and Jackson just radioed that he's bringing in four prisoners. I've got to get the cells ready, which means I won't get a wink of sleep tonight. Could you fill in at Candace's?"

"Certainly." Elizabeth paused, obviously hiding her relief. "What time?"

"Seven," Darlene picked a time out of thin air.

"I'll be there." Elizabeth sighed. "Night."

"Night." Darlene dropped the receiver into the cradle. Elizabeth would call the other ladies. Then, they'd wait for one final call before they all called it a night. The one Darlene would make, telling them Conlee's second team was cooling their heels in Jackson's jail cells.

Frankly, that time couldn't come fast enough to suit her. These men were trained operatives and there were four of them. They could take Jackson down.

Cold fear gripped her heart. Darlene gritted her teeth and went to check the cells, hoping she wouldn't regret the ladies' decision to not just shoot them. The thought of killing turned her stomach, but not so much as Jackson being hurt.

★　★　★

Max opened the front door and couldn't believe his eyes. "Candace?"

"Hi." She stepped inside, dressed in white slacks and sandals and a pale green sleeveless top. Dark circles rimmed her eyes and she appeared weak and weary but determined.

"You look a hell of a lot better than the last time I saw you." Blunt, but true. Her recovery was nothing short of a miracle.

"Don't be fooled. You should feel it from the inside." She touched his arm with a shaky hand. "When the fever broke, the symptoms started to ease up. I'm tired as hell, someone's still playing baseball inside my head, and my days and nights are mixed up, but I think I'm going to make it." She walked through the entryway into the living room.

"Elizabeth is worried about Gabby. I wanted to see her myself."

Max was worried about Gabby, too. She certainly hadn't made Candace's kind of comeback. "She's sleeping now. Her temperature is down. It's not yet normal, but it is better."

Candace nodded, looked as if she wanted to ask something, but then thought better of it.

"Sit down." Max motioned toward the sofa. "Would you like something to drink?"

"Maybe some juice, but not now. In a minute." She dropped onto the sofa, crossed her long legs in front of her. "I wanted to thank you for taking care of things at L.I. I don't know what I'd have done if you and Gabby hadn't come."

"Glad to do it." He sat down in a chair across from her. He should dig a little before risking a bold move, but there was too little time left to waste it on typical tactics. He didn't totally trust the ladies, but they hadn't exposed Gabby and he didn't have a lot of options left to try. One thing he didn't doubt was that the ladies had *not* made the attempt on Gabby's life. Nothing about them was consistent with those who hired Global Warriors. "Candace, something strange is going on here. You do realize that."

"Yes." She didn't hesitate or try to avoid the truth.

That encouraged Max to take the plunge. "Elizabeth and I have been very frank. I need to be frank with you, too. I'm nearly out of time."

"By all means, Max."

She didn't ask "time" on what. That was an excellent sign. "Are you aware of any leaks that might have come from the ladies about Gabby?"

"No, I'm not." She leaned against the sofa arm, braced her head with her arm. "If there had been one, we'd all know about it, Max. And we'd take the necessary steps to nullify any complications caused. That's how we operate."

"No secrets."

Her eyes twinkled. "Not from each other."

He believed her. It fit with everything he'd seen in all of them. "Your recovery is nothing short of a miracle."

She nodded, dipped her chin. "Ask what you really want to know, Max. If I can answer, I will."

Her willingness relieved and worried him. "Do you remember anything special about Erickson caring for you?"

She dropped her gaze to the coffee table, to the magazines Gabby had laid out.

Max's gaze followed. *Judicial Review, Weekly Standard,* and a variety of other magazines that all had oak trees on the covers, lay fanned there. Something hitched in his chest at knowing he was the only person in the world other than Gabby who understood the significance of those oaks. "Candace?" he prodded. "It's important."

"I know." She took in a heavy breath then looked up at him. "Do you want to know for Gabby, or because you're after Erickson?"

Max could and should lie, but she deserved better. "Gabby needs help, Candace. But if Erickson is doing something he shouldn't be, then both."

"I'm sorry, then." Her expression turned somber, her eyes distant. "I can't help you."

Erickson *had* given Candace and Gabby something. It had saved Candace and was helping Gabby. But why the different reactions? Why hadn't Gabby made a full recovery, too? She hadn't been as critically affected by the infection. Candace was protecting Erickson because he had saved her life. Max understood that, and yet . . . "There are seventeen other people in Carnel Cove's hospital with this now, Candace. There are more in south Florida and even more in Texas and Mexico."

"I heard on the news where they'd tracked some of the cases back to a flight from Paris."

"Yes." He should leave it there. "But there are others,

too. This isn't a local problem. If we don't stop it, it's going to become a continental crisis, if not an international one."

"Keith told me there had been isolated cases reported in nineteen countries."

"Twenty-one, last I heard." Max had her attention; guilt and fear had replaced the resolve in her eyes. He used it, and drove his point home. "If Erickson can help save them, then he must do it, Candace. How can he justify not helping them? How can you?"

Candace slid him a level look meant to pin him to the proverbial wall. "The same way I can justify hunting down the bastards who pulled me into this mess at Logan Industries."

Fabulous. A rich and gutsy vigilante. Now he was certain nothing more could possibly go wrong on this mission from hell because everything already had.

The commander would not be happy, which meant the rest of SDU would be miserable.

★   ★   ★

Voices in the living room awakened Gabby. She crawled out of bed and headed to the door. When she put her hand on the doorknob, her instincts shouted not to interrupt. She opened the door a crack and blatantly eavesdropped, too confused and afraid to feel shame.

Why did Candace think Max would harm Gabby? Why hadn't he taken exception?

She listened, trusting her instincts and lacking confidence in anything else, but the conversation was as cryptic as the one between Max and Elizabeth. Gabby felt like a player in a game where there were only secret rules. The talks were as confusing as Max's treatment of her.

He said the right things. He was attentive and caring but distant, almost afraid of her. And he certainly didn't look at her the way a man normally looks at his wife.

Maybe she wasn't married to him. Elizabeth had said she wasn't, and Max hadn't denied it . . .

No, that was absurd. Gabby might be uncertain about a lot of things, but being married to Max wasn't one of them. Unless the marriage was a trick of her mind—and it could be. Max *hadn't* denied it. Yet why would he bother? Surely he considered the comment as absurd as she did. Their wedding photo, complete with tux and bridal gown and veil, sat on the fireplace mantel, for pity's sake, and she vividly remembered—what? The wedding ceremony? Their honeymoon? Them living together?

Gabby paced between the window and bed. Not a single image came to mind. She glanced at her reflection in the windowpane, wishing the moon were out so it wasn't so inky dark outside, and tried to remember something—anything.

She failed, and tried again. And then again. Frustrated and fearful, she turned her back to the glass. Why couldn't she remember them living together? Why could she remember all the *words* of the wedding ceremony, their honeymoon to Paris, but not recall a single *visual image*?

A shiver rippled through her back, up her spine to her neck. It was possible, she supposed, but they had made love. That she recalled physically, emotionally, and spiritually in minute detail. Yet if they weren't married, why pretend they were? And why was pretending so important even she was unsure of the truth?

Okay. The infection could be responsible. She'd been really sick. But Max hadn't. If there was a pretense, he was a party to it. She'd just ask him.

Max's voice carried to the bedroom from the living room. "I love my wife, Candace."

"Glad to hear it," Candace said. "Now tell me that your wife is Gabby. Because word on all fronts is that you act like a lover and friend, but not like a husband."

Obviously she knew the truth about this, too. So why push? Testing him. Had to be. "Yes, Gabby is my wife."

Shaking, Gabby eased the door closed. Max had confirmed their marriage and Candace's questions clearly had offended him—they would've offended Gabby, too—but she didn't quite believe him, and she couldn't just walk up to him now and say, "Are we really married, or for some odd reason just faking it?"

A spouse was a pretty important thing to forget. If he posed that question to her, she'd be devastated and angry. She didn't want Max devastated or angry.

But Gabby did want the truth. She *felt* married to him; would have sworn she was married to him. And the thought of it's being a sham caused pain that ran so deep inside her she couldn't tell where it started or stopped.

It couldn't be true. She paced her bedroom, shutting out the pain, her mind racing. Pausing at her dresser, she stared at her reflection, scouring her memory, her eyes wide and haunted. She prayed for answers, failed to find them, and then for any tiny clue, but again failed.

Her instincts strummed. It was vitally important, urgent, that she find the truth. She dug through the closet, the dresser drawers, the nightstands. She found a lot of unexpected items, and one shocking one: a gun in her purse. But she was a judge. Often threatened. She had a permit to carry it in her wallet. She didn't recall getting the permit but obviously she had; it was there. And if she had a permit, she apparently knew how to shoot the gun, though she couldn't remember that, either.

Trying to be quiet, to avoid being heard by Max and Candace, she tugged at the nightstand drawer. Something jammed it. She tugged harder and finally jerked it loose, then pulled it out. Taped to its underside was a heavy brown envelope. Her heart beat fast, thumping against her ribs, and she swallowed hard. Her instincts again hummed. Once she opened the envelope, her life would never again be the same. Yet she couldn't deliberately live a lie. Since college, Sybil had warned Gabby that she couldn't shut out what she didn't want to hear, though over the years, God knew Gabby had tried.

She stilled. She *remembered* that conversation with Sybil—from college. How could she remember that but not her wedding?

Frightened and vulnerable, Gabby sat on the edge of the bed and tugged her robe over her chest. She closed her eyes, took in three deep breaths to calm down, and then opened the envelope—and wished to hell she hadn't.

Five sets of passports, marriage licenses, and drivers' licenses spilled across her lap.

All five sets had her photograph and description.

All five sets bore her signature.

And all five sets had been issued under different names.

Pain, sharp and swift, stabbed through her. Sadness chased it. She should call Sybil. She would know the truth. Gabby reached for the phone, dialed the first three numbers, and then hung up and jerked away as if the receiver had burned her hand.

She couldn't call Sybil. Not about this. In the past, they had shared everything: Sybil's lousy marriage to and divorce from Mr. Snip-It, her falling in love with Jonathan Westford. Gabby had been scared to death Sybil had died in the swamp—she'd mourned. They'd cried together over Gabby's brother's losses in his battle with drugs, about Gabby being an outsider in her own family, about Sybil's parents' deaths. They *had* shared everything, but Gabby knew down to her bones she couldn't share this. Calling Sybil would be dangerous to others, to Gabby and Max, and to Sybil. Unfortunately, that left her with only one confidant.

Max.

Even more unfortunate, he would be hurt. But she

had no choice. She had to know the truth. For some reason not yet clear to her, the truth was vital.

Before she could lose her nerve or her resolve, she scooped up the documents and shoved them into the envelope, then strode into the living room. Max and Candace sat on the sofa, drinking from glasses of juice.

"Gabby?" Max jumped to his feet. "Are you well enough to be up, honey?"

"Sit down, Max." She turned to Candace. "I'm glad you're better. You are better, right?"

"Getting there. It's good to see you up and around, too."

She looked like death, bedraggled, and maybe even worse. "I'm almost fine. I think. Maybe." Exasperated, she frowned. "Go home, Candace. I need to talk with Max."

Candace looked surprised, but not hurt. Actually, she smiled. "Well, that's clear enough, I'd say."

Max looked shocked. "Gabby, that's a little rude, don't you think?"

"Yeah, it is. I'll apologize tomorrow." Gabby hiked up her arms. "I'm not myself."

"I know exactly what you mean. Hazy as hell, right? Don't worry. It gets better fast."

"I hope so." Gabby just didn't think she could deal with any more upset right now.

Smiling, Candace set down her glass on the coffee table and stood up. "Good to see you back to normal, darling. You had me worried." She brushed a kiss to Gabby's cheek, then slid Max a relieved look. "Gabby *is* rude, Max. You of all people should know that."

"I do," he admitted. "But I hoped she'd be a little more civil with her friends."

"Right." Candace grunted, and then left through the front door.

Candace wasn't insulted. Why? "Women," Max muttered. "Who can figure them?"

When the door shut behind Candace, Gabby turned on Max. "I want to ask you something, and I want you to tell me the truth."

"Okay." He eyed her cautiously, which just made her more jumpy and made her feel even guiltier than she already felt. "Listen, Max, I don't mean to hurt you, but I have to be sure about this. It's important."

"All right." Max had no idea what to expect, but her temper was building and she wasn't going into her classic, meditative calm-down mode, which cautioned him to brace for the eruption. It came in short order.

"What is this?" She waved an envelope at him. "And what *exactly* does it mean?" She sounded furious, and she might well be, but her chin trembled, and letting him see that weakness really ticked her off. "Are we married or not?"

Max froze. An impossible situation just got more impossible. How did he answer her?

"I'm waiting." She stood, arms folded over her chest, glaring at him.

"You haven't eaten," he said softly. "Let's get some tea and toast and I'll tell you everything I know."

Maybe by then he'd have a clue what that should include.

★   ★   ★

"Commander Conlee?"

Sitting inside Home Base's secure booth reviewing Intel tapes, Conlee recognized Vice President Sybil Stone's voice, hit pause to stop the tape, and then tilted the phone receiver away from his chin. All of the lines inside Home Base were secure, but he waited an additional twenty seconds for the satellite scrambler's relay to kick in as an extra precaution. "Yes, ma'am." He turned his back to the wall of screens and stared at a black spot on the wall.

"Has Agent Grayson reported in?"

"Yes, ma'am." Conlee couldn't predict her reaction to the news with any degree of certainty. As a human being, she'd be thrilled Gabby was still alive. Secretly, so was he. But as the veep, she gave him no idea what to expect. Sybil Stone took her duties seriously; as well she should, even when they personally cost her more than anyone should have to pay. "Things are more complicated in Carnel Cove than originally expected, ma'am. He's sorting them out."

"So Gabby is still alive?" Her tension crackled through the phone.

"Yes, ma'am."

"Grayson reported it to you?"

"No, ma'am." Conlee hated admitting that. It wouldn't bode well for Grayson. "Dr. Keith Burke, Burke Pharmaceuticals, has been on the scene, treating Candace, and apparently Gabby, for the Z-4027 infection she contracted in—"

"The broken-window incident at Logan Industries' lab?"

"Yes, ma'am."

"Gabby has the infection?" Horror filled the veep's tone.

"Apparently so, ma'am. Grayson reported challenges in obtaining a full out-briefing from Gabby. My guess is it's due to the infection, though he hasn't formally reported it."

"And the second team you sent down?"

"They reported arriving, ma'am. They'll gather intel before reporting again."

She hesitated a long moment. And then another. Finally, she said, "I see." Her tone was noncommittal, giving no indication of her reaction. "Keep me posted, Commander."

"Yes, ma'am." He dropped the receiver into its cradle, pulled the cigar stub that never had been lighted from his pocket, and clamped down on it, snagging a fleeting thought.

The veep had wanted Grayson specifically assigned and sent to Carnel Cove. Conlee had intended to assign another operative to handle the cancellation—one who hadn't been Gabby's partner. But the veep had insisted on Grayson, and since he never had been activated as Gabby's partner, Conlee hadn't seen any logical reason to object. After all, she was the head of Oversight for Home Base, and carrying out her orders, not disputing them, was his duty.

Until now, he hadn't had a reason to wonder why she had issued any of her orders. In this case, at the consensus briefing, she had specifically issued Grayson a cancellation order on her best friend. But a thought occurred to Conlee now that should have occurred to him then.

Had she specifically chosen Grayson because she knew he would carry out the cancellation order?

Or because she had somehow known that he wouldn't?

Chapter Twenty-nine

Gabby showered and dressed in a red silk blouse and slacks. Her stomach seemed stuck in permanent "rock and roll," and it was only by the grace of God that she wasn't throwing up.

It's nerves.

Of course it was nerves. She jerked a brush through her hair and looked at her pasty reflection in the bathroom mirror. She was either married or she wasn't.

From all those sets of IDs, you could be married, all right. Six times, under six separate identities, to six different men—including Max.

And if that wasn't enough to make her toss her cookies, she didn't know what was. But Max hadn't seemed shocked by the evidence. He'd seemed resigned. Surely if they were really married and he loved her, he would have been stunned that she could be a bigamist.

Weak in the knees and seeing stars, she clutched at

the edge of the sink. Squeezed her eyes shut. Okay. So she was married or she wasn't. She was a judge or she wasn't. She was in love or she . . . She looked into the mirror. No, that was one thing she felt sure of; she did love Max. That was real.

"Lie to me, you heartless bitch," she muttered to herself through clenched teeth. "I'm scared enough without bringing love into it."

She stared angrily into her eyes, ignoring the dark circles smudging the skin under them. She loved him. She'd never allowed herself to love any man, but she loved Max. "Damn."

She hated and resented the truth. She feared it.

God, did she fear it.

She walked out of the bathroom, slammed the door, and rounded the corner into the kitchen. Max stood at the counter near the toaster, waiting for the toast to pop up. He looked good, standing there, drying his hands on a nubby dishtowel—though not actually familiar, natural and at home. Because she liked that more than she should, at least until she knew the truth, she looked away.

"Do you want some eggs, or just toast and juice?"

"Toast and coffee. I hate orange juice." The venom in that remark brought her up short. She did hate orange juice, didn't she?

"It's cranberry," he said, lifting the pitcher. "You always drink cranberry."

Finally! Something verified real. She *did* hate orange juice. Mmm, if they weren't married, would Max know that about the juice? "I definitely need coffee."

She reached for a cup, closed the cabinet door, and a flicker of movement outside the window caught her eye. She scanned and strained. Something had shifted in the long, deep shadows, but it was that odd time of day, where you could see but couldn't define. That shift could have been anything, or nothing. All the wildlife was out of sync from the storm. She held her glance on the distance a moment longer, but saw nothing unusual. "Is it getting dark or daylight?" For the life of her, she couldn't tell.

"Dawn." The toast popped up and he retrieved it, putting it on a plate.

He already had a cup. She poured for herself and mixed in milk. "Did you sleep?"

"Not much for a few days."

Who would have believed that dry toast could smell so good. Her stomach rumbled. "Because I had you worried?"

He nodded. "Among other things." He moved closer, stroked her cheek. "We'll talk about them after you eat."

She lifted her face to his hand. "I think we'd better talk now." She was trying to be brave about this, but not knowing truth from fiction about herself was extremely unsettling. She wanted this resolved.

Worry flickered through his eyes. "Are you sure you're okay, Gabby?"

Okay? She was a nervous wreck. A jumbled mass of live-wire nerves, all frayed and snapping. She was a terrified maniac. "I'm fine."

He searched for what that meant, as if the truth lay hidden in her face. "Don't lie to me."

There was something in his eyes. Some secret gleam that promised he understood her—at the moment, better than she understood herself. She stepped closer, looked up at him. "I'm scared to death, Max. All those identities. All those names. What am I? Some kind of sextuplicate bigamist or something?"

"Of course not." He cupped her face in his hands. "But that you don't know means we've got even more trouble than we thought."

She couldn't stand the suspense another second. "Am I your wife?"

He motioned for her to sit down at the table. When she sat, he put her toast before her. "Yes, you are my wife."

A sigh of pure relief escaped her. "Whew! Okay. Okay."

He put the butter and a jar of red-raspberry preserves in the center of the table. "And no, you aren't my wife."

"What?" She paused, knife midair, and looked up at him.

He sat down in a chair beside her, placed his coffee cup near the jam jar. "Gabby, what I'm about to tell you is extremely sensitive information. I know you're having memory problems because of the infection—well, we think it's actually from the vaccine you were given for the infection—but either way, you have to understand that if you screw up, we're both dead."

"I'm not a judge."

"Actually, you are," he corrected her. "You're also a pilot, a special operations officer, and a senior covert operative for the U.S. Secret Service's Special Detail Unit."

"Special Detail Unit. SDU." No way could she swallow. Not even dry toast. "And Conlee? Who is he?"

"Our commander."

"You're a covert operative, too." A lead weight buried her heart. "We're not married."

"I've been your absentee husband a lot of times, Gabby. All those licenses and passports you found—those were your insertion identities from previous missions." Max explained the Global Warrior attacks on the flight from Paris to Florida, the fruit and cruise ship infections in Texas, and the infestation of the vineyards in California. Then he went on to explain why Gabby had come to Carnel Cove, to investigate Judge Abernathy for judicial corruption in the three Global Warrior cases. Max talked until he told her everything he knew to tell her, and though she hadn't responded, she no longer looked at him as if he'd lost his mind and she was debating bolting out of the house.

"I believe you—about almost all of it, Max." She motioned for the carafe of coffee.

He refilled her cup, watched the steam lift off it. "What don't you believe?"

Ignoring the butter and jam, she bit down on a piece of dry toast, chewed slowly, and finally swallowed. "It's not that I don't believe you—you can quit looking offended. It's that I'm having trouble reconciling my instincts with what you're telling me on . . . one point."

He refilled his own cup and set the carafe back onto the table. "Everything I said is true, Gabby. I swear it."

A frown creased her skin between her brows. She reached over and touched his neck, let her fingertips slide up his nape, cup his chin, and then she kissed him. Just a taste of a kiss, but when she met with no resistance, she deepened it, and Max responded to her.

She parted their mouths and sat back on her chair. "That's what doesn't fit, Max."

"What?" Breathless from the kiss or confusion, he couldn't think straight.

"The way I feel about you. The way you react to me. How could this just be a job between us? It doesn't feel like just a job. I know you and your body. I know it, Max."

He stiffened. "Yes."

"So are we really married, too?"

"No, we're not."

"Are you telling me we're just having an affair?" She looked incredulous. "I don't believe it. I know better than to get involved on the job, Max, and so do you."

"It's not like that."

"So what is it like?" She clearly hated his being evasive. "I heard Elizabeth and Candace. They asked if you were here to kill me." Gabby clenched her fingers into a fist atop the table. "Is that true, Max?" Fury blazed in her eyes. "Did you come here to kill me and end up in my bed instead? Am I still breathing only because I slept with you?"

"No, Gabby." He slid back his chair, stood up. "It's not like that."

She crowded him and, nose-to-nose, shouted, "Did you come here to kill me?"

Max glared back into a face that looked fragile, on the borderline of being devastated. He had hoped telling Gabby who she was would stir her memories, but that hadn't happened, and if he answered her question now, he wasn't likely to be around long enough to keep her alive. "I'm your partner, Gabby. You contacted Commander Conlee at Home Base and asked him to activate me. I'm here because you asked me to come."

"I work alone." She said it emphatically, and immediately knew it was true.

"You have worked alone," he countered. "Until now."

"Why did I activate you?"

"I don't know. You told me you had evidence, that I'd get it whether or not you lived, but I haven't been able to find it." He leaned back against the counter, some of the steam leaving his voice. "Gabby, we need that information to prevent an imminent terrorist attack."

"A terrorist attack?"

He nodded. "One threatening the public and our economy."

He could see the wheels turning inside her mind. "These Global Warriors in Carnel Cove are manipulating the U.S. economy," she said. "Is that what all the attacks have in common?"

"I think so, yes."

She sipped from her cup, cradling it in her hand, needing its warmth. Inside, she felt ice cold. "And by extension, they're manipulating the stability of the U.S. government."

"By extension," he agreed, folding his arms over his chest.

A memory winged through her mind. A memory of wet footprints on a concrete floor. Of a man in her garage attacking her. A memory of her killing him.

Gabby dropped the cup. Coffee splattered on the floor,

on the hems of Max's jeans, and the cup shattered. "Oh, dear God, no. No!" Her uneasy stomach slammed into full rebellion.

Gagging, she rushed from the kitchen to the bathroom, and the coffee and toast she'd just swallowed came right back up.

When she stopped heaving, Max came in, wet a washcloth at the sink, and then passed it to her. "Here."

She took it, swabbed at her face. "Oh, God."

"You're too active. You've been seriously sick, Gabby." He passed her a glass of water.

"I feel fine." She took the cup, stood and rinsed her mouth, then flushed the toilet and turned to the sink.

"Right." He backed up a step. "That's why you're in here vomiting your guts up."

"Could you be a little less graphic? My stomach is still flipping cartwheels." She glared at him in the mirror. "It's not my health, Max. It's this nightmare."

"What nightmare?"

She checked his eyes in the mirror. Unfortunately, the man seemed sincere, which meant she'd used good judgment in not activating him before now, if in fact she hadn't. "My life, for God's sake. All this? I thought I was a judge. A small-town judge married to a man who spends too much time away from home. Now I find out I'm this . . . this   " She faltered, unable to bring herself to say murderer.

"Covert operative," he filled in for her.

"Right." She gobbed toothpaste onto the brush, inserted it into her mouth, and then began scrubbing her teeth. "It's a lot to take in, Max. I mean, cutting a man's throat. It's not exactly top of the list on marketable job skills."

He stepped up closer behind her. "Does it help to know you're really good at it?"

"No!" She tossed the towel at him.

He caught it, laughed in her face.

"What an asinine thing to say to a woman." How could he imagine something so vile was funny? "You're a pig, Matthew Grayson. A pig," she said from around the toothbrush, her mouth full of foam. "I can't believe I was upset that I'm not really married to you."

He looked pleased by that comment. Too pleased for it to not be genuine. "I meant you are good at your job, not at killing." He shrugged, leaned a shoulder against the door casing. "Though, to be honest, you're good at that, too."

She bent over and rinsed, shoved the toothbrush back into its holder. "You'd think if I was that good at either, I'd remember it."

"You'd think so." He rubbed his neck. "Elizabeth said you kept mumbling, 'Don't tell.'"

"What does that mean?" She dabbed her mouth dry with a towel.

"Even when you were out of it, you didn't break your cover. That's proof of how good you are at your job, Gabby."

"If you ask me, that's proof I've spent too much time undercover."

"You thought that, too."

"I did?" Why couldn't she remember that?

He nodded. "You told Sybil you were burned out."

Bristling, she turned and leaned a hip against the counter. The space between them was crowded and the smell of soap on his skin triggered a memory of them making love. That memory was too vivid to not be real. "Max, what exactly is going on here?"

"I told you. The Global Warriors are planning—"

"No. I mean with us. I might not know for sure whether or not I'm married to you—"

"I told you. You're not. It's our cover."

"—but I know I don't fall into bed with just anyone."

"I'm sure you don't." His expression grew somber and he picked up the towel and dried some water spots on the marble counter.

"You know what I think?"

"What?" He draped the hand towel through its ring to the right of the sink.

"I think you're deliberately misleading me. I think you're maybe even protecting me."

"I'm not."

"I think you are." She crossed her arms over her chest. "I think we are married—"

"Why would I lie, Gabby?"

"I don't know why. I just know my life with you feels real and important. It feels . . ."

"Special?" he asked, his voice deceptively soft.

"Yes." She glared at him. "Yes, exactly. All this SDU operative nonsense—it has to be a joke. Why are you doing this to me, Max? It's not funny."

"I'm not, honey. I swear it." He reached out for her.

She twisted out of his grasp. "No. It's not true. None of it. I would know."

He grabbed her arm, turned her to face him, and then held her pinned between his body and the sink ledge. "I don't lie to you, and I don't play cruel jokes on you. Not now, not ever."

Her heart shattered, leaving a gaping hole in her chest. Her life, all she knew and all that was familiar to her, was . . . gone. How could that be? How could any of this be?

She stood there, looking up at him, trying to take everything in and make some kind of sense of it. But nothing seemed to fit. Nothing felt right. Except Max. Max felt right. She stepped closer and hugged him, pressing her cheek against his chest.

A flash of them in the lab, of Candace stretching her blouse across a window trying to keep mosquitoes inside, raced through her mind. Max and Gabby in bed, making love. She leaned up and planted little kisses on his neck, jaw, and face—wherever her lips touched.

He lifted her and turned in a circle.

A deafening sound startled them. The window glass shattered.

Max dropped to the floor, and covered Gabby.

Gabby hit the floor hard. Max's hand cupped her head, slammed her nose to his chest. "What happened?" And what was soaking her ear? It smelled like—

"I've been shot, Gabby."

★   ★   ★

The director picked up the red phone in his study. There was no need to dial. It was a direct link between him and the Consortium and the security on it was tighter than that provided for President Lance at the White House.

"Yes?" The chairman sounded half asleep.

Considering the time, he probably had been. "Sorry to disturb you."

"Do we have a problem?"

His phoning near dawn made that a logical deduction. "Yes and no. It's a mixed bag."

"Unmix it."

"The vaccine is proving to be highly effective against the Z-4027 infection. Candace Burke is fine."

"Burke's version, or Erickson's?"

"That's part of the mixed bag. It could be either. Dr. Swift is investigating now, trying to make a determination."

"I'm not even going to ask why we don't know. Just fix it." The chairman grunted, as if sitting up in bed. "What about Lady Justice?"

"Who?"

The chairman sighed, clearly impatient with the director's performance on this venture. "The lady judge—Gabby Kincaid."

"That's the other part of the not-so-good news in the

mixed bag, Mr. Chairman. It looked as if the infection would kill her. But Cardel—"

"The Warrior we haven't lost?"

Wincing at the sarcasm, the director stiffened. "Yes, sir. The live one." This was bound to tick the man off. "We haven't yet located Jaris Adahan's body, though Cardel has been keeping a close watch on Kincaid. She's better."

"Better as in, she's going to live? Or better as in, she's not yet in a coma?"

"Better as in, she's been sitting in her kitchen having coffee and toast with her husband."

"So you're convinced now that he is her husband?"

The chairman was asking if she was a judge or the Justice Department investigator Andrew Abernathy suspected her to be, and that question the director still couldn't answer. He hedged. "Cardel is convinced." The director rubbed a knot of tension out of his neck. "They were up in the middle of the night arguing."

"Sounds married." The chairman paused, and then added, "Have Cardel take her out."

The director swallowed back a groan. He'd hoped to avoid reporting yet more bad news. "Killing her right now probably isn't wise. I heard at the Silver Spoon she has no memory. With no memory, she's no threat. So why increase suspicion by killing her?"

"Is this memory loss permanent?"

"Drs. Swift, Erickson, and Burke think it could be. In earlier studies, Z-4027 caused long term memory challenges. It didn't just destroy the paths to specific parts of the brain storing memories. It destroyed the brain cells."

"Don't be wrong about this."

"The doctors all agree."

"No." The chairman suddenly changed his mind. "I have a feeling about this. Have Cardel take her out. Make it look like an accident."

There was no way around it now. The director stared at

the antique desk lamp on his desk. "He failed once already and winged her husband."

"Is there any more bad news coming down the pike?"

The director cringed. "I'm afraid so. A second SDU team is in transit to Carnel Cove."

"Okay, here's what I want you to do. Kill Gabby Kincaid—forget the accident, just make sure she's dead. Find out which of the vaccines worked. Tell Swift he's out of time. And find that body!" The chairman slammed down the phone.

The director's ear rang. He slumped back in his seat and closed his eyes. He wasn't a freaking magician. Where hadn't Cardel Boudreaux already looked?

He made the call to Boudreaux.

"Yeah?"

"Kill Gabby Kincaid. Forget form and just get it done. By dawn, an assassin team of SDU operatives is going to be crawling all over the Cove looking to bury you. And find Adahan's body, for Christ's sake." Soon Gabby would be dead. Maybe then Andrew Abernathy would back off. He had had enough of people crawling down his throat and up his ass.

"I've looked everywhere. Even dove in the mucky water in the cove. Kincaid or that husband of hers must have dumped Adahan in the gulf."

The water was so stirred up from the storm, an elephant could be in it and not be found.

"I'm finishing this job, but pass the word. After this, I'm retiring."

Boudreaux could just . . . disappear. And he would. But there was too much money yet to be made. "I'm right behind you."

"No, you're not, though your island and redhead probably seem appealing right now."

The director was impressed. He hadn't made the paper trail easy to follow. "One island and redhead aren't quite enough. I want two. Then I'm right behind you."

Cardel grunted. "Then you'll want three."

He was probably right. "Maybe a blonde."

"Anything but a brunette. Your perfect wife is a brunette."

Surprised, the director paused. Cardel Boudreaux was worth every penny of his fee. "Call me when Kincaid is dead."

"You've got it," Cardel said, accepting his orders.

The director flipped the phone he'd used for two weeks—that was his limit on any cell phone—and tossed it onto his desk blotter.

"You bastard."

His wife.. *Bad break.* How much had she heard? The director looked over toward the study door. Three steps inside the room stood his perfect wife, and the look on her perfect face was of perfect horror.

"Islands? Redheaded whores? Orders to murder Gabby?" She grabbed her head and squeezed, as if what she was hearing threatened to explode her mind. "What have you done?"

He didn't say a word. Just sat there and let her rant and rave, his arms resting on his stomach, his expression calm and collected. He had nothing to fear from her. A perfect image was the ultimate concern in her life, and she wouldn't let anything—not even murder and other women—destroy it.

"Oh, God." She gasped, her hand to her chest. "What have you done to the children? To me?" She backed up, bumped a shoulder against the door casing. "Their father, the murderer. Me, married to a murderer. Good God, that's what people will say!"

He held his silence.

"You're a monster. A monster! I hate you! Do you hear me, you son of a bitch? I hate you!" Sobbing, screeching, she turned, stumbled, and ran down the hallway and then up the stairs to the second floor.

He lighted a cigar and rocked back in his desk chair. At least they had that one thing in common. They both knew how to hate well.

Lasting marriages had been built on less.

★　★　★

A relentless hard knock at the front door had Candace hurrying to answer it. She peeked through the viewer and saw Gabby and Max. Both looked like death. Opening the door wide, she stepped back so they could come in and saw the blood soaking a tourniquet on Max's left arm. "What happened?"

"He's been shot," Gabby said. "Get Keith."

Gabby led him into the living room, though Candace couldn't be sure who was actually holding up whom.

"She's panicking, Candace," Max said. "It's in the fleshy part of my arm. Nothing life-threatening."

Gabby glared at him. "Four inches in and you'd be dead, Max. That's not panicking."

"Keith!" Candace bellowed at the hall.

He came running, bare-chested, his pajama bottoms slung low on his hips, bleary-eyed and hair rumpled. "What's wrong?"

"Max was shot." Candace got on the other side of Max, dragged him to Keith, and then went back to Gabby and sat her down on the sofa. "You're about to drop."

"I'm weak. Really weak," Gabby said.

"Clammy, too." She got Gabby a cool cloth while Keith took Max to his makeshift clinic at the back of the house. "This will help." She passed the cloth. "Now tell me what happened."

"We were in the bathroom." Gabby rubbed the cool

cloth over her face and neck. "Max was hugging me. If he hadn't turned, I would have been hit."

Candace narrowed her eyes. "When did this happen?"

"Ten minutes ago. Maybe a little more," Gabby said. "We looked around outside, trying to catch the bastard, but didn't see anyone."

"Did you call Jackson?"

"No. Max said there was no sense in it. If we couldn't find anything, Jackson wouldn't be able to either, and he's swamped with the spraying."

Candace didn't get it. Something had happened to throw a wrench in the works. According to Elizabeth, Conlee's second team should be in custody. Had they gotten away?

The phone rang. Candace stepped into the kitchen and answered it. "Hello."

"You sound great," Darlene said. "Call the ladies. The team is now on ice, cooling their heels in Jackson's cells."

Oh, boy. "How long have they been there?"

"Twenty minutes. I've been busy, helping process them and get them settled. Why?"

Worry replaced confusion. Candace swallowed a sip of water and set her glass on the counter. "Because about fifteen minutes ago, someone took a shot at Gabby and winged Max."

"Oh, no. There's someone else after her, too."

Candace swiped at a water spot on the stainless steel countertop. "Sounds like a logical conclusion to me."

"Any idea who?"

"Not a clue." Candace checked to make sure Gabby was still on the sofa, out of earshot. "Keith is patching up Max. Gabby's on the sofa. I can't call the ladies with them here."

"I'll take care of it," Darlene said. "The battery on my cell is low, but it's not dead yet." She blew out a sigh. "There's more, Candace."

"What more?" God, this had to be the night from hell.

"The bank robbers put up quite a ruckus. Jackson tagged them for resisting arrest without violence and for damaging the ATM and stealing the jewelry. Their fearless leader is demanding Jackson get Elizabeth down here. He says she can vouch for them."

"But she didn't see them. Miranda picked them up, posing as Elizabeth."

"I know. Because they're going to insist Jackson call Elizabeth and they believe she'll vouch for them, but they won't know her and she can honestly say she's never seen them. I'm not worried about Jackson in this, but when Commander Conlee—"

He would show the team photos of all the ladies and they'd identify Miranda. "We need some kind of justification."

"Like what? No matter what we tell him, the man is not going to appreciate us intercepting his operatives, setting them up as robbers and jewel thieves, and getting their asses thrown in jail, Candace."

"He might. It depends on motive," Candace said. "And Max's shooter might just be it."

"We were protecting them?"

"Exactly."

"He's not going to buy that, Candace. Why would he?"

"Because someone else really is after Gabby and Max. His own team canceling them is one thing. But a stranger taking out two of his best operatives isn't going to sit well with the commander. We'll blame the shooter, claiming Miranda was drugged and incapacitated, too, and say we intervened to protect the team. We're sleepers, not trained to the extent these operatives are. We're given latitude for less than stellar methods and judgments in this type of situation."

"I hope you're right. Because I am absolutely too tired to die."

"You're not going to die," Candace said. "But if you do, I'll have teabags put over your eyes to keep the swelling down."

"Only you would do that to a corpse in her coffin."

"Anything for a friend."

Chapter Thirty

Gabby shoved away the tangle of covers, stretched over Max to the nightstand, and reached for the ringing phone.

"No! Let me get it." Max grabbed the receiver from her and answered. "Hello?"

"Merlin is reporting another twenty-five EEE cases at Carnel Cove Memorial Hospital."

Commander Conlee. Max digested what he'd said. Another twenty-five was too many cases to reasonably attribute to a normal spread of the infection. The missing black-banded canister had to contain Z-4027, and the trucks spraying the Cove had to be laced with it. Human trial studies. That's the only thing that made sense. "Has Stan reported on the chemicals?"

"All tested. All normal." Conlee sighed.

Normal? Max couldn't believe it. "How can that be possible?" Gabby sent him a questioning look. He lifted a finger, motioning her to wait and be quiet. Conlee had to know she was still alive by now, but they'd be crazy to flaunt it in his face.

"Apparently more infected mosquitoes than we estimated escaped from the lab."

The memory replayed in his mind of Candace, spreadeagle, covering the opening with her blouse. She had been in the building and heard the alarm, which had been set off by the window being broken, and she had gone directly to the lab. "I'd bet against it."

Gabby crawled out of bed, shrugged into a robe, and walked to the window, facing the front of the house. The rumble of a large truck rolling down the street vibrated the walls. It passed by the window. One of Carl Blake's trucks, spraying Area Three.

A chill crawled up Max's backbone, and Gabby instinctively rubbed at her arms. She had the feeling, too.

Operatives' instincts were honed. They had to be to survive. One of them could be getting a false reading and be overreacting to an intense warning, but not both of them. The commander finished his update, Max briefed him on word from the Silver Spoon he'd gotten from Erickson, Candace, and Elizabeth, and then added, "I'll report in as soon as we've got something solid, sir."

"Well, move your ass. I've pulled operatives off active missions across the country and put them on this, bodies are piling up everywhere, and our underbelly is still exposed."

"Yes, sir."

Conlee paused, then his voice dropped lethally low. "Did you say 'we' have something solid? *We?*"

Pretending not to have heard Conlee, Max grimaced and hung up the phone. *That was a rookie slip. Gibson was a trainee and he wouldn't have made such a stupid mistake.*

Brad Gibson wasn't sidetracked by a lot of emotions, either. Or worried that the Gabby he had fallen head over heels for would recover her memory and recall that she didn't love him. That he was just her friend.

Max tossed back the covers, thoroughly disgusted with himself for getting that close. But, he had been in trouble with her a long time before coming to the Cove. What she thought mattered. It always mattered. That's why her lack of faith in him and his ability to do his job rubbed him so raw. Since he couldn't deny it without lying to himself, he jerked on a pair of khaki slacks and reached for a shirt.

"I'm supposed to be dead." Gabby stood statue still, her back stiff against the bronze drapes. She folded her arms over her chest and held them tightly against her body, restraining herself by sheer force of will. "That's why you were shushing me. I'm supposed to be dead."

Max pulled a black shirt over his head and tugged it down, then met her gaze, steeling himself against the pain he saw there. "Yes."

He still felt it, even though relief that he hadn't lied to her shone in her eyes. "Where does Dr. Richardson think the victims contracted the infection?"

"Are you remembering, or going by what I told you?"

"I don't know." She grabbed a pair of jeans and a top from the closet. "Does it matter?"

"It could." He watched her pull on the jeans and then a soft blue blouse that clung to her breasts. "Do you remember the evidence? What or where it is?"

She hesitated while buttoning the blouse and thought a moment, and then zipped her jeans shut. "I don't." That brought obvious frustration, and she dug through the closet for a pair of white sneakers. Pulling them out, she repeated her original question. "Where does Dr. Richardson think the victims contracted the infection?"

"They don't think it's the spray, Gabby. Commander Conlee says it tested clean."

"My gut says it isn't. You saw Candace and so did I. Mosquitoes escaped, yes, but not enough to cause this many infections this fast. Dissemination would take longer, Max."

Now the relief felt was his. "I agree with you."

"Then let's prove we're right."

"How?"

Gabby walked over to the nightstand, picked up the phone, and dialed.

A woman answered in sleep-fogged mumble. "Who died?"

"No one's died, Candace."

"Then why in God's name are you calling me at the crack of dawn? I just got to sleep."

Gabby glanced at the bedside clock—seven o'clock. "You've slept an hour, and I need help now."

"What's wrong? Are you okay?" She sounded alert now. "Is it Max?"

"We're great." Someone was talking in the background. Keith, Gabby supposed. "But there is trouble." She licked at her lips. "Listen, there are about forty victims at the hospital diagnosed with EEE."

"Oh, God, Gabby!" Candace was wide awake now and horrified into shouting. "Tell me it's not from the lab. Please!"

Gabby put the receiver back close to her ear. "I don't believe it is. But some disagree. That's why I'm calling. I need information, and I can't get it through my usual sources without revealing more than I want to reveal."

"What do you need?"

"Addresses on those patients."

"Elizabeth's on the hospital board. But she'd have to go through channels."

"I'd rather not do that."

"Then you're on Miranda's turf. She can do anything with computers."

"Without getting caught?" Gabby stared at Max, who looked extremely skeptical if not downright disturbed by what she was doing. "If she gets caught, we tip our hand and the bad guys win, Candace. That means all of us lose in a big way."

"Define all of us."

Gabby cut to the chase. "The people of Carnel Cove, within months, the people of the United States, and of course, the government."

"Wow. That's big. I knew it, but hearing it—"

"It's huge," Gabby interrupted. "Can Miranda do this without getting caught?"

"Sure."

"Are you positive? This is not the time to be overconfident."

Candace paused, and then asked an amazing question. "Are you on a secure phone?"

Startled, Gabby pulled the receiver away from her ear, looked at it as if it were alien, and then put it back. Did she answer honestly? She shouldn't. But could she afford to lie? "I don't know."

"For God's sake. Ask Max."

Gabby covered the receiver with her hand. "Candace wants to know if this phone is secure."

Max sat up, worried at his lip for a second, and rubbed at his arm above the bandage Keith had put on his arm. "Tell her, yes."

Gabby sent him an "are you nuts" look.

"I ran a check on it," he assured her. "Tell her, Gabby."

Extremely uneasy, Gabby uncovered the phone. "He says yes."

"Okay." Candace took in a deep breath, then let it out slowly, sending static through the phone. "Gabby, you don't really know who you're dealing with, darling. Over a year ago, Commander Conlee hired Miranda as a subject matter expert."

"What?" Gabby couldn't believe it. "Why?"

Max walked over to her, hiking his brows. "What is it?"

She waved a hand to shush him, confused and in knots. Should she relay that stunner or not? How would Max react to it?

"Because Miranda kept showing him how easy it was to breach the Department of Defense's secure systems," Candace said. "She was all over the place in areas classified way above Top Secret, and never left the first footprint. He puts in a new security measure. She breaks it. That's what she does. Breaks his systems to show him where they're vulnerable."

"Wow."

"You knew she was good at that stuff."

"This is a little more than good, Candace."

"What is?" Max asked.

"Shh, I'll tell you in a minute." Gabby had decided. "I'm sure this will be a cakewalk for her."

She had to think. This was serious stuff. "It's illegal as hell," Gabby warned. "If she gets caught, she'll go to jail, and from what Max has told me, the commander won't lift a finger to help her. Make sure she knows that."

"That brings risks that complicate things, but I'll tell her. Don't hold your breath though, Gabby. Only one person is more terrified of jail than Miranda, and that's Elizabeth."

Being a judge's wife, Gabby could certainly understand that. "Do we have an alternate?"

"Sure. Darlene Coulter."

Max caught the name and rolled his eyes heavenward. "The sheriff's wife?"

"Tell Max to stop freaking out. Darlene is the head of the Sunshine Committee at church. She always checks on patients to send them cards and flowers and such."

"Try her first, then." No felonies. Gabby smiled. "Tell her I need the info fast, okay?"

Candace's tone changed significantly, somber and serious,

etched with fear and regret. "Innocent people are going to die, aren't they?"

Gabby swallowed a hard lump lodged in her throat. "I'm afraid so."

"I'll call Darlene now."

"Thanks." Gabby put down the receiver and faced a glowering Max.

"You realize we just signed their death warrants," Max said. "They're friends—good friends to both of us—and because of the position we've put them in, Conlee will cancel them."

"No, actually, he won't, but I love this compassionate side of you, Max." She stroked his face. "Apparently Miranda already works for Conlee. Candace does, too, through Logan Industries, and I strongly suspect Elizabeth might have been brought on board since William died in February."

"She told me Conlee was no stranger to her," Max said. "But how can that be?" The training was exhaustive, and none of them had crossed the doors of SDU at Home Base headquarters; Max would bet his career on that.

"Subject matter experts," Gabby told him. "Candace said Commander Conlee hired Miranda to breach SDU's security systems. She's a computer guru with amazing skills. How would Candace know that unless she worked for SDU, too? Conlee wouldn't let Miranda advertise it; he cancels people for that, right? And you said I killed a Global Warrior and Elizabeth removed all evidence from the garage. How did she know how to do that? Being married to a judge might help her learn to examine evidence, but not to sanitize a crime scene."

"You think all the ladies of Carnel Cove are SDU subject matter experts?"

"Maybe." Gabby cocked her head. "Or it could be a ploy."

"Candace, Elizabeth, and Miranda?" Right now, Max

could use a stiff drink. "I don't buy the ploy. Not after all they've done. They're sincere, Gabby, and totally devoted to you. Elizabeth threatened to shoot me if I harmed a hair on your head."

"Elizabeth? Now that's a shocker."

"I swear," Max said. "She had a thirty-eight in one hand and her little rosary bag in the other." Her jaw gaped, and Max nodded, confirming his claim. "I'm sure if they're in, Paige is, too. Her special skills could be really helpful to Conlee."

"He wouldn't blink before factoring empath consultations into his decision making," Max said, shifting his sore shoulder. "And Darlene Coulter, too. Married to the sheriff, working in his office. She has an inside line to everything going on in the Cove."

Gabby walked to the bedroom door. "But not Sissy Blake. The ladies would never agree to trust her."

All fluff and no substance. "Elizabeth told me." The truth hit Max right between the eyes. "Gabby, do you think Conlee recruited the ladies and created a special SDU cell here?"

"Would any seasoned operative call it differently?" She went into the hallway and, realizing she couldn't remember being an operative, seasoned or otherwise, she yelled back at him, "Don't answer that. In the mornings, I need coffee before criticism."

Max was having trouble taking it all in. He sat on the edge of the bed and mulled it over. Conlee always had operated on a "need-to-know" basis. He always had used subject matter experts—Max had conferred with them on many occasions. But an entire cell of them? Why would he have an entire cell, especially in a small tourist town like Carnel Cove?

Home Base. The truth hit Max like a sledgehammer. Because of the recent missile crisis, Conlee had to move Home Base out of Washington to a less densely populated area. He *was* moving Home Base's headquarters to Carnel Cove.

Suddenly it all made sense. Conlee would need contacts here. A physical site. Logan Industries had four sublevels, two of which were currently under construction. It was already doing government contracts, so it had security clearance, and so did Candace and Miranda. Elizabeth obviously had known about SDU through William, so she was a natural insider. That left only Paige. The empath supposedly so talented she often assisted on challenging cases—probably Conlee's cases. And Conlee had said he'd investigated them on another matter.

"Well, well." Conlee could have told Max. But it was another of his "see how sharp your operatives really are" tests.

Max got on the cell phone with Stan Mullin for an update. After a quick briefing and information exchange, Stan said, "Blake says they should be through spraying Area Three by dusk. Sheriff Coulter says most of the roads have been cleared of debris enough that the trucks can get down them."

"You verified the chemicals being used aren't tainted with Z-4027?" Max still had a bad feeling about them. It was the only rational explanation.

"Yes. They ran the tests twice, and I ran them a third time so I could certify them."

"Stan, something is wrong here. It's got to be in the chemicals."

"I know there's something wrong, Max. I've got knots in my gut, telling me something is wrong. But those chemicals tested fine all three times and that's a fact."

Max was unconvinced. He stared at one of Gabby's shoes on the floor next to his. He liked the look of their things being together. Them being together. Hell, he might as well face it. He was crazy about the woman. Totally nuts.

"Who ran the tests?" The answer had to be in the chemicals. There was nowhere else for it to be.

"Erickson and Swift. Mayor Faulkner and Carl Blake acted as impartial observers."

All the usual suspects. A stray thought took hold. "Did you test the same chemicals they did? In the same truck?"

"They tested two trucks. I tested the canister, before it went into the truck."

Normally that was a good practice. Canisters could be contaminated and so could trucks. Stan had tried to cover all bases. Unfortunately, because of who the testers were and who the observers were, this time that had been a severe mistake.

But knowing a mistake existed and identifying it were two different things. Max glanced at the bedside clock. Seven-thirty. There was a lot of ground to cover and they didn't have much time. "Keep me posted."

"Will do."

Max tucked the cell phone into his pocket and joined Gabby in the kitchen. A map of Carnel Cove was tacked to the wall across from the table. At the counter, with the phone crooked at her shoulder, she wrote furiously. "Thanks, Candace. Thank Darlene, too."

Gabby hung up the phone and held up the paper. "Darlene came through for us. We've got the patients' addresses."

He smiled. "Remind me never to give you any kind of flack that'll have the ladies coming after me."

"I'll do that." She grinned and planted a quick kiss to his chin. "Grab some coffee and let's see what we've got."

"To peg a pattern, we need to color-code hospital admittance times." Max poured himself a cup of coffee and managed a total of one quick sip before Gabby shoved a box of pushpins at him.

"Start with red. I'll tell you when to switch colors." Gabby began reading off the patients' addresses.

By the third one, a cluster was forming that had Max's hand and her voice shaking. And it wasn't in Area One, where the lab incident most likely caused infections.

"Switch to blue," Gabby said. "Sixteenth and Main."

Max put in the pins, the dread he had felt instinctively dragging down on his stomach, and from her expression, on Gabby's, too.

"Switch to white, Max. These are the last to be admitted." She read off three additional addresses. It wasn't many, but it was enough. "Oh, God."

He backed away, looked at the two clusters of red and blue, and the small one of white.

"Red is Area One, blue is Two, and white is Three, right?"

She nodded, horror flooding her eyes. "This is the attack, Max." Proof stared her in the eyes. She didn't need memory to verify it. "They're using the spray to infect people." She turned on him. "Didn't you have Stan check this? Didn't Richardson double-check it at the Home Base lab?"

"Yes, I did. Stan just told me that Swift and Erickson ran the tests, Mayor Faulkner and Carl Blake observed. Then Stan ran a third test on the canister. All tested clean."

"What about Dr. Richardson?"

"Commander Conlee said he ran a double-check at the Home Base lab. It was clear there, too." This wasn't the time for it, but her comment steamed him. "And don't talk to me like I'm incompetent, Gabby. I know my job."

"I'm sorry, but someone's manipulating something, and we'd better find out who and how—now. The freaking truck just came down our street. We can't stop spit if we're dead."

"Call Keith at Candace's and warn them. Elizabeth, too. Keep them on the line until I get Stan." Max had Stan on speed dial and pushed the button. When he answered, Max said, "Halt all spraying, Stan. Immediately if not sooner."

"Why?" Even with the background noise, he sounded stunned. "You know why we—"

"Just do it," Max interrupted. "I'll explain when I get there."

"How the hell am I supposed to contact the fleet? Storm damage has communications down between headquarters and the trucks."

"Don't they have cell phones?"

"No. Blake didn't equip them with phones, and we didn't have them on hand to spare. He replaced CB radios with hi-tech systems that have been down since the storm. Satellite time is at a premium, he says. It wasn't cost-effective." The grumble in his voice made his feelings clear about that decision. "The best we can do is to reach them individually. It'll take time."

"We don't have time." Max dragged a hand through his hair. "Are you in Area Three?"

"Yeah. At the park on the cove."

"Get Sheriff Coulter and every available man out to those trucks and shut them down. Do it now, Stan."

"You got it."

Max turned to Gabby, who was on her cell phone, and lifted a finger.

"Hold on, Candace," Gabby said. "I don't know why! Don't you think if I knew why I'd tell you? Just hold on."

Max interrupted. "Tell her and Keith to get to the park at the Cove and not to drag their heels getting there."

"Why?" Gabby asked automatically.

Max frowned. "We've got to do a mass evacuation—fast—or a lot more people are going to die."

*　　*　　*

Andrew Abernathy left the Silver Spoon Café and drove to his fishing cabin. Anguish was tearing him apart and his conscience was carrying so much guilt that any moment he expected it to burst, cause a stroke, and kill his vindictive ass.

The cabin was empty, dark, lonely. But it was the only place memories of Liz and Douglas didn't nag him for making a deal with the devil and selling his soul in the name of revenge, which is why when he'd left the Spoon, he'd driven the twenty miles to the lake cabin rather than just go home.

Carnel Cove wasn't a safe place to be anymore. Especially not right now. And that Andrew knew why and had become a part of it was his greatest sin of all.

Being dead would be better than living with this, Andrew. You know it.

Liz. Even here. Nagging him from the grave because he had failed to remain the man he had become in their life together. The man with faith in the system, with purpose and dignity, ethics and integrity. He'd sold it all. And not once in his mind since had his beloved wife looked at him with love in her eyes. Only regret. And shame.

He'd rather be dead.

Determined, he walked across the hardwood floor to the kitchen wall phone and dialed the director. When he answered, Andrew said, "Jackson has everyone meeting at Carnel Cove Park. Stan Mullin called the police station and ordered Jackson to stop the spraying. Everything. All of it. Total shutdown."

"And you know this because . . ."

"I was having breakfast with the sheriff when he got the call. He looked worried as hell. Mullin told him there are forty-eight cases of EEE at the hospital. They're all dying. All of them. What the hell are you doing killing our own?"

"Would you think, Andrew? I'm tired of your whining. In trial studies some of the mice die. It's a fact. Because they're sacrificed, many others live."

"You're not God. You don't get to choose who lives or

dies. What, did you draw it out on a map? Figure out who was dispensable and who wasn't by where they lived?"

"By their financial status, actually," the director said coolly. "We don't want to upset the economic stability of Carnel Cove, Andrew."

"You cold son of a bitch. These mice are men, women, and kids. Families. They have lives and people who love them. They love other people. Don't you care how much hell you put anyone through?"

"I care." His tone was even, deceptively calm, and assured. "As much as you do."

That remark knocked the wind out of Andrew. He collapsed onto a kitchen chair, deflated and devastated because it was true. For all that had been good, he'd poisoned. And now he was left with this ugly truth. "Oh, God."

"Just for today."

Andrew clenched his jaw. For today, he supposed, the director did feel like God. He chose who lived or died. He controlled people's lives and fates. And he did it for money. Bristling, Andrew rebelled. "No. No, more. This is going to stop. I'm going to stop it."

"Don't even try," the director said. "You know exactly what will happen to you, and nothing at all will change. We'll move forward as if you never existed."

"Not this time."

"Andrew, do not do something stupid. You can't fight us and win. You know it. I've been easy on you because of Liz and Douglas, but stop screwing with me. I'm tired of it."

Andrew stared out the window. The director didn't issue idle threats. But neither did Andrew. It began to rain. Soft and gentle, like cleansing tears. "For the first time in a long time, I know exactly what to do."

"You can't stop this, Andrew. There's nothing you can do and if you think there is, then you're a delusional fool."

"Maybe. Maybe not. I guess we'll see about that, won't we?"

"Big mistake." The director hung up the phone.

★   ★   ★

Cardel Boudreaux stood in the woods behind Gabby Kincaid's house. His rifle was mounted on a tripod, and he stood bent, looking through the scope. She and Maxwell Grayson had left the house and were getting into her red Jeep. He was going to be doing the driving. Cardel had had to speculate on that—who would drive—and set up in the woods accordingly.

He had gotten lucky, and now Gabby Kincaid was firmly fixed in Cardel's crosshairs. "Okay, baby. I've got you now." He rubbed the trigger with the back of his fingertip, a quirk he'd developed coming out of training. "Time is up."

His cell phone vibrated against his hip.

"Son of a bitch." Cardel blew the shot. She was inside the Jeep and that husband of hers was already pulling out of the circular driveway. Frustrated to the tips of his ears, Cardel answered the phone. "What?"

"Did you take care of that matter?"

The director. Calling about Gabby Kincaid. "If you'd waited ten seconds to call, I could have said yes. As it is, you cost me my shot."

"How unfortunate."

"Yeah, that's what I was thinking." Cardel put the rifle in its case. Collapsed the legs of the tripod. He was getting tired of sleeping in the woods to avoid leaving a trail and he was ready to be done and get the hell out of this sweltering hellhole.

"Get over it, Boudreaux. I'm paying your organization a lot of money for your services and they don't include an attitude."

"What do you want?" Cardel didn't take this shit. Not off anybody.

"Forget about the woman. Meet me at Abernathy's fishing camp right away. We've got a fire to stomp out."

Another hit. Another seven-figure fee. Cardel could eat a little dirt and take a little lip for another seven-figure fee. "Yes, sir. I'm on my way."

Chapter Thirty-one

The park at the cove was hopping.

Gabby got out of the Jeep and walked with Max past a trash drum, overflowing with debris someone had gathered since the storm, and into the knot of about sixteen people standing near their cars and trucks. Two motorcycles were in the group. One she recognized as Paige's, and the other was a decked-out Hog covered with Hell's Angels stickers. Stan Mullin nodded toward Max. "More help is on the way."

"Good." Max stepped into the center of the group.

Gabby stopped short, next to Candace and Elizabeth, saw a man she recognized as Candace's ex standing at her side. "Keith? What are you doing here?"

Candace touched Gabby's arm and whispered, "Saving our asses, darling." She nodded toward Max. "Pay attention and be quiet. You're still not yourself."

Smelling the briny water, Gabby focused on Max.

"Where's Sheriff Coulter?" Max asked Stan Mullin.

"Jackson, his men, and the volunteer firemen have spread out to search for the trucks. They're all in Areas Three and Four."

"Both areas?" Max asked.

Stan nodded.

Max stifled a curse. "Who sent them into Area Four before Three was finished?"

"It wasn't me," Stan said. "Judge Abernathy called Jackson and asked why the trucks weren't following the plan, or we wouldn't have known they were in both areas."

But Faulkner would. He knew everything that happened in Carnel Cove. Max slid a look in his direction, but the mayor wasn't paying attention. He was whispering something to Carl Blake. What it was, Max couldn't hear, but it was clear Sissy Blake didn't much like it. Her expression would have to soften to pass for stony.

Max glanced back to Stan, who had that "I know what you're thinking and I agree with you" look in his eye. "Where is he?" Max didn't have to say Abernathy's name. Mullin knew.

"An hour ago, he was at the Silver Spoon. No one knows where he is now."

They already lacked the manpower to pull off this evacuation effectively. Areas Three and Four encompassed half the county. Running down Abernathy would have to wait. "Do the trucks have testing equipment?"

Stan nodded. "Yes, sir."

"Okay." Max turned to the group. "Here's the problem. Testing shows the mosquito spray we're using is fine, but we have reason to believe it's contaminated. Hurricane Darla has severed communications with the trucks, so we have to manually hunt them down and halt the spraying. In the meantime, we have to evacuate as many people as possible from Areas Three and Four." Max looked from the crowd back to Stan. "What are current wind conditions?

Do we have to worry about the chemicals blowing back into Areas One or Two?"

"Southeast, ten to twenty," Stan said. "NOAA considers all areas high-risk."

A disgruntled mumble rippled through the crowd. "Okay," Max said. "Let's divide into four groups. Each group covers an area. Recruit help along the way. Move house to house through neighborhoods and densely populated areas first. Elizabeth," Max shifted his gaze to her, "can you get the women from the church in Areas One and Two to start a phone chain and warn people in Areas Three and Four to leave immediately?"

"Of course. Darlene has a street address index. We'll get on it right away."

"Thanks," Max said. "The goal," he announced to the entire crowd, "is to get as many people out of Carnel Cove as possible."

"Some aren't going to want to leave." The man belonging to the Hell's Angel Hog rubbed his T-shirt. There was a skull on its front that matched one on the shirt of a woman standing beside him wearing glued-on jeans. "They didn't evacuate for Darla and they won't evacuate for this."

"Yes, they will," Max said. "This is a mandatory evacuation authorized by the federal government. Anyone here have a felony against them?"

Half the group looked at Jeans and Skull. "I got busted for DUI three years ago," he said.

"You been drinking?" Max asked bluntly.

"No." He smiled. "I'm a Baptist preacher now. We don't drink alcohol."

"That works for me." Max nodded. "Everyone raise your right hand and repeat after me." He deputized them and they repeated the oath. "Put anyone who refuses to evacuate under arrest and haul their asses out of Carnel Cove. If we're right, then later they can thank you for saving their lives."

"Now, hold on there, Grayson." Mayor Faulkner stepped away from Carl and Sissy at the back of the group and moved forward.

Gabby watched him shoulder his way through the crowd. Carl didn't look pleased; he hadn't since he and Faulkner and Sissy had arrived. But Sissy looked strained, as if she had to work to project her public persona when all she really wanted to do was scream. That would not happen. Gabby couldn't imagine Sissy allowing herself to scream in private, much less in public. She gave all three of them another glance. Actually, none of them looked pleased.

"What are you doing?" Faulkner shouted. "You can't evacuate my town."

"I'll be right with you, Mayor." Max held up a wait-a-second finger and then turned to the group. "Move!" He pointed to Gabby. "You stay put."

People scattered, and Gabby kept her distance from the group. If she still wasn't herself, she couldn't afford to mess up. Max had warned her that would cost them their lives. He was totally in charge, and when he had raised his voice, even Faulkner had backed up a step. If anything could have amused her in this situation, which it couldn't, seeing Faulkner rattled would do it.

"Grayson, you don't have the authority—"

"Actually, I do," Max insisted, his expression as steely as his voice. "Stan will verify it."

Stan nodded, and Gabby looked down at the ground. Everyone's shoes, including her own, were caked with wet earth. But Faulkner's dirt wasn't sand. Odd, considering the shoreside park sat on sugar white sandy beach. There was no clay in the area, and yet his shoes were covered in red clay. Suspicions aroused, she wondered if maybe that too was a result of Hurricane Darla damage, and looked from Faulkner through the half-dozen people still in the immediate vicinity. Everyone's shoes were caked with sand—except for two others.

Carl and Sissy Blake.

Where in the world had the three of them been to run into red clay?

"That's it, Grayson. I'm going over your head. You have no right to usurp my authority here. I've got nearly fifty Covers in the hospital with EEE. We need that spray."

"Go to anyone you like, Mayor." Max squared off on him. "I issued the order to preserve the health and safety of Covers. It stands."

Faulkner stared hard at Max, the veins in his neck raised like snakes crawling just beneath his skin. "Who *exactly* is your immediate supervisor?"

Max crossed his arms over his chest and lowered his voice to just above a whisper. "That would be Sybil Stone, the Vice President of the United States, sir."

The wind collapsed from Faulkner's sails. Clearly, it had dawned on him that far more was going on here than he realized. "You've got some explaining to do, Grayson. A lot of it."

"In due time." Max stood his ground. "I suggest you evacuate, Mayor. This park is in Area Three, and Area Three is contaminated."

Gabby watched Faulkner's face pale. But Carl Blake's reaction was far more interesting. He turned red. Almost blue red. Gabby had never seen him look so angry. Carl was a physically nondescript man with a nondescript personality, but today he was furious. And Sissy had an unusual look to her, too. Rather than her controlled, calm, and serene presence, she looked afraid. Truly terrified.

Max's cell phone rang. He answered it. "Grayson."

"It's Stan, Max. You'd better sit down for this one."

Following Max's motioning, Gabby got into the Jeep as Max climbed in the driver's side. Faulkner, Blake, and Sissy all left together in the mayor's sedan.

"A volunteer fireman called in. The truck was outfitted with dual tanks. The first tested negative, but the second tested positive. It's not pesticide, Max. The samples are bloodred."

"Z-4027," he whispered to Gabby. "We missed this? Weren't we testing both tanks?"

"According to the fireman, they're not normal dual tanks. They aren't mounted side by side or even vertically. They're configured with the second tank inside the first."

"Son of a bitch." Max hung up, slammed a hand against the steering wheel, and then hooked a sharp left onto Highway 98.

Gabby lost her seat and slid into him. "Hey! Where are you going?"

"Logan Industries." He shot her a glare. "David Erickson knows a lot more than he's telling, and he is going to talk to us now."

"I don't think—"

"Blake's trucks have tanks within tanks. They're spraying Z-4027 selectively, Gabby."

Mentally reviewing all the details Max had shared, she cringed, and a cold chill swept up her back. "Oh, my God, these heartless pigs honestly *are* doing trial studies on the public."

"Which means someone's black-marketing the Z-4027—"

She held on as he made a right into L.I.'s parking lot, circling the downed oak. "Or gathering the stats they need to market it."

"It's deliberate, Gabby. Americans doing this to Americans, and it's deliberate."

"I wish I could deny it." God, did she wish it. "Erickson has to know more."

"Yes, and he talks by whatever means are necessary." Max's jaw went tight. "Agreed?"

"Agreed." Her stomach didn't so much as flutter.

He pulled into the slot next to Erickson's Volvo. "I don't mean to push, but now would be a great time to remember where you stashed that evidence."

"I've been wracking my mind, Max. I swear I have," she said, letting him hear her apology in her tone. "I remember everything you've told me: all the mission details, the people involved, the goals here—all of it. I just don't remember any of it on my own."

"Nothing?"

"Just what you've told me." Right now, personal flashes ranked insignificant and unworthy of mention. Only what impacted the crisis had priority.

He pulled the keys from the ignition. "Are you carrying?"

She smoothed her hair back from her face. "Carrying what?"

"Your gun, Gabby." Max sighed. "If Erickson is up to his earlobes in this, he isn't going to be exactly cooperative. He could have been the one to hire the Warriors to assassinate you."

Her stomach lurched. "No, I'm not carrying."

Max reached into the Jeep's glove compartment and pulled out a second gun. "Take this. If you have to use it, don't think. Just let your instincts take over."

"You're sure I know how to use it?" She wasn't sure of anything herself. The alien feeling of the cold steel in her hand did nothing to reassure her.

"Trust me. You know how to use it. You're an expert marksman."

She cast him a blank look.

"A sharpshooter, Gabby," he clarified. "You're a sharpshooter."

That should have reassured her. Instead, her stomach flipped and wound into knots.

"Let's go chat with Erickson."

She stuffed the gun into the waistband of her jeans. *Oh, please, don't make me have to use this thing.* She left the Jeep. *Please.*

As she closed the door, she prayed again. *But if I have to use it, God, let me be really good at it.*

Chapter Thirty-two

Dr. Erickson was sitting at his desk in the lab, staring at a photo of his son, Jeremy, on his desk. His expression was solemn, somber.

When Gabby and Max walked in, Erickson didn't look up, yet Gabby sensed he was aware of them. "I came to thank you," she said.

He spared Gabby a glance; foggy and unfocused.

"For my life." She smiled at him, hoping that she wouldn't have to touch the gun now warmed by her body. She'd make nice with the devil himself to keep from putting her alleged skills to the test.

"Thank Keith Burke for that." Erickson said the words, but his voice lacked conviction.

He was a horrible liar—actually, an obvious novice at it—and yet if Gabby hadn't been watching for a telltale sign, she would have missed the flinch warning her of it. "No, I don't."

Their gazes locked.

When it became evident neither would break away, Max interceded. "We know you gave Candace and Gabby vaccine injections, David. We also know Keith Burke's injections failed. Yours worked."

He looked a little surprised. Gabby wasn't sure what to make of that.

"That's impossible," he finally said. "Every trial done in the lab falls short. Every one."

So he had given them injections. "Candace and I lived. So something you did worked, because what Keith had done alone did not. Don't you have any idea of what it was?"

"No, I don't." His tone was blunt, sharp, and full of self-recrimination.

Obviously neither she nor Max would need a gun. Gabby lifted the photo of his son. "Jeremy was an adorable boy, David. Was he always full of mischief?"

"Yes." Erickson seemed surprised by her observation. "But it was the kind that reminds you life isn't all serious and critical. Sometimes it's pure and simple and playful and fun. I loved that about him."

"I can see why you would," she said. "Even now his memory reminds you of all those things and all those special moments." An odd catch in her voice betrayed her, her not having a Jeremy in her life hit too close to home. "That's such a blessing."

"Did you ever meet my son, Gabby?"

The wistfulness in his voice tempted her to lie. But she couldn't. He was too raw and vulnerable. "No, I'm sorry to say I didn't have that privilege."

"Then how did you know that about him?"

"It's in his eyes," she explained. "Just as profound loss is in yours." Gabby spoke softly. "I know the looks of grief and loss. And regret." Boy, did she know regret.

He blinked hard.

Max softened his tone. "David, there are over forty people with Z-4027 infections just in Carnel Cove's hospital. We've got three other states now reporting cases."

"Three?"

"New York just recorded four. Texas and California are the other two. And we've got another outbreak in south Florida, in orange grove country," Max disclosed. "Listen, you did something right. Whatever it was, it helped Candace and Gabby, and if you don't do something right again, all of those other people are going to die."

"I wish I could. But even if I knew what I'd done, there was only one vial of test vaccine. I used it on Candace and Gabby." His Adam's apple bobbed hard in his throat. "There isn't any more." He waved a hand at the destroyed lab. "And I don't have the facilities to produce any more."

"We can provide a facility," Gabby said, and hoped to hell it was true.

"You don't get it, do you?" Erickson grunted. "You don't get any of it."

"Any of what?" Max asked before Gabby could.

Erickson again let his gaze slide to Jeremy's photo. Resignation turned to resolve in his eyes. "Dr. Swift has shut down my program. There will *never* be any more vaccine."

Gabby cut a look at Max who was clearly just as surprised by this news. "Whatever for?"

"A lack of funding."

"That's not true," Max disagreed. "The funding is available under federal grants."

A cold, hard knot of certainty settled in Gabby's chest. It infuriated and relieved her. Finally, she was getting a grip on this situation. "Swift has the vaccine now. He doesn't need David anymore, so he's cut the program. Swift can develop and market it without David."

"Marcus Swift is a peon," David said. "You really don't understand a thing."

Frustrated, he stood up and paced, window to sink, cupping a hand to his skull. "Swift isn't running this show, and the people who are running it obviously don't want to market the vaccine to the public." David paused, stared at the ceiling for a long moment, perceptibly debating the wisdom of saying any more.

"David, please," Gabby urged him. "People are going to die. They're all someone's son or wife or daughter or mother. If you can do anything, please!"

"I can't tell you, don't you see that?" He glared at Gabby. "Since Jeremy died, finding a cure for EEE has been my life's work. Something that I did in conjunction with whatever Keith Burke did cured you and Candace. But I won't know what until I confer with Keith, and if I tell you what I know about this whole situation, that conference will never happen."

"Why not?" Gabby asked.

"Because I'll be dead."

Gabby stepped closer to him. "Who's going to kill you, David? Dr. Swift?"

"No." He let out a rush of breath ripe with irritation. "I told you, he's a peon."

"David," Max interceded. "Peon or not, if Marcus Swift and the mysterious 'they' who are in control are through with you, you're a dead man anyway."

Erickson stilled, blinked hard, and the truth dawned in his eyes. "Yes, I suppose I am."

"So help us," Gabby clasped his upper arm. "Please, David. Help us. Who does Swift work for? And who's manipulating events?"

He sat back down. "The Consortium."

That disclosure meant nothing to Gabby. She looked to Max, but his nearly indecipherable shrug proved this was a new name to him, too.

"It doesn't want to market the vaccine publicly. It wants to black-market the superbug and then pick and choose its buyers for the vaccine and the pesticide." Erickson looked up at them. "The Consortium is playing God, choosing what crops survive and fail and who lives and dies. It's all about economics. Money and power."

Which equates to governmental control. The economy going south always took the stability of the government with it. Gabby frowned, certain he was telling the truth. "Who, what, is the Consortium?"

He cocked his head. "You do not know how badly I wish I couldn't answer that."

"But you can," Max prodded, leaning a hip on the edge of Erickson's desk.

"Yeah." He rocked back in his desk chair. "At least, part of it. I only know what Marcus Swift has told me about it, which isn't a lot."

"Who's involved?" Gabby asked, trying to get David focused.

"It's a small group of wealthy businessmen here in the Cove. They make things happen that they want to happen, using whatever means are necessary."

"The Consortium is located here, in Carnel Cove?" Gabby slid Max a glance and saw in his eyes they were thinking the same thing. Suddenly, Conlee's having an SDU sleeper cell in Carnel Cove, moving Home Base here, made more than perfect sense.

"That's my understanding. The Consortium arranged for Candace Burke to buy Logan Industries and Marcus Swift to run it—they made sure no one else qualified applied, so I wasn't sure if Candace was one of them or not. She's a financial whiz, no doubt about it."

"You *weren't* sure if she was one of them," Gabby said. "Does that mean you are now?"

"She can't be involved. Candace doesn't know anything about what we do here. It was a good investment and she made it. Then she did what she always does in her business ventures—at least in the ones I've researched trying to figure this out. She hires an excellent manager to run operations for her, and a kick-ass compliance auditor like Carl Blake to keep everyone walking the straight and narrow. But until the lab incident, I still wasn't really sure." He blinked hard. "She put her life on the line to protect the Covers. That tells me she didn't cause the problem. You don't sacrifice your life to prevent infections you're causing."

Relieved, Gabby nodded. "Did Candace hire you, then?"

"No. Swift brought me in to develop the vaccine. I'd been working on an EEE vaccine for over a year—ever since Jeremy died." David let out a self-depreciating laugh. "I was in up to my earlobes before I even knew the Consortium existed. Once you're in, you can't get out."

"Who's in this Consortium?" Max asked.

"I don't know. I wish I did. I'd kill the bastard leeches myself. They'll do anything—I mean anything—for money. But I don't know exactly who they are."

Hoping something David said would trigger her memory, Gabby paid close attention, but still she recalled nothing of value and came up dry. Profoundly disappointed, she gave in to sheer frustration and plopped down in a chair across from David's desk.

"Talk to me about the black-banded canister," Max said. "The one you and Swift were arguing about when I came into the lab."

David looked up at Max, the light from his desk lamp streaking the shadows across his face. "It was Z-4027. Access to it was highly restricted, of course."

Which made Gabby wonder why Home Base hadn't picked up on the problem. Or maybe it had. Maybe Commander Conlee had been aware of that and that's why he had activated Max when Gabby had put in the request.

Erickson continued. "I was ready to do some studies on a prototype vaccine. So I pulled a few samples from the canister—all documented, just as they're supposed to be. But when I tested the vials, there was no Z-4027 present."

"Someone had switched the bands," Max said.

David nodded. "That's what I thought, so I reported it to Marcus Swift."

"Did he report it to the CDC and DOD?" Max asked.

Gabby scanned a mental list of the acronyms Max had shared with her—Centers for Disease Control and Department of Defense—then continued tracking the conversation.

"No, he didn't." Erickson swallowed hard and his gaze slid to his desktop, as if what he next had to say embarrassed and shamed him. "That wasn't the first time Z-4027 security had been breached, Max." His eyes looked haunted in his gaunt face. "It was the third."

"The third?" Gabby reacted before she checked herself. "When were the other two?"

"The first was in January," Erickson admitted. "The second, the last day of June."

"And Marcus Swift refused to report both incidents?" Max asked.

Again, David nodded. "He also ordered me to forget about the breaches. I insisted I was going to the DOD with it. That's when he told me about the Consortium and that, if I went up the chain of command, they would kill us both."

Gabby made the connections. The first had been stolen right before Judge Powell's death; the second, right before the July 4 incidents. She risked a glance at Max and knew he'd connected the dots, too.

"Marcus Swift says the Consortium hires Global Warriors to assassinate anyone who gets in its way. They're mercenaries. Apparently, very successful ones, or Swift wouldn't be terrified of them. And he is terrified of them."

"You saw these Warriors?"

"No. But I found a U.S. flag pin at the base of the canister, when I pulled the vials for the studies. Marcus freaked out when he saw it. I don't know for fact what it meant, but he knew." David paused, remembering. "I think that pin was a signal, and that's why he wouldn't report the security breaches."

Gabby sifted through all Max had told her and concluded that David Erickson was right. It had to have been her running tests on Powell's tissue samples that had the Global Warriors attempting to assassinate her. The timing of the breaches fit perfectly with events. They must have caused Powell's death, and the New York incident as well as the July 4 "natural outbreaks." It seemed amazing that a small group of businessmen in Carnel Cove could have such far-reaching impact on the U.S. economy, but after the events of September 11, it didn't take a genius to know a small group could cause a lot of death and damage. Give them significant resources, and of course they could manipulate the economy.

"I wanted to live to continue my work," Erickson said simply. "So I forgot about the pin and the canister—until people started dying. Then, I had to do something, so I went to Judge Powell. Everyone in the Cove knew he was a man worth trusting."

Max rested a hand on his knee. "After you talked with Judge Powell, he turned up dead."

"Yes!" The agony of that had David dragging in a breath that heaved his chest. "I gathered all the gossip about his death at the Silver Spoon, and I found out he had been with the mayor, Judge Abernathy, and Carl Blake when he had contracted the infection. What was I supposed to do then? There was no one left to talk to about this."

"You could have talked with Jackson Coulter." Gabby was certain that the sheriff wasn't in this Consortium. Not because she knew the man so well, but because she knew his wife. Darlene Coulter wouldn't tolerate her husband being involved in anything like this. She was too much the idealist.

"Jackson would have been fired on the spot and nothing would have changed—except the Consortium would have had those bastard Warriors kill him and me, and I'd be responsible for leaving Darlene without a husband and their daughter without a father."

"What about Judge Abernathy?" Gabby had been sent here to investigate him, and David seemed to have a wealth of insight on others. Maybe he did on Abernathy, too.

"Before his wife and son were killed, I might have gone to him," Erickson said bluntly. "But something happened to him after that. It wasn't just grief. Trust me, I understand grief. He was . . . different."

Max stood up. "We'll work on putting the pieces together. You need to get with Keith at Candace's and put your heads together. What he did didn't work. You say what you did didn't work. But the combination of what both of you did *did* work. Figure out why so we can stop other people from dying."

"All right." David stood up and shrugged out of his lab coat. "I realize my reputation is shot because of this. But I swear to God, I just didn't know what else to do. I had to continue my research. I had to."

"For Jeremy," Gabby said. "I understand. We'll sort it all out. Just get with Keith and find out what the two of you did right."

David left the lab.

Gabby and Max stood squared off, facing each other. "It's plausible, Max."

"Yeah, it is." Max moved toward the lab table, pulled out an earpiece and lip mike, and touched base with Commander Conlee. "Did you get all that?"

"Yes, we did," Conlee said. Obviously, Intel had alerted him to monitor the moment Max and Gabby had entered the lab. "Do you think he's shooting straight?"

"Absolutely, I do. So does Gabby."

Mentioning her earned him a grunt, but no surprise and no immediate threats. "Intel is already working on establishing firm connections between the thefts and the incidents."

"We need a stock analysis of the California vineyards. That could be our connection."

"Gibson is on that. We're running cotton, too. That's a major crop in Texas, and the growers are already reporting unusually high stats on crop failure. Same goes with the orange groves in Florida."

"My gut's telling me these incidents are all connected to this Consortium, Commander."

"I've suspected it since February, when William Powell died," he admitted. "Get me the evidence to prove it."

Oh, yes. He'd created a sleeper cell in Carnel Cove of subject matter experts, all right. Likely he did intend to move Home Base here, too. Killing multiple birds with one stone was Conlee's style. "Yes, sir."

Max removed the earpiece and mike. Gabby stood waiting for him at the door leaving the lab. He walked over.

"Any flak about me not being dead yet?"

"Not at the moment."

"Well, we'll take that as a good sign and press on." She walked out of the lab, and headed down the hallway toward the exit.

"My head's still spinning, putting everything together." Max fell into step beside her. Reaching to clasp her hand seemed natural. "Where do we go first?"

"To talk with Judge Abernathy." With her free hand, Gabby pulled her cell phone out of her handbag, but she waited until they were seated in the Jeep to dial. Seconds later, the call connected. "Miranda, it's Gabby."

"Hi. You okay?"

"I can't remember spit, but Max is watching out for me, so I'm fine." That earned her hand a gentle squeeze from Max, who clearly appreciated the trust. "Listen, Miranda, I need some information fast. There's no time to research. What happened to Judge Abernathy's family? Do you know?"

"Of course. They were killed in a car accident by a drunk driver," she said. "He rammed them right through the guardrail on the Mid-bay Bridge."

"Where's that?"

"Next door, in Okaloosa County. The bridge connects Destin to Niceville. Liz, Judge Abernathy's wife, had a fondness for charter fishing. She and their son, Douglas, used to go often. That's where they'd been—on a fishing trip. The accident happened on the way home."

"Who was the drunk driver?"

"That I don't know. But I'll check and call you back. You on your cell?"

"Yeah." Gabby looked over at Max, driving toward Abernathy's house.

"Give me a few minutes to find a computer that isn't tied up with the phone chain evacuation plans, or one I can commandeer."

"Thanks." Gabby looked at Max just as he hit his right blinker. "Where are you going?"

"Abernathy's."

"He's rarely at home these days, Max. He spends most of his time at the cabin." She gave him directions that had him driving north, out of Carnel Cove.

A few minutes later, the cell phone rang. Gabby answered. "Hello."

"Sebastian Cabot was the driver," Miranda said. "But if you're hoping to talk to him, you're out of luck."

"Why is that?" Gabby glanced at her watch. Ten forty-five. How long would it take to stop all those trucks?

"Sebastian Cabot is dead, Gabby."

Gabby relayed that to Max, and then asked Miranda,

"What happened to him?" Was his death due to natural causes, or the Consortium's Warriors?

"He drove off a cliff in the Sierra Nevada Mountains in California."

"Was he drunk?"

"No, he wasn't. A trucker saw it happen. He said Cabot deliberately drove off the cliff. Never hit his brakes or tried to turn."

Gabby's stomach dropped and then filled with acid. An ice-cold warning flooded her. "When did this happen, Miranda?"

"Let me see   July July fourth." She paused. "Hell of a way to celebrate Independence Day, wasn't it?"

"Yeah." Thoughtful, Gabby agreed. "Thanks, Miranda."

"Sure thing."

Gabby put down the phone, looked at Max who anxiously waited. "Sebastian Cabot died by suicide the day of the biological outbreaks in California. Max, it's a long shot, but I want to follow a hunch. How do I reach Conlee?"

"Are you nuts?" He clasped her hand, squeezed. "Gabby, mentioning you and reminding him that you're still alive is one thing. Getting into his face with direct contact is another. It's definitely not in our best interests. Definitely not."

"If I'm right, it's in America's best interests, and that supercedes us." She shook doubt off her shoulders like a wet dog slings water. "Give me the number."

Max reeled it off, and Gabby dialed. When Conlee answered the phone, she hoped she wasn't making the second-biggest mistake of her life. If he asked her anything outside the scope of Max's briefing, she was screwed. Of course, he wanted her dead anyway, so when you got right down to it, what else did she have to lose? "Commander, it's Lady Justice."

"Yes."

If he was stunned, he didn't sound it. She licked at her

lips; her mouth suddenly had gone dry. "Have Intel run a manual check on the security tapes for both ends of that July fourth Paris flight, and on the customs' U.S./Mexico and U.S./Canada borders crossing tapes."

"What are they looking for?"

"Jaris Adahan, other Global Warriors on the watch list, and Sebastian Cabot."

"Who is Cabot?"

"The drunk driver who killed Judge Abernathy's wife and son. He deliberately drove off a cliff in California on July fourth. What he was doing in California is still a mystery, but my instincts are shouting that there's nothing natural about the grape louse infestation in Napa Valley. He had access."

"So did millions of other people, Gabby."

"True, but they didn't have a direct-link connection to a judge who fixed cases on three suspected Global Warriors." She spoke with a certainty that came across stronger than her current evidence warranted. "They're biological attacks, sir. And they're all connected."

"You have proof of that?"

Did she? Maybe she did. Somewhere. "In progress, sir."

"I see," Conlee said, then paused for a moment. "It's the economy."

The Consortium David Erickson had warned them about. "Exactly, sir."

"Why aren't you dead?"

"I told Grayson he could kill me later. There's too much work for him to do alone right now, and bringing in someone to replace me wouldn't be an efficient use of manpower for interacting with the locals. They're good people, but they close ranks against outsiders."

"I see."

She didn't know what to make of that, but brazened it out. "If you intend to send Housekeeping for me and Max, give us forty-eight hours first. Otherwise, we don't stand a chance of putting this all together for you, and I guarantee that you won't be able to do it yourself. There are too many threads, Commander, and America will get screwed."

He didn't respond. Just disconnected the phone.

"Well?" Max asked. "Did he agree to wait?"

"No, but he didn't refuse."

"So we don't know if he's sending a second team in to wipe us out or not?"

"Unfortunately, we don't," she said, gently patting his hand to soften the blow. "Max?"

"Yeah?" He looked from the road to her.

"Either way, I'm glad you're with me." Her expression crumbled. "I don't mean that I want you dead, I don't. It's just that something this awful, well, it's—it's . . . well, you know. It's nice to have someone special with me."

"Special?" He looked pleased and as dopey as Jonathan Westford when he looked at Sybil sometimes. Absolutely awed.

Which was really kind of wonderful when that look was coming in your direction. "Very special."

He brought her hand to his mouth and brushed a kiss to her knuckles. "Yeah, I know what you mean. I don't want you dead, either. But, well, me, too."

"Yeah?" She felt herself smile and bit down on her lips. "Oh, yeah."

Dopey was looking better all the time. She could get used to it. Hell, she could probably get addicted to it.

And to him.

Chapter Thirty-three

Three miles north of the gulf, Sheriff Coulter intercepted Max and Gabby in his patrol car. Lights flashing, sirens wailing, he pulled them over.

Max veered over onto the shoulder of the road, and Jackson stopped alongside. Both men lowered windows, and Jackson shouted across the car. "Half hour ago, Darlene radioed that Doc Erickson warned us the low-income housing unit just north of here was high-risk. Bobby and some volunteers got right on it, and one of Blake's truck drivers said he was ordered to go directly there and spray, even though it wasn't on his list."

"Who issued the order?"

"We don't know. A garden-variety-looking guy in a FEMA jacket," Jackson said. "But it wasn't Stan Mullin, Max. I've been looking, but he seems to have disappeared off the face of the earth. Bobby and crew are nearly through evacuating."

"We'll keep an eye out." Max tapped the gearshift back into drive.

"That second Warrior," Gabby said, gritting her teeth.

Pulling back onto the road behind Jackson, Max stomped the gas. "That'd be my guess."

At a fork in the road, Jackson veered left; Max, right. When he drove over a crest, a white truck that had been parked alongside the road pulled in behind him. Max watched the rearview and quickly got agitated. "The idiot is trying to crawl up my butt." He tapped his brakes, but the jerk didn't back off.

The road leveled, and the truck whipped into the left lane to pass him. Max saw a gun barrel aimed his way through the passenger's window. "Get down!" He shoved Gabby into a crouch and swerved onto the grassy shoulder.

The masked shooter changed his aim and rapidly fired, shooting out the left rear and then front tire. The Jeep pitched wildly, and Max fought to keep it on the road. The bandage on his arm stained bright red.

Gabby raised her gun and put two bullets through the truck's rear window. Unfortunately it was an extended cab with tinted windows, and she'd not gotten a clear shot at the driver; he gunned the truck. His tires screeched and he pulled away, out of range.

"Get going, Max. We're not going to catch that Warrior jerk sitting here parked in the grass." She braced on the dashboard, steadying her aim. "I'm tired of this ass trying to kill me."

"Honey, we're in a Jeep. He's in a V-eight. We're not going to catch him."

She looked over at Max, then at the blood soaking his arm, and her face paled. "Are you okay?"

"I just opened the wound. It's all right."

"Let me fix it. There's a first-aid kit in the back."

Max agreed, more to reassure Gabby he was fine than

because the bandage was in dire need of changing. She looked genuinely worried about him, and there was a part of him that was awed by that. Awed and humbled.

When it was done and she had gotten some of her color back, he said, "Now what do we do about the flats? We've only got one spare."

"One spare and a case of tire inflators. That'll get us to Abernathy's camp."

"You're a hell of a woman, Gabby Kincaid." Max smiled.

"Of course." She smiled back, her heart full. "About time you noticed."

At just after six P.M., Max spotted the dirt road that led to Abernathy's cabin on Clearwater Lake and turned. It was narrow, and reedy weeds spiked up beside shallow drainage ditches that ran alongside the road. Hurricane Darla's remnants were still being felt. The ditches were full and the water gushed through them at a good clip, keeping the muddy roadway passable, provided you were in four-wheel drive.

"That's it." Gabby pointed to a black mailbox on a post that stood beside a five-foot break in the thick trees that passed for a trail up to the cabin itself.

Max turned then drove to the cabin. It was wooden, freshly stained a cool beige, with a front porch that ran the length of the house. Gabby knocked on the front door.

No one answered.

She rapped again, and they waited.

Still no one answered.

"Let's try around back."

They stepped off the porch and made their way around the side of the cabin to the rear. Beyond a stretch of cleared lawn was a deep area that had been left natural and led to the lake. At the shoreline, a long wooden dock led out over the water. Birds chirped in the oaks and pines, squirrels jumped tree to tree overhead, and the sounds of the water lapping against the wooden dock carried back to where they stood. Under ordinary circumstances, it would have been a welcome retreat and a soothing place to be.

Today, it was not.

Gabby tried the back door. It wasn't locked. She peeked inside. "Judge Abernathy?"

No answer.

Max headed toward the water. There was no boat at the dock. Scanning the lake, he saw several little bends, and in one, he glimpsed a boat's stern. "He's on the water, Gabby."

Gabby cupped her hand over her eyes and squinted against the glare of the low-slung sun. Judge Abernathy was in the boat and slumped halfway over its side. "He's in trouble."

They ran full out across the wet grass and down the wooden dock; in midair, just before they plunged into the water, Gabby screamed, "Max, can I swim?"

"Yes!"

She hit the water, sank beneath it. It should have been warm—it was August, for pity's sake—but the storm had dumped so much rain and stirred up the lake, the water felt frigid. *Don't panic, you can swim. Just do it.* She broke the surface and took a stroke. When she didn't sink, she took another.

Max reached the boat first. He pulled himself up and over its side. When Gabby grabbed hold of the hull, Max had his fingers in place on Abernathy's throat, checking for a pulse at his carotid. "Well?" she asked, breathless and swiping water from her face.

Sober, Max looked down at her. Whatever Abernathy had known was lost. "He's dead."

Gabby's insides turned to ice. Treading water at the

side of the boat, she looked at Abernathy's neck. "Oh, Max."

"What?"

"Mosquito bites. Three of them." She looked up at him, hunched over Abernathy's back to see his neck. "Just like Judge Powell."

Max did a quick check of Abernathy's nails, eyes, and joint movements. "Maybe not the guy in the truck. The judge has been dead since early morning, I'd guess."

Gabby caught a glimpse of Abernathy's hiking boot. It was brown with thick, heavy-tread soles that cut deep. Treads that were caked with red clay.

She shot a glance back at the shore, looking for breaks in the weedy grass that lined the lake edge. "Max, there's red clay here. His shoes are covered with red clay."

"Yeah?" Max looked at her over the side of the boat, obviously not following.

"At the cove, the dirt is sandy, not red clay."

He tugged his clinging shirt away from his body. "What's your point, Gabby?"

"Mayor Faulkner and Carl and Sissy Blake were at Cove Park, when we were organizing the evacuation. Their shoes were all covered with red clay."

"Honey, the dirt in half this county is red clay. So Faulkner and the Blakes were somewhere in it, but that doesn't mean they were here."

"It doesn't mean they weren't, either." Gabby turned to swim away. "I'm going back to the Jeep for my cell phone."

"You calling the commander?"

"No. He'd just send Housekeeping sooner." Treading water, she swirled to look back at him. "I'm calling Sheriff Coulter."

"He could be involved, Gabby."

"He busted his ass to evacuate Areas Three and Four," she reminded Max. "And Darlene wouldn't marry a jerk. She'd straighten him out or leave him. It's that simple."

"No marriage is ever that simple."

"Don't be silly. Put the rules on the table and live by them and any marriage is that simple," she contradicted him. "Darlene is still there, so Jackson Coulter is a good man."

"Are you willing to stake your life on it?"

"Why not?" He'd have to stand in line to take her out. Behind Commander Conlee, the Global Warriors, and only God knew who else.

"What about *my* life?"

She had been protective, and Max had just proven that he knew it. She thought for a second, recalled Darlene and Jackson together on different occasions and just having coffee at the Silver Spoon. Darlene admired him. It was in her eyes. "Yes," Gabby told Max. "I'm willing to stake your life on it."

"Then call him."

Max trusted her judgment. She might not remember spit about her supposed real life, which made her wonder if she actually had one, but in her cover, she had gained Max's respect. That meant a lot to her, though it probably shouldn't. Of course it shouldn't. But it did. Ordinarily, that might upset her. But with everything going on right now, it didn't rate above a nagging gnat on the worry scale.

At the dock, Gabby climbed the ladder out of the lake and then rushed across the boards to the lawn and then to the Jeep. The door creaked open and she reached inside and grabbed her cell phone. Dripping water, she shook, slinging droplets onto the drying mud and dirt. Droplets of water pinged on the Jeep's fender.

The sheriff answered on the third ring. "Coulter."

"Jackson, it's Gabby." She leaned back against the side of the car. "You need to get up to Judge Abernathy's camp and don't announce it to anyone else just yet."

"What's going on?"

"Abernathy is dead." She swiped dripping water back

from her face, plucked at her clinging clothes. "Like I said, Jackson, keep it to yourself until you get here and check it out."

"I'm on my way," he said, then dropped his voice. "I'm afraid there's a lot going on in Carnel Cove that I don't know, Gabby. None of it looks good. And I think we may have some local power players up to their eyeballs in it."

"I'm afraid you're right."

"I will find out, and whoever they are, they're going to jail." Steel edged his voice. "My family lives here, too, you know?"

Relieved that her gut instincts about him had been right, she nodded. "I know, Jackson."

$$\star \quad \star \quad \star$$

Sitting in her library at home, Elizabeth hung up the phone and checked off the name on her list, preparing to move on to the next one. Her phone rang and she answered. "Elizabeth Powell."

"Where the hell is my team?"

Commander Conlee. *Oh, dear.* "They're here," she said, trying to avoid saying any more than was absolutely necessary. "Can I call you later, Commander? We've got a federal emergency evacuation going on, and I'm supposed to be telling people to evacuate right away."

"Why?"

Now what? Inspiration hit. "Because Max said." Let Conlee call Max to get his answers. That was safe. Max and Gabby had no idea there was a second team in Carnel Cove. "I really will have to get back to you, Commander."

Before he could object, she disconnected the call and dialed the next number on her list. For a second, she considered giving Gabby and Max a warning call, and then decided against it. It would be best for them to remain in the dark. Then Conlee couldn't hold them responsible for getting some of his hotshot operatives arrested for breaking and entering, grand theft, bank robbery, and whatever else Jackson had tacked onto the impressive list.

Elizabeth just hoped her plan to get the team out of trouble worked as well as the one that got them into it.

Chapter Thirty-four

Darkness fell as Max turned into the circular drive at Gabby's.

She had an uneasy feeling in her stomach. "Are you sure it's safe to come back here? This is Area Three and we know for a fact they sprayed it."

"David and Keith say yes and Dr. Richardson backed them on it, Gabby," Max said. "All effects of the spray should be out of the air by now. So long as we don't wallow in the dirt, we're good. Besides, you've had the vaccine, and if I didn't get it at the lab, odds are I'm not going to get it—at least, according to Erickson and Burke. Some people have a natural immunity, and apparently, I'm one of them."

He parked the Jeep and they went into the house. Both of them automatically ran a security check to make sure the place was clear of intruders and listening devices. When confident it was, they met up in the kitchen.

"Are you hungry?" Gabby opened the door and peered into the fridge, hoping for a six-course meal to suddenly appear and willing to settle for anything semihealthy and mold-free. When had she last eaten a decent meal? Her stomach felt plastered against her backbone.

"Starving." He nudged her over at the fridge. "I tossed out most of what was in here—"

"Whatever for?" She glanced at him, then peeked into the nearly empty fridge. Bare shelves had her fighting a rush of disappointment, and her stomach growled in full-fledged protest.

"The storm," he said. "Electricity went out and every thing had spoiled."

"Ah." The smell of his skin and the lake and the wind competed with her stomach for attention and won. Bent at the fridge, she stood up and faced him, the open door between them. "I'd forgotten about the storm."

Did she really say that? How could she actually say that? Worse, how could she mean it? It was true but, God Almighty. Forgetting a hurricane when evidence of it was all around her? Heat rushed up to her face.

"You feeling okay?" Max brushed a hand against her face.

It wasn't really a personal touch, just testing her temperature, but it felt personal. Almost like a caress. It had been a long time since she'd felt a caress. "I'm a little tired, but okay."

"You're lying to me, Gabby." He stepped around the door, stood before her, and clasped her shoulders, then gently squeezed. "Be honest."

Be honest. Easy for him to say. He knew who he was, and what he was, and where things stood between them. All she had to make those judgments was his word and a few instinctive hunches, and considering the confusing signals she was getting—from him and from herself—that just wasn't enough. Still, he looked so . . . concerned, and interested, and approachable. He looked as if he really cared. "I'm confused."

"About what?"

She wished he would back up a step. Just a step. It was too hard to keep her head clear and her guard up when he stood this close, and hemmed in by the fridge door, she couldn't step back. "About us." Unable to stand it, she skirted around him, leaned against the kitchen counter, her back to him. "I remind myself over and over that this life isn't real, that we aren't married, that I'm not really a judge, but the problem is I don't believe it." She risked a look back at him. "It's not that I think you're lying to me, Max. I know you're not. It's just that . . ." Words failed her and she shrugged.

He stepped closer and clasped her shoulders again. "What?"

She looked up at him, let him see the truth in her eyes, and called herself forty kinds of fool for doing it. "My mind and my heart don't agree. I feel connected to you. When you look at me, I feel special. And I know it's not just my imagination, or that you're faking it, Max. I know it, just like I know your body as well as my own. How can we not be real? How can I imagine that all this between us isn't real? It's the most real thing I've ever felt in my life."

He cupped her face in his hands, stroked her jaw with his thumb, and cocked his head. "Would it help to know that my head and heart don't agree on us, either?"

"Really?"

He nodded.

"And your body, too?" She groaned. "I mean, you know my body."

His eyes warmed. "Intimately."

She couldn't help herself; she smiled, and wrapped her arms around his waist. "If I told you that I think I love you would it shock you?"

"Absolutely." He masked his expression, hiding even a hint of his true feelings from her.

She needed a grip here, and she intended to get one. "Would that be a good shock or a bad one?" she pushed.

He hesitated before responding; looked as if he seriously considered not answering her at all. Finally, he said, "That would depend on whether or not you're in control of yourself."

He meant her memory. "What if I never remember completely? Do we hang in limbo forever, then?"

He looked annoyed by that question, and sounded annoyed answering it. "I don't know."

"I don't either, Max. Keith said it could be permanent. So did Erickson. But it might not be. Candace's memory wasn't affected." Gabby stroked the front of his shirt, running her fingertip along the center tab between the third and fourth buttons. "I might never remember. Then again, I might remember any moment. Either way, I don't want to live my life on hold."

"I understand that." He stroked her face, dropped a kiss to her forehead, then her cheek. "I'm going to be really honest here, Gabby."

Her heart felt as if it was squeezed in a huge fist.

"I could love you," he admitted. "I love the way you look at me and the way you stroke my neck, like you're doing right now. You let me know you want to be close to me, and not because you're really thinking about it—it's just an instinctive thing. I love it that you snore, that you didn't even slow down when you were running down that dock and you asked me if you could swim. You trusted me, and jumped. I love a lot of things about you."

The truth of what he was saying hit her. "But you're afraid I'll remember and then I won't love you anymore?"

"It's possible." He lifted his chin, stared at the ceiling a second, then looked back down at her. "It's probable. You didn't trust me."

Gabby couldn't believe it. She felt so much for him, so deeply. "I know everything about you, Max, and I've always trusted you implicitly."

He searched her eyes, seeking the truth. "Do you remember now?"

"Not in my head." She felt a little foolish and a lot nervous. "But I know in my heart."

A strange blend of relief and disappointment flooded his eyes. He pulled back and stared at her from the other side of the table. "Don't you get it? You don't remember, but I do. I could get suckered into loving you forever. But I only have one heart. I can't risk giving it to a woman I'd mourn losing forever."

"Yes, you can, Max." She spoke gently to soften that harsh reality. "You have to risk it because you can't not risk it." She paused a second, then added, "That's the problem with love. It's not rational or wise or even just. It's mostly a fickle pain in the ass. But when it's there, it's there, and it just stays put until you get weary of fighting it."

He stood statue stiff, stared daggers at her. "I disagree."

"Okay." She walked back to the fridge, seemingly dropping the subject. "So what do you want to eat? Miraculously, it looks like the chicken is still good, but nothing else." Bent double, she peeked up at him over the fridge door. "You love chicken, don't you?"

"Yeah, I love chicken." Frowning, he crossed over to the sink, got a drink of water, and then set the glass down. "How can you just drop this with an 'okay' and then go on like everything is normal?"

"Do I have any choice?" She shrugged, set the chicken on the counter, then washed her hands with hot, soapy water. "What do you want from me? I feel one way, you tell me I feel another—I don't know what to do. It's hard."

"It's hard for me, too."

"I wish I could spare you, but I'm stuck. If you have a

solution, I'm all ears." She tensed, afraid he'd withdraw and she'd never be close to him again.

"I want you." He pulled her to him, closed his arms around her, and kissed her hard and long and deep. "I just want you."

★   ★   ★

Commander Conlee's voice on the phone sounded impatient, stiff, and stern. "I'm waiting for an explanation, Grayson. We both know you disobeyed a direct order and now Gabby's giving me lip, wanting me to hold off sending in Housekeeping to take care of you two for forty-eight hours so you have time to resolve things. What is going on?"

Max frowned at the bathroom mirror. He had a towel wrapped around his hips and a razor in his hand. "I was told to make a determination, and if necessary, to cancel Gabby. I've determined that's not in the best interests of the United States." Not to mention his own. He dabbed the edge of the towel to the water dripping shaving cream from his chin down his throat. "She's fine, her cover is fine, and we're following so many different threads on this mission I can't keep up. I need her." Never were truer words spoken.

"I see."

Max couldn't do it. He loved her and had made love to her. He couldn't kill her and that was the bottom line. Conlee's tone proved he knew it. "Yes, sir. I guess you probably do."

"Vice President Stone will be glad to hear it."

Max stilled, stared into his own eyes in the bathroom mirror. "Sir?"

"She said you would kill Gabby only if there was no way around it, and if anyone could find a way to let her live, you would. That's why she insisted on you taking the assignment."

The Vice President had *insisted*? "What made her think—? How could she be convinced I wouldn't kill Gabby? When I got here, I had every intention of carrying out that order."

"I have no idea. Maybe it's woman's intuition. Hell, what man really understands them anyway? Bottom line is it doesn't matter. What matters is that you'd better be right about her cover or a lot of good men, including you and me, are going to die, Grayson."

Max swallowed hard. He'd made the call, and he had to stand by it—and by her. "I accept full responsibility, sir."

"Yeah, well, that and a buck will buy me a cup of coffee, but it won't do a thing to get either of us through the pearly gates."

Max resumed shaving, stroked a lick down his cheek. "I'm not wrong about this, sir."

"All right, then. I sent a second team down there to assist. They arrived, but haven't reported since. Find them and send them back to Home Base. We'll consider the matter of Gabby closed. But if it becomes necessary—"

"I'll handle it." He rinsed the razor in the sink, beneath the faucet of running water. "You have my word, sir."

"Fine." Commander Conlee paused, and then shifted topics. "Intel sent me the tape of your conversation with Dr. Erickson. Have you sorted it all out yet?"

"Not yet, sir. We're working on it, but we've had a few complications."

"Serious ones?"

"Oh, yeah." Max rinsed the last bits of shaving cream from his face and blotted it dry. Then he dropped the towel tucked at his waist and shrugged into his clothes. "We found tanks inside tanks in Carl Blake's sprayers on the trucks." Max propped the phone in the crook of his ear and buttoned up his shirt. "Someone switched the canisters in the lab, so the trucks were spraying Z-4027. The testing was pulled on the outer tanks. That's why they came back clear. The inner tanks held the Z-4027, which was being sprayed in specific, handpicked locations."

"Who picked them?"

"My guess, the Consortium Erickson warned us about. One of the drivers was told to spray a low-income housing area not on his list by an unknown man wearing a FEMA jacket. It wasn't Stan or any of his guys, so we're figuring it was that second Warrior."

"Logical deduction. Have you gotten a fix on him?"

"We think he was the masked man who shot out two of the Jeep tires. He escaped. This man's like a ghost. He's avoiding the hotels, resorts, and apartments around here. Elizabeth and Miranda have been canvassing them." Paige sensed he was still in the Cove, but always moving. Max grabbed a comb and ran it through his hair. "Wherever he is, he's lying low."

"What about the spraying?"

"It's stopped now, and Erickson and Keith Burke have accounted for all the chemicals. But the consequences of what was already done are going to be steep."

"How steep?"

"I wish I knew." Max put the comb back into the drawer and closed it. He splashed on some aftershave that smelled tangy and not sweet. "After we made the link from the Consortium to Abernathy to Sebastian Cabot and his suicide in the Napa Valley region, we went to put the pressure on Abernathy. Gabby was convinced he knew a lot more than he was telling, and I think he did, too."

"But?"

"He's dead, sir. Three mosquito bites on the back of the neck, just like Judge Powell."

"Z-4027?"

"That's not verified yet, but if I were a betting man, I'd say odds look reasonably good. I've, um, been unable to locate Gabby's test results on Judge Powell."

"Why don't you just ask her?"

Oh, here it came. "Remember the lab incident, sir?"

"Grayson, how could I forget it?"

Max winced. "There were repercussions. Candace and Gabby are fine. Well, mostly fine, but Gabby is experiencing some . . . residual effects."

"What kind of residual effects?" Steel ranked softer than his tone.

"Long-term memory loss, sir," Max confessed, lacking any alternative to lying, and he just couldn't bring himself to lie to the commander. "Keith Burke gave them both injections. Neither responded to them, but then Erickson secretly injected them both. They got better. We've got the two of them consulting now to see if it's Erickson's alone—which he says it isn't—or a combination of the two vaccine injections that arrested the infection."

"So Gabby was infected." Conlee seemed menacing, holding onto his temper by one frayed thread. "And you didn't inform Home Base?"

Now Max was totally screwed. Not that he had any more to lose, but it bugged him to have his reputation tarnished. For a lot of years, he had been a respected, highly decorated, and trusted operative. "Under the circumstances, I couldn't report it until now, sir."

"Grayson, I should bust you to hell and back."

"Yes, sir," Max agreed, and lifted the tube of toothpaste from the countertop and dropped it into the drawer near his comb. Gabby's hairbrush lay beside it. He hated how good seeing their things together made him feel. "But first could you get Dr. Richardson to consult with Burke and Erickson? They've got to figure out what they did that worked and generate more vaccine, or our death toll is going to climb by forty-two people—maybe a lot more—just in Carnel Cove. Add south Florida, New York, and Texas to that, and—"

"I've got it, Grayson." Conlee was obviously talking around his stump of a cigar. In six years, Max had never seen him without one, or seen one lighted. "When this is over and it's convenient, I'm going to knock both of you on your cocky asses."

When it was over. Convenient. "Yes, sir." Max hung up the phone. A devastated Gabby stared at him from the door. "What's wrong?" She looked as if she'd lost her best friend.

"I remember Commander Conlee." Gabby's throat filled with tears she swallowed back.

Max smiled. "That's fantastic!" He started toward her.

"But I still don't remember the evidence," Gabby said, frustrated. "I don't remember the judicial challenges with the Global Warriors' cases and investigating Judge Abernathy for corruption. I don't recall anything on the Global Warriors you haven't expressly told me, though I have a flash of killing a man in the garage you say was one of them. I don't remember anything on the Consortium Dr. Erickson talked about, though it does ring true to me and the name—the Consortium—feels oddly familiar. Maybe. I need to know *all* of that and I can't remember *any* of it. The one thing I *don't* want to remember is not being married to you. So naturally, that's the one thing I *do* remember." She shrugged and lifted a hand. "I know your ass is on the line with mine now, and if we don't find out who is behind the dead Warrior—" She stopped mid-sentence and frowned at him. "Where is that dead Warrior now?"

"I buried him at the park."

At least that mystery had been resolved. She went on. "Well, if we don't find out why he was here and get all this

Z-4027 business under control, we're going to be buried next to him, so I hope you picked a pretty spot."

"Lovely." Max smiled at her.

She bristled. "What are you smiling at?" The man had lost his mind. They were in so much trouble it was outrageous and he was grinning at her like an idiot. Maybe *she* had lost her mind. She'd fallen in love with an idiot. "You know, insanity is looking pretty good right now."

He laughed in her face. "You can't choose to be insane, Gabby."

"Yes, I think I can. I can't imagine anyone doubting me on it. Not right now."

Laughing, he stepped up to the counter and swept his arms around her, then nuzzled her neck. "You're just bitchy because you love me."

"Most definitely." She smacked his shoulder—and then wrapped her legs around him to keep him close. "You're going to hold it over my head, too. I can see that you're going to use it to make me miserable. I wish I hadn't told you."

"But you did." He planted a row of kisses along the arch of her neck, then drew in a deep breath as if he were taking her scent down into his soul. "It's okay to love me, Gabby."

Easy for him to say. He wasn't the one who had lost his memory and had wished for insanity as a respite. "Okay or not, it's there, Max. So let's just accept it and drop the subject before I get nauseous."

"You really do need to ease up. My ego can take the strain of your not totally knowing yourself and swearing you love me, but your obvious joy about it just knocks me to my knees."

"Oh, shut up and kiss me, then take me to bed." She lifted her face and closed her eyes.

Still smiling, he kissed her hard and deep. She pressed into him, and he seriously considered taking her up on her offer. "No bed," he said. "Another time. Right now, we have a country in crisis to consider."

* * *

It had been a bitch of a day, and the night wasn't looking much more promising.

The director sat in his favorite wingback chair in his robe and slippers. His perfect wife was still upstairs locked in their perfect bedroom and not speaking a word to him— perfect or imperfect. A wise man was grateful for the silence. And today, he needed it.

"To you, Andrew." He lifted his glass of Jim Beam in a salute, and then took down a healthy draw that burned his throat and warmed his chest. "Ah."

Killing a man you'd known more than half your life was a bitch, all right. But some things couldn't be avoided. Andrew had known the rules, and he'd played the game and made his choices. Still, he'd be missed.

Half an hour later, the director checked the time: It was a reasonable hour now in Eastern Europe. He phoned the chairman and informed him about Andrew and about Grayson interfering and stopping the spraying.

"We got enough hard data to prove our point," the chairman said.

"I wanted more. I wanted to wow the buyers."

The chairman let out a low laugh. "Ah, you'll never learn. You're a greedy man. That can be good, I agree, but only if you learn to be philosophical about these projects. We made fortunes with the cotton and wines. Time to cut our losses on marketing the vaccine and pesticide—at least for a few months."

"You're right, of course." Carnel Cove was too hot to do anything else, thanks to that hurricane and all the feds it brought in with it.

"Have a pleasant evening."

Visions of his redhead floated through his mind. She gave the best massages. Maybe he'd pay the island a visit next week.

Something made of glass crashed upstairs. Again. His wife was systematically destroying every object in the house.

Maybe he'd leave tomorrow. . . .

Chapter Thirty-five

The doorbell rang.

Max looked at the clock—three A.M.—grumbled, crawled out of bed, threw on some jeans, and answered the door.

Sheriff Coulter stood in the mellow porch light, grim-faced. "Max, sorry to wake you."

"No problem." He stepped back so Jackson could come inside.

He stepped through and shut the door, his shoulder swiping a ficus Gabby had just inside the entryway. "Carl Blake has committed suicide."

"Blake?" Bank president. Model citizen. Owner of the fleet of trucks used to spray the chemicals—including the ones outfitted with tanks inside their tanks. Local real estate mogul. One of two men who'd had red clay on his shoes at Cove Park. Close associate of the deceased Judge

Andrew Abernathy. *And now apparent Consortium member.* "What happened?"

"A couple hours ago, I finally caught up to Carl and Sissy. I saw the red clay on their shoes—just like Gabby said. I pointed it out and asked if they'd been up to Abernathy's cabin. They denied it, though Sissy looked disturbed about my asking." Jackson shrugged. "Next thing I know, I'm at the Silver Spoon grabbing a cup of coffee and Bobby—my deputy—comes running in hell-for-leather, telling me Blake's dead and he left a suicide note."

Max pinched the bridge of his nose. "What does it say?"

"That's why I'm here," Jackson said. "It doesn't make sense."

Max waited. Gabby came out of the bedroom fully dressed in jeans and a green top and nodded at Jackson.

He nodded back. "Sorry about the intrusion, Gabby. It couldn't be helped."

"No problem, Jackson." She offered him a smile.

Jackson then went on, talking to Max. "The note said, 'I didn't know.'"

Max looked at Gabby, who hiked her shoulders signaling she didn't grasp his meaning either, and then they both looked back at Jackson.

"I asked Sissy—you have to figure if anyone knows a man's mind, it's his wife—but she didn't have any idea what Carl was talking about."

Max was totally lost. "So why are you here?"

Jackson's cheeks reddened. "As you might imagine, Sissy is pretty upset. She's asking for Gabby and Candace to come to her house right away."

"Did she say why?" Gabby asked.

"No, she didn't. I assumed it was just one of those times when a woman needed to be surrounded by her friends."

Odd, Gabby thought. Sissy Blake was not her friend, nor was she Candace's. "Tell her we'll be right over."

"Sure will." He turned back to Max. "I ran into Stan Mullin as I was leaving the Silver Spoon to come over here. He says he needs to talk with you as soon as you have a second. The guy in the FEMA jacket who told the truck driver to spray the low-income housing community wasn't one of his. Darlene's at the station running a search on the description of the man, but so far we haven't matched him up."

Max nodded. "Thanks, Jackson."

He turned to walk out and paused, his hand on the doorknob. "I still don't know what is going on here, Max, but I think you have a good idea. I'm trusting you not to put the screws to my town." Jackson gave him a long, intense look. "I'll have your word on that."

"You've got it, Jackson."

Apparently satisfied with what he saw, Jackson nodded and left.

Two minutes later, Gabby and Max were walking out the door. "Drop me off at Candace's," she said. "You can take the Jeep to go see Stan."

"Okay."

Max drove them over, and when Gabby was ready to get out of the Jeep, she leaned over and gave him a quick kiss. "Love you."

Before Max could respond—if he could have responded—she was climbing into Candace's car. His heart knocking hard against his ribs, Max just sat there and watched them drive away. For a lot of men, he supposed, the little gesture wouldn't mean a thing. But it was a major event to Max. A first. Significant because it was Gabby making that gesture toward him. Toward *him*. Definitely significant.

You're making a sucker bet, Max. She didn't love you before, and she won't love you when she gets back to normal.

You want a broken heart, fine, go ahead and let yourself love her. But when she walks, don't come bitching to me. She will walk, Max. You know she will. The women in your life have always walked.

They had. Always. Why would Gabby be any different? When she was in her right mind, she didn't respect his skills, much less have any trust or faith in him—not even enough to be a professional partner, much less a personal one. She'd walk, too. Eventually. It was inevitable. And knowing it hurt. Deep.

Max put the Jeep into first gear, and headed to the Silver Spoon to meet Stan.

★ ★ ★

"Did I just hear you tell Max you loved him?"

Gabby looked over at Candace. She was beautiful, blond and lanky, and while she could have stepped right off the pages of *Vogue* for her looks and fashion sense, she had stepped off the pages of *Fortune* for her astute business acumen. Gabby saw no physical signs that Candace had been ill, much less at death's door, but that didn't surprise her. Candace was Candace, and perfection was as natural to her as sunshine and humidity were to Florida.

Of course, Gabby looked like something the cat wouldn't even drag in. T-shirt, jeans, and running shoes. Hair bed-wrecked. But she had slowed down long enough to wash her face and brush her teeth while Max had called Candace and given her a heads-up to get ready. Still, Gabby was half surprised Candace allowed her to get into the car. Usually she sent her back to "freshen up," which was her polite way of asking if Gabby had bothered to look into a mirror in the last twenty-four hours. "Yeah, that's what you heard." Why bother denying it? She did love Max. Whether or not he believed it didn't have a thing to do with whether or not it was real.

"Mmm." Candace kept her gaze on the road and stopped for the red light on South Main.

"Mmm, what?" Gabby snitched Candace's brush and tugged her hair into a ponytail.

"Oh, nothing." Candace adjusted the temperature control and then clicked on her blinker to turn right.

"Don't say that," Gabby told her, pulling her hair back and up and capturing loose strands. "I hate it when you say that because it's *always* something."

"I'm surprised, that's all." Candace didn't take offense at Gabby's shouting. It was just Gabby. "That you love him, I mean."

"It's not a novel concept, Candace." Gabby twisted the band into her hair. "I am married to the man."

Candace held her gaze firmly through the windshield on the road. "Right."

Sarcasm wasn't Candace's style, but her voice was riddled with it. Had Gabby taken her into her confidence and told Candace the truth? That would have carried serious consequences for both of them. Surely she wouldn't have jeopardized Candace that way. "Right, what?"

"It's just that you guys don't act married. More telling, you look at him hungry-eyed. If you were married to him, that gleam would be satisfied, not starved."

Gabby grunted, turned the tables on her. "So Keith and you were married, and you look at him the same way."

"Yes."

No denial. Interesting. "But you divorced him."

"Actually, he divorced me." She looped an arm over the steering wheel.

"You're kidding." Gabby had seen the way the man had looked at Candace. She couldn't believe it.

"Not kidding." Candace pulled up to the curb outside Sissy's two-story brick home. "Keith loves me, Gabby. He always will. I still love him, too. But we just can't love each other and live together."

"Why not?"

"Well, if I had that figured out, then I could fix it, now couldn't I?" She cut the engine and snagged her purse. "This bit of business reeks to high heaven. There's no way Carl Blake would just kill himself. He had everything to live for and no reason to want to die." She frowned. "None that we know of, anyway."

"Maybe. But outsiders seldom know everything about anyone." Gabby got out and shut the car door. Falling into step beside Candace, they walked by the mailbox—which sported stickers for both the Gators and the Seminoles, which signaled life must be hell in this house during football season since the two were major rivals—and up to the front door. There were four cars in the drive.

"Any idea why she wanted to talk with us?" Gabby rang the doorbell.

"Not really," Candace said, then lowered her voice. "She's always wanted to be one of the ladies in our little group, but she's so hung up on being perfect. It wouldn't have worked."

The front door swung open. Mayor Faulkner nodded and invited them inside, clearly relieved to see them. "She's in the library. Nothing I said made any difference to her. She's asked fifty times if you two were here yet."

Two other men stood in the living room. One turned away, to look out the window into the night. There was something oddly familiar about him, though Gabby instinctively knew they hadn't met. The second man, dressed in a charcoal gray suit and tie, was one of the men from the bank. Gabby had seen him there several times, though she didn't know his name.

"Where are the children?" Candace asked Faulkner.

"It'll take a while for them to get home from college. Their daughter is down in Gainesville. Her boyfriend is driving her home. Their son is in Tallahassee at FSU. He'll be here in another hour or so."

"What happened?" Gabby asked.

"I wish I knew," Faulkner said, keeping his voice low so Sissy wouldn't overhear him. "Carl put a thirty-eight in his mouth and pulled the trigger. That's all we know right now."

Gabby flinched because Faulkner expected it.

Candace didn't, and Gabby wondered why not.

"Go on in," Faulkner said. "Gloria just brought in a fresh pot of coffee."

"Gloria?" Gabby asked.

"Their housekeeper," Candace said, walking into the library.

Sissy sat on a burgundy leather wingback chair that seemed far too large for her to be comfortable. It looked like a throne. "Oh, girls. I'm so glad you've come."

"Of course, Sissy." Candace hugged her. "I'm so sorry for your loss."

Sissy let go, wept a little, and then hugged Gabby.

"I'm sorry, Sissy." Because there wasn't any more that could be said that wasn't redundant, Gabby fell silent, though she thought losing a spouse had to be one of the hardest things a human being could ever experience.

Sissy sniffed and swiped at her face with a soggy tissue. "Have some coffee."

Candace poured, and Gabby sat down on a matching chair across a lamp table from Sissy. "Is there anything you need?"

"I just don't know what could have gotten into him. How could he do this?" Horror spread through her eyes. "What am I supposed to tell the children?" She sniffled and got a fresh tissue, crimping the old one in her palm. "There's just no way to explain something like this. They'll be crushed."

"They'll survive it," Candace assured her.

"Kids are resilient." Gabby had heard that a thousand

times—usually in connection with those serving time in Juvenile Hall. *How did she know that? Was that a memory?*

"But suicide!" Sissy's pale face turned pink and she dropped her red-rimmed gaze to her lap. "How can I ever again face anyone in Carnel Cove? How can I, knowing I've spent thirty years of my life married to a man who'd rather be dead than married to me?"

"Sissy," Gabby said. "Suicide is rarely a family member's fault. Usually, the person feels overwhelmed and too weary of battles to fight anymore. You can't let what he did affect you this way."

"But it's a mortal sin." Her eyes stretched wide, owl-like. "I can't bury him in consecrated ground. The children and I may not be welcome at St. Mary's."

"Of course, you will," Candace said. "You've been a member since you were born and Father McDowell knows it." Candace sipped from her cup. "Where did this happen, dear?"

"I don't know." Sissy stilled, shocked by that realization. "Jackson told me he'd found Carl, but I don't know where. Oh, my God. How can I not know where it happened?"

"It's okay. It's the shock. It happens to everyone." Gabby hoped she sounded reassuring. "Jackson will tell you again. Mayor Faulkner is here. I'm sure he knows."

"Ronald. Yes, he'll know." She looked at Gabby. "Have you shown anyone else Carl's notebook? He noticed it missing the morning Hurricane Darla made landfall. I have to know that it wasn't my fault he killed himself, Gabby. That nothing in that notebook made him do it."

Notebook. What notebook? Obviously, one Sissy had given Gabby that she was supposed to know she had. "No, I haven't shown it to anyone else," she said, certain it was true since she didn't know where it was herself.

Sissy slumped in relief. "Thank God." She smoothed her hair, as if the strokes soothed her. "I didn't think so, since the storm hit so soon after I gave it to you. But I had to be sure."

"Not a soul," Gabby said emphatically.

She smiled. And it seemed so odd to see a smile in her tearstained face that Gabby instinctively looked at Candace, who was casting an equally suspicious look at Sissy.

They talked for another half hour, and then Sissy's son came home, so Gabby and Candace left to give the family some privacy.

When Gabby walked back into the living room, the vaguely familiar man was gone. The man from the bank was sitting on the sofa petting a beagle, seeming wooden and out of place.

Faulkner saw them out and they got back into Candace's black Porsche. When Gabby closed the door, Candace turned in her seat and looked Gabby right in the eye. "Do you remember anything about the notebook?"

Gabby felt trapped, but decided to answer. "No. Nothing."

"I didn't think so." Candace pursed her lips and cranked the engine. "Sissy said she gave it to you just before the storm." She shifted into first and pulled away from the curb. "The day before, your Jeep broke down on the road to Abernathy's cabin. The dealer towed it in and I picked you up."

"Did we go straight home?"

The notebook wasn't at Gabby's house; after finding the passports and licenses, she'd ripped the place up from stem to stern searching for her real past but found nothing except her memory box, which was pitifully close to empty and very depressing because it was. Carl Blake's notebook had to be in her courtroom.

Candace stomped the brakes and made a U-turn in the middle of University Avenue. Gabby's shoulder thumped against the door. "What are you doing? Geez, Candace, you're driving like a maniac."

"I was not. I was just turning around."

"At fifty miles per hour?"

"Oh, stop. It wasn't."

"Well, do you mind telling me—before you turn me into roadkill—where you're going?"

Candace looked at her as if she were slow on the uptake. "The courthouse. Obviously, you left the notebook there if it's not at your house."

"I never said it wasn't at my house."

"Gabby, get real, okay?" Candace rolled her gaze and hit the brakes hard to swing into the courthouse parking garage. "You had no memory, darling. If the blessed thing was in your house, you'd have found it." She whipped into Gabby's parking slot and stopped. "Or are you going to tell me you didn't look?"

"No." Gabby got out and fished her keys from her purse, not at all comfortable that she had become so predictable to Candace. "I'm not."

*   *   *

Cardel Boudreaux drove into the judge's parking area at the courthouse. After he verified that the black Porsche parked there was Candace Burke's, he drove out onto the street, stopped curbside, and dialed the phone.

When he got what appeared to be a fax line, he punched in the chairman's code number. He didn't like reporting directly to a client—the buffer of his boss doing the conversing made him far more comfortable—but for double his fee, he had agreed to lose the buffer and take on the extra risk of direct contact with the head of the Consortium.

"Yes?" The man answered.

"She's at the courthouse. Sissy Blake asked her about the notebook. She said she hasn't shown it to anyone else."

"Do you believe her?"

"I do." Cardel fingered the blinker stem. "She got it the day before Darla hit and she's been sick ever since. This is the first time she's been to the courthouse." He should tell the chairman that he'd bugged Candace's car and Gabby didn't remember the notebook, but that could diminish the danger to the Consortium and jeopardize Cardel's doubled fee, so he kept that tidbit of info to himself. "It's the final possible link to you or anyone outside of Carnel Cove."

"Sever it." The chairman paused and then added, "I have serious doubts it's authentic, but I want that notebook in my hands by dawn."

"Yes, sir." Cardel hung up. If everything went as planned, Cardel would have it just as soon as Gabby and Candace returned to Candace's car.

They'd never leave the parking lot alive.

★   ★   ★

"Find anything?" Candace walked up the center aisle to the gap between the prosecutor's and defender's tables.

"Nothing." Gabby propped her hands on her hips and blew out an exhausted breath.

"Mind if I call in reinforcements?"

Gabby would call anyone short of the devil to find that notebook. "Who?"

Candace pulled out her cell phone. "She who knows all in Carnel Cove, dear heart."

She who knows all? Gabby lifted her arms. "Who the heck does that mean?"

"Miranda, darling." Candace smiled. "If it's going on in or near the Cove, Miranda Coffield knows it or can find it out."

If that were the case, Gabby should ask her who's

heading the Consortium, where that second Warrior was, who killed Judge Abernathy and William Powell, and a dozen other important questions. Miranda was informed, but how could she know this? Gabby couldn't imagine, but Candace had insight she lacked because the woman never praised lightly.

"Hey, it's me," Candace said into the phone. "Listen, Gabby and I are at the courthouse. Are there secret compartments, safes, false walls, or anything where someone could hide something here?" She paused. "No, not the whole courthouse. In the courtrooms." Candace listened and then looked at Gabby. "Is this Courtroom A or B?"

"B." Now what exactly should Gabby think of this?

A few minutes passed. "Thanks, Miranda." Candace winked and shut off the phone. "There's a cubby under the bench."

"You're kidding." Gabby couldn't believe it.

"Does this look like the face of a woman who's kidding?"

It didn't. Candace looked dead serious. "How did Miranda know this?"

"She pulled the original plans, from when they built the courthouse. It's on the plan." Candace walked over to the front of the bench. "Miranda can do anything with a computer, Gabby. Anything at all. I thought I'd already mentioned that."

"You did." Gabby ran her fingers along the outside of the bench. "But you know, she's so good it's almost scary."

"In the wrong hands, she could be scary. But Miranda is one woman you don't have to worry about. She's straight as an arrow all the way."

Finding nothing, Gabby moved on, let her fingertips glide along the wood under the kneehole in the bench. On the far right, she bumped into a lever. "This could be it." She pushed it, not surprised she'd missed it before. It was hidden under a lip. A wooden panel about two feet wide slid open, revealing a small cubby. "Oh, yes!" She shot Candace a glance and then pulled out a black leather notebook. "Got it."

"Yeah, yeah. What's stuffed inside?" Candace stretched across the bench to see.

Gabby unfolded the papers, scanned them. "Judge Powell's test results." Remembering doing the tests, she looked over at Candace. "I ran them in your lab, didn't I? You let me in."

Candace nodded.

The Consortium. The notebook *is* the evidence. "Oh, God. We've got to get this to Max." Gabby ran around the front of the bench, grabbed Candace by the arm, and they ran out of the courtroom.

Clearing the elevator, Gabby felt dread drag at her belly. "Candace?" She didn't know how to tell her this. How did you tell a woman who had put her life on the line to save others that she was in serious jeopardy of going to jail?

"Give it to me straight, Gabby." Candace watched the elevator light above their heads mark off the floors. "Honey, you've had that tone in your voice exactly twice. Once, when you told Elizabeth and me that you couldn't tell us anything other than what you already had but you believed us about William being murdered. The second time, when you told Max you loved him. I figure that was bad news to you, considering how hell-bent you are on not loving anyone. So both times, that tone carried bad news. It's a reasonable assumption this time's no different."

"Unfortunately, you're right. It appears Logan Industries is up to its armpits in all this subterfuge, Candace. There's no way around it."

Candace pursed her lips, stared off to the wall for a second, but kept right on walking. "Sweep out the clutter, then."

"That's it?" Gabby lifted a hand. "That's all you have to say about it?"

"What do you expect me to say about it, Gabby?" She shrugged. "I don't know a thing about medical research. I figured the DOD would keep everyone in line—we are on full-monitoring status. If it didn't, and they didn't catch it, how could I?" Candace hitched her purse strap back up over her shoulder. "Am I happy about it? No. But I'm a realist and a practical woman. I'll nail the son of a bitch who did this to me to the jailhouse wall—after I break him financially." She stepped out of the elevator and paused at the door to the parking area. "Do you know who at Logan Industries is corrupt?"

"Not exactly," Gabby admitted. "Not yet, anyway."

"Well, find out, will you?" Candace frowned and stepped into the garage. "Like I said, you sweep out the clutter. I'll pray I don't find my assets in the dustbin or my backside in jail."

Candace pressed her keyless entry button and they walked from the door toward the car. Gabby automatically checked to make sure the area was secure—the two-story parking garage had always given her the heebie-jeebies. No one else was in sight, and no other cars were on level one. The place was deserted.

Halfway to the car, the hair on her neck stood straight up. "Wait." Gabby looked around, heard a car pull away from the curb outside. "Run, Candace!"

They ran toward the street, cleared the corner, and were down two buildings when Candace slowed down. "What the hell is going on?"

Gabby pulled her. "Just move!"

The car exploded.

Chapter Thirty-six

Max didn't recognize the car pulling into the drive.

It stopped near the Jeep, and Gabby got out. "Thanks for the lift, Bobby."

Bobby wore a deputy's uniform, but drove an unmarked white sedan. In the front seat beside him sat Candace. She looked shaken.

Gabby didn't. Perplexed, Max waited on the front porch for Gabby to reach him.

She lifted up on her toes, smacked a kiss to his lips, and then turned and waved good-bye.

Max looped an arm around her waist. "What happened to Candace's car?"

"It blew up."

Surprise streaked up Max's back. "What?"

"It exploded, Max."

"What do you mean, it exploded?"

"All I know is it was intentional. Someone put a bomb

in it—no idea who; I didn't see anyone. It's a miracle we weren't killed."

"Candace's car exploded curbside at Sissy Blake's house?" Max followed her across the porch. "And Sissy's house was deserted?"

"No, not at Sissy's. A self-respecting weed wouldn't dare grow in her grass, much less a car dare to explode near her home."

Clearly lost, Max held up his arms. "Where were you, then?"

"At the courthouse, looking for the evidence Sissy said I had." She waved him off. "I'll get to that later. Candace and I were walking from the elevator to her car. I heard this car pulling away from the curb, and all these alarms went off inside my head. I don't know why. I didn't think, I just acted. I told Candace to run. She took off toward the car. I jerked her around, and pointed her outside. We ran. The car blew up. And that's all I know." Gabby walked inside and went straight to the kitchen. Reaching up into the cabinet above the stove, she pulled out a bottle of bourbon and poured herself a stiff drink, then kicked it back. Her hands were trembling. She poured herself another.

Max stilled her hand on the counter and hugged her to him. "Thank God you're safe."

She slumped against him and held on tight, amazed at how much safer she felt just being with him. She'd rather have him as her husband, but if he wouldn't and refused to be, then having him as a partner would be a decent consolation. Not great, but decent. Somehow she just knew she was fed up with going it alone.

She stepped away and drank her second drink in a single swallow.

"Slow down on the juice, Cinderella," Max said. "Otherwise, you'll miss the ball."

She glared at him, plopped the glass on the counter.

But seeing no condemnation in his eyes faded her anger and piqued her curiosity. "What ball?"

"We've got art." He picked up a stack of papers from the kitchen table. "Intel came through with connections to the July fourth infestations."

"Finally, some good news." She skirted around him, bumped into him and snagged herself a kiss, then sat down in a chair at the table. "Show me."

He put a photo of the Global Warrior she had killed in her garage in front of her. "Jaris Adahan left a cruise ship in Mexico and entered customs in Texas under an alias. But the photo is definitely his."

He was wearing a hat with a U.S. flag pinned to its brim. Seeing it on him ticked her off. "He got the cotton crops, then?"

Max nodded. "We connected him through the contaminated fruit shipment."

"How?"

"On a hunch, your favorite trainee checked out the customs inspector in the photo with Adahan. He was dirty, Gabby. When the Justice Department brought him in, he started talking."

"I knew Gibson had potential." Gabby smiled. "What's the market done on cotton?" That could lead to a human connection between the incidents.

"Egyptian cotton prices have tripled."

She pulled Carl Blake's notebook out of her purse. "We can verify who made the most money on those stock transactions. This could help tie them to the Consortium and give us a connection to the Global Warriors. Maybe."

"What is it?"

"Carl Blake's notebook," she said. "I haven't yet read it, but if it contains what I think it does, we'll know who was running the Consortium, and I'm betting we can see who made out like bandits on the trades. That could tell us the identities of the other Consortium members."

"Sounds promising."

"What else do you have there?" He passed her a photo of Sebastian Cabot, the drunk driver who had killed Judge Abernathy's wife and son and then killed himself in California. "Which customs site is this from?" she asked.

"Canada to U.S.—within proximity for the grape louse infestation. Dr. Richardson says the timing is consistent and there were empty pâté tins in Cabot's wreckage. A lot of them."

Gabby frowned, not making that connection.

"The louse needed a host. Pâté was a natural choice."

She nodded. "So Intel's tagged the infestations as biological attacks."

He poured himself a cup of coffee and sat back down. "Based on testimony and what they've uncovered so far, Intel feels confident that this Consortium is a group of Carnel Cove businessmen who manipulate major events through third parties—like the Global Warriors—to serve its financial interests, just like Erickson said. They think Faulkner is the head of it, Gabby. And I have to say that he looks very guilty. He's done everything short of issuing Stan Mullin a direct order to resume the pesticide spraying."

"Nothing happens in the Cove without Faulkner knowing it." She looked down at Carl Blake's notebook and flashes of memories stormed through her mind, fast and furious, and explicitly clear. "Oh, God."

"What?" Max reached across the table and covered her hand with his. "Gabby, what is it?"

"Carl's journal. It tells it all. About the Consortium, Faulkner, about Judge Abernathy suspending the Warrior sentences in return for the Consortium dealing with Sebastian Cabot for killing his wife and son. About them making sure Dr. Marcus Swift was hired to run Logan Industries by keeping out all other potential applicants. About Swift recruiting Erickson so he could steal the patent on the Z-4027 vaccine and pesticide. It's all there,

Max. All of it. Including Carl's suspicion that Judge Powell had been murdered."

Yet something didn't feel right. Something felt very wrong.

"What's not connecting, Gabby?"

Not at all surprised Max had picked up on it, she looked up at him. "Faulkner being the Consortium director."

"You said yourself nothing happens here without him knowing it, and we know they had strategy sessions at the cabin. He made everyone's business his business. It fits."

"No, actually it doesn't," Gabby insisted. "He dodges responsibility. He takes credit for successes, but not fault for screwups. You've seen that."

Max thought it through and frowned. "He lacks the leadership abilities, doesn't he?"

"Yes, he does." Gabby's neck felt stiff. She rubbed at it. "I'm not sure why, but I feel certain the mayor didn't order or commit the murders. He respected Judges Powell and Abernathy. He really did. I don't think he had the guts to order either of them killed."

"But Blake wants us to believe he did."

"Maybe. But, you know, he was funny about things. I think if he'd had a choice, he wouldn't have wanted us to know anything. And I'm not at all sure he'd leave incriminating notes like this."

Gabby slid back her chair. Its legs scraped on the floor, and she reached for the telephone and dialed. Moments later, she spoke. "Candace. Hey. Listen, tell me how you came to buy Logan Industries."

"Mayor Faulkner gave me the initial heads-up on it being vulnerable. I followed up on the lead, decided it was a great investment, checked with Keith for objections on the due diligence, and then bought it."

"Otherwise you'd have had no idea it was vulnerable?"

"No. Last reports out on it, it looked financially stable. I met with the owner, had my compliance auditor take a look at the books, and made an offer. He was happy, I was happy, and Faulkner was happy. Faulkner was worried about the loss of jobs if poor management let L.I. go under. If he hadn't contacted me, I wouldn't have known L.I. was ripe for a hostile takeover."

"Okay, thanks."

"Gabby, how much trouble am I in?"

"I'm not sure yet. Try not to worry. We'll make it right." She hung up the phone and turned to Max.

"Faulkner," he said, beating her to the disclosure.

"Yes."

"It's not looking good for him, Gabby."

"That's the problem." She put on a fresh pot of coffee and waited at the counter for a cup's worth to filter through and fill the pot. "He's such a politician, Max—always mindful of reelection. He wouldn't tarnish his image or risk turning voters against him. Faulkner is a pain in the ass, but he is extremely protective of Carnel Cove and Covers. His great-grandfather founded the town, so he feels strong ties to the place. He wouldn't ordinarily pass on a hot tip on a specific local business. They're all special to him. At worst, he'd have someone else do it—like Carl Blake. Being the bank president, it would be more natural for him to know about this. But Candace says Faulkner gave her the lead himself."

"Maybe he didn't want the business to go down the tubes. That costs the Cove revenue, jobs, stability, and he would want to protect against all that. I don't see the conflict here."

"You're missing my point," Gabby said. "Faulkner would see to it that Candace got the lead, but he wouldn't give it to her himself. He'd be afraid that the other businesses would feel slighted. More likely, he'd have Carl Blake tell her—especially if Faulkner was manipulating events for the Consortium. He'd never risk that direct tie to himself. It could compromise him."

"Yet he did tell her himself. So your theory is that since he did, he can't be the director of the Consortium?"

"Exactly." She nodded. "Faulkner could be faking it, but he genuinely doesn't seem to know the truth about the lab incident, which is amazing in itself since he typically knows everything that goes on in Carnel Cove. If he were the director, it stands to reason that Dr. Swift would have told him. If he brought Dr. Swift onboard at L.I. he would answer to Faulkner."

Max mulled it all over in his mind. "He grilled me, looking for answers. He doesn't know the truth; I'd bet on it. As the director, Faulkner just doesn't work."

Gabby reached over and flipped a strand of hair away from Max's eyes. "You know what does work?"

"What?" He cupped her hand, twined their fingers.

"The director issuing Faulkner an order he couldn't refuse." Gabby slid off her chair and nudged Max's side until he slid his chair back from the table. Then she eased onto his lap and rested her chin at the crook in his neck. "What if Carl Blake was the director?" Max's arms closed around her and his heart beat hard and fast against her side. "What if Blake arranged for the Warrior to attack me? Forced Cabot to infect the vineyards and Faulkner to give Candace the Logan Industries stock lead? I could see him squelching likely CEO applicants so Candace had no choice but to hire Dr. Swift."

"Swift probably was already in the Consortium's pocket."

"Yes."

Max sighed and rested his cheek against her head. "I'm not connecting all the dots, honey. Why would Blake kill Judge Powell? Judge Abernathy?"

"Because Judge Powell was in New York—according to Blake's journal—to report Judge Abernathy to the Justice Department for judicial corruption."

"The suspension of the three Global Warrior cases."

She nodded. Rubbed small circles on his shoulder. "When the fourth Warrior case came up and Faulkner told Abernathy to handle it, I had already been inserted here as a judge. Abernathy sensed I was more than a judge. He balked about hearing the case. Faulkner insisted, so Abernathy retired from the bench to avoid having to hear the case."

"That put the case in Judge Powell's lap," Max surmised.

"According to Blake's book, Faulkner approached Judge Powell, looking for a suspended sentence. Powell agreed to think it over."

Max's eyes gleamed, linking the connection. "But then Powell went to New York to meet with the Justice Department, so the Consortium got the Global Warriors to arrange the elevator incident to stop Powell from making the meeting."

"It worked, too. Powell recognized that incident as an attack meant for him, and he returned home without going to the meeting. He went up to the cabin to talk with Judge Abernathy. To confront him with his suspicions."

"Faulkner was there, of course."

"So says Carl Blake. It's hard to make him a scapegoat if he's not around. But I say Faulkner wasn't there. Carl was, and he killed Judge Powell. Carl released the Z-4027-infected mosquitoes in the lab *and* he killed Abernathy—to frame Faulkner as the Consortium director."

"But you had done the testing on Powell and thrown a wrench into the works."

"I think so. That's why he sent the Global Warriors to murder me. I was a risk too high to him to take."

"Only instead of dying like a nice little judge, you killed his Warrior."

"And his second Warrior missed me and winged you. The only thing he's murdered is the Jeep's tires and maybe Candace's car—provided the people in that housing unit live." She sat up, looked at Max. "The final nail for Carl was when his journal went missing."

"That's why he killed himself. He feared exposure through it."

Gabby studied the matter long and hard. Carl Blake thought he was brilliant. He was clever, but only clever. His biggest challenge was appearances and ego. "No, Max. That's why he didn't kill himself," she said. "Don't you see? Carl Blake thought he could conquer the world and everything in it. He was domineering, master of his world. He wouldn't leave it voluntarily. There's no way he would have killed himself, Max. No way."

"So this too was murder?"

"It has to be," Gabby said. "Nothing else makes sense." She scooted off his lap and raided the fridge, which had been miraculously restocked—she assumed by Max. Hauling out smoked turkey breast, baby Swiss cheese, mayo, pickles, and mustard, she glanced back at Max. "Grab the lettuce and tomatoes, will you?"

"Sure." He went to the fridge, grabbed the items, and then joined her at the sink, where they worked side by side to prepare sandwiches.

Gabby loved working in the kitchen with Max. It felt cozy, comfortable.

"You know, in light of everything we've learned, it makes sense that Dr. Swift substituted the black-banded canister in the lab." Max snitched a slice of pickle off a plate holding them, slivers of onion, and wedges of tomatoes.

Gabby withdrew two plates from the cabinet and then closed the door. "How's that?"

"Swift had Erickson's vaccine, right? He didn't need him anymore."

"Right." She pulled out knives and forks and set the plate of cold cuts on the table.

Max carried over the rest. "What didn't Swift have, then? What couldn't he get?"

Gabby slathered mayo on a slice of bread. Bit into a piece of onion and pondered. Max's point hit her like a hammer strike, and excitement bubbled in her stomach. "Trial studies."

"Yeah." Max took a bite of sandwich, chewed, and swallowed. "He had already gone through the allotted funding for them. So he couldn't get more money off the DOD contract. He also couldn't finish the contract without the studies. He was screwed."

"Then when Hurricane Darla hit, and the mosquito population increased as it always does after a hurricane, he saw an opportunity to get his trial studies and to get FEMA to pay for them." The excitement got buried under the heartless act of a man willing to kill innocents for his own purposes. "God, Max. He's a monster."

"Spraying Z-4027 on the public for money qualifies in my book."

"David Erickson would know it, too. So Swift had to shut down his program for the vaccine and get him out of Logan Industries. Swift had to discredit David to get rid of him to get the vaccine patent, and to have authorities blow off anything David might report to them as sour grapes. That's why Swift set it up to look like David's lab had the security breaches and David, not Swift, didn't report them."

"That's my take on it." Max got up, fixed them glasses of iced tea, and then returned to his seat and shoved a little white bowl of lemon wedges toward Gabby.

For a man who wasn't married to her, he knew a lot of her habits. She squeezed two wedges into her glass. "But Swift screwed up on the timing."

"He did." Max wiped at his mouth with the edge of his napkin. "When he claimed David was switching the canisters, he was here, with you and me and Elizabeth. Naturally, when all hell broke loose at the lab, Carl Blake realized his pesticide-spraying trucks had sprayed the superbug and not pesticide. Forty-two people in the hospital, no cure . . . maybe the reality of killing people, doing trial studies on the public and getting caught at it, were more than Carl could handle, and so he killed himself. It's possible."

"It's not possible." Candace came in from the living room and snagged a plate from the cabinet. She sat down across from Gabby. "Pass the bread."

"How long have you been here?" Gabby passed over the loaf of bread.

"Long enough to know you're going down the wrong road." She made herself a sandwich, took a bite, and then got herself a glass of tea. "I'm not buying it—Faulkner, that is. He doesn't have what it takes. Carl does. He hired the Global Warriors to kill people—including you." She paused and slid Gabby a glare. "I'm totally pissed about my Porsche."

"Be glad you're alive."

"Tomorrow." Candace spread a napkin in her lap. "Today, I want revenge."

"Which is why you're here?" Max asked.

"If Carl Blake killed William Powell and Judge Abernathy personally—which I believe he did—then forty-two strangers dying meant nothing to him. I'm betting he didn't kill himself. I'm betting someone else killed him." She looked knowingly at Gabby.

"Who?" Max asked, not following.

Gabby sucked in a sharp breath. "Someone who wanted the truth to remain buried even more than Carl wanted it to remain buried."

Candace nodded.

"Faulkner is the obvious choice."

"True," Gabby agreed. "But that's exactly why he wouldn't do it."

"Then who are you two talking about? Obviously, you've got a grip on who did this."

"Yes, I do," Candace said.

"For all the reasons Faulkner wouldn't do it, Sissy Blake would—and why she would create the incident at the lab."

Max swallowed a bite. "Share your insights. I'm not making the leap."

Gabby touched a hand to his forearm. "Sissy knew Carl was the Consortium director—in the same way Elizabeth knew William was SDU—"

Candace frowned. "What's SDU?"

"Never mind," Gabby said quickly. "The point is, Sissy knew and she hated it. Likely, she hated him for it."

"She is extremely into appearances, Max," Candace explained. "If Carl were exposed doing something illegal or embarrassing, the humiliation would be worse than death to Sissy. She honestly couldn't take it."

Gabby went on. "Sissy knew about it all, and she wanted it to stop. She wanted the ugliness to just go away. She killed Judge Powell to keep the truth about Carl buried. She rewrote Carl's notebook, framing Mayor Faulkner—simple handwriting tests will prove it—and she gave it to me so I would bring Faulkner to justice. Then Hurricane Darla gave Sissy exactly what she needed to force Carl to cease and desist on all Consortium activities."

"What did she need?" Candace asked. "Now, I'm lost."

"Outside authorities," Max said, clearly putting the pieces into place.

Candace's eyes stretched wide. "So she created the lab incident to get outside authorities involved." Candace grimaced. "God, that woman is twisted."

"Desperate, Candace," Gabby said. "Carl was respected. As his wife, Sissy was respected. If he died, then his sins died with him, and she became his respected widow."

Max interceded. "If his sins were exposed, then she

lost her husband, her family and home, and her respect in the community. Everything that mattered to her would be gone. That's why she killed Carl. She wanted to retain her respect more than she wanted to keep her husband, marriage, and family intact."

"Sparing herself and the kids." Candace nodded, thoughtful. "She'd think Jackson would go easy on her—they had a thing years ago. Yes, it all fits."

"Just get your butt in gear and you can help us prove it to Sheriff Coulter and then the FBI." Gabby stood up and took her plate to the sink. "But why would she assume that 'thing' years ago would make a difference to Jackson now?"

"First loves are never forgotten, Gabby." Candace looked at Max. "What your wife doesn't know about relationships is amazing. Educate her, will you?"

Gabby snorted, grabbed Max's sleeve, and ushered him to the door. She tossed Candace a cool glare and a sniff. "Max and I are doing just fine, thank you very much. Right, Max?"

Hey, it didn't take a real husband to see the danger in disagreeing on that one. "Absolutely, honey."

Candace giggled, low and throaty, but turned her head to keep Gabby from hearing it. Max decided then and there he really liked her. Unfortunately, he also discovered he didn't just like Gabby; he loved her.

Even more unfortunate was that loving her left him parked firmly between the rock and the hard place.

Chapter Thirty-seven

"Gabby, I've done everything I know to do, okay?" Jackson Coulter's face reddened like a three-hour overdone sunburn and he plopped down onto his chair behind his desk. "Sissy won't move off the dime."

"She's guilty, Jackson." Gabby stood in front of him, her arms folded over her chest. "Let me talk with her."

"I can't do that, any more than I can arrest her. She's just here for questioning. Besides, you're a judge, not her lawyer."

"Has she asked for a lawyer?"

"Not yet."

Gabby hiked her brows. Sissy wanted to talk; Gabby had sensed it at her house, and she would have done it then if her son hadn't arrived home from college. She had no intention of not talking. She was the victim here. Her husband's victim . . . maybe. Or maybe not. "Ask her if she'll talk with me on tape. If she agrees, then you're in the clear."

"Why would she do that?"

"I don't know that she will." Gabby elevated her voice. "Jackson, would you just ask her?"

"Getting loud, honey," Max said from behind her, the cell phone at his ear.

She paused to roll her gaze heavenward so he wouldn't miss it, and then looked back at Jackson. "Will you just ask the woman? Please."

"All right. All right." He left the office and entered the interrogation room down the hall where Sissy had been sitting for over five hours.

Any moment, Gabby feared, the woman would ask for an attorney, or insist she be charged or released. Gabby had to talk with her first, or Sissy Blake would never admit the truth.

"Okay, Stan." Max turned to look at Gabby, pacing a short path from Jackson's desk to the office door. "Have HazMat verify the tanks test clean before you resume normal spraying. Verify the chemicals, too." Max paused, running a mental checklist to make sure he'd covered all hazardous material procedural requirements and then added, "No, you can't trust the bands. I don't care where the pesticide comes from, you run it personally and check the tanks before any truck is loaded and dispatched."

He hung up the phone. "Gabby, you're going to wear a path in the carpet."

"Is Stan up to speed on things now?"

"Yes, he is." Max tucked the phone back into his pocket. "The commander, too. He's still searching for his second team."

Darlene piped up from Christie's desk. "They're in the cells."

Gabby looked at Max and then they both turned to

Darlene. "Show us," Gabby said, wondering how this had happened. Conlee would have a fit.

Jackson walked her and Max back to the cells and Gabby nearly lost her lunch. "Jackson, what are you doing?"

"Holding bank robbers and jewel thieves."

Gabby shouted, "You're holding Justice Department investigators! Turn them loose."

"I can't just turn them loose, Gabby. I caught them with the jewels and the money."

"You'd better explain," Max said, steel in his voice.

Jackson did. "And that's it. They were caught cold with the jewels and the money."

"Oh for pity's sake, Jackson." Gabby huffed a sigh. "It was a setup—probably by the same man who shot Max, took the potshots at us on the road to Abernathy's, and blew up Candace's Porsche. I swear it wasn't these guys. They're highly decorated, above reproach."

"So they said." Jackson sighed. "But they claimed Elizabeth could vouch for them and she'd never seen them and they'd never seen her. We haven't been able to verify who they are."

"Damn it, Jackson," Gabby said. "I just did."

"I'm backing that." Max stepped to her side. "We're vouching for them."

"Okay." Jackson took the keys from his belt, opened the cell door. "I'll get Darlene to handle the paperwork." He walked down the hall to the office.

Max looked over each man on the team. "Forget your orders, they've been changed. Get back to Home Base."

"Gabby." Jackson stuck his head in the door. "Sissy will talk with you."

Gabby tried not to act surprised, but she figured she had a one-in-five-thousand shot. Why Sissy agreed to talk with her on tape, Gabby couldn't imagine. But she didn't linger. The last thing she wanted was for the woman to change her mind.

Jackson led her to the interrogation room, started the tape, and then closed the door.

Gabby sat down. Sissy looked pale and weary, but whether from grief or fear or a combination of the two, Gabby couldn't be certain. "I'm supposed to remind you that this conversation is being taped and that anything either of us says can be used against you in a court of law, if things come to that."

"Jackson told me, Gabby." She sipped water from a white plastic cup. "My poor children. Who's going to comfort my children?"

"You will, Sissy. You've always been there for your children."

"Don't patronize me." The sadness in her eyes hardened. "We both know why you're here. And we both know I'll be in prison, nowhere near my children." She cleared her throat, but her voice still shook. Obviously her thoughts troubled her deeply. "Soon they'll never want to see me again or even speak to me. Do you know what that's going to be like, Gabby? To watch the children you raised turn against you because you protected them?"

"No, I don't," she answered honestly. "I know what it's like to feel alone, though, and I imagine that's what you're feeling now."

"You all know the truth, don't you?"

Gabby nodded.

"It's so humiliating. I heard him on the phone, talking about the Consortium and his women and—and . . . oh, God, it was horrible. I couldn't believe he would do such things. He destroyed our family!"

She sobbed, long and hard, and when she regained control, and the wails turned to sniffles, she dabbed at her eyes and the tip of her nose with a crushed tissue. "I had to release the mosquitoes at the lab. I learned what they were doing, and I had to stop them. I hated putting Covers in that kind of danger, but I just had to get this to the attention of authorities outside the Cove. I didn't know everyone involved here, or what else to do. So I waited until Candace was in the building. I knew she'd hear the alarm and stop them from getting out." Sissy's tears spilled and anguish contorted her gentle face. "Then she got so sick and I was so afraid I'd hurt her, too. That's why I asked her to come with you to the house when Carl died. Miranda said Candace was really okay, but I just needed to see for myself." She lifted a hand to her face. "Poor Elizabeth probably hasn't been off her knees since all this started." Sissy's voice caught, choking on tears. "She's probably worn out her rosary."

"She and Candace are okay, Sissy." Gabby didn't elaborate. The less she said, the better the odds Sissy would keep talking.

"I had to do it, Gabby." Resolve settled over Sissy like a shield. "I couldn't stop Carl, but he had to be stopped, and no one in Carnel Cove could do it. He would have killed Jackson, too." She sucked in shuddered breath. "So I broke the lab window and smashed the tanks."

Something was off. Seriously off. Sissy was too forthcoming. Or she would be if she were anyone but Sissy. She was weary of the deceit and lying and pretending everything was fine when inside she was falling apart. This burden was just too heavy for her to carry.

"I thought Carl was having an affair, so I waited until he was asleep and I read his journal. He was. She was a redhead, Gabby. That's what he called her—*his redhead.*" The shock of learning that drained from her face and disbelief replaced it. "I thought I wanted the truth. That's why I violated his privacy and read his journal. But I got a lot more truth than I bargained for. I saw Carl's dark side in it, and it was the most evil thing I've ever encountered in my life." She shivered, crossed her chest with her arms, and wiped the goose bumps from her skin. "He had already killed Judge Powell, and it was clear that Abernathy would be next."

Gabby had to ask, and prayed she wasn't making a mistake by interrupting the flow. "Was it Carl who killed Judge Abernathy?"

"He was there. But he had one of his thugs do the actual killing." She stared down at the table. "Carl wouldn't dare to dirty his own hands." She looked at Gabby as if she were a child who needed to be led by the hand. "William Powell was a fine man. He would have talked to the Justice Department in New York, and Carl knew it. He hired those animals to kill him. And then Judge Abernathy retired— you terrified him. He told Carl you could destroy them. Frankly, I couldn't see it. I mean, you're a local judge and you weren't in the Cove when they started all this. You couldn't hurt them. But Abernathy swore you could. And he convinced Carl, too. He was going to get those awful men to kill you, too, Gabby, and only God knows how many others. He had to be stopped."

"So you stopped him." She was in shock, but she wasn't falling totally apart. She knew she was sealing her jail cell door, but oddly, it didn't seem to matter. That struck Gabby as strange.

"I couldn't stop him. He was the father of my children, and there's no way I could have left him and taken them with me. I threatened to, when I first found out what he was doing with that Consortium group of his. But he swore he'd hunt me down and kill the kids, too. I had to stay. Then I didn't know what to do."

"That's when you gave me his journal," Gabby said. "Why did he keep one? It's such damning evidence."

"Insurance. None of the Consortium members could turn on him. He had hard evidence implicating them." Sissy pulled a fresh tissue out of the box on the table between them. "'The chairman always covers his assets,' he used to say."

"Chairman?" Gabby frowned. "I thought he was the director."

Sissy paused, paled. "Director for the Consortium, chairman for the bank."

Truth? Or protecting her children? Gabby wondered. It felt like a lie. "Are you sure Carl was the head of this Consortium?"

"Oh, yes. Read his journal. You'll see." She sniffed. "I was terrified, but I stole the journal, praying that the hurricane would keep him too busy to notice too quickly. I brought it to you, and then went to the lab. Outside authorities would fix everything. They could stop Carl."

"So what triggered his actual death?" Gabby leaned across the table, folded her hands together atop it. "Did he miss the journal? Was he afraid he'd been caught? What?"

"He shot himself in the mouth," she said, not meeting Gabby's eyes. "I don't know why." Her red face flushed brighter. "I hated him for what he was doing to our family. Long before his death, we were barely on speaking terms. Maybe his redhead knows why. I don't."

Definitely lying. "Sissy, you know Jackson is going to run tests on your hands. He'll find powder residue that will prove you pulled the trigger."

Sissy dipped her chin, looked down at her lap for a long moment and then checked her watch. That struck Gabby as an odd thing to do. It wasn't as if Sissy was going anywhere. She had been stripped bare and broken, lost everything that mattered, and she had nothing left to lose.

"It's time, Gabby." She lifted her gaze, calm and resigned. "I'll spare Jackson the trouble. I shot Carl in the mouth with his own gun. I don't regret it, either. I'd do it again. He was deliberately hurting people, spraying those god-awful chemicals. Destroyed so many lives. He didn't care. It was about the money. Always about the money." She scowled. "Greed made him a terrible bastard and horrible man. A monster. I killed the monster, Gabby."

"He just sat there and let you shoot him?"

"Of course not." She took in a deep breath and sat back at the table. "I waited for him to fall asleep in his chair. Every evening after dinner, he takes Baxter for a walk. When they get back, he snoozes in his chair and Baxter curls up at his feet."

Their beagle. "So you waited for him and Baxter to go to sleep, and then what?"

"I had a cup of tea."

Gabby tried hard to remain patient. "And then?"

"I heard him snore," Sissy said. "Carl has a horrible snore." She pulled her purse into her lap, and opened it.

Gabby automatically reached for the gun in her waistband, but Sissy was fishing for her lipstick, not for a weapon.

She pulled out a compact and, looking in the mirror, applied a swipe of coral. "I intended just to shoot him and take my chances with telling the children and Jackson why. But when I got the gun and went in there, he was rocking back with his mouth hanging open, and I remembered hearing on TV that a lot of men shoot themselves in the mouth, so I shot him in the mouth." She closed her compact and dropped it and the gold tube of lipstick back into her purse. "It made a horrible mess of my antique rug. The children will never get the stains out."

Gabby had no idea what to say to that. Obviously Sissy had snapped. Shock made people react in bizarre ways, and worrying about rug stains definitely ranked as one of them. A pungent scent caught her attention. There was no food anywhere in the interrogation room, so why in the world did she smell almonds?

Sissy shrugged and smiled at her. "Well, that's about it, Gabby. You can feel badly for my children, but don't waste any sympathy on Carl." The look in her eyes turned dark, hard. "He got a lot more mercy than he gave anyone else. Do you know he bought his redhead an island? He thought

I didn't know for the longest time, but I did. I've known since the very day he signed the contract to buy it." Smoothing her hair down, she sniffed. "Remember to tell the children about the island, will you, dear? The deed won't show up anywhere. It's in Carl's private box at the bank. I don't think the children know he has a private box."

"You can tell them, Sissy. You'll see them."

"No, dear. They might see me, but I won't see them."

"What do you mean by that?"

"It doesn't matter."

The woman was heartbroken and raw, and it touched the compassion in Gabby. "I'm so sorry, Sissy." How tragic to feel betrayed and driven to murder, knowing it would cost you your kids and the life you'd built. By ending Carl's life, Sissy had ended her own. Figuratively, of course, but all she had known until that point was gone.

"I wonder if Jackson will let me call and say good-bye to the children."

"Good-bye?" Something was seriously off. So far off, it gave Gabby the creeps. Sissy spoke with such finality.

"Yes, Gabby." Sissy smiled. "When you came into the room, I was drinking water, remember?"

Gabby nodded, a cold fear crawling up her spine. That almond smell when she had opened her purse. *Oh, God, cyanide! The woman had swallowed cyanide!* "Tell me you didn't, Sissy. Your kids can't lose you, too. How can you let them lose you, too?"

"A mother who killed their father? A mother in prison for the rest of her natural life?" Sissy snorted. "They'll be relieved and we both know it. It'll be so much easier for them without me here reminding them of what happened." Tears shimmered in her eyes. "I would like a nice funeral." She dabbed at her eyes. "I won't be buried in consecrated ground, of course—suicide is a mortal sin, you know." That worried her into eating a streak in her coral lipstick. "Father McDowell will tell the children how best to handle it. Tell them not to put me near Carl. Not even in the same cemetery. Promise me, Gabby." When she nodded, Sissy went on. "I want pink roses with white baby's breath. Three dozen—no more. Soft pink, not that brassy blue pink. I like the gentle ones."

She'd definitely taken cyanide. Gabby ran to the door, shouted, "Jackson! Jackson, hurry!"

Sissy smiled. "Calm down, dear. It's too late." She stiffened, grimaced, and tears leaked out of her red-rimmed eyes. "It'll all be over in a matter of . . ."

Sissy Blake slumped forward and died.

Chapter Thirty-eight

Two hours later, Gabby and Max went to the Logan Industries lab to do a secure remote report to Commander Conlee.

On the walk from the building to the lab, Gabby tried not to let dread overwhelm her. "He's going to be supremely pissed that Sissy Blake poisoned herself in my presence, Max."

He clasped her hand in his. "Technically speaking, she took the stuff before you entered the room. Diluted, true, otherwise she would have been dead before you actually talked to her, but still, before you got there."

Gabby glanced over at him. "Do you think that'll make any difference to Conlee?"

"No." Max answered without hesitating. "But he'll be more supremely pissed that the second Warrior got close enough to you to bomb Candace's car and you didn't take him out."

Gabby bristled. "Did you have to remind me of that right now?" The one nerve she had left was frayed. "My head's already on the platter, remember?"

"So is mine." He smiled at her.

The man was actually smiling? He knew Conlee had to be ruthless, and yet he could smile about this? "Did you get one whiff too many of that pesticide, Max?"

He stopped, tugged her to him, and planted a sound kiss on her lips. "Maybe. I'm thinking that if I have to die, I'm glad it's with you."

"You want me dead, too?" She smacked his chest. "You really know how to make a woman feel special, Grayson."

"You know what I mean." His playfulness disappeared. "You are special, Gabby. To me, you're very special, and you make me feel special. I want you to know that. It has nothing to do with the job, or anything else. It's just the truth."

She stilled and just stared at him, caught somewhere between terror and awe and a joy that ran so deep it warmed the marrow of her bones. The back of her nose burned and her eyes stung. She blinked hard to keep welled tears from falling, and whispered, "Thank you, Max."

He nodded once, and then moved toward the lab door, as if what he had said surprised him as much as it had her. But it was a good surprise. And one she'd hold close in her memory for a long, long time—provided Conlee didn't kill her.

Fifteen minutes later, they were standing before the lab table, side by side, briefing the commander. When they finished, he was, as predicted, pissed. While he ranted, Max eased his hand to Gabby's under the ledge of the lab table, lacing their fingers, pressing their palms. It was the most pleasant ass-chewing Gabby had had in her entire career.

"Kincaid, why the hell are you smiling?" Conlee shouted, nearly blowing out her eardrum.

"Every moment is precious, sir." She looked over at Max. "I'm not wasting them."

"Oh, for God's sake." Conlee snorted. "I've rescinded the cancellation orders. Now can you two please give me your full attention?"

Rescinded them? Gabby's heart knocked hard on her chest wall, and she felt the same reaction in Max, who squeezed her hand until she swore he'd break the bones. "Yes, sir."

"Of course, Commander."

He was happy. They were happy. It was an odd time for a perfect moment, but Gabby had had too few perfect moments in her life to squander even this one. She stroked Max's thumb. "Have Burke and Erickson been successful on their vaccine?"

"If you're asking if they've discovered why the combination worked, the answer is not yet." Conlee sounded irritated by that. Of course, he would be. He took every aspect of his mission to protect the people of the United States very seriously—as indeed he should. "Dr. Richardson recommended we manufacture both and give double injections to everyone infected. Since we can't really do anything else, and if we don't do that their situations are pretty much hopeless, we're going that route. We'll have what we need to vaccinate everyone infected shortly. Strictly voluntary, of course."

"Considering the alternative is certain death, I think the response will be good, sir." In her book, anything looked better than death.

"I agree, Gabby." Conlee harrumphed, clearly not happy with what he had to say next, but too much the realist to deny it. "The nature of this attack being not in the lab incident but in the spraying as a response to the lab incident warns us that we're in yet another new era."

It did. And there had been far too many new eras since the attacks of September 11. The Consortium and Global

Warriors had had the Special Detail Unit and FEMA do ninety-five percent of the work for them, ordering, arranging, and paying for the spraying. It was an awful thing, seeing government programs bastardized by terrorists to harm the very people those programs were charged with protecting. Maddening and frightening, too.

"It's a challenging development, sir," Max said. "All the Consortium really had to do was substitute the chemicals. If Sissy Blake hadn't created the lab incident, Dr. Swift or the missing Global Warrior would have done it. It was an extremely low-budget mission for them."

"Unfortunately, it was, which means we've got to make it substantially more expensive for them—to act as a deterrent. At least Carl Blake is dead now and his Consortium is shut down. Lieutenant Gibson is following the paper trail. Mayor Faulkner is clean, though he was clearly manipulated by Blake, as is Dr. Erickson. He's as devoted to finding a cure as any man on a mission I've ever seen." Conlee's tone shifted, became weary. "We're not a hundred percent convinced about Candace Burke—"

"We are, sir," Gabby interrupted. "Aren't we, Max?"

"Absolutely, honey," Max said without stopping to think.

"Honey?" Commander Conlee said. "Grayson, did you just set me up for all the paperwork that goes with harassment charges?"

"Deep-cover hazard, sir." Max explained, his expression straight.

Oddly hurt, Gabby let go of his hand. He didn't try to stop her, and that hurt her more.

"From all we've been able to determine, the Consortium has been dismantled. We'll know more as time goes on, but Intel feels confident it won't be functioning again before we can round up any residual parties."

Candace stepped out of the storage room and up to

the lab table. Gabby and Max tried to act normal, despite their surprise.

"Get Burke an earpiece," Conlee barked.

Gabby passed hers to Candace. She tapped it into her ear, and then snagged the mike. "Hi, Commander."

"Ms. Burke," he said stiffly. "Where's my boat?"

"My guess is the second Warrior used it to bug out after he set the team up with the jewelry theft and bank robbery."

"Is that a fact?"

"Seems reasonable enough to me, sir." She frowned up at the remote viewer. "I realize I've breached etiquette by letting Max and Gabby know I'm aware of you and you're probably going to kill me for it, but I can't leave the rest of the country vulnerable to protect myself."

"What exactly are you talking about?"

"Carl Blake." She frowned up at the remote viewer. "Your Intel people need a wake-up call on the Consortium and I'd just as soon they didn't get it in the form of another biological attack—or worse, a chemical one."

"Your point, ma'am?" Conlee urged her, oddly stiff and formal.

"My point is that Carl Blake might have been a bank president and a minor player financial whiz. He might have owned a couple companies and a ton of real estate. But, Commander, that man did *not* have the skills to mastermind these kinds of attacks. He wasn't a strategic thinker. Take him away from money and he was lost. He related to everything by the bottom line and dollar signs. Everything. And speaking quite frankly, sir, he didn't have the balls to take these kinds of risks. Someone is above him in this Consortium, sir. Someone sharper, stronger, wiser, who is willing to take more risks and is better able to protect himself from detection while doing it."

Conlee grunted, softened his voice. "I understand you feel strongly about this because you were personally used,

Candace. Logan Industries is your company and Blake put your reputation and life at risk. Outrage is normal, but—"

"Screw my reputation, Commander. This isn't an ego thing. Didn't you hear me? I knew Carl Blake, and he didn't have what it takes to pull this off."

"Intel feels confident the Consortium stops with Blake."

"Well, Intel is wrong." She parked a hand on her hip and stared up at the viewer lens. "Keep digging, Commander, or you'll be leaving the U.S. wide open. That's just a friendly warning. Intel *is* wrong."

"Thank you for your input, Ms. Burke."

Gabby knew that things were getting tense and touched Candace's arm, cautioning her to back off. "Max and I will keep a sharp eye out for developments. Sissy mentioned 'the chairman' and referenced it to banking. She, Erickson, and Swift said only 'the director' about the Consortium. We'll check it all firsthand."

Candace glared back at the viewer and then nodded, satisfied. "That works for me, Gabby. I trust you and Max. And of course, I'll be doing what I can—"

Conlee didn't care for that snub or the indignant sniff that had come with it, and evidence of both came in his heated interruption. "You'll stay out of it, or I'll put your ass in jail."

Candace didn't appear worried, or forgiving. "When William Powell was dying," she said, ignoring his threat, "he said you could be trusted, so I'm trusting you to keep an open mind on what Gabby and Max report on the Consortium. It *is* bigger, Commander." She then looked directly at the viewer, letting him see her sincerity. "If you're going to kill me for coming out of the proverbial closet, would you please give me twenty-four hours' notice?"

"Excuse me?" Conlee sounded bewildered, as if his ears had deceived him.

"Notice. You know. A heads-up that you're sending Housekeeping for me."

Max and Gabby turned their heads away from the viewer. Max cringed, Gabby grinned, not at all surprised. Candace would go toe to toe with anyone short of God.

"Get the hell off my viewer, Candace Burke."

"Yes, sir. But kindly remember that *your* viewer is in *my* building. Perhaps things are different there, but in the South, it behooves one to be gracious. Civility is still expected—and appreciated." She removed the earpiece and mike and returned them to Gabby. "He's prickly sometimes, isn't he?"

"We all have our moments." Gabby couldn't help herself. "Just out of curiosity, why do you want the notice?"

Candace shrugged. "I love banana splits."

"What?" Totally lost, Max glanced at Gabby to interpret.

But she didn't have a clue what Candace was talking about, either.

"I love banana splits, but I don't eat them." She tapped at her hip. "You might as well just plaster the pounds on your buns and save your stomach the trouble of processing. If Commander Conlee is going to kill me, then I want time to eat myself sick on the suckers."

Conlee's muffled chuckled sounded through the earpiece, and watching Candace leave the lab, Gabby felt oddly comforted. Conlee wouldn't cancel or jail Candace Burke.

"So where is Dr. Swift?"

"Sheriff Coulter has him in jail," Max said. "FBI will retrieve him in the morning."

"Fine. You two stay put for a few days while we mop up, just in case. Keep watch for Cardel Boudreaux. We had a sketch artist work with that truck driver and we think Boudreaux ordered him to spray the low-income housing community. Customs has been alerted. My guess is that since his client, Carl Blake, is dead, he's going to make a run for the border."

"In his position, I would," Gabby admitted. A snapshot of a man in Sissy's living room flashed in her mind. A man wearing a hat with a flag pin in its brim. "Son of a bitch."

"What?" Max asked.

"What?" Conlee mimicked him simultaneously.

"Cardel Boudreaux." She remembered the flag pin in his hat at the airport, when he'd come into the country. "He was at Sissy's. I didn't recognize him with the hat. It was pulled low over his eyes. I should have had him, sir."

"Go from where you are, Gabby." Max sighed. "Between the car bomb failing and his client being dead, he had little incentive to hang around. I'm sure he's out of the area by now. Hopefully, he hasn't yet left the country. He's the only link we've got to Sissy's Consortium chairman—if Candace is right and Sissy lied about Carl being its top-level manager."

"The alert's been issued through Homeland Security channels. You guys stay put there."

"Yes, sir."

Max took off his earpiece and mike and looked at Gabby.

"I feel like an idiot. The man was ten feet away from me, Max."

He curled an arm around her shoulder. "Welcome to the human race, honey. You're beautiful and smart and no more perfect than the rest of us."

"I never thought I was perfect." She hiked her chin, offended.

"No, you just demanded it in others." He kissed her to take the sting out of what he'd told her. "But I adore you anyway."

She didn't believe it. Didn't trust it for a second. "Right. Easy to say to a woman with a spotty memory."

He laughed out loud and led her out of the lab.

"Laughing about that? Have you no shame, Maxwell Grayson?"

"None. You remembered my name. That's enough."

★　★　★

"Gabby?" Max called out through the bathroom door.

She turned off the water so she could hear him, grabbed a thick towel, and began drying off. "What? I'm still in the shower."

"Sybil's on the phone," he shouted from the doorway. "Do you want me to have her call you back? It'll be a day or two, she says."

"Just a sec." Gabby stepped out of the shower, bent forward and wrapped the towel in a turban around her head, then shrugged into her robe. Tugging at the tie at her waist, she opened the door and reached for the phone.

Max passed it to her. "Cute hat, honey."

"Go away." She rolled her gaze heavenward as if annoyed, but inside she was smiling. "Sybil?" she said into the phone. "Where are you?"

"In Washington. I'm glad you're alive."

"Me, too." She walked out of the bath and down the hall, then into the bedroom. "I know this whole thing has been hard for you."

"It was awful. But I hedged my odds," she confessed.

"How? For crying out loud, Sybil, you sent Max to kill me."

"I did," she admitted. "But I knew he wouldn't do it unless he couldn't not do it."

"Oh, really?"

"You're crazy about the man, Gabby. He'd have to be dumb as a dead stump to not know it, and knowing it, he couldn't kill you. It was low risk—for a high-risk proposition."

"Well, thank you so much for that comforting thought."

She plopped down on the bed, tumbled to her back, and then stared up at the white squiggles on the ceiling. "So is he crazy about me, too?"

Sybil didn't answer.

Gabby waited, but when it became obvious she wasn't going to answer, Gabby nudged her. "Sybil, are you still there?"

Worry filled her voice. The kind of worry that passes between two women who have been friends too long to hide anything of consequence from each other. "What's wrong?"

Wishing she'd kept her mouth shut—Sybil would obsess, she was so protective—Gabby glared at the globe on the light fixture. "Conlee didn't brief you about me getting the infection?"

"He did. But you're cured. So why are you asking me how Max feels about you?"

She'd always been too observant and sharp to deceive. "There's a little residual effect."

"What kind of residual effect?"

The phone bumped Gabby's chin. "My memory needs a few patches. Max is helping me fit them in."

"Patches?" Her voice bordered on hysteria. "What the hell do you mean 'patches'?"

"I don't remember some details. But don't worry. Nothing that would jeopardize anything. It's personal stuff."

"For example . . ." Sybil prodded.

"I remember my cover, okay?" Gabby let out a sigh of pure frustration. "I don't remember not being married to Max or not loving him or not being a judge or not really living in Carnel Cove."

"You think your cover is your life?" Sybil sounded stunned.

Hell, she had to be stunned. Gabby was stunned by it, too. "I did. I don't anymore."

"Oh, Gabby." Fear, regret, concern, worry. So much worry.

"Don't start, Sybil. I mean it. I'm fine." Gabby plucked at the coverlet with her forefinger and thumb. The rich texture felt good next to her skin, oddly comforting. "Sybil, was I really crazy about Max?"

"Oh, yeah. Definitely."

"Well, I guess that's it, then."

"What?"

"I love the man. I thought I was married to him, but he said no. I believed him—well, not at first, but after a while—and yet . . ."

"You still felt married to him."

"Yeah." She rolled over onto her side, scrunched a pillow to her chest. "But that could have been because we've been married so many times."

"True," Sybil agreed. "But if even knowing that, you still love him . . ."

"Shut up." Gabby groaned. "What the hell am I supposed to do with this? He'll make me crazy."

"You're already crazy."

"I'll be worse."

"You'll be better." Sybil laughed. "Trust me on this."

Sybil and Jonathan Westford had been down this road. It hadn't been an easy one for them, either, but Gabby had to confess, they both seemed happier than ever. She grunted. "I'm not sure I like this, Sybil. Not at all."

Sybil laughed harder.

Gabby lost it. "You could pretend to be sympathetic, you heartless bitch. Remember how crazy you were when you were going through this?"

"Yes, I do. And I also remember you were about as sympathetic as a stone. You laughed at me, too. Now I see why." She gave Gabby a sniff of a snort. "Suffer, darling. It's worth it."

"I doubt it."

"Oh, it is, Gabby." All teasing left Sybil's voice. "Absolutely."

"You know, you're as goofy now as you were when we were in college and we used to sneak down to Miller's Pond to skinny-dip. You got stuffy for a time—Mr. Snip-It's lousy influence, no doubt. I'm glad you divorced him and you're back. I couldn't stand that man."

"Gabby!"

"What?" Good God, Sybil couldn't defend her jerk of an ex even now, could she?

"You remembered Miller's Pond," Sybil said. "You remembered college. You remembered that you always called Austin Mr. Snip-It."

"Yeah?" And that meant . . . What?

"Gabby, those are real memories. They're not part of your cover."

Gabby stilled. Blinked hard three times, and struggled to keep up with all the flashes of scenes of her life playing through her mind. All at once, she remembered everything. Activating Max. The details of this mission and of others. "Oh, God, Sybil. I was lovesick. Can you believe it? I can't believe it. But it's true. It is. I kept all those passports and identities because in them I'd been married to Max."

"I know, Gabby." Sybil's voice softened. "You two have a few days there. Relax and give things time to settle."

"Right." The odds of that were about a million to one. "I felt dopey and I hated it. I really hated it, Sybil."

"I know you did. Look, give Max a chance. That was something you were never willing to do before. Take the risk, my friend. He's worth it."

"But am I?"

"Of course, you are. Gabby, don't you know he thinks you're amazing? He's always thought you were amazing. That's why you drove him nuts."

"That makes perfect sense." Gabby didn't try to bury her sarcasm. "And you know this because . . ."

"You do the same thing. It's human nature. You dislike anything or anyone who gets too close. You always have."

She had. How did she come back with something clever on that? It was the truth. "I don't like you very much some times."

"I love you all the time."

She frowned, groused. "Me, too."

"Look, you did nothing and had nothing. If you want something, then take the risks. If you don't, then don't whine about it. Either way, get off the dime, Gabby. You've got guts. Use them or lose what you could have with Max. The choice is yours."

"I just love how you beat around the bush and express such compassion and gentle understanding."

"You do enough bush beating for both of us. Especially when it comes to Max. If you want him, dear heart, go get him. Otherwise, let him go."

"It's not that simple."

"It's exactly that simple." Sybil paused a second and then went on. "I've got to run. I need to be on the Hill in fifteen minutes."

"Desert the sinking ship. Go ahead."

"You're not sinking. Your ballast just needs a little fine-tuning. Decide what you want, Gabby. Then go get it. I'll check in with you later to see what you decided to do. In the meantime, will you please try not to stomp around and make Max nuts?"

"What?"

"When you're scared, you stomp around like a bear with thorns shoved between its toes."

"I do not."

"Yes, you do. You always have."

Gabby frowned. "Okay, so I do. I won't."

"Thank you," Sybil said sharply. "I'm glad you're not dead, Gabby. I would really be lost without you."

"Me, too." Gabby swallowed hard. "Now get going and make Congress tow the line."

"Jonathan sends his love."

"Me, too," she said. "Bye."

Gabby hung up the phone and just lay there. She couldn't make herself move or think.

She couldn't make herself face Max.

★   ★   ★

Max hadn't meant to eavesdrop. He hadn't meant to hear any of the conversation between Gabby and Sybil. But he had. And he'd known the very moment Gabby had begun to remember. The very second. How much she remembered, he didn't know, but how much did it take for her to realize she didn't give a damn about him?

A sour knot formed in the pit of his stomach that left a bitter taste in his mouth and dread in his chest. He walked back to the kitchen, his steps heavier than they had been just moments earlier, when he'd felt pretty good about the success of the mission and his relationship with a woman who was unlike any other woman in his life.

She remembers now. You're no one special to her again. You're nothing to her again. Just the partner she never wanted.

That hurt like hell. He hurt like hell. He sat down at the table and stared out the window above the sink. Maybe it hurt so much because he'd never had that kind of connection to anyone else before in his life. Maybe because he had always been attracted to Gabby, even before he understood why she played the Queen Bitch at the unit. Maybe it was because he hadn't really known before what he had been missing in feeling special to one woman who looked at him with love in her eyes and touched something good inside him he hadn't even known was there.

So what, you're just going to back off? Forget her and what she means to you?

What else could he do?

Come on, man. Think about it. Commander Conlee assigned you—with Gabby's best friend's blessing—because you wouldn't follow their cancellation orders. You were willing to fight for her life. Why aren't you willing to fight for her heart?

Why wasn't he?

Max stood up, paced a path between the stove and the fridge, alongside the table. He took life-defying risks all the time. It came with the job. If he could do that, he certainly could do this. The question was how?

He thought about it. Downed a cup of steaming hot coffee, and thought some more. Finally he knew what he needed to do. Grabbing the phone, he punched in the number and waited for the telltale ring.

"Gibson."

"It's Agent Grayson. Agent Kincaid and I are proud of you. That was quite a hunch you had, connecting the customs official and the fruit shipment. Catching the detail of the U.S. pins being used as a signal was decent work."

"I'm just glad it panned out."

"If you have a few minutes to spare, I need a quick favor."

"Sure, Agent Grayson."

"I need a photo—a recent one—of a man named Harlan T. Crumbsfield," Max said, and then went on to explain where he could likely be found. "As soon as you get it, fax it to me at Gabby's house."

"Sure thing, sir. What's the priority level?"

"One." Max gave it the highest ranking without the first pang of guilt. For the first time in his life, his heart was on the line. To him, that made the cut and warranted the ranking.

The question was: Would he make the cut with Gabby?

Chapter Thirty-nine

Max was working in the yard, clearing the remnants of Darla's revenge. He had bagged and stacked twigs and broken branches, and had moved on to raking up strewn leaves. The sunshine felt good on his back and the physical work was a healthy outlet for the inner tension. He had no idea how things would go with Gabby, whether they'd end up together or apart, and he hated not knowing.

She came outside carrying a glass of lemonade. "You've got an hour, then we've got to get ready for the fund-raiser at Elizabeth's."

"What is this one for?" Max asked. Gabby had told him that whenever Carnel Cove needed something, they held fund-raisers until they got it.

"Jackson needs money to hire a standby receptionist so Darlene and Christie can have a little time off. The budget is stretched too tight, so one or the other of them has to be on duty at all times." Gabby smiled. "That demands a party, in the ladies' book."

"I kind of like that about them. They don't complain, they find solutions. It's . . . good."

Gabby nodded. "Very good."

Max bit his lower lip. "Miranda said something about the youth center needing a new boat motor, too."

"A Yamaha," Gabby said. "I forgot the numbers." Cocking her head, she gave him a mischievous look. "Wanna buy them one to celebrate?"

"What are we celebrating?"

"That depends." She passed the glass. "I thought you might be thirsty."

He took it. "Thanks." Parched, he swallowed a long draw, appreciating the cold sliding down his throat. She looked gorgeous . . . and scared to death. "You okay?" What did she want to celebrate?

She blinked hard and the green in her eyes darkened nearly to black. "No."

"What's wrong?" He leaned the rake against a stump and set the glass on it. She looked close to tears. Over the years, he'd seen many emotions from Gabby, but genuine tears hadn't been among them. He didn't like it. "Has something else happened?"

She toed the dirt at the base of the stump. "Commander Conlee called. Cardel Boudreaux got out of the country. Intel was reviewing customs tapes and found it a few hours ago. Apparently, he hit the border right after he blew up Candace's Porsche. We lost track of him in South America."

Was that what had her close to tears? That they'd missed Cardel Boudreaux? "We'll have another shot at him. You know these guys always lay low for a while and then crawl out from under their rocks. When he does, we'll find him, and we'll follow him to the Consortium's chairman— if there is a chairman."

"I know." Gabby sighed. "Patience. Persistence. Perseverance."

She didn't look more at ease; if anything she looked more upset. He reached over and hooked her chin with his thumb. "Talk to me, honey."

"I didn't lie about the evidence. I saw to it you would get it, even if you had killed me."

"So you said."

"I mailed you a note, Max, telling you where to find it. It'll be waiting for you at your office when you get back to Washington."

Definitely the memory return. Was that what she wanted to celebrate? Remembering? He wanted her recall restored, of course, but he didn't want to lose her. His heart again rebelled at the possibility, and he patted at the piece of paper folded in his pocket. Dutch courage was better than none. But before he could decide what to do, Gabby claimed his attention.

"Commander Conlee is in negotiations for Home Base's new headquarters."

"Really?" He lifted the glass from the stump and took a drink. His throat felt parched. He could lie and call it thirst, but it wasn't. It was fear. Fear of losing her and never again feeling what he felt with her.

She nodded. "You're not going to be surprised."

"Sublevel floors at Logan Industries?"

"You got it." She smiled. Caressed his arm. "I think watching him and Candace is going to be entertaining. She doesn't take anything off him."

"He's taking it easy on her because they're negotiating. He wants tighter control on the lab; he has to get Home Base out of Washington and into a small town that's relatively isolated from primary targets for security reasons; and there's a perfect place between here and Abernathy's cabin on the Federal Reserve for an underground bunker."

"More than any of that, I think the commander is impressed with the resourcefulness of his Carnel Cove cell."

"Another reason he wants Candace where he can watch her. He knows she's going to track Cardel Boudreaux to the ends of the earth to bust his chops for intruding on her turf."

"No doubt about it." Gabby frowned then shrugged. "It'll also allow him to let her live and keep her out of jail."

Max nodded. "Seems fair, considering how she tried to keep those infected mosquitoes in the lab, knowing they would kill her."

"Yes, it does." Pleased, Gabby stepped closer to him and looked straight up into his face. "As partners go, you're good, Max."

"Yes, I am."

"When you got to Carnel Cove, why didn't you just kill me?" She sounded somber, not sad or accusing or angry, just serious.

"At first, I wasn't convinced it was necessary, and I'd promised Vice President Stone I'd do all I could to avoid it."

"You said at first." She didn't touch him, but she wanted to; she was squeezing her hand open and closed at her side. "What about after that?"

This is it. The big plunge. Swim or drown time, Max.

The last thing he needed was that reminder. "I didn't want you to die," he said simply.

"Why?" She pushed, knowing she was pushing.

He took her hands in his, thought for a moment for the words, and then let her see the truth in his eyes. "Because you're the only woman in my whole life who has ever made me feel like you'd harness the universe for me." He let his thumb slide along her jaw, earlobe to chin. "That's too rare to lose, Gabby."

"What about you?" She licked her lips, stared openly into his eyes. "Would you harness the universe for me?"

"I'm a mere mortal, honey."

So he wouldn't. Fighting disappointment, she trudged on, intent on making her case. "You know, of course, that I remember some things now. I'm not sure I remember everything, or that I ever will, but my past isn't a total mystery to me." She let her gaze drift up to the trees, lifting her face to the gentle breeze. "Having cancellation orders issued on me had me looking into my memory box, Max. It was a real wake-up call."

"It was for me too."

She grunted. "I'm sure you were looking at more than a note from a fifth grader, a pair of wings, and a bunch of photos of oak seedlings."

"Actually, I don't even have a memory box."

"Not at all?"

He gave her a negative nod.

"Well, I don't know about you, but I'm not wasting a good wake-up call. I want more." She stuffed her hands into the back pockets of her jeans. "So much so that my mind played tricks on me. It wasn't the virus, Max. Candace was worse and it didn't impact her memory."

"Keith said his researchers noted memory challenges, honey."

"Short-term, true. But I didn't remember you weren't my husband, because I didn't want to remember it." She paused a moment, tried and failed to gauge his reaction, then went on. "I loved being married to you, Max. I loved feeling special to you." Here was the hard part. *God, keep me strong enough to get this out. Please!* "I know we aren't married now. But you are still special to me. I love you, Max."

He stared at her, his jaw loose, his glass tipping.

Confusion twisted her expression, riddled her tone. "Are you okay, Max?"

"Um, yeah. Yeah, I'm, um, fine." He passed her the folded piece of paper.

"What's this?"

"A gift for your memory box."

She unfolded the page and saw a man she didn't recognize, who had obviously lived hard. He looked about fifty pounds overweight—jock gone to flab—and half drunk, chugging down a long-necked beer. "Who is this?"

"Harlan T. Crumbsfield," Max said. "He's twice divorced—cheated on them both—and he's remarried again, though things aren't going too well."

"Oh?" Gabby tagged along to see where Max was going with this.

"Not well, at all, I'm afraid," Max said. "Harlan had a little trouble with his women. Seems his wife took exception to his mistress coming to her home for a visit. The women brawled, and ended up sharing adjoining jail cells for a weekend. They're out on bail now and after Harlan. He's spent the last two weeks in protective custody at a shelter."

"Ouch. That's not such good news for Harlan, now, is it?"

"No, I'd say he's going to have to be a little careful for a time."

"Maybe forever."

"Maybe." Max brushed a thumb to Gabby's cheek, smiled into her eyes. "Now aren't you glad you saved being special for me? You could have been married to him."

"Oh, Max." Gabby laughed out loud. "Where did you find out all this?"

"Your favorite trainee and my conspirator, Gibson, got it for me." Max nodded at the paper. "Did you read the note on the back?"

She flipped it over and read aloud. "I love you, Gabby. You'll always be special to me. Marry me, and let's build a life that keeps your memory box full."

Her heart soared and she nearly floated. "Is that note from Harlan T.?"

"No, honey. It's from me." Max circled her in his arms and pulled her close. "Marry me, Gabby."

"Why not?" Smiling from the heart out, Gabby looped her arms around his neck. "I've already married you five times. What's one more?"

The corner of his mouth curled. "Right."

"Right." Gabby laughed aloud, happy and showing it.

Not that she thought for a second that life with Max would be a cakewalk; it wouldn't. They were both strong people with strong wills. They shared dangerous jobs with very high risks. There would be hard times. Lots of them— it was inevitable.

But they would have love to soften and sustain them, stamina and determination to hold them steady to their course, and lighter burdens for sharing them with someone who cared. Together they would build a good life.

And share a memory box crammed full.

About the Author

VICKI HINZE lives with her family in Florida, where she's working on her next novel. Visit her website at www.vickihinze.com.

The Very Best in Contemporary Women's Fiction

SANDRA BROWN

___28951-9 Texas! Lucky $7.50/$10.99   ___56768-3 Adam's Fall $6.99/$9.99

___28990-X Texas! Chase $7.50/$10.99   ___56045-X Temperatures Rising $6.99/$9.99

___29500-4 Texas! Sage $7.50/$10.99   ___56274-6 Fanta C $7.50/$10.99

___29085-1 22 Indigo Place $6.99/$9.99   ___56278-9 Long Time Coming $7.50/$10.99

___29783-X A Whole New Light $7.50/$10.99   ___57157-5 Heaven's Price $6.99/$9.99

___57158-3 Breakfast In Bed $7.50/$10.99   ___29751-1 Hawk O'Toole's Hostage $6.50/$8.99

___57600-3 Tidings of Great Joy $6.99/$9.99   ___57601-1 Send No Flowers $7.50/$10.99

___57602-X In a Class by Itself $6.99/$9.99   ___57604-6 Riley in the Morning $7.50/$10.99

___57603-8 Thursday's Child $7.50/$10.99   ___57605-4 The Rana Look $7.50/$10.99

TAMI HOAG

___29534-9 Lucky's Lady $7.99/$11.99   ___29272-2 Still Waters $7.99/$11.99

___29053-3 Magic $7.99/$11.99   ___56160-X Cry Wolf $7.99/$11.99

___56050-6 Sarah's Sin $7.50/$10.99   ___56161-8 Dark Paradise $7.99/$11.99

___56451-x Night Sins $7.99/$11.99   ___56452-8 Guilty As Sin $7.99/$11.99

___57188-5 A Thin Dark Line $7.99/$11.99   ___57960-6 Ashes to Ashes $7.99/$11.99

___58252-6 Dust to Dust $7.99/$11.99   ___58357-3 Dark Horse $7.99/$11.99

NORA ROBERTS

___29078-9 Genuine Lies $7.99/$11.99   ___27859-2 Sweet Revenge $7.99/$11.99

___28578-5 Public Secrets $7.50/$10.99   ___27283-7 Brazen Virtue $7.99/$11.99

___26461-3 Hot Ice $7.99/$11.99   ___29597-7 Carnal Innocence $7.99/$11.99

___26574-1 Sacred Sins $7.99/$11.99   ___80326-3 Divine Evil $22.00/$32.00

....

Please enclose check or money order only, no cash or CODs. Shipping & handling costs: $5.50 U.S. mail, $7.50 UPS. New York and Tennessee residents must remit applicable sales tax. Canadian residents must remit applicable GST and provincial taxes. Please allow 4 – 6 weeks for delivery. All orders are subject to availability. This offer subject to change without notice. Please call 1-800-726-0600 for further information.

Bantam Dell Publishing Group, Inc.	TOTAL AMT $_____
Attn: Customer Service	SHIPPING & HANDLING $_____
400 Hahn Road	SALES TAX (NY, TN) $_____
Westminster, MD 21157	
	TOTAL ENCLOSED $_____

Name _____

Address _____

City/State/Zip _____

Daytime Phone (_____) _____